THE
THOUSAND-HEADED
SNAKE

By the same author

The Hong Kong Foreign Correspondents Club
May and June

THE
THOUSAND-HEADED
SNAKE

ANTHONY SPAETH

WEIDENFELD AND NICOLSON · LONDON

First published in 1993 by Weidenfeld and Nicolson
An imprint of the Orion Publishing Group Ltd
Orion House, 5 Upper St Martin's Lane, London
WC2H 9EA

A catalogue record for this book is available from the British
Library

ISBN 0 297 81356 0

Filmset by Selwood Systems, Midsomer Norton
Printed in Great Britain by Butler & Tanner Ltd
Frome and London

For Ajay Singh

ACKNOWLEDGEMENTS

The epigraph from *Remembrance of Things Past* is from the translation by C. K. Scott Moncrieff and Terence Kilmartin; and by Andreas Mayor. Chatto & Windus Ltd, 1981.

The translation of the Khushhal Khan Khatak poem, entitled 'Carpe Diem', is by Sir Evelyn Howell, contained in *The Pathans* by Olaf Caroe, Oxford University Press, 1958.

The Bessie Head letters are from 'Bessie Head: Two Letters', by Charles P. Sarvan, published in *Phoenix: Sri Lanka Journal of English in the Commonwealth,* Sri Lanka Association for Commonwealth Literature and Language Studies, Dept of English, University of Kelaniya, Kelaniya, Sri Lanka, Vol. 1, 1990, editor D. C. R. A. Goonetilleke.

Alice Giles's quote on page 34 is from Edward Seidensticker's translation of *The Tale of Genji,* Martin Secker & Warburg Ltd, 1976, p. 918.

The geography of Drews' India trip is purposely fanciful. The caves of the Barabar Hills, which E. M. Forster visited on 28 January 1913, are located near the town of Bela in Bihar state.

And so we ought not to fear in love, as in
everyday life, the future alone, but even the
past, which often comes to life for us only when
the future has come and gone . . .

— *Remembrance of Things Past*

THE PRESENT

I am returned to Hong Kong. Restored and reconstituted. In any other circumstance I would raise a glass!

The commonest tourist, returning with camera and troubled bowel, would feel a thrill. The towers of Hong Kong still standing, the harbour still churning, the shops busy, the pubs busier still. Take a picture, George, you oblivious, God-lucky sod. The Chinese scurry like there is no tomorrow. (Which makes excellent sense if you contemplate it.) They dive into the underground, rush off to their crummy offices, wait in the rain for double-decker buses that career through narrow streets. They check wristwatches, peering suspiciously down the avenue. The bus roars into sight and skinny arms flail like so many fowls. Listen: they actually cluck. For night is coming. The blessed night of the present. When preoccupation with the future can be drowned in brandy and the tidal rush of mah-jong tiles. The towers blaze bravely still: incandescent emblems of the colony's prosperous past. Emissaries of crimson and emerald extend across the mirrored Hong Kong harbour. From Kowloon come complementary colours. They merge midway and blend silently and harmoniously until dawn.

When everyone awakes with a headache and a dry mouth. (Or almost everyone: hangovers, blast it, are behind me.) The Cantonese fly to office. George, the common tourist, wonders whether to shop or ferry to the outlying islands. He could visit the border to peer into mainland China. But few choose that trip anymore, or so I understand. The border packed up a few years ago and shifted south with terrifying speed and uncertain purpose. Which helps explain the impatience of the Cantonese: moving ever faster to somehow outrun it.

That desperate dynamism has infected even me. I'm outracing my story. Which is intolerable in a narrator with plenty of pages and all the time in the world. Allow me to blame Hong Kong. There's no dot on the globe where the future has such powerful magnetism, pushing and

3

pulling the present, the past and the six million inhabitants caught between like so many iron filings. My position is above it all, describing the patterns that form. My qualification is unique: removed from the present and future, though admirably ensconced in Hong Kong's past. There's a corner named for me at the Hilton Grill. How many ex-governors can say the same? Better than a dental hospital. A racecourse would have been ideal.

Indulge me a minute! The commonest tourist thrills to return to Hong Kong: to find it intact, towering, the most admirable erection of twentieth-century mercantilism and, in one humble opinion, the most beautiful. So consider me, Timothy P. Marquand, who departed painfully and against his will. Rudely, one might say, bloody rude. How could I have expected to see the runup to 1997 when the wave from China ceases rearing and foaming and finally engulfs? But here I am, amidst my towers and my friends. Which were the only things I missed except for the pint or two on a Saturday, or a Wednesday, or Monday night. Gin Sundays at the Dickens Bar with the jazz band – who began that custom? No plaque there: just sticky beer rings and crisps crumbs. Memory has always been short in Hong Kong. The present was always so compelling. And now the future.

When the future is an icy, airless peak, however, there's a tendency to tumble back into the past. To an earlier age. Which I am here to toast and enshrine. It's all a kind of prehistory, unfortunately, for there are no documents. I never acquired the habit of a diary and, as far as I know, neither did Danny Drews. 'Talking to myself,' he scorned. 'Who can write without a reader?' Danny and his damned 'reader'. How he believed in him. How he relied on that primitive notion: that there was always someone out there watching or listening. Diaries did seem solitary, midnight pursuits and Danny and I rarely kept our midnights to ourselves. So it all went unrecorded. There are snapshots, of course, but disappointingly few: fresh-faced students in stuffy pubs; baggy-eyed hacks in cane chairs hoisting glasses. Cigarette smoke, ceiling fans, eyes turned rabid by the flash. The cameras are never there when the important events occur. Only memory: of an earlier age when love entwined with impossible hopes. The Original Age. And of all that came later: lives, death and the failure of those twisted, marvellous dreams. This, of course, is the Succeeding Age.

My story straddles these two ages and, in the great tradition of the human heart, shuttles hopelessly between. And now it begins. But there's a final thing you should know about your narrator. My last address was the third floor of Canossa Hospital, also known as the chronics ward. I died at dawn on October 12, 1989, after what is jokingly described as a very long illness. My funeral at St John's was packed and the requiem party at the Hong Kong Foreign Correspondents Club boisterous. Or so I understand. I was only corporeally present at the former and totally absent from the latter. Which was ironic for requiems were my traditional favourites. At St John's, my eulogy was delivered by Daniel Drews, Founding Editor of Hong Kong's very own *Orientweek* magazine, who wore a tie in my honour. Danny called me a scholar, a professional, the best China-watcher of our generation and a true friend. Lastly, sombrely, he dubbed me a tale-teller. 'That,' he proclaimed, 'is the ultimate testimonial to a fellow journalist.' (I can picture the tie: navy blue with wide, red stripes. I remember it from our days in London. I would wager it's the only tie he owns.) 'For at the end,' Danny said, 'in our maligned and misunderstood profession, that's what we are all about: our tales.'

That's the idea, good reader. At the end of my eulogy, or so I'm told, Danny Drews wished me Godspeed.

Which I now intend to claim.

Like most living news organizations, Hong Kong's *Orientweek* magazine had its traditions. And while none could claim great age – the magazine itself was barely a teenager – they were handed down by the staff as if they were venerable heirlooms. Perhaps genuine traditions would have been loved less. The *Orientweek* staff was young – snot-nosed kids, really – and they didn't yet admire things too distant in time or experience. They had the immigrant's craving to combine old with new and everything at *Orientweek* was tacky, pliable, needy of a final alteration or a distinctive pinch. Admittedly some newcomers, fresh off the boat, reacted against the magazine's determined quirks. But their disdain was soon overcome by the desire for something solid and shared, yet something still in the process of being formed. That was the special thrill of toiling for low wages and long hours at *Orientweek*. It was young; each contribution counted; most of the magazine's staff were fellow refugees and exiles. All had come to Hong Kong alone.

Never, but never, could the word 'reveal' appear in print. Drews claimed it had a dirty sound. (The proper alternative was 'disclose'.) Hong Kong was a 'territory' or a 'bustling business centre' and never a 'colony', for Drews said the region's most contemporary magazine shouldn't even acknowledge the era of colonialism. There was the newsroom ban on the necktie, of course, derived from Drews' famous cover, which hung in an outsized blow-up behind the receptionist's desk. It was the first thing visitors saw. The necktie cover had been the magazine's coming of age, everyone said, the succinct summation of *Orientweek*'s cheekiness, its claiming of the Orient as home and its admission that home needed some alterations. *Asia Without Ties!* The photo showed three Asians at office desks: a Sumo wrestler in a loincloth, a coyly naked bar girl and a skinny clerk ripping off a necktie. The receptionist's least pleasant task was to command visitors to remove their ties, no one excluded, even Japanese and Koreans. *Orientweek* lost several advertisers that way and countless receptionists. Surprisingly, the Japanese enjoyed the ritual. The Koreans did not.

Not all the magazine's traditions were Drews', as Drews himself admitted each Monday morning, or at deadline time, or whenever else tension rose in the newsroom. He'd jump from his desk – you could spy him through the vertical glass pane – fling open his office door and bellow: 'Let's get some *weather* into this goddamned stuffy newsroom!' It was a tribute to the legendary Indian proofreader, Mr Ramalingaya of Mysore, who had long ago withdrawn his odd idioms back to India. The reply from across the room was always the same:

'Iran or Iraq?'

This derived from Luis, a Macao–Portuguese makeup man with an imperfect grasp of geopolitics. Luis had issued his famous blunder in an era when the Middle East was a blur to all. Luis was less than sober that night, or so it is said. Nonetheless, it was a night destined to solidify his position at the magazine.

'What's our style?' Luis had scratched himself in a rude place. 'Iran or Iraq?'

Indeed, some called Luis indismissable.

Luis still worked at *Orientweek*. When his famous *faux pas* was bellowed across the newsroom, he wrinkled his brown forehead, rubbed a hand over his greying hair and grinned the same grin as on that renowned night. In recent years, Luis has taken on the nickname of 'Saddam' D'Souza, much to the embarrassment of Madame D'Souza at *Orientweek* parties. Or so I'm told.

The tales from that misty time were repeated frequently – the night the lights were cut off, Drews' famous taxi fights, the banking reporter with the eternal hard on: 'Thank you, I prefer to sit!' – but if you counted them up, few veterans were still around. There was 'The Missing Link' in Jakarta, of course, who's gone native in at least five Asian lands, and durable Ellen Weigner in Tokyo, poker player *par excellence*. In the Hong Kong newsroom it was only Dolly Leung, the librarian, and Saddam D'Souza. 1997 was approaching and its toll was reverberating. Never had the Chinese staff seemed so precious until they started disappearing. There must have been a kind of border, crossed before anyone noticed, and after that no one knew how to fix the *Orientweek* computer, or work its telephones, or man the printing press, for everyone was new and stupid.

With the exception of Ho, the maintenance man with the melted ear, who was old and stupid.

'Never listens to a thing I say,' Drews insisted, folding his own ear downward. 'I *told* him not to go to Nagasaki in 1945.' On buoyant days, Drews jumped from his desk – you could see him through the pane – opened his office door, cupped his hands to his mouth and feigned hysterical shouting while Ho stolidly emptied *Orientweek*'s garbage.

Yes, yes, it was said far too often: Drews was *Orientweek* and vice versa. He was Franco, Tito, Castro and Santa Claus all rolled into one, but alive, real and hardly middle-aged. And if he tended to tyranny it was a tyranny that seemed more crucial with each moment approaching 1997. Many saw Drews as a saviour that could put it all right. He was bright – the photographic memory was always cited – he was worldly and, at the same time, ceaselessly and childishly enthusiastic. To the male staff, he was a paragon of what could become of youth and idealism after seventeen years in the Far East and two decades in journalism. To the female staff, he was alternately frisky and needy and, despite his oversized wedding ring, many succumbed to one Drews or the other. (It took but one syllable to discover whom Drews had conquered: Dan.)

His less admirable qualities were recognized and endlessly excused. His stinginess about housing allowances, say, or his exquisite memory for people's flaws. It was one of the most famous remarks of one Timothy P. Marquand, China-watcher extraordinaire, that when you gossiped with Drews, you could feel his listening. On the phone, you could hear it: a tense, expectant silence from the other end.

'The eyes and ears of Danny Drews,' proclaimed Marquand, 'hark back to a time before data banks, people, before tape recorders, before quill and papyrus. They remind us of when man lived or died on memory alone! Little brethren, tell Danny Drews the things you want remembered only in perpetuity.'

'Perpetuity?' asked Reuters. 'Is that near Corfu?'

'Paoshun,' corrected the famous China-watcher. 'Before pinyin.'

'Paoshun?'

'Been there! Nipped in over the border in '81! Now drink to Chill Wills, one of the great *artistes* of his times. May he rest in peace!'

It should be clear by now: within his newsroom, Drews was the ringleader of a failing circus. He was a charm against impossible times and a totem the staffers could long for, puzzle over and spy upon, hour after hour, through the pane in his office door or in the corridors of Central at lunchtime or at the trusty Hong Kong Foreign Correspondents Club, where he drank late into the night with loud, opinionated, tantalizing people, seedy men and women with ivory cigarette-holders, journalists all. 'Drews News' was the staple of the *Orientweek* newsroom, 'Drews Love News' the gravy.

News about Miki Drews – the marble-faced enigma, 'Drews' Hiroshima' as she was known – was *Orientweek*'s priciest spice.

At the Hong Kong Foreign Correspondents Club, or FCC, Drews' stature was never disputed but its specifics tended to fragment under those tireless ceiling fans. Some insisted he was an editor of genius but no great shakes as a reporter or writer. To this, loyalists would cite the famous series on Vietnam, the Imelda Diary, his Daim crusade. Others said he spread himself too thin. To which loyalists would describe the legendary Drews hours and his various kindnesses to the dwindling Chinese staff, the earless Mr Ho conveniently forgotten.

And some said he seemed, well, kind of cold, unhappy, not the 'old Drews'. No one could even remember the last time Drews did his rendition of 'Joe Cool' in five verses from some Wanchai tabletop. This was a comment most hurtful to current staffers. Loyal heads shook, tears came to eyes, and often, too often, an earnest female voice described the concern Drews lavished on the basket-cases that arrived at the *Orientweek* newsroom, only to be sent back to Kai Tak airport within weeks, occasionally in wheelchairs. Sometimes that telling monosyllable made its appearance: Dan. And everyone would smile or give under-the-table kicks.

Drews' greatest genius was his ability, with tribute to Mr Ramalingaya, to bring new weather to the stormiest newsroom. Newspapers and magazines are moody places and the moods are gloomier than generally thought. Drews was able to counter the biggest blows to *Orientweek* morale: the painful resignations, the totally wrong cover stories, the weeks in which eight confusing events broke on deadline day, three of them on the subcontinent. It was partly his determined youth boosted by the agelessness of his staff. All that was needed was a Drews memo attached to one of the foul Australian cartoons he collected in the top drawer of his desk. Or one of his telephone tantrums in which a caller received abuse straight from the Founding Editor. Or the famous Drews desktop stomp: he was the only editor in Hong Kong, who, from a standing position, could leap atop a desk with both cowboy boots. He did so often, honouring all the reporters in turn, but only those engaged in serious phone interviews, preferably long distance, to the subcontinent whenever possible.

Major crises called for a blowout night at the Ball, Drews' private sleaze club, where the girls had rubbery nipples but didn't smell from the crotch, or weren't supposed to, no matter how close they got. 'And that's more than I can say for the Foxtrot,' Drews proclaimed, blowing smoke from the cigarettes he smoked on Ball nights. Hangovers were the great levellers and Drews held his Wanchai blowouts only before deadlines: he wanted the staff to both frolic and suffer together. And it worked. The Ball cushioned some of the magazine's worst blows, including the premier hospitalization of one Timothy P. Marquand.

Which was, as I wisely proclaimed, the first tremor of a midlife crisis at *Orientweek* magazine.

The second tremor came straight from the bedrock of Hong Kong island via Tiananmen Square. Life stopped in Hong Kong for several days in June 1989. Ever after it hardly seemed sufficient to be young, to work late, to make piles of money – not an option for *Orientweek* staffers – or to beat the *Far Eastern Economic Review* on a regular basis. For the future was on the march, intending, it appeared, to trample all that had come before it. To make matters worse, *Orientweek*'s coverage of the Tiananmen slaughter was a rout. Claudia chose that moment to have her baby. (And within weeks, she lost both the story of her career and her job despite numerous appeals to 'Dan' – a fuck-up in journalism can kill both salary and love.) The invaluable Tim Marquand was in Canossa, attached like a wilted parachute to varicoloured tubes and wires. Rusty Graves was in place, of course, living up to his nickname. In desperation, Drews sent in the Missing Link from Jakarta, whose stories never again contained the left-leaning assuredness of his pre-Tiananmen files. Drews spent a week shouting into telephones and shaking copies of the *International Herald Tribune* over his head, which no one had seen him do before. The *Far Eastern Economic Review* had been shaken over Drews' head. The *Bangkok Post*, the *Philippine Inquirer* and the *Indian Express*. But the *Herald Tribune*?

To be blunt, *Orientweek* forfeited the story of its life to the networks and the mainstream papers, which Drews despised.

'The *New York Times*!' he bellowed. 'We're behind the *New York Times*? Why the fuck are we in this business?'

Then came the photo foul-up. Sammy unplugged the photo-receiver in favour of the coffee-maker. Of course, Sammy was new: his predecessor had emigrated to Australia.

'Someday we'll laugh at this,' whispered Kelvin Chu.

'I won't,' said lovely Marietta.

Everyone admitted the pencil-sketched Tiananmen cover was not one of *Orientweek*'s most attractive, although it wasn't true that Drews did it himself with a ruler.

'With just one more hour we could have had colour,' maintained Kelvin.

'*This* would have looked better in colour?' asked Marietta.

'I'm sorry,' said Kelvin.

'So am I,' said Marietta. 'Jeez – so is this cover.'

When Rusty Graves came to town for R & R, he found Drews barricaded in his office. A week later, the Missing Link visited en route to Jakarta. The chill had yet to thaw.

'God, it was a disaster up there.'

'Tell us,' said Marietta.

'Anybody want to go to Wanchai? I have stories that would curl your hair.'

'It's curled,' said Marietta, whose hair was very long and very straight.

'And I thought Indonesia was brutal. We look like a paradise now. Honkers, fuck, it's sunk.'

Kelvin winced. 'We were hoping for an invitation to the Ball.' He gestured toward Drews' door.

But the door was sealed. Drews' sweater hung over the back, obscuring vision through the glass pane.

'What about the Foxtrot? That's not such a bad place.'

Dolly, asked to call, reported that the Foxtrot had closed.

'For good?' Kelvin seemed appalled. Even bar girls were deserting the ship. 'Something to do with Tiananmen?'

'It's closed,' said Dolly. 'That's all they would say.'

They all looked at Drews' door and the sagging sweater.

'If this goes on much longer,' said Marietta, 'I might as well go back to the *Review*. We need some goddamned *weather* in here.'

The breakthrough was the Tim Marquand cover 'Mao Lives', heavily rewritten by Drews and, some said, pulled through tubes from the ailing Tim. There was no trouble with the cover art this time – Marietta saw to that – and when the story came out, you could see no other face at the FCC but Mao's as the correspondents devoured their noodles behind fresh copies of *Orientweek* magazine. By cocktail time those correspondents would be accusing the ailing China-watcher of being a famous reactionary, or apologist, or middle-of-the-roader. But that didn't matter. For several hours, *Orientweek* was once again supreme.

The next Thursday, after lunch, the staff found a communication from Drews on the bulletin board. It outlined the rules for a treasure hunt to be held the following day.

'A treasure hunt!' marvelled Kelvin. 'There hasn't been one since . . .'

'1979,' said Dolly, who functioned as both librarian and *Orientweek* antiquarian.

'Before all of our times,' said Marietta. 'Wasn't there that famous fuck-up?'

Dolly giggled, covering her mouth with her hand. The fuck-up was, in some opinions, Drews'. His clue, a dried red chilli, had been too clever. An over-zealous team captain, scanning the CAAC schedule, spotted a flight to Luchou that very afternoon. Hadn't Drews always maintained the best chillies came from Luchou? He boarded the flight and didn't return for a week. (Drews' intended destination: the Red Pepper restaurant in Causeway Bay.)

' "Wrongway" Wong. Where is he now?'

'Canada,' said Dolly. 'His brother-in-law has a restaurant.'

Marietta sighed. ' "Wrongway" no more. Pity us. Pity Hong Kong. He was such a good reporter.'

Drews' instructions were more precise this time. The treasure hunt would take no longer than one day. All the clues were available on the north side of Hong Kong island or by telephone from Hong Kong island. No one, Drews instructed, should board any airplane or, indeed, even wander in the direction of Kai Tak airport.

'That holds for the clues,' Drews wrote. 'The grail itself could be located anywhere in the territory or anywhere atop our "fragrant harbour".'

'Oh Lord.' Marietta pressed her tummy. 'I get seasick.'

There were only three teams because of staff shrinkage. The memo didn't state it but everyone knew that, like last time, Command Central would be at the *Orientweek* newsroom. Drews would hold court, accompanied by his cigarette-smoking wife, offering clues to those who, at one time or another, had called him Dan. The memo concluded with a warning: treasure hunt expenses would not be reimbursed by *Orientweek*.

'Oh Lord, who put in last time?'

'The Missing Link,' said Kelvin. 'I'd bet on it. Cabs and food.'

Dolly nodded. 'His popped tyre. $150. That was a lot in 1979.'

'It doesn't say what we're searching for,' said Marietta. 'Last time it was a Vietnamese refugee.'

'I guess Drews will tell us tomorrow,' said Kelvin.

'Wouldn't it be nice if it was a night on the town?' Marietta twirled around the newsroom. 'Or a housing allowance? After all these years? We could move to the Midlevels.'

'A green card,' sighed Kelvin.

But the next morning at ten o'clock, the newsroom was empty. Three envelopes with identical clues were pinned to the bulletin board. There was no Command Central and no Drews. Extra clues seemed unlikely: no teases, taunts, day-long jokes. There was no Miki Drews and no revelation about the grail.

'Oh Lord,' said Marietta. 'You know what that means.'

'What?' demanded Tisch McAuliffe, a team captain. Tisch was bossy, fattish and had pointy teeth. She wore bright sports clothes with little pink socks. Her nickname around the office was 'Death'. Her partner, in life as well as treasure hunts, was Philip Knisely, who worked on the business side. Philip's newsroom nickname was, inevitably, 'A Fate Worse Than', except to the Chinese staff, who referred to the couple as 'Left Cheek' and 'Right Cheek' in guttural Cantonese.

'Don't you see?' Marietta flicked a cigarette. 'We're searching for goddamned Drews himself!'

The first clue brought all three teams, simultaneously, to the ladies room of the Macao ferry. The cleverest clue was: 'Synonym for animosity.' (Answer: pique, or The Peak.) The most difficult was the ultimate: 'Home to Macarthur, Iran or Iraq.'

'What the fuck does that mean?' Dusk was approaching. The sweat on Kelvin's T-shirt was evaporating, leaving an undulating circle of salt.

Marietta clicked her fingers. 'Where's Luis? Which team is he on?'

'I think he's on his holiday.'

Marietta rushed to a payphone. After negotiations with the long distance operator, she shouted into the receiver: 'Can you hear me? Manila Hotel? Do you have a guest by the name of D'Souza?' Her little finger was in her ear and she grimaced with the effort of shouting across seas. 'Luis D'Souza? From *Orientweek* magazine?'

There was a pause and then a familiar voice. 'Is it Etta? You're the first. You're going to win!'

The final drive was long and surprisingly lovely.

'I've never been this far north,' said Marietta. 'After four years in Hong Kong.'

'My parents brought me here so long ago. I wonder who comes anymore.'

At the end of the road was, of course, a border. But before that came a blackened sign and a neglected parking lot. A dirt path led through a former picnic ground. Ancient, decapitated barbecues dotted the site. A row of skeletal huts lined the path: abandoned souvenir stands.

The final high ground of the Crown Colony of Hong Kong was a prominent hill with trees. Beneath the lacy silhouettes, sitting in trampled dirt, was a tall man in a T-shirt that read, from the back, 'Asia Without Ties!' Drews was gazing north to an expanse of rice paddies and a small village. Workers pushed tiny implements and led miniature water buffaloes. They inched between fields heading for home.

Marietta placed a hand on his shoulder. He looked up. 'Etta, I hoped it would be you.' If it wasn't for his eyes, one could consider Drews ageless. He was the overgrown leprechaun, the hairy elf, who loomed so large in his staffers' imaginations. The eyes still sparkled, though they were set in small pouches of fine wrinkles. His hand, long and veined, stroked a flecked beard.

'Sit with me. Looking lovely – I don't know how you do it.' Drews craned around. 'Kelvin, sit on this side.'

He gestured at the rice paddies. 'Can you believe that's what it's all about? That's China. And this is us.' Drews looked up at the trees. He placed his hand on the mound of dirt. 'That's what I've been thinking all day.'

Marietta said: 'It seems so peaceful.'

'Miki and I came here on our first day. Our first day in Hong Kong! Timmy insisted. He boarded us on this ancient steam train. The trip took hours. It was our honeymoon, believe it or not. Miki and I were married two days. She bought squid on the platform, like you get in Japan. I had forgotten it until today.'

'Weird place for a honeymoon,' said Kelvin.

'This place was jammed with people,' said Drews. 'They stared across into China, took pictures, gloated over the fact that they were here and the Chinese were there. For the three of us it was everything. Timmy was the rising China-watcher — watching *that*.' Drews pointed. 'I was the new journalist. We were young, we were in love ...'

'The three of you,' whispered Marietta.

'Yes.' Drews faltered. 'The three of us.' He shook his head. 'Hong Kong was going to be our own little kingdom. We knew it. We could see the future. Timmy was so excited he couldn't sit. Someone had died the day before: was it Walter Brennan? Or Bud Abbott? I remember Timmy striding through these trees, saying goodbye to Walter Brennan or Bud Abbott and sounding his new theories about China. The other people thought he was a madman. We thought he was a genius.'

'Poor Tim,' said Marietta.

'On the ride home, Timmy decided he'd write a spy novel beginning on this hill and ending here. Under these trees.' Drews looked up. 'What kind of trees are they? I've never known trees and flowers.'

'I only know the Chinese name,' said Kelvin.

'He was going to dedicate it to Bud Abbott. Yes — it was Bud Abbott who had died. We spent night after night, the three of us, plotting the book on a huge piece of cardboard in Timmy's apartment. I have that cardboard still, with all these boxes connected by lines. I was in favour of a tragic ending, a single rifle shot from that rice paddy. But Timmy wouldn't hear of it. "A happy ending, my friends! Nothing else will do! Not for us — not for *our* book." That's what he always called it. Our book.'

Drews shook his head. 'I realized today, sitting here, this place means nothing anymore. You couldn't set a scene here. The earth has shifted beneath our feet. Tourists don't even come here anymore.'

Marietta put her arm around her boss's shoulder.

'It looks exactly the same,' Drews murmured. 'It's the same picture.' (The reference was to his photographic memory; Drews was comparing mental images from fifteen years apart.) 'And yet everything has changed on our side, changed completely. Do they know it over there?'

'You could always write another novel, Drews. Without Tim. Major motion picture.'

Drews looked at her. 'That's not it. It's like your child has been diagnosed with some incurable disease. All you do is hover over the bed ... I mean, the magazine ...'

Marietta squeezed him.

'And we worried about Philippine film stars, Cabinet reshuffles, Indian insurgencies ...'

'And neckties,' said Kelvin.

Drews gave a surprised laugh. 'Neckties? If I had to do it all over again, that's the only thing I'd repeat.'

There were shouts and car-door slams. Crates of Carlsberg were hauled up the hill.

'We spent a fucking hour trying to find the Iranian and Iraqi Consulates,' protested Tisch. 'Did you know the Iraqi Consulate is all the way in Baguio Villas? God I hate losing.'

'What about Macarthur, Death?'

'Philip got it all confused with Macarthur Park in Los Angeles. We went to the US Embassy, then to Statue Square.'

'The US Consulate,' said Philip.

'Consulate,' Tisch barked. 'Okay, Mr Genius?' She turned her back on him. 'I remembered the song, of course. "Someone left the cake out in the ra-ain ..."' But how should I know it was a real park? I'm not West Coast, I'm Philadelphia.'

'Poor Death,' said Kelvin.

'Don't call me that.'

'Her name is Anastasia,' said Philip.

'From my grandmother,' said Tisch. 'Named after the tsarina, before she was shot.'

'Your grandmother was shot?' asked Drews. 'I'm very sorry.'

The beer ran out and Dolly, with a demure giggle, asked to be driven home to Happy Valley. The rest decided to adjourn to the FCC. Drews was the last to head toward the parking lot. Marietta joined him for a final glimpse of the rice paddies across the border. He peered through the trees as if he could, with proper concentration, find some distinction between the mental image of fifteen years before and the scene before him.

'They need some new weather up there, Drews.'

He showed pained, hollow eyes: the leprechaun suddenly aged. 'We need some umbrellas down here, Etta.'

Marietta shook her head dolefully. 'I, um . . .' Then she burst out laughing.

'What?'

'I'm sorry,' Marietta said. 'It's just . . . oh, I'm terribly sorry. I just thought of that song. And it seemed so appropriate.'

'You mean . . .'

Marietta nodded eagerly. She hummed nine notes.

'Yes,' Drews said. 'Our cake is a fucking mess.'

They drove on an illuminated highway until black fields gave way to enormous housing blocks with rows of bright windows. At the harbour, the car descended into a fluorescent tunnel. They emerged onto the rock called Hong Kong, a world of endless, receding light and shining, hard concrete. Except, as every local engineer knows, the foundations in the colony are dangerously shallow. Beneath that concrete skin there was little to rely on: a fragile tube carrying a subway. Sewage lines. And undisturbed Chinese rock.

At the FCC, Drews got into a drunken quarrel with Erhard Dietrich over Tim Marquand's Mao cover. He concluded the argument with a desktop stomp on the Club Table. Shortly afterwards, Drews went missing. It was his peculiar habit: he never intimated his departure, never bade farewell and always left alone, except on nights when a new romance was to be consummated. And even then, technically, Drews left alone, to meet his paramour in one of the two dark lanes connecting Ice House Street to Queen's Road. Where, rumour had it, lovemaking frequently began and not merely foreplay. Some claimed to have seen it, or nearly seen it. They heard scuffles and scowls, signifying *interruptus*, and saw a couple fleeing into a taxi, including a tall, bearded, curly-haired man.

But this wasn't easy to credit, for at the FCC there was someone who claimed to have seen most any event in history if you asked around and the hour was late enough. Every single event in the history of local journalism had been witnessed, including Gutenberg's visit to the colony to have a suit made. If you inquired at the bar.

Soon, the club started to empty. 'Death' departed with her 'Fate Worse Than'. Kelvin put his hand on Marietta's petite shoulder and said: 'Work tomorrow.'

From the taxi window, Marietta scanned the pedestrians along Lower

Albert Road. It had become habit. Everyone at *Orientweek* looked for Drews on the early morning pavements of Hong Kong. Most party-night post-mortems concluded with a description of Drews striding energetically through Wanchai, or pacing the deserted streets of Central, or morosely walking home to Shu Fai Terrace, the skyscrapers leaning in on him. Even on regular worknights people watched him depart and described the sight the following day. Was he weary? Was he happy? What direction did he take?

'Funny Drews mentioning a child,' said Marietta. 'I never thought he was interested. We all know about Miki's miscarriage. But that was when?'

'Too late now,' said Kelvin.

Marietta spied a tall male walking near the Governor's mansion. She touched the cabbie's shoulder and asked him to slow. But it was a homeless beggar.

High above that road, in Canossa Hospital, a light shone in a third-storey window. A dark-haired woman in pearls stood at the window smoking a cigarette.

'He's down there, you know. Wandering those mean streets.'

'Don't talk, Tim. The nun said. Just try to sleep.'

'He may be on his way up here.'

The large, expressionless face of Miki Drews, Daniel Drews' Hiroshima, moved slowly from side to side. 'He'll be here tomorrow.'

'If I'm to sleep, just flick that switch. Over there. The itty bitty one.'

'We want you to wake up in the morning,' Miki said. 'Sleep. Soon I'm going.'

'He's having a drink.'

Miki Drews smoked. She turned and saw the huge man asleep, his swollen face open at the mouth.

'Yes,' she whispered. 'A big drink.'

Drews was drinking in a bar with a plaster elephant head above its door. He drank until 4.30 and never again remembered those last three beers, or the money he loaned six Pakistanis for cab fare, or the noodles he ate, or the glass he dropped, or the pass he made at the woman with the hairy mole.

At 4.30 am, there were no *Orientweek* staffers awake to witness Drews' journey home. And little to see: a tall man with long black curls and an impressive beard waiting for a taxi in the neon sunshine of Wanchai. His mask-like face as the taxi wound its way past Adventist Hospital. The generous tip, the over-fond salutation, the usual trouble with the key. And then the passage that no staffer had ever witnessed, which all were curious about. Into the high-ceilinged flat. Across the Afghan rugs and down the corridor, into the shadows at its end. A door opens, and closes. Was it the master bedroom – still? – or the guest room? After all these years, still, that was the big question at the *Orientweek* newsroom.

For those refugees and exiles had all come to Hong Kong alone and they knew the symptoms of solitude. They watched out for each other and made it a point to concern themselves with each other's pasts and presents. The future, they knew, was beyond their reach.

Imagine from the Hong Kong sky the sound of a big, sloppy nose-blow. Cloud-sized tears thundered aside. A deafening clap of celestial happiness. For all this is as bloody new to me as it is to you. I was indisposed the day the *Orientweek* staff wasted a day, on company time, searching for their elfin idol. Faithful Dolly Leung, giggling nervously behind a dwarf hand, as her team races through the Lion Rock tunnel; Tisch and Philip at Statue Square with matching sneakers and spare tyres; lovely Marietta with glittering Irish eyes and her pinkie in an ear as she shouts down the line to Saddam D'Souza in, of all places, Manila. My fond, foolish friends: how I missed them, goddammit! And what about Danny, the self-anointed hairy grail: for what was he searching? A new mental picture? Is this the curse of the photographic memory: an addiction to mental photo collecting? Was Drews collecting his own triptych of Hong Kong, Past, Present and Future? The Past was 1975, his first day in the Crown Colony. The central image was Hong Kong on the brink in 1989. The frame on the right would remain empty until the future bought its ticket and boarded the southbound train: the Steamroll Express. But Danny chose his subject poorly. The border was meaningless. The changes he pursued occurred closer to home. His wife Miki in 1975: young, full-faced, wearing that impossibly wide smile and sitting on a barstool, a small pearl bracelet on the arm that clasps Drews' shoulder. The centre frame in 1989: Miki, aged and wearing expensive, long pearls, dealing herself cards at the dining-room table in Shu Fai Terrace. She is alone and she pushes away with her toe a small, sad dog. The Future . . . well, again, that must remain blank. What might it be? The same woman, merely older, dealing her worn cards, the dog dead or disposed of? Or is it a dining room empty altogether? Is the subject chosen too decorously? Why not the Drewses' marriage bed, Past, Present and Future? Where is *Orientweek*, or my own flat in Conduit Road, which encapsulated so much of Danny Drews' life? Can Danny be content with a series of photos when something larger is required: a mural perhaps? At the very least a one-reeler with the jerky movements of the past, single room sets and faces, eternal faces, with black-rimmed, emotion-filled eyes.

Danny is rummaging around in the past. Dare I suggest something unsatisfactory, something unspeakable: that the future is best found in the present? That sounds smug, no doubt, the wretched wisdom of a dead loudmouth. But even when alive, I warned people against malingering in the past or the future. I had a philosophy I energetically proselytized, not only at midnight but on midafternoons in the newsroom as Dolly Leung nibbled custard cups over pieces of salvaged copy paper. Did none of them learn from the China-watcher's oft-quoted verse? *Roses, wine, a friend to share* . . . (It's my signature poem.) *Time is heedless, time is heartless* . . . And then in a room at Canossa Hospital, located on the lofty Peak itself, above the futile scurrying and worrying of Hong Kong island, I gave them the ultimate proof at dawn on October 12, 1989. Which, one would think, would be bloody hard to ignore.

> *Life, our mortal life, hath sweetness,*
> *As its sweetness, so its fleetness . . .*
> *Abstinence I do abhor,*
> *Cup on cup, my Saqi, pour.*

But the future is powerful. And down there in Central, in the basement bar named the Nullah, with its plank tables and its eternal aroma of old beer – which a billion Chinese cadres will be unable to exorcise – the future's ugly magic is being worked on two of our 'friends'. That's the term at the magazine: 'Friends of *Orientweek*'. This included bankers and advertisers, Japanese and Koreans, trusty sources and, on occasion, competitors of the feebler sort. Along with old 'friends' turned less friendly with the passage of years. Unfortunately, a magazine can't choose its friends as a man can, or a woman. Particularly in retrospect.

The Nullah can wait: that should be its motto. The Nullah is on the edge of Hong Kong island, almost in the water, in a low-ceilinged, below-sea-level basement that appears on no known ordinance map. When one of the colony's bankers or stockbrokers lost his emotional balance in Central or the Midlevels, he would roll down the hill into the Nullah to be accosted by toothsome, jabbering interior designers or female journalists best described, in the broadest sense, as 'freelance'.

The Nullah was more anonymous than the Foreign Correspondents Club. Not because the people were any different – they were the same – but because its lights were dimmer, its cigarette smoke thicker, the hour later. If the clock could be turned back in Hong Kong, the first people to jump at the chance would not be six million Cantonese eager for extra days in the moneymaking sun but a handful of expatriates desiring to erase a few dark memories from that sour-smelling cellar.

I propose we back up a few hours. We must back up literally, up the hill into Central, in the direction of the FCC and, beyond it, Victoria Peak. But not too far, for rents in Hong Kong climb with the altitude and just as steeply. In a small alley, two blocks from the FCC, there is a narrow building sandwiched between white office blocks. The alley is totally unlit: a mere shortcut where drunken lovemaking has been known to commence. The garbage trucks stop there nightly to collect an odoriferous pile that appears at 9 pm sharp. Most people in Hong Kong would be surprised to learn that a human actually lives in this alley: that someone remains when the office lights are extinguished. But there are a few residents in the anonymous building and one has just stepped from its doorway. He takes the long way around, for the garbage waits at the top of the alley, prompt as always, which is more than can be said for the garbage truck.

Our friend walks with the deliberate stride of someone accustomed to being recognized. When he hits Queen's Road, the shadows drop and we see why. It's a profile instantly recognizable to any reader of the Sunday *South China Morning Post*. That hawk-like beak: that head of silver hair with rakish sideburns. If he put his forefinger to his temple and pouted, he would perfectly match the photo appearing atop the column 'Nick's Beat'. The silver-haired man turns and labours up a hill. He enters the big, double doors of the FCC. We shall pause. I can easily describe what is happening under those ceiling fans. It's as familiar to me as my round face used to be in the men's room mirror. There is some backslapping, a wave from the far side of the bar. Some strained smiles, perhaps, and several glares from the Club Table. The FCC bar is long but one can go around it in an uninterrupted loop if necessary. Within minutes, insufficient time for the swiftest drink, Nick Naversen re-emerges with a slightly less confident step. Could he not find the person he sought? Or was there someone in the room he was forced to avoid? A creditor? An angry former colleague? Or his ex-wife Fran?

Fran Naversen is nearly as famous as her former husband and as staunch a regular at the expatriate haunts of the colony. 'The Baby Lady', they call her. The words aren't everything: the tone is important.

Nick Naversen flags a red taxicab and manoeuvres himself into the back. He wears his usual blue striped shirt with the white collar, custommade. But the shirt is strained by a belly the tailor hadn't foreseen. If the light was better, or if we were closer, we could see fraying on the white collar. Perhaps we could spy the belly itself, or its bushy grey navel, peeking between valiant buttons. Nick and I patronized the same Chinese tailor, Sunny, in Wanchai. From the looks of it, Sunny hasn't seen Nick in many years. The taxi heads uphill from Central and we lose sight as it disappears into the Midlevels. Where is Nick Naversen going? To the very Peak itself!

We've time for an amble in the opposite direction. The gates of the Hongkong Bank Building are down, so we have to skirt around. Statue Square is dark and abandoned. The Furama looms to the right, lit handsomely. Ahead we see the dark waters of the harbour and the final Star Ferry from Kowloon, the crimson glare of Tsim Sha Tsui catching on its corrugated wake. We're nearly at water's edge. There is an alley behind the Hong Kong Club, dark but for a doorway oozing yellow light. We don't have to wait long. Another taxi, the longer, older model, screeches to a halt. Nick Naversen lumbers out. He arranges his worn belt, jabs the blue-striped shirt under it, reaches the doorway of the Nullah and disappears.

At the bottom of narrow stairs, Nick enters a tunnel that leads to the Nullah proper: a wide, square beer hall with a parquet dance-floor and a Philippine trio with moustached, wicked grins. Nick orders a gin at the bar. Next to him is an anaemic Englishman, too young to be a Nullah habitué, but times are wearying in Hong Kong these days, even for the young. No one greets Nick or seems to recognize him. But his anonymity won't last long. The *Morning Post* readers know him, as do the TVB watchers. Anyone who has spent time in Hong Kong knows him intimately. Nick Naversen has knocked on most doors over the years, offering the proverbial shoeshine and his wolfish grin. He came to Hong Kong as a young journalist of energy and ambition and enjoyed a brief season of fame as one of the three founders of *Orientweek* magazine: the junior member of the troika, perhaps, less renowned than Daniel Drews and less popular than the China-watcher. But he was there at the beginning, one of the first to suggest we break from the *Review* and go it alone. 'Go it alone' – the phrase suited Nick and, in time, came to characterize his life. His stint on the news side didn't last long and he switched to the business side. That didn't last long either. He clinched a corner office at Sun Hung Kai, becoming the colony's first and foremost financial PR man. But the surf of time kept coming with higher and higher swells for prosperous Hong Kong until Nick found himself barely within sight of shore. He even left Hong Kong. But inevitably he returned. ('On the next bloody boat,' went the line at the Club Table.) Technically, Nick remained a PR man. His media training course for executives, he said, was a booming success. He also read the weekend news on TVB in a confident, caustic tone that some women found attractive. There was his *Morning Post* column, of course: racist, chauvinist, maliciously witty when possible, maliciously outrageous when not. Added to this was the growing fame of ex-wife Fran, the Baby Lady, who was regularly discussed on Radio Hong Kong's call-in show. A strident Filipina called her an exploiter of Third World poverty. A timorous, low British accent said she was a saviour to the colony's would-be parents. Fran's own voice could be heard on the radio, harsh and insistent or laughing a half-Nelson laugh. She sometimes featured in the Sunday *South China Morning Post*. Her photos could be frightening for those with a hangover: defensive, with blank eyes where the flash caught her spectacles. The camera gave her extra pounds: an angry mouth on a leaden, gigantic torso.

The usual comment was that Nick and Fran Naversen were 'made for each other'. This wasn't meant kindly and people continued saying it long after the couple had separated. Especially when Fran's adoption business picked up. 'She sells babies,' went the sneer at the FCC bar. 'Those two are made for each other.' Marriage was unable to hold some people together: Nick and Fran Naversen, in contrast, were incapable of being rent asunder by mere divorce. Something bound them together. Some called it insecurity, others talked about 'evil'. Greed, of course, was a given.

Nick Naversen sipped a drink. The Englishman beside him stared at the dancers on the dance-floor with undisguised longing. Nick gave an audible sneer. The song changed and the dancers returned to their tables. A sole male took to the floor wearing an open Hawaiian shirt. He began twirling to the music. He was deeply tanned. A Mexican hat hung down his back.

'Look at this turkey,' said Nick loudly. The Philippine band broke into huge smiles.

'Tourist, obviously.' The Englishman gulped nervously. For he recognized his hawk-nosed, silver-haired drinking companion from the television and the newspaper and feared to say anything more committal.

The man's solo dance became more robust and exhibitionist. He twirled around the whole floor.

'This is disgusting,' said Nick. 'Why do they let these people . . .'

With a crash, the tanned man lost balance and crashed through a row of empty chairs and tables. Waiters rushed to help him up. His Mexican hat got tangled in a chair. Nick snorted happily and offered the Englishman a drink. Nick felt a heavy tap on his shoulder.

'Hey!' It was a broadly-built woman with glasses magnifying poached-egg eyes. She wore a bulky sweater over black slacks. Gold dangled from her wrists and over her sweater. 'Funny meeting you here. Ha ha.'

The young Englishman recognized the famous Baby Lady and marvelled at her giant elbows, knees and hips. He wondered how to survive an introduction to what was known as the most hated couple in Hong Kong. A bartender delivered his drink.

'Enjoy. You owe me!' Nick guided Fran toward a booth in a far corner. 'I haven't seen you in dog years, Big Girl. What are you having – the usual?' A waiter flipped open a pad. 'One Drano, please.'

'I'll start with a Bloody Mary.' The waiter nodded. 'Spicy.' Fran pointed at the waiter threateningly. 'Got it? Spicy.' She slid into the booth and put two large elbows on the table. 'I thought you'd sworn off this place, Nick.'

'This is my neighbourhood now. I've moved.'

'Again?'

Nick nodded.

'Why?'

'Why do you think? I'm broke.'

Fran gave a forced laugh. 'I've heard that before. What about the media training?'

'Not working out, to tell the truth.'

'I noticed the advertisements growing smaller and smaller until . . .' She pursed her lips. 'Poof!'

'Such potential here in Hong Kong. Few corporations have more to hide.'

'And TVB?'

'They're still sitting on my proposal. The magazine show.'

'You've been talking about that magazine show for four years.'

'They're total shit for brains over there. Take it from me. Three years, not four.'

'Where did you move?' He told her the address. 'Behind Citibank? People *live* there?'

'None that I've managed to see.'

The cold poached eggs narrowed with thought. 'That's David Courtney's old flat. I've been there. It's tiny!'

'What were you doing in David Courtney's flat?'

'I handled it for the agency.'

'Didn't make much moolah on it. If only it had a room or two. I have to put my television on the toilet seat.'

'Yes,' said Fran. 'So did David. I remember his saying so. I thought it such a good idea. I put my own television on the toilet. And every Saturday night I watch you on TVB, your face coming up out of the bowl.'

Nick couldn't restrain a chuckle. He made a mental note to use the theme in his next column, replacing his own flat with that of a convenient 'friend' ('Real estate prices are really through the roof, as a friend recently found ...') and his newsreading face with that of a colleague recently arrived from London. Fran asked for a new drink, her 'usual' Guinness. Nick ordered a refill of his gin.

'How's *your* business?'

'Fantastic!'

'Bringing out a new model? You ought to try white babies – match the parents.'

Fran's eyelids fluttered impatiently.

'Revolution in the industry. Or designer babies.'

She leaned forward: 'It's nothing more than supply and demand.'

'Send me a card when you have your end-of-year sale.'

Fran lowered her voice. 'I've had a real breakthrough, Nick. My own judge. In Iloilo. My margins are about to double.' She tried to snap two yeasty fingers.

'What about Korea?'

'I talk Korea on the radio because everyone wants a North Asian baby.

But the supply . . .' She made a raspberry. 'The Philippines is the place for babies. Indonesia's possible, but still expensive. I'm thinking of branching out into South America. Chile's a great market.'

'Tough quality control.'

'That's a racist remark.'

Nick shrugged. 'Everyone's racist.'

'Don't tell *me*. You don't know how tough it is to get these parents to accept some of the babies. And I'm not talking about hare-lips. I've stopped hare-lips. Not worth the agony.'

Nick hummed agreement.

'Take India, for example. Big possibilities there. But I wouldn't even mention India on the radio. The phone would stop ringing like that.' Again the large hand rose: the fleshy fingers rubbed together.

'You could use some voice training, my dear. You sound like you're selling killer dogs, not babies.'

Fran gave her mirthless 'Oh yeah?' laugh. 'You've been on the radio too, dearest. You caught real heat for that column about the white bathroom attendant in the Chinese nightclub.'

'I interviewed him myself. Went to Kowloon. Amazing story. Wimpy kid from Los Angeles. The Chinese love him. They use the toilet several times each night. Towel bill is enormous. And the place is packed. Talk about racism. The stall door swings both ways.'

'Is he, you know, gay?'

'Hope so,' said Nick.

'And I saw your column from New York. About the working women of the Big Apple. With their "well-filled blouses". Radio Hong Kong got several calls.'

'Big apples indeed.' The wolf smiled. 'Damn. You always think of the best lines after the column is published.'

'The big question, Nick, is why you went to New York. Expensive trip. What's going on, dearest?'

The initial tension dissolved between the Naversens for they were back on the comfortable ground called business. The two were business partners still. They were directors of a major Hong Kong corporation. Its name, of course, was Orientweek Holdings Ltd. Nick, as one of the founding trio, had owned a third of the magazine's shares until Fran claimed half during the divorce. At numerous times in his career, Nick had attempted to sell his *Orientweek* shares. But the magazine had never paid big dividends. The other shares were cemented up in the friendship of Drews and the famous China-watcher. The only value of *Orientweek* shares was if the magazine was bought.

'So that's why you went to New York!' Fran's eyes widened behind her spectacles. 'To try and sell *Orientweek* again!'

'Try, yeah.' Nick ordered another round of drinks. 'And try like a bugger. I went to the three biggies.'

'Like . . .'

'Like *Reader's Digest*. In Pleasantville. Which is an unpleasant cab fare, believe me, from almost anywhere.'

'Big bucks!' Fran rubbed her thumb and forefinger together.

'Forget it,' said Nick. 'I got a big lecture on 1997 and Deng's window of opportunity. Have you heard of Deng's window of opportunity?'

'No. What is it?'

'Fran!' cried Nick.

'Okay, okay. Who was next?'

'The great Robber Barons of Dow Jones, the *Wall Street Journal*. Dow Jones was all practicalities. They couldn't get off the printing press. Our "big debacle", they called it. Knew the price down to the penny. Can it be gotten out, they asked?'

'Well?'

'We got it in, I said.'

Fran stared at him.

'Well, what was I supposed to say? I don't know a thing about printing presses.'

'Go on. Tell me about *Time*. I know you went to Time Inc. They're the big catch. What did *Time* say?'

'*Time* was like the State Department. Big oak doors. An absurdly large boardroom. There were five of them, all in shirtsleeves. All men.'

'What happened to the great working women of Manhattan? With their well-filled blouses?'

'They were near my hotel. Damned expensive too.'

'I don't want to hear about it.'

'Surprisingly good-looking. Anyway, *Time* dismissed 1997 as an inconvenience they could overcome. The printing press never came up. We even talked a price range: a very satisfactory price range.'

'What price range?'

'Keep your bra on.'

'Tell me!'

Nick raised a fist and uncurled a thumb, forefinger, and all the remaining fingers. Fran squinted suspiciously. Then he raised a second fist and opened the fingers simultaneously.

'Ten million!'

'But wait. *Time* was very unhappy about the negotiations of 1984. I tried to tell them Drews would see sense now, after Tiananmen. There was this strange silence. Then everyone looked at one guy, a bland, buttoned-up creature with razor lips. Apparently he was sent to discuss a sale in 1984. A *tête-à-tête* with the Founding Editor himself. And apparently Drews closed the meeting with a desktop stomp. The *Time* guy had this tight smile and these furious eyes. He was still humiliated, years later. He mentioned Drews' cowboy boots. He still saw them landing inches away from his nose on Drews' desk. Someone else said: "He's not a man to do business with." Razor lips said: "He's a madman." '

'Didn't anyone laugh?'

'Funny you mention it. Yes, someone laughed. I did. But no one joined me.'

'The sale is off?'

'*Time* is still interested. That's what they say. "*Very* interested." But they don't believe Drews will sell. They told me, in effect, to return when I had Drews' head on a platter.'

'I knew as much. So why did you even bother?'

Nick gave his famous smile. 'You're getting a little dull these days, Fran. What happened to that killer instinct I used to love?'

'Ha!' Her expression tightened with offense. 'Nick, why are you smiling like that?'

'I told them Drews didn't matter any more. Or wouldn't. Soon. They were interested in that. Most interested.'

'What do you mean Drews doesn't matter?' Fran's puffy eyes widened. 'Oh my God! Tim!'

Nick whispered vehemently: 'They say he's nearly dead.'

'I wondered about that item in your column. About his Tiananmen cover.'

'A little puffery. Thought it would make him happy in his last days. He's in Canossa, you know.'

'He's been there a million times.'

'I tell you, Fran, he's never leaving Canossa again.' Nick's voice dropped. 'Drews and Miki have moved furniture from Conduit Road into the hospital room. You should see it . . .'

'Who told you?'

'They've moved his bed. You remember those abacus lamps? From Stanley Market?'

'You visited! You dog!'

'I had to see for myself. I went there tonight. Blown up like a blimp. I've never seen anything like it. Makes you wonder about this.' He jiggled his glass. 'I think I'll switch to beer. Waiter!'

'What did you say?'

'He was asleep.'

'Chickenshit.'

'I would have talked to him if I had to. Christ, I brought supplies.' He patted his pocket, producing the sound of clinking glass. 'From the airplane. Figured it couldn't hurt him now. Wish someone would do the same for me someday.'

Fran showed baby-like teeth. 'My pleasure.'

'The point is, Fran, when Tim ups it our day has come. We've finally got a chance. To sell *Orientweek*.'

'A chance.' Fran wagged a milky finger. 'Don't forget the board.'

Then the conversation was consumed by corporate arcania, which Hong Kong residents learn by osmosis, as Milwaukee understands beer and Wisconsin knows its cheeses. They counted director seats on eager fingers. When *Orientweek* was established, each of the initial troika had been made directors and asked to nominate one other. Nick had named Fran. Drews had chosen the loyal banker who provided *Orientweek*'s financing. Tim Marquand had nominated Miki Drews, making it all one happy family.

'Who inherits Tim's shares?'

'Best bet is Saqi,' said Nick. 'He's taken the board seat, remember, from the last meeting.'

'So even if we get Saqi on our side,' said Fran, brow wrinkled in concentration, 'and he presumably wants the money – he is Cantonese – we still have Miki Drews to worry about. Technically, Saqi could ask for a change in directors, but that would take an extraordinary meeting.' Fran shook her head. 'He won't change her. And that leaves us with three: you, me and Saqi. Three isn't enough. We need four: four out of seven.'

For there were seven directors of *Orientweek*, as per Hong Kong company law. Drews had chosen the seventh director with typical fancy, and, to top it off, named him chairman of Orientweek Holdings Ltd.

'We need the old man,' said Nick.

'The old man,' said Fran. 'How are we going to get the old man?'

'Fuck knows.'

'I mean, what does he get if *Orientweek* is sold? *Nada*. He owns what: ten shares? And he loses his position.'

'I know, I know.' Nick put his head in his hands and spoke to the plank table. 'I know what you're thinking. And I don't like it any more than you. We'll have to offer him a cut.'

'A big cut,' said Fran.

'From both our shares.'

Fran laughed, forced as always, but with a touch of genuine mirth. 'I don't need the money like you do.'

'For God's sake,' said Nick. 'Let's worry about that later. We have to get Saqi first and then the old man. Does anyone know where he is these days? Does anyone fucking care? And let's get this straight from the start: this cut has to be as small as possible. This is my last windfall. This is Aunt Ethel kicking the bucket, this is Hollywood calling. This is my fucking future. I don't want to give it away to some decrepit old ...'

'Has-been?'

'Has-been?' Nick Naversen laughed loudly. 'I'm a has-been. Nothing wrong with that. Rather comforting at a certain age. That old man stopped being a has-been twenty-five years ago.'

I know where the old man is and only I know. There is an old café behind the Lee Gardens Hotel rarely patronized by expatriates of the Naversen variety. It's on a small lane and looks like a cheap rendezvous from old Shanghai. A recessed door with blackened glass; chipped painted letters spelling out a forgotten name. The waiters are old Portuguese half-castes. The tables are timeless and colourless and, let's hope, moderately clean. The old man sits in his corner drinking coffee laced with brandy. He is totally erect, as always, his chair sideways, his starchy, white head tipped against the window and the busyness outside. He seems in a kind of daze, staring intently through the dim room but seeing nothing. What is he thinking about this night? What does he think about any night? What has he thought about for the past twenty-four years? Many have speculated over the decades and few have claimed success. Is he thinking of the poet's words, which sum up his strange life?

> *Doth time tarry for thy prizing,*
> *Or make speed for thy despising? . . .*
> *Abstinence I do abhor,*
> *Cup on cup, my Saqi, pour.*

Only I know where Evan Olcott is tonight. Only I know his full, true story. In retrospect, I wish I had passed it along before I said *au revoir* at dawn in a belch of black blood. Told it to anyone – to Danny, to my Saqi even. What a difference that would have made to the story I am now forced to tell.

But perhaps I wasn't the only one who knew Evan Olcott's story. That's what I believed: that's what the old man insisted. But there are other ways of knowing than being told. There is guile and there is greed. There is desperation and flattery. So too is there wisdom and empathy: bonds that come from life, which I did experience – let no bloody fool say otherwise – and age, which I happened to bunk. I learned this from another remnant of Hong Kong's past, another of journalism's has-beens, and I learned it in a most appropriate venue: high above the present, with a clear view of all we called life in those towering concrete canyons. Alice Giles was a regular on Canossa's third floor. She checked in frequently, hobbling along the green corridor followed by a plump Philippine maid who carried jars of a viscous brown liquid that, apparently, Alice Giles lived on. There was a time when she was the worrisome case and I would visit her on my discharge days. She could be very weak: a horse-faced woman, too tall for the hospital bed, with bangs of greasy white hair. Over time, the pattern reversed: Alice would visit me on her discharge days, trying to ignore the awful sight in the bed before her. Her maid was proven right, I guess. 'She fine.' The maid danced slightly when she spoke, a heavy woman's jig. 'She always like this. Just fine.' Alice was fine, after all. Her only problem was that life made her sick from time to time.

Alice had been in Hong Kong forever, or so it seemed. In the old days, she was one of the few non-China-watchers. Business was her speciality and she exposed some of the colony's earliest scoundrels. I met her on my first night at the Foreign Correspondents Club when she was still a towering legend. She was there at the Club Table, eating a sundae at midnight and trading the wickedest barbs in her beautiful, girlish whisper. I was preposterously young and had never seen a journalist eating ice cream at midnight or, for that matter, anytime during the day. I hoisted my drink and said, in the anxious boisterousness of youth: 'That stuff will kill you, ma'am.' Alice looked up with joyous eyes. Her hair was already snowy white.

'What a way to go!' she replied. It occurs to me now: Alice Giles was the only foreign correspondent with whom I never shared a drink.

The legend faded over the years and Alice became a kind of ghost, labouring through the FCC with thin, unwashed hair, swinging an oddly bulbous belly under her tunic. A lively exchange could revive those red-rimmed eyes: Alice Giles never lost her talent for ripostes, slipped through the ribs in that little girl's whisper. But the past had something on Alice Giles, which it claimed very early. It's no wonder she frightened the boys at the FCC. One had to wonder about the wicked little girl and what had trapped and encrusted her. Few had the courage to investigate in fear it could occur similarly to them.

A late-life scoop resurrected Alice's career and her standing at the FCC. But Canossa continued to press its claim. And that's where we became friends.

She started visiting me, usually at night, with music for my tape recorder. We had similar sentimental tastes. I introduced her to Gordon MacRae's reprise of 'If I Loved You'. She played 'Peter Pan' for me and a jazz song with the memorable lyric: 'I like to tinkle on an old piana . . .' Once, with a clumsy, accompanying jig, she performed 'Love Potion No. 9'. Her maid was always there, sometimes accompanied by an alert, brown-skinned daughter. After an initial period of suspicion, my own cupbearer struck up a friendship with the maid. They conspired for hours in the hallway: a fat, giggling Filipina and Kin Wah, my dourly Cantonese acolyte. Alice liked to stand by the window taking strength from the incandescent skyscrapers beneath us. I lay in bed in the glaring light of a hospital room or, much later, the lamps from my own flat.

'I've always adored this place,' she said one night, staring toward the harbour. 'It's the only spot on earth that feels like home.'

'The great escape,' I said. 'You've heard it all these years at the FCC, old girl. Those people claiming they never could "go back". Pay attention to the choice of words. I think everyone comes to bloody Hong Kong for the same reason: to cut themselves loose from the past. To move ahead, to find the present, totally unencumbered.'

'To find a future.'

'The hell with the future!'

'Yes.' She whispered a line from a Japanese poem.

It is the autumn wind that hurts most.

I responded with my own verse:

> *Time hath all young lovers slain,*
> *Time is heedless, time is heartless –*
> *Saqi, fill and fill again.*

Then I asked: 'Did you know Evan Olcott?'

'In the old days. I know you're his friend. I've heard.'

'Yes I am.'

Alice looked at me with sympathy.

'The wisest man in Hong Kong. Evan Olcott has got it right. He says he's empty of the past.'

Alice was silent. Then she spoke in a whisper. 'Evan had his past taken from him in some terrible way.'

I said nothing. For I was the only one who knew the whole story. Or so I thought.

'It's a mistake to live in the past, I agree,' she continued. 'But the past is always there when the present fails or when the future, oh, turns on you. It has to be. It's like the plant world. When the weather turns hostile – too rainy or too hot – they shift their growth underground. To their roots.'

'That's another Evan-ism. He is the rootless man. "Look at me! I am rootless!" That's what he told me. We travelled once, for a bloody long time, in India.'

'No one is rootless.'

'Except Evan Olcott.'

'Except Evan,' she agreed reluctantly. 'But there is a danger in losing your past. No matter how painful it is. What can replace it?' She pointed to the deep canyons leading to the harbour's edge. She turned those reddened eyes to me and whispered: 'Demons, Tim. I'm sure the most awful demons are out there, ready to rush in and fill the vacuum. Just look at Evan!'

The hour is late and if those lights down in Central are vibrant and seemingly eternal there are other lights less lucky. One is wavering on the Peak. Perhaps the doctors realize it, perhaps not. Do they know, as no one else does, or nearly no one, that it's a matter of mere hours? Do they know that the scattering of dawn's rosy petals on the harbour will come unnoticed by all, or almost all: by the frantic nurses, the aghast friends, by the occupant himself, fatally swollen with intermingled present and past? That the tubes will stop pulsing, the oxygen tank cease hissing, the malfunctioning call switch, which I dubbed the 'penis on a wire', will never be grappled for, never be needed, that its repair can be postponed until the next terminal patient starts his epic journey? That that wide, hairy mouth will open one last time – and not for a drink – before it closes forever? That Tim Marquand's outrageous bill can be prepared for ... whom? Do journalists leave estates? What do they bequeath but snapshots of sideburns, drunken grins, double chins? Old typewriters. And clips, of course, the all-important clips: a life contained in a bundle of jaundiced newsprint. How fast it can be flipped through. How infrequent the stories that halt one. Those big stories from the past – the revolutions, the palace *coup d'états* – have utterly lost their charge. Only a handful of pieces retain some pulse. The review that surpassed the book under discussion. The fond colour piece. And, most surprising, the stories we winged. 'And winged damned well, me friends!' (The words come from a younger Tim Marquand, tonight's dominant shade, healthy, relatively lean, unengorged by invasions of his past.) 'Quite indistinguishable from the truth! Makes you wonder about this stuff.' He hoists a glass of clear liquid gone yellow in the light, peers at it, sniffs with bobbing, comic eyebrows. 'Bottled clairvoyance! Nothing less!'

Magazine clips, yes, Tim Marquand has a mountain of them stuffed in the closets of his Conduit Road flat. But he also has magazine shares worth $3.3 million. Something to raise a glass to. Especially if you are the inheritor.

From the shadows of the hospital room emerges a thin figure. His haircut is boyish but his walk is middle-aged. He goes to the bed with a cup in his hand. He lifts it to the beard. But there's no response. The linen has shifted, exposing the China-watcher's groin. The thin man looks unflinchingly at the painful thighs and the massively enlarged scrotum. The body hair, once ginger, etches dark lines in the swollen flesh. The veins scream for attention. He puts the cup on the bedside table and adjusts the linen with thin, swift hands. He retires to his backless couch and sinks into the shadows, wrapping a blanket around his legs.

The hospital bed moans. The Chinese man barks out the time.

'When . . .?'

Soon, says the Chinese man. Very soon.

'The hotel . . .'

The Chinese man smiles: that silly confusion. A hospital is not a hotel. The doctor, he explains, has waived the rules. Visitors will be allowed tonight.

The body on the bed is motionless. Its swollen eyelids haven't parted all day.

The Chinese man leans forward on his couch, his hand pinching the edge of the blanket. It has become dark; another lamp could be lit. But the black silence touches him, silences him, presses him back to his couch, where he exhales quietly.

No, trusty cupbearer, my *saqi*, light no lamps. Not on this night. The lights torment your friend as the darkness does a man struggling to live. They distract from the other lights that beckon yet remain distant.

It is, it will be, it would be the ripe sun of the tropics, filtered by graceful palms, spreading colour on a pounding surf. No, no surf. This would be in the hills, on a remote river, in some odd archipelago or a new continent. Wherever. A thatched house sits on a small rise: not a mere house, a rambling thatched palace. Around it staves are arranged with queer, crowning ornaments. They look like human heads. But never mind. A mere detail. (It can be changed.) The important thing is that the trek is complete. Success is within reach. The path has started winding among the staves. The native helpers fall silent with fear. (What colour is the skin of those helpers? Black? Brown? And the decapitated heads? What colour shows in their bulging, frightened eyes?) The doorway is directly ahead: a forbidding black rectangle. But inside, within the bamboo palace, bathed in the light of a tropical dusk, he is there, at the end of this endless path, he will be there, would be there, must be there . . . my Danny.

If their skin is yellow, where would that be – such tropical light? Not in Wuhan, where the light over the wheat fields was so thin. It was about to rain, you could tell from the window of that ancient train. Everything was flattened except the spirits of the visitor, the newcomer, the graduate student, the fresh-faced foreigner, ready for anything the Middle Kingdom would throw his way for the rest of his China-watching days. For the rest of his . . .

The door to the room hisses open. Through the shadows a visitor moves toward the hospital bed. The dying man's hand rises. *'Danny!'* The lids part, exposing cat eyes: helpless blue marbles in an evil yellow sea.

But it's just a nun bleeding from the shadows in reverent slowness. Something has made a profound impression on Canossa's nuns, the enormous swelling perhaps. They approach him like a magnificent dying despot.

The eyelids rejoin. The tropical light dimmed, as if by a switch. The sun slipped behind a small black cloud. A fleeting summer rain fell on the bus stop near the Yacht Club. The cloud hovered directly above the green-topped Excelsior Hotel . . .

Miki Drews comes in, her moonlike face glowing in the darkness, and takes her chair. She lights a cigarette. Drews arrives with a plastic sack heavy with green cans of Carlsberg.

'Peaceful night.'

Miki exhales smoke.

Drews extends a can to the shadows. 'Sure, Saqi?' He raises his eyebrows, shakes his head. 'You need a break? Walk around?'

'He doesn't seem to hear us.' Miki motions toward the door. 'The nurse called it' – she hesitates – 'hepatic something. Can't really talk.'

'Timmy unable to talk. The end *must* be near.'

Miki has her thick paperback. She reads and smokes. Drews scowls at some pink sheets, scribbles with a pencil, curses.

'Shhhh,' Miki says.

Drews sighs.

'Okay,' mutters the distended mass on the bed. 'Okay men . . .'

It is the sigh he hears: the signpost to the past. It was a contented sigh heard through a thin wall in that long-ago, eternal flat in London. The light was yellow, straining through a mist. The windows were fogged but only at their lower edges. He edged his feet along the pantry shelf so as not to scrape the wall. Or Danny would hear. Low humming came from the other side. Danny's body was stretched out, languid, youthful. The water became still. His muscles were subtle, his penis long and soft. Tim had never seen it hard. Danny said he masturbated infrequently. Could he imagine the solitary exertions on the other side of their dividing wall? Nature: so cruelly asymmetrical. Tim took a deep breath, grabbed the windowsill, shook it and yelled:

'Fire!'

The water roiled and the young man, shanks lean, slipped onto the bathroom floor. Tim pressed his face against the glass and leered. *He'd never bathe in peace again! Listening for someone behind the wall, climbing the pantry shelves . . . Listening for me!*

'You know,' says Drews, 'we've been saying goodbye for so long, we've never really said it.'

'A long goodbye.'

'I mean, if he just had another day sitting up in bed.' He runs hands through his black curls. 'I've forgotten the last time he called. Was it about that Chinese herb shit?'

'That was Saqi.' She looks around the room. The Chinese man is gone. 'Kin Wah.'

As for childhood, there was a mother, of course, and that father -- the tree maliciously avoiding the apple -- and schooling and fractures and long bicycle trips to other counties. There was meanness but he was the extraordinary boy who couldn't be pressed down. There was always something overflowing about him. He made an early vow, fulfilled by a scholarship and a friendship with an American: they got and stayed away! The house: unremarkable from the outside and unique within. Today -- tonight -- it remained for him. The bookshelves and books, far more enduring than their master. The upstairs wallpaper with its tiny blue blossoms; the dark closet with the shrunken, preserved coats. All were unchanged, patient, timeless, unlike the man who holds their key in a fast-faltering grip. The past was being sheared from the future. The present will soon swallow them both, along with what should have been.

The Chinese man returns to the room and wraps himself in his dun-coloured blanket. He coughs drily. Miki closes her novel and lights a cigarette. Drews' head bobs, beard scratching at his collar. The hospital room, lockless and permeable during the day, is secured by the night. The memory chamber is sealed. The bearded man on the bed is laughing, typing, bragging, playing the raconteur. He was telephoning, now he's banging the telex machine, soon he will leave the hotel to board a shoddy-looking airplane dismissing fears of fiery, airborne death. *Death! Who could care? There's a story to be captured!* His inflated arms lie frozen at his side. Miki glances up, stares at the beard with the hole in the centre. She looks to the chest and is reassured by its slow heaving. Her gaze shifts to the edge of the golden light thrown by the abacus lamp. Tropical flowers shiver against the black windowpane: royal blue with fuzzy, drooping pistils. Beyond them a few pinpricks of Hong Kong's eternal light.

In the misty, yellow light of the common bathroom, Tim reclined in the bathtub, conscious of his plump, ginger-streaked thighs. Drews, wrapped in a towel, was at the mirror. His beard had been choppily cut. He was scraping off the remnants, a man reverting to boyhood. He was preparing to go home.

'I'll grow another one,' Drews vowed, wiping the mirror with his free hand. He looked to Tim in the tub. 'You've *got* to come over. I know we can raise the dough.' He peered at his image. 'I wondered if there were pimples under there.'

Drews bent, cleared his face with water from the basin and turned to the man in the tub. 'Well? A face only a mother could love?' He extended the razor. His face was pink and shining. 'Your turn.'

So pink, so shining. The cloud hovered above the Excelsior and although the rest of the sky was clear and bright, rain pelted down in its distinctively rude Hong Kong manner. Tim held a *Morning Post* over his head. Everyone else had run from the bus stop, jabbering and laughing, or almost everyone. He looked to a roadside tree offering partial shelter. He felt frantic – he had an interview in thirteen minutes – but didn't move except to impatiently rock back and forth in the downpour. He looked back to the bus stop and motioned with his head toward the tree. The Chinese boy finally smiled. They met under that tree. Tim boomed out an obscenity, the boy smiled again. He seemed so young, jailbait, but Tim wasn't much older. He spoke in Cantonese. The boy replied in deliberate, proud English.

His hair was too long on the sides, plastered down with the rain. His eyes were shy. Tim reached out and touched his rain-beaded hand. His name: the nicest name Tim had ever heard. The characters the most beautiful. Kin Wah. It might have been the finest day of his life.

A rattle from the Venetian blinds. Kin Wah is at the window. The dark skyscrapers below have become visible: grey, exploded teeth in a shiny black mouth. The sky is lightening.

'Lee Remick died,' said Drews. 'Did you read?'

Miki nodded.

'Timmy would have held a party.' Drews starts to whisper. 'He's so frantic about that pillow. At the end, he's left with a goddamned pillow.'

The sun is, will be, would have been setting. The palm fronds are gone: the landscape is no longer tropical. The thatched hut has turned to mud. It looks like northern India. The heads on the staves remain, however, flanking the final path of Tim Marquand's searching life. He tries to ignore them but can't. It's the teacher who was so harsh. A neighbouring boy. That disapproving father. The blond-haired man in the loo, inviting, potentially corrupting, rebuffed – corrupting all the same and astonishingly enduring in memory. The dark doorway beckons. The stout man calls ahead in his booming voice – '*Danny! I've come!*' – and wipes his brow against the harsh sun. He barks at his helpers but they have all disappeared, or almost all.

He passes the final head on the stave. It has starchy white hair and a distant, removed gaze. The head speaks slowly, casually: 'Don't go in. Empty yourself of the past.'

He hesitates but feels a hand on his back. It's the last helper, who speaks in deliberate, proud English. 'Go in. It's your time now.'

The interior of the mud hut is dark in a wrong way. There are lamps made from abacuses, Chinese propaganda posters, framed photos of journalists in scuffed wicker chairs. There are green velvet drapes, floor to ceiling, corner to corner, pulled against the evanescent night. The room is empty, or almost empty. And then the bell rings. The familiar bell. Tim tries to spin but is impeded. A different door is opened by a shadowed man, who steps inside, smiling, bearded, holding a plastic sack of beer cans.

'No!' cries Tim. 'I can't fucking get up.' Tears stream down his wide, flushed face. 'This isn't it! This isn't right!'

He makes the largest effort of his life and returns to that head-lined path. He is alone at the dark doorway. He re-enters. The room is shady, not dark, with trapezoids of sunlight slanting from rough windows in the mud. It's empty. He would be, has to be here! Where *is* he? Tim looks and, in the corner, spots him. He is dirty and thin, like a hostage. Tim inhales, holds his breath and whispers tenderly:

'Danny?'

The anterior sound has drained from the scene. The hostage rouses. His face is shiny and beardless, pink and heartbreakingly young. The face from that morning in London at the washbasin.

'Timmy?'

'I told you, Danny. I told you I'd be the one to find you. At the end.'

The Chinese man stands at the darkened window staring at a pink Tsim Sha Tsui. He looks at his watch and the coughs begin. He moves to the bed and stands behind the two visitors. Tim Marquand's eyelids part for the last time: two yellow globes, flecked with blue, not shrunken but burstingly full. There is a black, soundless explosion. Drews feels it in his hair, sees it on Miki's embroidered blouse. He looks at Tim's distended jaws and a machine-like shout shatters the silence. The mental camera clicks. And then swift, white professionals move in to displace them. Before they know it, they are on the other side of the hospital-room door, alone in the corridor in the milky light of dawn. Miki goes in search of a nun. Kin Wah swabs Drews with paper towels. Drews tries to catch Kin Wah's gaze, to see if those slanted eyes are filled with the same mental image as his own: the whale of a man, the bruise-coloured flesh, the bursting eyes, the distended jaws, open, pregnant, fiery, anointing them. But Kin Wah is staring at the blood as it comes off Drews' skin and onto the paper towels. The blood, which resembles coffee grounds, seems to fascinate him.

I apologize for such a rude departure. Bloody rude. Deepest regrets from your humble narrator. (Imagine a stately bow.) But life goes on, or so they say, starting at the FCC, where a requiem was held in honour of Timothy P. Marquand, the veteran requiem-holder, the evening of his jampacked funeral. 'Afterwards,' the engraved invitations might have read, 'home away from home.' It was crowded and boisterous with the proper mix of liquor and tears. By comparison, the follow-up observance at the Ball was a painful rout. It was hosted and financed by the Founding Editor himself and open to select 'friends' of *Orientweek*. But the girls were new and, Drews claimed later, as malodorous as those at the defunct Foxtrot. To many the party was ruined by the battle-axe tears of Ellen Weigner, hauled from Tokyo on *Orientweek* expense. An old, true friend. And an estimable poker player. It certainly wasn't aided by Johnny Chen, the replacement for Sammy, who six months earlier had plugged in Mr Coffee instead of the photo machine to ruin the Tiananmen cover. (Sammy had then migrated to New Zealand.) Johnny got too close to two of the girls, refused to pay his bill and tried to force a war between the Ball bouncers and the puny *Orientweek* staff. And puny it was: few over twenty-two and none on the staff longer than a year, except for the small band of veterans.

'Their first night at the Ball,' scorned Ellen Weigner, wiping her eyes, 'and probably their last.'

'Dolly!' yelled Drews, spotlight centre, cigarette dangling from his mouth. 'Where's Dolly? I want Dolly up here on the bar!'

Dolly Leung waved a demure hand. She giggled and pulled her chair closer to the table. You never knew with Drews: Dolly looked toward the door.

'I really wish Drews could let it out in some other way,' said Marietta, shouting over the raunchy music. 'Not just drinking and jumping on tables. I haven't seen him shed a single tear.'

Kelvin eyed Drews on the bar. 'This is a "Joe Cool" night. All five verses.'

The clincher was the unexpected arrival of Nick and Fran Naversen. It's possible they were invited as 'friends' of *Orientweek*: in Hong Kong friendship is often measured in the number of shares one owns in a company. But it was equally possible they gate-crashed. All the proper elements for a Naversen outrage were there: rudeness, bad taste and free drinks. Silver-maned Nick made the rounds with glass in hand, dropping lascivious comments with a smirk. Fran spent the evening in conversation with Kin Wah, the China-watcher's 'acolyte', as he called him, or catamite as he was known at the FCC. They made a strange pair in the shadows: formidable Fran, blue neon discs flashing from her spectacles, and skinny, aging Saqi, wringing his hands and listening intently to Fran's urgent pitch.

Later, there was the usual grumbling from the excluded about irreverence in the face of journalistic demise, which foreign correspondents take more gravely than anything except hostage-taking and expense-account fraud. Especially death by drink. But the complaints ended and Tim Marquand became a mere memory. His 'Mao Lives' cover was framed and hung at the FCC. A local literary agent collected his columns with the cooperation of Drews and overtime hours extracted from Dolly Leung. Soon that memory faded except in a few spots. The Hilton Grill was one. The FCC, of course, where I became a cautionary tale accompanied by much head-shaking. (And no measurable decline in gin sales.) And the *Orientweek* newsroom, naturally, where Tim Marquand tales enjoyed a reverent renaissance.

And so my memory pulsed, like the light bulbs in the dormitory in old Wuhan, until it inevitably dimmed. Except in one spot where it remained constant and vibrant, less a memory than a haunting. It was a flat on Conduit Road. An old building with the original high ceilings and disgraceful servants' quarters. The fourth floor. The door is unlocked. As it always was.

Orientweek's accountant, boyish Henry Fok, was troubled by the new charge on the company books but couldn't dispute that emphatic signature. Henry Fok was unconcerned about propriety, being both Cantonese and an accountant. But something niggled at him, upset his sense of history, one might say. For it was dogma at *Orientweek* that the magazine didn't pay rent. This applied to staff housing, mostly, and no one had ever been exempt including the Founding Editor, which explained his unglamorous quarters in Shu Fai Terrace. It applied to office space, purchased by the magazine at outrageous prices in 1976, which, of course, became the wisest decision in *Orientweek* history, until Tiananmen at least. It applied to all other assets except some extremely expensive computer equipment and that decision took months and was only clinched, as were so many things, by the epoch-ending slaughter in Tiananmen Square. Henry Fok knew other companies had different philosophies. But Henry Fok had been at *Orientweek* for a long time. (Too long: he was awaiting his immigration visa to Australia.) Which made each month's rent cheque, payable to some Shanghainese landlord residing in Kowloon Tong, hard for him to sign.

Not that the rent was expensive. Timothy P. Marquand had lived in the same flat for a lifetime. It had been, in the pre-Tiananmen real-estate market, a steal.

Henry Fok's pen hesitated above each month's rent cheque for yet another reason. He was awaiting the memo from Drews that would explain it all. The memo that announced, say, that a staffer would soon move into the flat, totally empty, or nearly empty, for more than six months. The memo that justified not only the empty flat but a houseboy's salary as generous as the rent was modest – higher, in fact, than any other servant's salary Henry Fok and all his friends and family had ever heard of. A crazy salary. Although lunacy was something Henry Fok had grown resigned to at *Orientweek*. The memo he coveted never came across his desk. He signed and mailed the two cheques each month, one to the Shanghainese in Kowloon Tong, the other to the houseboy on Conduit Road, shaking his head and complaining at family gatherings, where he was comforted by much spitting and whining. Once he made a detour by the building and peered up at the windows on the fourth floor. There were no lights, unsurprisingly, for the flat was that of a dead journalist. It would have been an unbearable affront if the overpaid houseboy was turning on all the lights. Henry Fok would have felt obliged to report the situation to Drews. Goodness knows what would have happened then. One of his terrible bellows across the newsroom, his long arms flailing facetiously toward the newsroom ceiling; one of Drews' ludicrous songs. Perhaps a song would have been dedicated to him, Henry Fok. And wherever he went in the future, he would be sung about in the

Orientweek newsroom until the Communists trooped in on July 1, 1997, with cannons and little red books. Perhaps the song would spread to Australia – white men had inscrutable ways.

Could Henry Fok ever have understood? He was twenty-nine years old and fourteen breathless months away from his immigration visa. *Orientweek* magazine was only fifteen years old. Daniel Drews was forty-one. Hong Kong was a venerable 148. And yet all, in the shadow of Tiananmen Square, were facing the same midlife crisis. Perhaps Henry Fok would have understood. It was a terrible time and empathy was in the air, even among the emphatically unempathetic Cantonese.

It was a time at *Orientweek* when 'Drews News' became distinctly less sexual. Someone in the newsroom made a count and there were, for the first time in the magazine's history, less than three staffers who employed the telling monosyllable, Dan. One was Anne McDermott, who hardly counted anymore. The other was Bethany Griffin, whose affair had been so brief that Bethany herself, in impatient moments, forgot her privileged monosyllable and sighed, 'Oh, Drews!'

The staff continued its nocturnal watch on Drews' movements, spotting him in the usual places: staggering from the FCC, painted in neon at Pussycat junction, walking rigidly toward Shu Fai Terrace. Funny enough, no one spotted him on Conduit Road itself, or walking up Robinson Road, or down from Po Shan Road. Only later did they realize how much time he had spent pacing these roads and how many Drews disappearances led, inevitably, down Po Shan Road or up Robinson Road, through the narrow elevator shaft and the fourth-floor door that still bore, in faded script, the name of a famous China-watcher who had died of acute, aggravated, some said wilful cirrhosis of the liver. Marietta conjured the theory that Drews may have spent more time walking to and from the flat, or circling around it, than he did inside. It was a kind theory, sweetly concerned and utterly false. Drews sometimes jogged up Robinson Road to get to Tim's flat. He hailed cabs when the distance was walkable. He cut short evenings at the FCC and was, on more than one occasion, sober upon reaching that door: the door that had never been locked, which bore the name card that should have been removed 200 days earlier but which remained – a card as old as the flat's occupancy, scrawled with the pride of youth, faded, which had for several years intimated premature aging and death.

Only Kin Wah knew where a rusted key for the door could be found.

Drews pushed it open. He flicked a wall switch and a pair of abacus lamps came to life, illuminating the Maoist propaganda posters. Green velvet drapes, floor to ceiling, covered the windows. Drews turned on another lamp and it directed his attention, as he knew it would, to the wall of photos: of smiling Chinese peasants; of Tim and Drews side by side on a tilting ferry in scuffed wicker chairs; clean-shaven in long-ago London, standing with arms around each other's shoulders at a kebab stand. The living room was empty, or almost empty, and unaltered in 200 days.

Kin Wah stood in the kitchen doorway.

'Hi, Saqi.'

'Good evening.' Kin Wah disappeared into the shadows of the kitchen. He returned with a can of Carlsberg.

'This is the photo you want, isn't it?'

Kin Wah nodded.

Drews held the corner of the frame. 'If we could only find some negatives.' He skirted the worn wing chair in the room's centre and took his chair. He opened the beer.

It was relatively early. Everything else was the same: the velvet drapes that shut the true night out and the promiscuous night in, the dappled light of the abacus lamps, the Maoist heroes gazing unironically from the walls. The wing chair was empty but it had often been, especially when it was late, when the cupbearer was asleep and alcohol needed to be fetched. The stereo was silent. Drews stood, walked around the wing chair and reached for a record sleeve. He waited for the familiar overture with its stirring violins and triangles playing 'You Did It'. Tim Marquand had a preference for overtures. He claimed all singers, with the exception of Richard Burton, Rex Harrison and Gordon MacRae, ruined the rest of the songs. He'd sit in the wing chair, head back and mouth open wide, singing a whole overture and conducting the middle parts with plump, ginger-streaked hands. Then he'd leap to his feet, delicately pluck up the needle and sing it all over again.

Drews and Tim Marquand had shared much: everything but lovers. To Drews, there were three things at the centre of their semi-merged lives: night, booze and a room. A succession of rooms. As some people's days lead inexorably to the typewriter, the refrigerator, the television, the days of Daniel Drews and Timothy P. Marquand all sloped into a room, windows blackened or masked, stocked with various alcohols to sustain talk and kill the strangeness of a foreign land. The best of those rooms, of course, was Tim's on Conduit Road, which uncannily recaptured the spirit of the room that brought them together in London. Deliberately so: Tim had searched Hong Kong for the right velvet and bought enough to cover the entire wall, as it had been covered in London. Other features of the room dated from later parts of the two friends' lives, but always shared parts. There were no family photos in the flat of Timothy P. Marquand, not even a framed photo of Kin Wah (except in the tiny bedroom). The London spirit reigned, enshrined and evoked by that photo on the wall showing two students at a kebab stand, fresh-shaven, on the morning they parted for different parts of the world: to journalism school in Missouri for Drews and to Wuhan for the nascent China-watcher. It was several years before the two reconciled their divergent paths. But come together they did, in that grubby, towering colony on the South China Sea, in a newly-decorated room on Conduit Road with shiny velvet drapes and a record player booming the overture to *My Fair Lady*, triangles chiming sweetly, as a reunion welcome.

As Miki had often remarked, there was a male atmosphere to the room and a whiff of the ecclesiastic. It had something to do with the drapes, the monkish mustiness, the wing chair located, so oddly, in the centre of the room (as it had been in London). Tim played his music with liturgical solemnity; his acolyte moved silently to and from the kitchen replenishing the wine.

Drews sprawled in his wicker chair loudly singing 'A Hymn to Him'. Timmy had been dead for 200 days, coming up on 201. Had he been alive he would have done the bellowing and Drews would have beat time with a pencil on the wicker. Drews' only comfort this 200th night was in the room itself, the music, the endless beer, the elastic night, stretchable far beyond 200 days. When the song ceased, he picked up the needle and played it again.

Orientweek had been conceived in that room one summer. Its subsequent birth was accomplished elsewhere, in a maternity theatre crowded with the Naversens, bankers and public-relations executives. But its conception had been private, behind heavy green drapes, the accomplishment of merely two. (Not counting the Oriental consorts, Miki and Saqi.) Everyone knew the story. They had heard it, with embellishments, from both Drews and Tim Marquand in various venues. At *Orientweek* celebrations – the magazine's birthdays or Tim's requiems for obscure film stars – the two would perform an epic version. Waiters would hover, wondering what kept the group sitting so long. If the reel could be rewound, we could watch *Orientweek* lifers being born on those saga nights. We could pinpoint the exact moment when the hook caught: when sceptical, ambitious salary-pullers metamorphosed into bright-eyed partisans, hungry forevermore for that unique grace exuded by Drews and Tim when they sat side by side, twin beards wagging. Always side by side: for when a real jaw began, one of them, and sometimes both, would rise and change places to get closer to the other. The better to interrupt, disagree, to tell the tale with alternating, often conflicting, details.

If the reel could be rewound. Tim's drapes managed to exclude sound, Hong Kong's most dominant element, and, of course, time. Drews' beer had grown warm to the touch. He picked an album – *Manhattan Tower*, another of Timmy's favourites – and placed it on the turntable. The music built and time started running backwards.

'. . . *we had a wonderful waiter – a waiter named Noah!*'

For Tim, London had been the apotheosis of their friendship and Hong Kong the recapturing. But for Drews, London was a mere seed and the jungle of dependence and love that grew in Hong Kong depended on a different sun, new shoots and stickier vines. In Hong Kong their careers took off, the magazine succeeded, and their twin love affairs, with Miki and Kin Wah, blossomed. The shoots became unruly and they were tended weekly in that Conduit Road drawing room, lavished with late hours, ceaseless talk and heavy intakes of beer for Drews and gin for Tim. The jungle got thicker and deeper and Drews followed his own barbed path. All Timmy could do was to watch him disappear – and hope that Drews would call from his tangled forest so Tim could triumphantly rescue him. (And here the curtain parts for an interruption from the narrator. Smile, goddammit. What is more knee-slappingly hilarious than unrequited love of the Saturnian kind? But it's love and only love that formed the Original Age, I posit. And the Succeeding Age owes less to age and death than it does to the fate of love of any kind.)

The record player had fallen silent. The ring of the telephone split the tomb-like atmosphere. Kin Wah appeared at the door, dishevelled and sleepy-eyed. Drews grabbed the receiver.

'*Wei?*'

Drews slammed it down. 'Wrong number.'

'You okay?' Kin Wah squinted. 'Tonight?'

Drews nodded.

'I need money.'

'You know I'll take care of you, Saqi, always. Sleep now. No, don't tell me the time.'

It was two years earlier that Drews had done the unthinkable: he started avoiding Timmy. He sought out new sanctuaries where no one could find him. But his exile was short-lived. Late one night he pushed through the door to find Timmy waiting in his wing chair. The record player blared old black jazz. From the chair, Timmy gave a monsignorial wave. He said something about long-lost friends. Drews went to the chair and knelt. He touched the China-watcher's feet. Then he withdrew from a pocket a piece of cloth, which he spread on Tim's elephant-foot table. It was a checked handkerchief with a dark stain in the centre.

'I have an excellent laundryman . . .'

'It's blood,' said Drews.

Tim reared in mock horror. 'Lock the door!'

'Miki's blood.'

Tim stared with narrowed eyes. 'Not . . .'

Drews nodded.

Tim raised a hand to his head, rubbed vigorously and then pinched the bridge of his nose. He rose and walked to the record player, switching it off in mid-song. He turned to the kneeling Drews, who had tears pouring down his face. Tim made three wide circles around the room. 'Wait.' From the kitchen came the sound of glasses, a bottle, a beer can being opened. He returned with a tray, which he poised above the table. Drews removed the handkerchief. 'Drink.' He returned to the far side of the room. Then he spoke in a strained voice.

'Danny, we've chosen never to talk about these things. I knew you didn't want to hear about my affairs. I repeat: my *affairs*. But listen to me, Danny boy, and listen carefully. I know about love. You've never believed it but I do. And I know something about infidelity and jealousy.' He fixed Drews with an intense look. 'Are you ready to listen to me on these subjects?'

Drews nodded.

'First,' Tim commanded, 'go to the kitchen and throw away that filthy handkerchief.'

Drews clutched the handkerchief.

'Or get out of my house.'

'I have to return it.'

'She knows it's bloody gone. She *knows* you know, for God's fucking sake. Throw it away. He – whoever he is – can get another snotrag.'

And so began the great search. The odyssey that will bring us into the parched landscape of the Succeeding Age, through the heads on their staves to that mud hut at the end of our path. It began with a faded, checked handkerchief stained with old menstrual blood. It seems frivolous when you trace it back to a father's slap, a schoolboy's caress, a stained handkerchief. Or a thick, dividing wall of plaster. But there it is, wrapped in nothing but a tissue of sighs: the incredible, inconquerable, stained past.

It began with Drews' discovery of the handkerchief in Miki's neatly arranged drawer. He instantly knew its significance. The things one saves: they are from new loves. Drews could see the handkerchief, newly ironed, as it was spread out by a pair of brown, masculine hands. He saw the hands positioning Miki, naked, atop it. He saw the brown body ease itself into her. Miki's love affair began on a menstruating day toward the end of her cycle, for the stain was small. How old was the blood? Time had stolen its odour.

Drews replaced the handkerchief, neatly refolded, in the drawer. When Miki was out, he spread out the handkerchief in search of an overlooked clue. He examined other drawers and found a shirt, not his own, smelling of sweat. The sweat: is that why she kept it? Next time, the shirt was gone. Finally, Drews stole the handkerchief and stored it in his desk at *Orientweek*. In quiet moments he shut the plywood door, hung a sweater over the glass pane, took the handkerchief out, smoothed it on the desktop and tried to absorb the emotion it captured for Miki. An emotion Drews had yet to experience: the joy of falling in love again. For in all of his renowned newsroom affairs, Drews had yet to fall in love. This is important: Danny Drews had known many women but he remained true to a single Japanese with an inscrutable, marble expression. For this is a verity: love comes in different shapes, which are unalterable. Drews' was solid, not very expansive, kept in a separate, well-guarded chamber. It was something he was proud of and considered, quite accurately, indestructible. For love does not have to be a wild English garden, needy of showers and sunshine. It can be small, dense and sharp-cornered, a heavy lump of true metal. Miki's love for Drews was also heavy and true. Unfortunately, it had a totally different shape.

Drews knew, of course, Miki's lover. He was his friend, his employee. He slept in the room across the hall. Their affair had been, if one likes to retrospect, inevitable. And now the handkerchief was gone. I was correct: Miki knew. Would she say something? And what would happen to the marriage as a result? For Drews' marriage was more important than the *Orientweek* staff understood. It was the centre of his gyroscopic, journalistic existence, the stability that allowed Drews his insanely inspiring life at the magazine. It became vital to know: who would Miki Drews choose? Her irresponsible, irrepressible, eternal husband? Or the lover of the shirt and the handkerchief?

One night, Drews feigned drunken sleep. He heard doors open and close. He waited and followed. The flat was old and it had, unfortunately, keyholes. He squatted and peered through a keyhole. It was his great mistake. A single image at the end of a dark tunnel would alter irreversibly his marriage and his life. He saw his wife's face, the face that had always been his, the face that only he could bring alive, smile. He saw her lips move. Beneath her face was the Filipino's.

'It was like something out of your worst nightmare,' Drews said.

I sat in the wing chair, fingers pressed together.

'That image, Timmy.' Drews tapped the side of his head. 'It comes to me whenever I lose concentration.'

'The curse of the photographic memory. You can't destroy the negative.'

'I just wonder, and I know this is fucking stupid, but I wonder if she scratches him.' Drews switched from beer to gin. 'With women, Timmy, I mean, is there one special cock? Do women spend their lives trying to recover some cock from their pasts?'

'Don't pigeonhole it, Danny, don't send it to another time or we're going nowhere and we're staying there for a good, long time.'

But Drews, drunk, shook his head. 'Or do women get stuck with one cock that is simply inadequate? The right key in the wrong lock? Even when there's love?'

'That's all I've been telling you through all of this, Danny boy: don't sacrifice the love.'

Once begun, the discussion had no end, stretching night after night. The keyhole: how often we came back to it. He described the vision in detail: the arrangement of the linens, the fall of Miki's hair. Drews rejected a confrontation with Miki, fearing the consequences. 'I don't know about a breakup, Timmy. It may destroy me.' And this brought us, in our dusty jewelbox, to a turn in friendship.

'Timmy, I'll snap. How can I go into that newsroom with those people peering in my office expecting me to be their little god? I'll run away. Disappear. And what will happen? Who will find me?'

I lifted the needle from a record. 'Gary, Indiana' was swallowed up by the endless night of Conduit Road. I put the needle in its holder, stepped into the middle of the room, threw my arms to the poster-filled walls and said: 'Who would find you? Danny boy! *I'd* be there. *I* would find you!' I stooped and grasped his shoulders. 'That's what I'm here for! After all these years. What do you think?'

And that was that. It ended as fast as it began. Drews was miserable for a few weeks and disappeared on a trip to Manila, where, I imagined, he sought solace in a succession of bar girls. The day after his return, he rushed to my flat to say that the Filipino had admitted the affair in a contrite, gushing letter. Miki had also confessed, concluding: 'I don't know what to do.' Drews and the Filipino had several summits at the Nullah over many drinks. Several days later, Drews announced he had solved the problem.

'Don't ask me how, Timmy.'

'Is he still living with you?'

Drews nodded.

'Is she still sleeping with him?'

He nodded again.

'He's set to return to Manila soon. At the end of the month.'

Drews shook his head slowly.

'Then . . .'

'I said don't ask.'

I didn't ask. But I knew. Danny had taken over the affair. He couldn't help himself: it was the only way for the great manipulator, the eternal ringleader and newsroom deity, and the only way to keep Miki. We can imagine his struggle. But soon Drews was happy: happier than I had seen him for years. The magazine prospered, a tribute to the shining power of a single electric editor. The staff was drawn together more tightly than at any other time since the early days. The magazine ran its most brilliant cover stories. How many desktop stomps Drews performed that summer! How many lunches he presided over! That famous deadline night when he performed, for the first time in *Orientweek* history, two versions of 'Joe Cool', English and Spanish, in ten verses. Dolly watched from behind her desk, hands cupped in her lap, and sighed. 'I feel like I've gone back to 1976.' Luis threw back his head and the fluorescent lights caught his bald spot. 'What's our style, Drews?'

'Fuckin' Baghdad!' Drews churned his hands in front of him, challenging Luis for more.

'Who's got a banana?'

'I wouldn't touch that one,' yelled Drews, 'with a ten-foot ...' He raised his eyebrows expectantly.

'Banana!' shouted the desk. (The allusion was to the former staffer who could peel a banana with his toes.)

Dolly giggled. 'That was one of my first duties here.'

'What, Dolly?' asked Marietta.

'The bananas.' She wiped a tear from her cheek. 'Drews said we had to have bananas on hand. Just in case.' She touched her bottom desk drawer: the former receptacle for the bananas.

No one could recall Drews so energetic and accessible: laughing and joking and swapping gossip with an unusual intensity. He began to leave open the plywood office door with its tantalizing glass pane. The sweater he employed to cover the pane disappeared. The Filipino started contributing stories of surprising quality – with heavy rewrites from the Founding Editor, according to Marietta.

I was certainly jealous: how could I not imagine what went on in that Shu Fai Terrace flat? I felt I had returned to those servants' quarters in London, my evenings consumed with feverish imaginings of what Danny was doing on the other side of our plaster dividing wall. But Canossa Hospital started calling more frequently and I had no choice but to answer. Drews survived his life's greatest earthquake. Life with Miki took new twists but continued. And he continued to call on me: Danny in his chair, beating time on the wicker arm. Over the months that followed I thought back to the night when Danny said he'd crack up and disappear. It was his weakest moment: nothing more than drunken self-pity. But my vow to rescue him wasn't drunken. Alone in the flat, behind the velvet drapes, I made it come true in a fantasy. I imagined the obscure parts of Asia to which he'd flee. I invented the pitfalls – natural obstacles, separatist groups, disease – and, being an experienced foreign correspondent, devised solutions. I sent Danny to lands of horrifying brutality and xenophobia. Then I put the needle down on a favourite record, flung my arms to the walls and sang, in a clumsy Polish accent, 'I Am Easily Assimilated'.

I went across the map from Borneo to Afghanistan in search of a new place for Danny and me, where the past was reduced to heads on staves and the future, that corrosive enemy, was permanently remote. I created a world, vast and yet stripped to the essentials, for our final union. And before long, 'I Am Easily Assimilated' became yet another *Orientweek* ritual. But no one understood the actual joke. Not even Danny. Only me.

Kin Wah stood in the kitchen doorway. He saw a long-limbed man with black curls and a beard kneeling at a worn wing chair, his face buried in its cushions.

Drews sat back on his heels. 'I was just . . .'

Kin Wah disappeared. He returned with a large, faded nightshirt. 'You can still smell him.' He disappeared again and returned with a fresh can of beer.

Drews looked around the room. The Maoist heroes stared down unpityingly. He held the shirt at arm's distance. He looked to the doorway. Kin Wah was standing there.

'The money?'

'Kin Wah, I promised. I'll send it this week.'

When he had gone, Drews brought the shirt slowly to his face. He inhaled and whispered: 'Sweet Jesus!'

Several days before my demise, I said to Danny: 'Do you remember that story I did, Jesus, it was more than ten years ago. From India?'

Miki had installed my bed in the hospital room. I was propped up, my head framed by the famous green drapes, also relocated from the Midlevels.

'From Punjab.'

I gave my famous ecstatic smile. 'Ah, Punjab! Glorious Punjab! The manliest place on earth.'

'India,' said Danny. 'Such a bizarre place.'

'Continuing,' said I. 'Our protagonist was a member of a martial caste. He was a bastard. He whipped his servants and did bad things to women. He drank like a horse. I forget what the story was all about.'

'Linguistic divisions.'

'Ah, important theme. But I remember the concluding anecdote. Do you remember?'

Danny ran hands through his black curls until they clasped his neck.

'The heavy-drinking bastard: the day before he died, he wept like a baby. Remember? On his charpoy. I always loved that. Imagine dying on a charpoy.'

I paused to cough. My throat was raspy: the doctors had recently removed a tube. 'He called for all his gear, one by one. He hugged his boots, his saddle, his whip and his reins. He said: "I'm leaving all of this? How can I leave all this?" I never forgot that story. The martial man parting with his accoutrements. He died with reins in his hands, remember, Danny boy?'

Drews nodded.

'That's how I feel, Danny, in this room tonight. I'm leaving all of this? Leaving you?'

He rose from his chair.

'But we kept our vow, didn't we? Our vow in London? We kept moving. God we moved, all over the Lord's map. That's what kept us happy, Danny.' I motioned to my swollen body. 'Attend, my friend, what it means to stop. Keep moving, Danny. For me. For us. Keep moving!'

Danny thought it over and, apparently, selected words for our evening meeting. But that was the day the famous China-watcher lapsed into a coma.

And then I died. Danny stood in the corridor of Canossa, bathed in the blue light of dawn. He allowed Kin Wah to swab my blood from his clothes. He had a single stunned thought:

No one will ever find me now. No one will even look.

A noise attracted Drews' attention. Kin Wah was in the doorway looking at his watch. Blue could be seen through the kitchen. The sitting room, with its drapes and ever-burning lamps, was suddenly old and stuffy. As always, the velvet drapes had failed. The eternal night was vanquished. Drews rose and folded Timmy's nightshirt. He returned it to Kin Wah. Waiting for a taxi on the sidewalk, he looked up and saw the green drapes being retracted. He headed back through the greasy dawn to Shu Fai Terrace, to the room where he always slept, the room where he had to sleep. Miki stirred in their bed.

'Where were you?' she asked.

'You've disappointed me, Big Girl.'

'He's not the dumb houseboy we thought,' said Fran.

'He was never really a houseboy.' Nick Naversen gulped his drink. 'He has an education.'

'So I forgot.'

'He agrees or doesn't agree?' Nick belched. 'Excuse me.'

'Of course he agrees. Who wouldn't agree? We're talking three million dollars.'

'Yes,' said Nick. 'Three point three.'

'That's a lot of babies,' Fran said wistfully.

'Lots of hare-lips. How much did you make on the hare-lips anyway? In rough terms. Ballpark figures. Must have saved a bit on pacifiers.'

Fran stuck out her tongue.

'Do that again.'

'What?'

'Your tongue. Stick it out.'

Fran showed the tip.

'All the way for God's sake.'

Fran opened her mouth and stuck out her plump tongue.

'Your tongue's mossy.'

'Oh, Nick.'

'It's all green. Have you been sick?'

'No!'

'Then why's your tongue mossy and green?'

'I don't know.' Fran poked a finger in her mouth, gently scraping the back of her tongue. She examined her fingernail.

'It's one of the first signs of AIDS. I read that in the paper. Have you been tired lately?'

'I'm never tired,' said Fran.

'I've been exhausted,' said Nick. 'Look at my tongue. Is it mossy?'

'It is a bit.'

'Jesus Christ. I knew it. Wait a minute. Let me go to the men's room.'

'Stop it, Nick. Let's get back to business.'

'Well what's the fucking problem with this guy?'

'Kin Wah doesn't want to decide anything before the closing of the estate and that happens first thing tomorrow. That's why I saw him tonight. At the old flat.'

'I wonder if I could get that flat. Those wonderful old ceilings. I could get my television off the toilet. Damned difficult in the morning.'

'Forget it, dear. Drews has the flat. He's paying the rent each month.'

Nick raised an eyebrow. 'Bringing around his young female friends? That dirty dog.'

'No, not at all. That's the weird part. Saqi nearly pushed me out the door. He was afraid Drews would come by.' She leaned across the table. 'He comes several nights a week. He just *sits* there.'

'No more ghoulish than an evening at the FCC.' Nick frowned thoughtfully. 'Is Drews paying or *Orientweek*? That would be bad for the bottom line.'

'Since when have you been concerned about the bottom line.'

'What a good name for a Hong Kong bar. The Bottom Line. I must remember that. When I get my three million dollars.'

Fran laughed. '*Our* three million dollars.'

'So how does it stand exactly?' asked Nick irritably.

'The estate is closing tomorrow. Kin Wah gets his shares. Once he gets them in his hand, I think he'll come around. But there's something more.'

'Don't tell me. Loyalty? Some erotic fascination with Drews' cowboy boots? That big, white dick bulging in those blue jeans? It's natural, in an unnatural way: two grieving friends thrown together in an empty old flat. A flat with a rent at 1972 levels. Who wouldn't be aroused?'

'Nick, I think Kin Wah is holding out.'

'Oh fuck. From zero to three million buckeroos in six months and now he wants something more. Only a Cantonese.'

'Nick dear, I have a plan. I know what he wants. He simply wants to migrate.'

'Dear Christ.'

'I mean, what's three million dollars when the Chinese are pouring over the border?'

'I'd be glad to write a letter. Character reference. Sign it with an alias if necessary.'

Fran shook her head with a smile. 'I can get him what he wants. If he plays ball.'

'You have a hare-lip at the American consulate or what?'

Fran smiled triumphantly. 'Adoption. That's the ticket. And I've got my own judge. I told you. In Iloilo.'

'Wonderful. All we have to do is find two people who want to adopt a greedy, forty-year-old Cantonese houseboy with a loose asshole. Where are you going to find those two turkeys?'

'Us.' Fran smiled.

'We're divorced!'

'Divorce isn't recognized in the Philippines.'

'I'm not ready to be a father. I'm working on a new girlfriend.' Nick shook the ice in his drink. He scraped his tongue with his pinkie nail and stared at it. 'I'd better start with the rubbers.'

'What about Kin Wah?'

'I don't want a son, Fran. Although a millionaire son is an idea I might get used to.'

Fran nodded smugly. 'Exactly. That's the whole point, dear. We can adopt him. But he'll have to pay.'

Both Fran and Nick Naversen had been busy during the previous six months. Fran's mission was to armtwist the aging Cantonese on Conduit Road. Nick's was more challenging: to capture the sympathy of the old man, *Orientweek*'s chairman 'non-emeritus', in Nick's term. The old man had nothing to gain from the selling of *Orientweek* and something substantial to lose. He would lose the title that had identified him in Hong Kong for fifteen years. The tag that had, in millions of conversations, staunched the flow of the past. For if Evan Olcott was not chairman of *Orientweek* magazine, how did one describe him? An old-timer? That wasn't a Hong Kong term. Journalist? It hardly fitted him now, not for the past twenty-four years. No, the past would inevitably resurface. 'That's Evan Olcott. You know him. He was imprisoned by the Chinese. So long ago.' That threatening sky seen through the bars day after day until it was seen in its entirety one morning, huge and grey with pregnant clouds. The hurrying and bustling. There was an explosion. Then everything went dark. And Evan Olcott's past, present and future were obliterated. The demons of human existence were banished with a single, instantaneous flash. Leaving him in an encompassing peace unknown to all humans except the saints, if they exist, and the eternally damned.

They lunched at the Captain's Cabin ten times, five, or was it only twice? The Captain's Cabin was one of Evan's places. On the first date Nick was nervy, smiling too much and looking into the corners for the enemies he perceived in all mainstream bars and restaurants in Hong Kong. The conversation hadn't gone well and the two men separated with no business discussed. Nick hurried away, silver head bowed in the rain, and Evan stared at him from the shelter of Connaught Centre. It had been a long time since someone wanted something from him. He walked contentedly to the minibus, tall and dignified, white hair springing buoyantly in the soft rain. Then came the fortuitous meetings in drinking spots rarely patronized by Nick Naversen. Again, the preliminaries never went far enough. And Nick was forced to retreat in surrender. Evan began to look forward to the chance meetings and Nick's tremendous clap on the back, speaking of the present and all its insecurities and joys. It was a wonderful slap of life. Evan became the only man in Hong Kong who relished a clap on the back from Nick Naversen. Plus the free drinks. Evan began placing himself in more accessible spots. He even returned to the Hong Kong Foreign Correspondents Club, where, late at night, Nick confided:

'I'm worried about the magazine. You know. As a shareholder.'

Evan pushed his chin into the air, stretching those tissuey, empty jowls. 'Powerless, really. Once a year. Letter in the mail.'

'With 1997 and all,' Nick said, giving a grin that said: *Far be it from me to bring up a serious topic, geopolitics, over drinks yet. But what can a responsible person do?*

Evan dissembled and accepted another drink. 'Lovely. Yes, thanks.' Nick brought the conversation back around and Evan lisped: 'Listen. Why don't you talk to Drews?'

Which led to shuffling and stammering on the part of Nick Naversen.

'He's right across the room. Should we have a word with the editor? Both of us?'

Nick coughed into his fist.

'Tell me, dear boy, to change the subject slightly, are these stories true about the Drewses?' Evan gave his odd smile with the overlapping front teeth, a discordant flash of adolescence in the weathered face. Nick said: 'If you believe the grapevine.' Evan said: 'Of course. But how did it, shall we say, come about . . .'

Later in his room, Evan laughed as he hadn't laughed in years. He steadied himself against the wall. How one waits! How unexpected is the moment when it finally comes. So he started to think and that took an effort. The thinking led to plans. Then Nick couldn't find Evan anywhere, even in the most godawful dives. He visited his filthy room but it was locked. The neighbours said he hadn't been seen in weeks. Nor had he started to smell. Nick sniffed delicately. Then he started sniffing avidly, pushing his beak into the window cracks. Evan's death would be inconvenient, for sure, but not as difficult as the alternative. Which was the reality: Evan Olcott had done one of his famous disappearances.

And then came the letter, or, more accurately, the aerogram. A single line, written in a halting, old man's hand.

I know what you want. I too want something now.

There was no signature. The aerogram had a reproduced painting of a dancing god on its front. Its postmark was blurred but readable. It was from India.

Back to Conduit Road, to the fourth-floor flat with the velvet drapes and the unlocked door. Drews was once again on the floor with his beard buried in the cushion of the wing chair. The doorbell rang: a violent, mysterious interruption. He rose, eyes puffy with emotion, and the front door slowly opened on its own.

The hallway was dark. The only light was thrown by the abacus lamps. Into the light came a tall woman in an orange tunic, stooping shyly with a pleading smile. Her hands were clasped before her. The eyes were horsy, framed by bangs of white, unwashed hair.

'Alice!'

'Drews, excuse me.' The voice was a comforting, girlish whisper. 'I don't mean to interrupt. Really, I don't.'

'Why have you come here, Alice?'

'To see you.'

'How did you know . . .'

'My maid.' Alice smiled shyly. 'Her name is Yrlinda. She's a friend of Kin Wah. She told me you've been coming here.'

'Saqi.'

'Yes, Saqi.' She said the word with knowingness.

'But why?'

'May I sit?' Alice was settled and offered a drink, which she refused. 'I recognize these lamps. And the drapes.'

'We moved them. To Canossa. My wife and I.'

'And this song. It's Gordon MacRae. I remember it from . . .' She sat nodding her head to the tune. 'I can see this building from my place, you know. On Bowen Path. You know the old girls' school?'

Drews nodded.

'But I never saw any lights. Now I know why. The drapes! That so puzzled me. I knew you were here. Night after night I'd look down. But there were no lights.'

Drews stared.

'I'm sorry. You must think me an old busybody. Miss Nosy Parker.'

'Journalists.' They both laughed.

'I have something you should have.' With shaky hands she withdrew from an envelope a sheet of yellow, ruled paper. She held it between them. Drews took the paper. He read aloud: 'For Alice Giles, a true friend.'

Then he stopped, scanning the page in editor's style. He read again. '"Roses, wine, a friend to share . . ." I can't take this. It's to you.'

'I want you to have it. I took a Xerox.'

'Thank you,' said Drews. The paper went limp in his hands. 'Timmy sent things to everyone that last week. He sent my wife a painting. Peaches in a bowl. She had always admired it.'

'And you?'

'A picture.' Drews walked to a photo on the wall showing two young men standing before a kebab stand. 'It's from our days in London. I've put it back. But I have so little of Tim's writing. He wasn't one for letters.'

'I figured as much.'

And so came a present from the past for my Danny. The old woman made her exit. She was alone for it was Sunday, the servant's day off. She waited patiently for the lift, hunched, smiling sweetly at Drews. She gave a shy wave as the lift descended. The last thing he saw was her white hair disappear down the shaft. Back inside, Drews read the piece of paper. It was hardly a letter, of course, just a salutation and a signature, in an obviously ill hand, with a poem between. Drews knew the poem as well as anyone. But poems mean different things on different occasions. He read it through several times. And now, I believe, it's time for you to read it in its entirety. Tim Marquand's signature poem. The poem that helped him lead his life. The poet was a Pathan named Khushhal Khan Khatak. And *saqi*, as you may have already discerned, is Persian for cupbearer.

Roses, wine, a friend to share —
Spring sans wine I will not bear,
Abstinence I do abhor,
Cup on cup, my Saqi, pour.

Hark! the lute and pipe! Give ear!
What says music to our cheer?
Time once flown returneth never,
Idle moments gone forever,

Wouldst recall them? Call in vain.
Life, our mortal life, hath sweetness,
As its sweetness, so its fleetness,
Count it nothing, 'tis no gain.

Doth time tarry for thy prizing,
Or make speed for thy despising?
Time hath all young lovers slain,
Time is heedless, time is heartless —
Saqi, fill and fill again.

THE PAST

Now they can be described: those sighs from the past, which linger like mists in the tall, jumbled forest. They are the chunks of bread we dropped along time's twisting path never to find again. Command the birds to go back and retrieve them: send them in a thick, black swarm. But they return with the unrecognizable: obscure stones or curled fern fronds. Dismiss them – give a giant clap of annoyance – and watch the sky darken as they flee. Try as we might, the path is lost.

But I have a special bird, whose claws pierce the skin of my shoulder. Its companion, Thought, has flown. Only Memory remains. His place is beside my ear, his beak darting in and out, telling where those mists linger. Memory and I will take you deep into the woods to point out the path's forgotten turns. This is a prerogative enjoyed by the dead. Absolute recall. And no need for discretion. For a dead newsman this is a veritable perk. No more 'sources say . . .' or 'observers believe'. I can see through another's eyes. I can tell it like it bloody was. I may demonstrate a certain disregard for those still living but they have enough. Sunday afternoons at the Dickens Bar, for example, the jazz band playing boisterously. Cool, bitter beer and mustarded sandwiches. For me there is no jazz, no sandwiches, no beer, for my *saqi*'s bottle is empty. It's memory: that is the smoky residue at the bottom of my cup. Come with me, my friend. Return to those lost moments and surrender to their evanescent beauty. Feel it on your skin: the crispness of an autumn evening in London, the night new, a warm, greasy gale from the kebab stand at the tube station and pinprick raindrops pumping the blood in your young veins. Place your palm on that impenetrable wall – cool, stained plaster between you and the only person you will ever love – and feel it in your exploding groin. Pass through a keyhole and feel it in your fingers as they grasp that moist member pushing frantically into the dampness of – yes! – *your* only love. We are in search of the sighs of love.

Of rooms we have had too much, I say. So I start with a face, a picture.

It's black and white, with the fierce clarity that captivates strangers and brings heartbreak to those who travel back with it through time. On closer examination, it's brown and white. It's in a thin green US passport, not very worn, buried in a cardboard box beneath old files and notebooks. Look at that elongated face with its surly, post-adolescent glare. The hair is of the period: dark curls stretched into a ponytail. The ponytail does something strange to Danny's face. There's a certain flatness to the cheekbones, a recession in the back near the ears. Perhaps it's the lights of the photo studio. The mouth is a tense, fleshy line and there are pimple marks on the long chin. The nose is round-nostrilled, as unformed as the signature running cautiously up the left of the photo. But the face is recognizable and not just to us who knew this gangling university boy. There's the high brow, the black, bushy eyebrows starting to meet in the middle. And there are the eyes: tensely narrowed, small and defiantly shiny. There are two tiny pouches under them: not pouches but wrinkles showing where the pouches would eventually be placed.

Like everyone, my memory plays tricks. When I recall those first days in London, I see the adult Drews in our servants' quarters or in the pub where we met. He's tall, confident, with black curls surrounding his face. He's laughing and bearded, of course. But the reality is different. It was a different face I first saw in London. A clean-shaven face with pimples, strange planes on the face. No, it wasn't the ponytail or the harsh lights of a photo studio. Those planes actually existed. The dead are above it all, perhaps. But we still have our memories to overcome.

How to describe Drews before London, before the Orient, before *Orientweek*? Should I describe the suburban Gothic house: three stories tall with dolorous dormers and a dark staircase leading from the kitchen? The wrap-around porch where the children sprawled on summer nights? Should I describe the seven brothers and sisters with identical joined eyebrows? The Catholic schools with their hysterical nuns and savage monks? Or the first stirrings of the real Drews: his talent for sports, his early decision never to play on a team? The years of running around a quarter-mile track, in heat and drizzle, never deigning to run a relay? I've seen photos of that young, skinny Danny with the serious mien. What did he dream about during those endless hours on the track? What was he escaping? Or should I concentrate on the momentous occasion when the high-school newspaper was revived – picture black-robed brothers, fussy and mutually despising, sitting around a conference table –

and Daniel Drews, lonesome track star, was chosen to run it? That was the real genesis of the later Drews. It was late in junior year. Drews was called into the office of Brother D'Ataglia and awarded the unexpected honour. Brother D'Ataglia was pleased with himself and expected thanks and perhaps more, for Brother D'Ataglia had a mixed reputation with the boys. Drews spent the summer running the beach of Breezy Point planning his year as editor. The first issue was dominated by a savage parody of Brother D'Ataglia, with emphasis on his fondness for the locker room. The next issue took on Drews' track coaches, beefy laymen who received the insult with all the female outrage of their clerical colleagues. The newspaper had never been more outrageous or popular. And although it was closed after Drews' final issue – with highlights of the year's satires, including some new libels against Brother D'Ataglia – no one had the nerve to close Drews down. For he stunned them into inaction: the quiet, negligible long-distance runner became the leading personality of the school. He showed an extraordinary political ability, assigning important football players to fictional positions in the staff box. He held court each day in the newspaper office, the door left open to exhibit his growing power. His famous prank: to watch for hated faculty members, wait for them to pass the door and then, in pantomime, to mouth the words: 'Three ... two ... one!' Then he and his followers would erupt into fake laughter. The teacher would falter – sometimes freeze altogether – and attempt to continue down the hall in a display of dignity. Which brought genuine, withering laughter from Drews' gang.

It was at this time that Drews became famous for his rendition of 'Hang Down Your Head, Tom Dooley'. He was voted graduation speaker and gave a thoughtful, merciless speech before the fluttering eyelids of the school's administrators. They were happy to see Drews go, undoubtedly. And yet they should have been proud. They had created a journalist, a personality, a man where none had been before with nothing more than a Gestetner machine, tubes of ink, a box of celluloid headlines and two IBM Selectrics.

Early college we can speed by. And onto London in the late 1960s, where we find the virgin expatriate searching for rooms. Rooms, rooms! We're back in their mouldy embrace. How they come to inhabit us: they contain, among the furniture, their own pasts and a foretaste of our future. Drews had his ponytail, two canvas suitcases, the miserable face of a stranger in a foreign city and an introduction. He walked up

Queensway consulting his shiny *A to Z*, past college archways of carved stone. Every building seemed to have a plaque with a king's name. He shifted his bags. And then he stopped at a series of shallow steps. Above him was a round hall with a neo-Greek frieze along the top. To its right was a Georgian building curved in obeisance to the hall. Drews was admitted by a uniformed doorman who escorted him, with a restrained smirk, to a hydraulic lift with mirrors and a plush bench for the weary. The doorman saluted as Drews disappeared up the caged shaft.

The lift stopped at the sixth floor. Drews exited and rang a doorbell stiff with paint. He heard a rough, echoing call. 'One more flight!' The voice was both husky and strident, with a Carolina accent. 'I'm up here.' The lift had hissed away so Drews dragged his bags up a flight of stairs. He found a smiling middle-aged woman beckoning from a doorway, a lit cigarette in her hand.

'Mr Daniel Drews, I imagine! Lordy, those look heavy.' It was a bright voice with a residual charm of sunny days, minted bourbon and slender, pretty cigarettes. Its unlikeable edge came from some later period of thick fog and cheap vodka. This was Mrs Bottom, Drews' new landlady and fellow countrywoman, leaning out the doorway of her own flat in an odd posture of anxiety. The woman's face was a horizontal oval with a broad, nervous smile. The smile bled up to her eyes, where it became aggressive. 'This is the back door, honey.' Her voice dropped and she peered left and right, aware of English people behind shadowed, cemented-looking doorways. 'Welcome to Albert Court. Come *on*.' Drews passed her with his bags. She took a drag on her cigarette. It seemed a final rebellion against an adopted land: the former plantation girl pushing it in the face of the mumblers and snobs. She slammed the door with a bare foot.

'Downstairs is the main entrance. But this is your door.'

Mrs Bottom led Drews down a hallway. Her steps became girlish, more so for the bare feet. Her arms danced and her head swivelled backward with intentional charm. 'I think we should have a cup of tea.' She spoke as if she were offering champagne. 'There's always tea here: as much as you can drink.' They entered an enormous kitchen with an old-fashioned stove and tall windows. 'And there is nothing more refreshing, even on a hot day. The English are right about that, honey.' Mrs Bottom laughed shrilly. 'About that anyway.'

Mrs Bottom needed boarders, Drews knew. Her life had collapsed and the only thing left was her former husband's lease on the Albert Court flat and her credit line at Harrod's, on which she bought groceries. Everything about her was subsumed. She was an unmistakable matron from the neck up. But her body had taken the opposite course toward sickly adolescence. She sashayed to the stove and Drews saw the seat of her slacks flap sadly, robbed of flesh that had once filled it. She slapped a kettle on the stove and had trouble lighting the fire. Momentarily, the smile disappeared behind oystery, disgruntled lips.

'*Voilà!*' Mrs Bottom poured tea from a dun-coloured enamel pot. One cup only: for Drews. She drew on her cigarette and faced him with a revived smile. 'The main bedrooms are downstairs. And the living room, the den, the dining room – I'm not using that much anymore.' Her hand waved in the direction of a doorway. 'But this is your floor, honey. Back there are the smaller servants' rooms.' She lit another cigarette with faltering fingers. 'They call that' – she motioned to a closet with a padlock – 'the wine cellar. And this – *this* is your room.'

She flung open a door. Drews saw bookshelves surrounding a fake fireplace with a blackened electric coil. He saw a diamond-shaped water stain in an upper corner. He saw a wing chair in the centre of the room and a settee in the corner covered in faded chintz. There was a very narrow bed against a wall. The windows on the far wall were covered in long, aging drapes of green velvet.

'Do you have any friends?' Mrs Bottom's hand was on her hip. Her gumball eyes glowed hopefully. 'Other nice young gentlemen?'

'I don't know anyone on my programme.'

'The rooms right through there' – she pointed at the wall above his bed – 'they're vacant. And they're only eight pounds a week. Yours is bigger. So it's more expensive. Breakfast, by the way, is all the bread and tea you can stuff yourself with.'

'You said so on the phone.'

'Plus an egg.' Her eyes narrowed. 'One per day. I count them, so no cheating!' Mrs Bottom wagged a naughty finger. She gave a husky laugh, flipped her colourless hair and swivelled with mock-youthfulness from the room. Her big voice came from the stairs. 'If the phone rings, please let me pick it up. That's one of the rules of the house. If it's for you, I'll ring the bell.' The voice receded. 'By the way, *Mission Impossible* is on tonight. I love *Mission Impossible*. They've just gotten it here.' Her footsteps shuffled down the stairs. 'The telly's in the den . . .'

Mrs Bottom's was the last of the great Albert Hall flats: the rest had been broken up into more economic units. She was the unlikely custodian of an earlier, more splendid age. Drews wandered the flat that evening, when the chimneys beyond his drapes had become black silhouettes. From the kitchen he found the other servants' quarters, mere cubicles with odd pieces of spare furniture. There was a bathroom with a clawed tub. Windows above the tub led, he discovered, to the kitchen pantry. Through another door he found the pantry, wide and dark. There was a tin of pie filling, another of kidney beans and canned soups with European labels. On the top shelf was a block of hardening Parmesan cheese. In the refrigerator he found milk, yellowed cheeses and a green substance in a bowl covered with plastic wrap.

From the flat's top floor, steps led to a duplex level. Drews fumbled for a light switch and descended. The first room was a den with stuffed chairs, books and a television. Next to the den was a huge dining room with a shrouded table. The final room was a formal, rectangular living room with two chandeliers, moulded plaster ceilings, furniture in Louis XIV style and, on two walls, oversized abstract paintings in matching reds and blacks. There was a stereo with a broken needle and a cabinet with glasses and a single bottle of gin. Drews was drawn to a series of framed photos on the wide mantle. They were portraits of a succession of Bottom children at different ages. A recent photo showed them to be a single son and daughter. The daughter took after Mrs Bottom, with long blonde hair. The son was sullen with sideburns and a clumsy middle parting in his hair. Mr Bottom, Drews knew, was a spectacularly successful American businessman but a failed husband. He appeared in that final portrait only, dangerously handsome. On a side table, Drews found photos of Mrs Bottom in silver frames, all taken on the same day before a grand, Carolina mansion. It was her wedding day. She wore a satin dress and she laughed as she put on, or took off, a wedding veil. Drews didn't recognize her at first, mistaking her for the blonde daughter. He was confused: the harsh smile was the only trace of the contemporary Mrs Bottom. And in the smileless photos, Drews found a woman of extraordinary, uncreditable beauty.

Drews lowered himself to a chair and looked at the darkened room. He imagined parties, servants, staid English guests enjoying or recoiling from Mrs Bottom's gauche charm. Mr Bottom would stand in a tuxedo across the room. The paintings would appear dramatic and expensive, not merely ugly and passé. Dinner is served. The provisions are from Harrod's meat and fish counters, not bread, butter and eggs from the general grocery section. He stepped into the hall and looked down the final flight of stairs, which led to Mrs Bottom's bedroom and those of her prodigal children. It ran directly beneath the kitchen and the servants' quarters. The lights were off and Drews peered into shadows. He climbed the stairs to his room, locked the door and examined the bookshelves. College textbooks from the children. A copy of the *Kama Sutra* with the son's name inscribed. P. G. Wodehouse in paperback; murder mysteries; crumbling horse books and proud Book of the Month Club titles aligned on a top shelf: *The Group*, *Voss* and Boswell's *Journals*. He heard a bumping up the stairs and that husky, smiling voice raised to a door-piercing holler.

'*Mission Impossible* time! For anyone who happens to be interested!' The bumps went down the stairs.

Drews dressed to go out. He descended to the den. Mrs Bottom was sunk in a chair, feet on a mismatched ottoman.

'Want some guacamole?' She gave her eager, lopsided grin. 'I make the best guacamole in London.' A colourless drink was at her elbow. The green stuff from the refrigerator had been put on a silver plate.

'I'll be going out.'

'I thought you'd stay in. On your first night. Here – here's *Mission Impossible*.'

Drews watched a few minutes to be polite.

'I'll be out for drinks,' Mrs Bottom said grandly. She took a gulp of her cocktail, hand shaking. 'But you enjoy yourself. Your first night in London.'

'I came Monday.'

Mrs Bottom shook her head. 'I know you young people. Swinging London and all. I'm not that old, not yet.'

Drews climbed the stairs, two at a time, and let himself out the servants' door. The lift lowered him to the grand entrance hall. Crimson rugs, brass planters, wide staircases with carpets and polished runners. A liveried doorman saluted from a distance and Drews gave an embarrassed acknowledgement with his paperback. The outside air was cool and moist as Drews had never felt before. It struck him as perfect weather: night-time weather, drinking weather, walking-home-from-the-pub weather, and Drews loved England from that moment on. He retraced his steps of that afternoon, past the sandstone colleges, down a hugely wide avenue with colonnades painted in succeeding shades of white, cream and beige. The parked cars were small and shiny. Drews passed mews with withdrawn, glowing pubs. He saw people strolling: middle-aged, timid but also somehow dignified. Gloucester Road brought him back to the world of laundries, pubs, teenagers, Indian restaurants and a brightly lit Kentucky Fried Chicken shop guarded by a plaster Colonel Sanders. He headed toward the tube station, which he considered the centre of his new world. And there he stopped, having completed his journey. He never considered going beyond and, in retrospect, Drews defined his universe for the next ten months on that one evening stroll. The mental camera clicked and England became for him a handful of snapshots: a succession of four streets with a station at one end and a warren of servants' quarters at the other. England's weather was the weather of Gloucester Road, its smell the smell of fast-food restaurants and launderettes, its class system captured by a newspaper vendor dropping change into the hand of a well-groomed woman with a dog on a leash. Drews saw commuters rushing from the station, crossing the street to avoid the unEnglish whiffs from the kebab stand. He saw an Italian restaurant with an American Express sign and decided never to patronize it. He felt the heavy coins in his pocket and entered a pub opposite the station. He was frightened and needed alcohol, God's gift to those thrust into a foreign land. He ordered a small lager and sat on a cushioned bench against a wall. We can see him sipping that beer: the ponytail hanging, those strange planes on the face, those tense, excluded eyes. A nervous swallow came every few seconds. He opened his book and started to read. The music was new and exotic: 'Sunshine Of Your Love', with its thick, impossibly sophisticated guitars.

And then Drews' reading was somewhat rudely interrupted.

'A Yank?'

Drews looked up. Standing between the bar and his table was a round young man with Irish colouring and frizzy hair allowed to grow too long. His arms were poised in the air as if conducting an orchestra.

Drews nodded.

'Friend or foe?' The Englishman guffawed and lunged at the table. 'What're you reading?'

Drews showed him. It was *The Fountainhead*, plucked from Mrs Bottom's bookshelf.

'Please say you're not a fanatic. You're not going to beg donations in the Underground for capitalism?' Another big laugh. 'Come join us.' A meaty, pink hand lunged at him. 'We're Communists. I'm Mao – they're Stalin.'

A group at the bar laughed.

The Englishman's handshake was insistent and electric. Drews swallowed nervously. 'Dan Drews.'

'Tim Marquand. You can call me Monsignor.' The Englishman withdrew his hand and held it as if waiting for it to be kissed. 'Leave your book. I'm sure no one will take it. Very, very sure. That jelly glass too. Only the girlies drink half pints. Don't say I never taught you nothin'.'

Drews rose, shaking his head. 'Is that supposed to be an American accent?'

The Englishman nodded.

'Americans don't talk like John Wayne.'

'My apologies, pardner. But shhh. Tonight is a solemn occasion.' His face hardened. 'We're commemorating the passing away of one of your greatest countrymen.' He started to introduce Drews to his companions at the bar.

'Who died? I haven't seen the papers.'

'Bert Lahr!' The round Englishman started making nervous circles around the pub floor. He threw his arms in the air. 'One of the gods of the American stage and screen.'

'Bert Lahr died last year,' said Drews.

'Quite so. We've all been very busy. Haven't we boys?'

The students at the bar nodded.

'But,' continued the round, restless Marquand, 'let us not forget Dorothy Gish. She died last week. Another titan!'

'I haven't seen a paper in ...' Drews shook his head. 'Who is Dorothy Gish?'

'Many consider her the more talented of the Gish sisters. The connoisseurs, of course. Any among us tonight?' The group laughed. 'This, by the way, is a pint. Now drink to Mr Lahr and Miss Gish. May they find happiness on that celestial sound stage, together perhaps for the first time in a truly unlimited engagement. May their eloquent eyes light up that heavenly theatre, may their priceless "business" convulse the angels on their comfortable clouds. "Rest in peace" – heavens no! May they pace the boards forever, poor miserable fuckers!'

73

And so began the friendship of Daniel Drews and Timothy Marquand, a swift beginning and a brief one, for the pub was closed with British brutality long before midnight. Drews retraced his steps past the Indian restaurants and the darkened launderettes, along the wide avenue of beige pillars, cream pillars, white, to sleep for the first night in his servant's room with the mildewed green drapes. The following evening, he positioned himself on the same crimson bench and tried to concentrate on *The Fountainhead*, distracted by every new arrival in the pub. He changed seats to get a better view of the door. And finally he saw the round, ginger-haired man bustle in the door, alone. The two young men drank until closing time and Drews made the offer he had considered for twenty-four hours and even dreamed of the previous night. Tim Marquand accepted without hesitation. Drews returned to the flat and went to the den, hoping to find Mrs Bottom. But the room was empty. He watched television until he heard the sound of the downstairs door. Voices followed. Shoes climbed stairs and Mrs Bottom appeared at the den door with an elderly English gentleman behind her.

'Oh, I think it's time for some introductions.' She was frantically gay and slightly unsteady. She kicked her shoes toward the television. 'This is Mr Daniel Drews, a young gentleman from my country who has come to stay as my guest.' She gave a kind of leer at Drews. 'Daniel is studying here for a year. And I'm going to make him just as comfortable as if he was at home.'

Drews stood and extended his hand.

'And this, Daniel,' said Mrs Bottom, 'is one of my oldest friends in London.'

The Englishman smiled reluctantly and gave a weak handshake.

'This is . . . this is . . .' Mrs Bottom's eyes narrowed. Her head bobbed. The Englishman, blank-faced, cleared his throat. Finally, Mrs Bottom admitted defeat with an averted glance. 'Well, anyway, let's get ourselves a little drinkie.'

'A little drinkie,' said the Englishman. The two headed toward the cavernous living room.

'Mrs Bottom,' called Drews. 'I have a friend. I think he wants to rent one of the other rooms.'

'Shhhh!' She darted a defensive glance toward the living room. 'That's *wonderful*. Keep your voice down. You told him ten pounds a week?'

'You said eight.'

'Okay, eight. But only one egg, honey.' She straightened and adjusted her shoulders as if readying for battle. 'I am counting, you know.' She gave her snarl smile and turned. 'Coming, Peter!' She stopped in her barefooted tracks and turned to Drews with proud eyes. 'That's it! *Peter*. Silly old me! I'm going positively bonkers.' She disappeared and Drews heard glasses clinking, a low mumble and Mrs Bottom's explosive, brassy laugh.

Drews spent the next few days eating eggs and drinking tea and staring at the jumbled rooftops of South Kensington. He sent his address to his parents. He found a kiosk near the tube station where a scarf-covered matron sold him cold cans of Coca-Cola. She called him 'luv' and was sharp with her change. He abandoned *The Fountainhead* and began P. G. Wodehouse. The day before classes began, a drizzly Sunday, Drews waited outside the Gloucester Road tube station and saw, several minutes early, Tim Marquand bound from the station carrying a small suitcase and a shopping bag full of record albums.

'Let's storm the castle, my friend.'

'This way,' said Drews. 'I think you'll really like it. It's a fantastic place.'

When Drews saluted the Albert Court doorman, Tim put down his suitcase, threw his arms toward the chandeliers and burst into laughter. 'Christ almighty! You should see yourself! The pauper as prince.'

Embarrassed, Drews said: 'This is our elevator. Our lift.'

'Wait one second. Let's take a good viewing.' Tim made large paces down the length of the entrance hall. He engaged the doorman in conversation. He disappeared up one of the carpeted staircases. 'The carpets stop there.' He shouted from the landing and pointed. 'After the first flight.'

'For God's sake, Tim!'

Mrs Bottom was waiting in the kitchen. Tim was all ecclesiastical charm. Mrs Bottom flounced her way down the dark, back passage to show him a cubicle with a bed, a chair and a narrow window. She had taken a lampshade from one of the other cells and even found a bedspread.

'It's wonderful,' said Tim. 'Christ! I forgot my hair shirt.'

Mrs Bottom looked at him suspiciously.

'I'm right through there.' Drews pointed to the wall above Tim's bed. 'My bed's on the other side. If you knocked, I'd hear it.'

'So let's see the glamorous Drews residence.'

'It's slightly bigger.' Mrs Bottom led the way through the kitchen. 'But only slightly.'

'I hope,' said Tim, 'I can control my envy.' Mrs Bottom threw open Drews' door with a queenly gesture. Tim went straight to the wing chair and sat. 'Wonderful. I'll take it.' He pointed to the wall between the two windows. 'A dartboard will go there. Oh yes, laddie, I'll make you a Brit if you give me the time. The Jesuits need seven years. Give me seven months.'

Mrs Bottom peered suspiciously. One hand was on her hip; the other was suspended in the air with a burning cigarette. 'What's this about Jesuits?'

Tim Marquand looked up and spoke to her in high-pitched Mandarin. Mrs Bottom's eyes grew wide. Cigarette ash dropped to the floor.

' "Power," ' Tim translated, ' "grows from the barrel of a gun." Mao Tse-Tung.' He put his hand into his jacket and withdrew a small red book.

'Oh lordy,' said Mrs Bottom, slowly shutting the door of the room behind her. They heard her feet on the stairs. 'I don't want Bolshies in this flat!' The voice diminished. 'That's all I need at this time in my life.'

Tim raised an eyebrow at Drews. 'So that is dear Mum.'

And thus Mrs Bottom received a nickname – never used in her earshot – and the two students took over her flat, or the top half, with power that grew from a simple outnumbering. 'Mum' made occasional raids, cigarette burning and trousers flapping, to demand the rent or count the brown eggs from Harrod's. But in effect, Drews and Tim had their own spread in Albert Court: a warren of cubicles, a magnificent kitchen, their own entrance and doormen who saluted. The dartboard went up the next week. Drews practised his aim while Tim fooled with the American's portable phonograph, made entirely of plastic. In the daytime they sampled the newest of music: languorous Vanilla Fudge, sweet and profound Simon and Garfunkel. When night fell, Tim claimed the phonograph to introduce his friend to the scratched glories of Rex Harrison, Richard Burton and Gordon MacRae. Tim sat in the wing chair booming out the words, his rounded lips raised to the ceiling. Drews sat on the settee beating time on the mahogany arm. He learned to drink tea; Tim experimented with Drews' efficient, electric egg cooker from America, concluding that it poached brilliantly but boiled erratically. The phone would occasionally ring, two or three times, and then cease portentously. Mum answered it downstairs. On her barefoot raids, Mrs Bottom looked around the kitchen with a kind of clenched defiance, to announce – girlishly triumphant – that she had a dinner invitation, had bought a new variety of bread at Harrod's, or that she was 'in the guacamole mood'. Drews would respond kindly while Tim invariably stole from her presence. It was an odd reversal: blunt-natured Drews played the sympathetic diplomat while courtly Tim Marquand turned his back. For Tim couldn't stand Mum.

'You could be kinder, Timmy.' Drews cut into a large loaf of bread. 'She's just down on her luck.'

'That woman,' Tim proclaimed, delicately cracking eggs into the electric cooker, 'smells of the bloody grave.'

And so it began: ten months that brought together two dissimilar men. They came together in isolation with no reminders of the outside world aside from the ignorable presence of Mrs Bottom, whose existence was subsiding a floor below them. It was the cottage deep in the forest from which all the paths extend. All of the paths being, of course, one-way.

With classes began a new ritual. The two young men bathed together each morning: one in the tub while the other brushed teeth or shaved. The bath was new to the American.

'I never feel completely clean.' Drews squinted at the fogged basin mirror. 'My hair in particular. I've even started washing my legs. I never bothered in a shower.'

'You never washed your bloody legs?'

'Not like you.' Drews pointed. 'You take five minutes on each one.'

'I've always washed my legs.' Tim sat up in the tub.

'Why?'

'Actually, I've always considered them my most attractive part.'

'Your fucking legs?' laughed Drews.

Tim considered his legs: plump but strong, streaked with pale hair. He covered himself demurely.

Before long, the two men decided to grow beards. It took weeks before the effect was desirable: satanic black for Drews and tightly-curled ginger for Tim. Both had weak moustaches, which they examined frequently in the mirror.

'I say we shave the bloody things off and start all over. The hair is bound to come in thicker.'

'I'm not going through that agony again,' said Drews.

Drews introduced Tim to his American classmates, awkward, virgin expatriates who regarded the loud Englishman with suspicion. Tim made each night a premier performance and he favoured uncrowded pubs with plenty of space for his wide, nervous circlings. Drews acted as a kind of interpreter, standing between him and the Americans. Tim's requiem pub party for Ramon Navarro was a failure. The American girls deemed it irreverent. Only the Puerto Rican boy with the pointy shoes seemed amused. He invited Tim and Drews to his favourite after-hours club, located down an iron spiral staircase off Cromwell Road. A password was required. The club was dark and sweet with the perfume of hashish. Most of the patrons were Asian. After-hours in London in the late 1960s – there were few thrills greater for a young person, especially those not fully initiated into sex. Hair was long, men wore beads and cowboy boots. London could actually seem like Europe after 11 pm, a cross between Berlin and Marrakesh.

Drews was more successful with Tim's friends and they were admitted to the Albert Court cubicles. On party nights, Gordon MacRae was vanquished by the Rolling Stones or Inna Gadda Da Vida. Hashish was smoked in a back cubicle reserved for that purpose, even though aged paint had permanently sealed its window. Mrs Bottom occasionally stumbled on the group as it moved from room to room or to and from the refrigerator. She was alert for the presence of women and always satisfied when she saw Tim's group. (For Tim Marquand had few female friends.) Once she offered guacamole, which Tim tried to refuse. But his friends overruled and ate with an enthusiasm that delighted Mrs Bottom and prompted reminiscences of her son Louis.

On those evenings Drews' personality took form. His early reticence in England faded and in its place stood a young man, cowboy boots digging deeply into the cushion of a faded settee, bellowing 'Hang Down Your Head, Tom Dooley' – for he had yet to discover 'Joe Cool' – to enthusiastic cries from pale, cigarette-smoking Englishmen. Or he played the talk-show host, directing, commenting, cementing feuds and dominating even Tim's elastic ebullience. Drews was poised between his days as high-school newspaper editor and his future as the totalitarian of *Orientweek* magazine. And Tim Marquand deserved much of the credit for his continuing evolution. The psycho-social buttresses had crumbled when Drews stepped off that plane in London but one had sprung up in the nick of time: a single, perfect friend who loved Drews unreservedly and, truth be told, could be dominated by him. With that single requirement, Drews was able to swell and grow. Tim's friends found Drews colourful, 'rather charming', pure Americana. Tim saw something altogether different: a young man standing on a settee in new cowboy boots, singing energetically and without facetiousness, a master of confidence, who would always, without fail, look to him for a significant nod midway through his performance. He saw the man who would sleep but inches from him on the other side of a thick plaster wall. What did he do in his dark privacy? Tim could only imagine, as he did night after night, reaching up with his free hand to feel the cold wall, wondering if it was possible – and if so, how – that Danny could be sleeping several inches away. The wall on Tim Marquand's side developed a stain in which one could almost see the print of a hand. And then, in the mornings, the two friends would come together and Drews would regain his original audience of only one. With whom he would talk, bathe, poach eggs. And that man was Tim Marquand.

Where does love come from? Is it born instantly in a pub and nurtured over eggs and tea? In a shared bath? Or does it grow slowly on weekday nights, when Tim and Drews went to the local pubs, drearily crimson and utterly un-swinging, to drink until closing time and discuss their plans for the life ahead? What about those walks back to Albert Court through the rain, the further discussions behind the green drapes – endless, rambling, adolescent discussions – the tea, the music continually playing on the tiny, plastic phonograph: the soaring violins of *My Fair Lady*, the ironic, mock-operatic sweeps of *Candide*.

'Here it comes, Danny, listen!'

Candide: '. . . You were dead, you know. Shot and bayonetted too.'
Cunnegonda: 'That is very true. Ah, but love will find a way.'
Candide: 'What then did you do?'
Cunnegonda: 'We'll go into that another day, now let's talk of you . . .'

'I love it!' Tim jumped up from the wing chair, plucked up the needle and looked at Drews on the settee. Tim crooned: 'You were dead, you know . . .' Then he played the song again.

One morning, Mrs Bottom arrived in the kitchen with an unusually withdrawn attitude. She sighed around the room, bit her lip and tipped her head back. And then, staring into a completely empty cupboard, she announced: 'I'm sure you heard those phone calls last night.'

Tim looked up from the *Kama Sutra*. 'Slept like a log. Thank you. Bit damp, as usual.'

Drews folded his newspaper. 'I did. I heard the phone.'

Mrs Bottom pulled a handkerchief from her pocket. She dabbed her eyes. 'They were from the doctor. In New York. I'm afraid Louis is in poor, poor shape.'

Tim smiled across the kitchen table at Drews.

'Is there something wrong?' Drews asked.

Mrs Bottom swivelled suddenly. 'He tried to commit suicide! He jumped out the window. Fortunately, it was only the third floor.'

'The third floor!' crowed Tim.

'He's always been sort of troubled,' sobbed Mrs Bottom. 'He took the divorce very, very hard. And we had that brief problem with *drugs*.' She appealed to the young men, anxious-eyed, for solace on the topic of drugs.

'What kind of drugs?' asked Drews clinically.

'Drugs are a killer,' said Tim. 'I knew a family, as happy as could be . . .' He clapped beefy hands. 'Never knew what hit them.'

Mrs Bottom sniffled, banged a kettle around the stove and departed barefoot down the stairs to her mock-luxurious dungeon.

'Timmy, you've got to be more understanding.'

'She's doomed, my friend, don't you see it? Don't tie your life to such people. They'll just drag you down.'

'She needs a little friendship.'

Tim slammed shut the *Kama Sutra*. He started walking around the kitchen. 'She's blown it, old man, don't you see it? Life is over for Mum.'

'Keep your voice down.'

'All that's left is the reprise.' He sang in a low, tender voice: '*Now I've lost you. Soon you will go in the mist of day . . .*'

'Give her a break.'

'Give *us* a break.' Tim spoke savagely. 'We're young. We can succeed where she failed. *We* can bloody soar. Haven't we decided? You and I? Haven't we taken a vow?'

The vow – our chosen path through the forest. The weeks had given way to months and the two men's friendship had deepened into love: an unbalanced love, for sure, but profound and mutual nonetheless. And because that love would never find a physical conclusion, it possessed a changelessness, timelessness even, that protected it from the corrosions that doom conventionally consummated love. It was and would remain a love expressed late at night with booze, music and powerful, addictive conversation behind floor-to-ceiling drapes of thick, green velvet that enclosed and excluded and brought the two men together in a symbolic embrace.

The freedom of living abroad had intoxicated Drews and he decided to make a life out of expatriatism. He would be a foreign correspondent – 'Epaulettes and all!' He implored Tim to join him. 'You can do it, Timmy. With your Chinese. You can move to Hong Kong. You can become a China-watcher.' The idea was thrilling but Tim Marquand had never left his own land and could only try to comprehend Drews' intoxication. Until the two men went for Christmas with the Marquand family. They planned the trip in all its details, even debating whether Tim should shave his beard.

'My mother wouldn't let me in the house,' said Drews. 'I'll shave mine if it makes it easier for you.'

'We go bearded or we don't go at all,' declared Tim. 'We must break these bourgeois chains!'

Drews drove, weaving into the wrong lane and bumping curbs on every turn. But Tim had the greater excitement. He wanted Danny to see his part of the country. And he wanted his family to see his American friend. But the trip was a misery and the two men cut it short, returning to London four days early. The house was the same, of course, as was the village, the neighbours, the gossip and the timeworn Christmas rituals. His mother was no more timid than at any time in the past. His father, always taciturn, wasn't measurably colder. Neither said a word about Tim's beard. But the unanticipated happened. Tim Marquand suddenly saw his home country, his house and most terrifyingly, his family, through a foreigner's eyes – through a loved one's eyes. And everything became small and mean and unbearably stupid. The house couldn't contain Tim's frantic energy. He embarked on long, incessant walks, showing Danny the landmarks of his childhood and adolescence, the bicycle routes, the early pubs. And one evening, when Danny was tired, he walked on his own. He saw nothing and allowed his legs to lead him in a wide loop that ended at the same, small house. He opened the door and found his father and Danny in the living room. Dad had his paper. Danny had a detective novel. Tim stood in the doorway and his father looked up. In his eyes, Tim Marquand found a look that caused him the sharpest pain in his lifetime. He saw it eternally – in London, in Wuhan, in Hong Kong, in that dimmed hospital room on the colony's peak. What was the expression in Mr Marquand's grey eyes, which he turned from Tim to his American friend and back again? It was a look of suspicion combined with distaste. Perhaps a better word is disgust: disgust for love and disgust for his only son.

On the way back to London, the city lights still far distant, Tim capitulated with a kind of explosive relief.

'Yes, we'll bloody do it, Danny boy. We'll get away. And I think we should make it a vow, as solemn as our lives: we'll keep moving until the day we drop.' He looked out the window at the shadowed hills and his voice softened. 'Maybe we'll be together, maybe not. I hope we will. But I don't care if I ever come home.'

'Don't worry about the journalism, Timmy. You can pick that up as you go along. Just keep up your Chinese.'

Tim nodded. He spoke in a low, alien whisper: 'We'll keep moving.'

It was sometime after Easter that Tim noticed the windows in the bathroom, high above the tub, that connected to the pantry. And one morning, when Drews was already late for classes, he entered the pantry silently, climbed the bare shelves and looked down through the yellow mist. Drews' hair was pulled back from his face. He wasn't rushing or even soaping. He lay with legs fully extended in the old-fashioned tub, humming tunelessly. Tim tried to wipe the mist from the window. But it was on the other side. Drews' humming stopped. There were several moments of complete silence. And then Tim heard a long, ancient-sounding sigh. His breath quickened. He looked down once more at the young man in the water. He steadied himself, taking care not to scrape the wall. He took a breath and yelled: 'Fire!'

Drew bounded from the tub. Tim pressed his face to the window and laughed as loudly as he could. Drews darted out of the bathroom and ran through the kitchen, naked, and into the pantry.

'You fucker!'

'Lying in the bath like a bloody king.'

'Just wait until next time.'

'Watch it: help me down.'

Drews went to his room to dress. When he came back to the kitchen, he found Mrs Bottom staring suspiciously.

'We were just fooling around,' Drews said.

Her eyes spotted the pools of water on the kitchen floor. She followed them, in a kind of angry march, into the pantry.

'I'll wipe up,' Drews called. Tim entered carrying books.

Mrs Bottom was in the pantry for several minutes. When she returned to the kitchen, she held aloft a tin of kidney beans. 'Which one of you has been swiping my beans?'

'Pardon me?' asked Drews.

Her eyes narrowed with the hatred of the scorned. 'I had two cans of kidney beans. Now there's only one.'

'We haven't had any kidney beans.' Drews looked to Timmy. 'Have we?'

'I'm sure it was him.' She wagged the can at Tim.

Tim gave a dismissing snort.

Mrs Bottom's eyes widened. She stood still for a moment and then, with a determined look, marched away, kidney beans dangling. 'This is my home.' She shouted at her right shoulder. 'I'm not going to be treated this way and eaten out of house and . . .' She reached the den, turned the corner and the voice faded. '. . . going through my things and not even paying for them . . .'

Several weeks later, when Drews was out with his American friends, Tim sat before the television in the den. He heard the downstairs door. Mrs Bottom appeared with an alcohol glow and dangling earrings and said: 'Oh, Timothy dear. I didn't know you were up.' She kicked off her shoes. 'I'd, uh, like you to meet my friend.' A middle-aged black man came from the shadows and extended his hand. Again, Mrs Bottom couldn't recall his name.

Things became worse for Mum. The phone rang frequently at night. The doctors suggested an institution for Louis. She started asking for the rent money early and, one morning, standing nervously in the kitchen doorway with a faltering cigarette, suggested a hike. The small number of tins in the pantry diminished until nothing was left but the hardened cheese on the top shelf. Then Albert Court served her with a summons. They were contesting her lease. One of their complaints involved her boarders, who had been reported by the doormen.

'You won't testify against me, boys?' Mrs Bottom was tearful. 'Will you? Daniel? Timothy dear?'

But the school year was almost over and the two men were busy forging their futures. Tim had received a grant to study for a year in Wuhan. 'Second prize,' he proclaimed, 'is two years in Wuhan.' Drews was applying to journalism schools. Goodbyes had to be prepared for. One morning in the bathroom, they solemnly shaved their beards. Drews put the plastic lid on the portable phonograph and wondered whether to leave his egg cooker for Mrs Bottom.

'Mum,' Tim replied, 'is out of bloody eggs.'

Drews removed the dartboard from his wall and said: 'Jesus, we made a lot of holes. It must have been you.' On the final evening, the two went to a pub and renewed their vow. The following morning, Tim walked Drews down those four avenues to the tube station. They lowered the canvas suitcases to the pavement beside the odoriferous kebab stand.

'I'm bloody hungry,' said Tim.

'It seems like yesterday.' Drews looked about. 'This is where I waited for you that Sunday. When you moved into Mum's flat.'

'There's our pub.' Tim pointed across the street. 'We should have gone there last night, in memoriam.'

'I never really liked that pub. I feel kinda pukey when I pass it.'

'There are bloody better ones,' agreed Tim. 'Whom did we toast that night? Ramon Navarro?'

'Dorothy Gish,' said Drews.

'Ah,' said Tim. 'One of the brightest in the constellation. Never seen one of her bloody films, I must admit. Silents bore me to fucking tears.'

Drews stopped a passerby and asked him to take a photograph. The two men stood by the kebab stand and Tim threw his beefy arm around Drews' shoulder. Drews did the same. The photograph was snapped.

'One more,' called Drews. 'If you don't mind.'

'Bloody bourgeois sense of history.' But Tim kept his arm firmly on Drews' shoulder. And it was Timmy who maintained the photos through the years and even hung one on his wall in Conduit Road. You can view it at any time: the tall man with the ponytail in the collarless shirt and the cowboy boots; the smaller, rounder man with the beatific smile, arms thrown on each other's shoulders. Both faces shine with emotion and freshly-shaved skin. Drews lugged his bags through the turnstile and turned to give a final goodbye. Timmy stood in the station doorway, waving both arms over his head and bellowing stoutly and unabashedly.

'This is not the end, my friend!' His arms criss-crossed, as if signalling for help. 'Danny – this is just the beginning!'

The beginning – it is portentousness itself! Out of the sylvan clearing and into the tangled woods. Or so it might seem. But was that sojourn in London such a cloudless idyll? What of the rooms, what of those thick, stained Albert Court walls, so many walls, extending into our dreams? What of those ghosts padding barefoot up the stairs – I'm aware of ghosts now and partial – oozing their pasts into our ears and pulling, beneath our bedclothes, on our very futures? The ghost in the kitchen doorway at 2 am, hand on hip, cigarette vibrating unsteadily, summoned by three frightening rings of the telephone, positing the notion that the grace of God might not be sufficient, might not even exist? *There's* a fright: that the rooms' walls follow us, with their scars and frantic stains.

But no one enjoys a bloody killjoy. And if the beginning has, in fact, already passed Timothy P. Marquand – the columns started to darken, the vines starting to choke, renaissance on the horizon, followed by decadence and you-know-bloody-what – it is still nascent for Daniel Drews. Both men endured graduate studies, in cloudy Wuhan for one and snowy Missouri for the other, followed by that inertia so unrecognized in universities: the tendency to continue once set in motion. Tim Marquand, of course, was fated for Hong Kong, the centre of China-watching and, perhaps, the source of that particular kind of inertia. Danny Drews was enduring a job in a rural daily, then a regional monthly. Finally, with advice from his friend in Hong Kong, Drews applied for the fellowship that would return him abroad. He specifically stated that his interest was not Japan or Taiwan or Indochina, the traditional favourites, but the shining Crown Colony in the South China Sea. He secured the fellowship, which, typically, sent him to Japan. But not without a sentimental stopover in Hong Kong. When Drews exited Kai Tak airport, he spotted a ginger-coloured mass of hair atop the body of a stout man – plump student no longer – bellowing greetings and pushing through chaotic crowds. The taxi penetrated the dismal skyscrapers of

Kowloon: Drews found himself in reaching distance, at fifty miles per hour, of Cantonese housewives preparing their dinners and scolding the babies. Then came a vibrating ferry ride across neon-painted water. And the final immersion into the constellation that is Hong Kong. The taxi stopped at a building darkened with mould. Tim dismissed the driver with happy, disrespectful Cantonese. The two men jammed into a tiny lift and ascended slowly. Tim pushed open a wooden door bearing a card with his name enscrawled.

'Feast your eyes, Danny boy. I can't describe how long I've waited for this bloody moment!'

Drews entered – carrying the same two canvas suitcases – and found a precise replica of his room in Mrs Bottom's servants' quarters. The green drapes were the main effect, of course, covering an entire wall and, concealed behind it, a panorama of the Hong Kong harbour. A wing chair occupied the centre of the room.

'Christ, Timmy, where's my old settee?'

'Nasty old thing. Wouldn't have one in the flat.'

'But everything else.'

'Look!' Tim pointed at a wall. And there they were in 8 x 10 beside the kebab stand, arms thrown about each other's shoulders, oblivious of the stray cuff and umbrella at the edges of the frame.

'Clean-shaven,' said Tim. 'Remember that morning, boy? Searching for your bloody pimples? Wait! I almost forgot.' He bustled around the chair. The room was filled with amplified scratch sounds, then stirring violins and happy triangles: the first intimations of 'You Did It'.

Tim bellowed, arms in the air. 'I knew we'd make it, Danny! I always knew. We've kept our vow. And now, nothing can stop us!'

Hong Kong was a place where vows could be fulfilled by sheer willpower. It was willpower on the part of the British that created it and the willpower of the greedy Cantonese that sustained it. In no other spot on earth did the topsy-turvy topography, the terrifying geopolitics and the greedy local ethos combine so fiercely to promote a religion of self-aggrandizement. It was a place everyone came to make their name or fortune or both and no one felt satisfied in any job: no clerk, no policeman, no bewigged judge. Hong Kong has always been a kind of confidence trick. And only those without confidence, along with the dullards and those with numerous mouths to feed, fail to see it. Daniel Drews and Tim Marquand had none of these disabilities. They were confident, restless, ambitious, and there was no *New York Times* in Hong Kong, no *Washington Post*, nothing but the venerable *South China Morning Post* and the moribund *Far Eastern Economic Review*. Nothing but Australian hacks and Indian subeditors, whom Drews could surpass for integrity and energy, and dedicated, competitive China-watchers, whom Tim Marquand was already outstripping with astonishing, boisterous brilliance. Excuse me: 'Timothy P. Marquand'. That was the byline starting to appear in scholarly quarterlies and magazines.

The steps seem so simple and logical in retrospect. Once the fellowship ended – or, to be precise, several weeks in advance – Drews fled the order of Japan for the ferment of Hong Kong, where he joined the *South China Morning Post*. He jumped to the *Far Eastern Economic Review*. Soon, Timmy was at the next desk, banging out a regular column proposed, with some insistence, by Daniel Drews himself. Within months – or was it days? hours? minutes? – Tim Marquand dominated the magazine's China coverage, routing several old-timers to the FCC bar. And then the truly inevitable occurred. The two men's dissatisfaction with the *Review* grew into an audacious plan to do it all on their own. To give Hong Kong, and all of Asia, a magazine that didn't only acknowledge the energy crackling through the region – acknowledged wearily, in soporific prose with a palpable yawn rising from toilet-tissue pages – but one born of that energy and bursting with it. To claim Asia as their own, and, a less difficult task, to steal all the members of the *Review* staff who showed even the tiniest spark of life.

'An Asian *Time*,' said Drews.

'God forbid,' said Tim.

'Well, it can look like *Time*. Glossy.'

Tim nodded.

'And read like it.'

'That,' said Tim, pacing wide circles around his living room, 'is what we have to avoid on pain of death.'

But your narrator has got ahead of himself again and, in total innocence, has turned his back on a new character in our story. For Drews did not leave Japan alone. When he landed at Kai Tak airport for the second time, on an identically muggy evening and met once again by his trusty, bearded friend, he was no longer the footloose former student with two light canvas bags. He had quite a lot of baggage, in fact, loaded on a trolley with a faulty wheel. When we reached Conduit Road, two trips were required up the narrow lift. For Drews was accompanied by his Japanese bride, Miki. He looked different when he entered my flat that evening lugging the final suitcase. Can I say that his face had finally changed: that those planes had disappeared, that the new Drews had emerged, or simply that my Drews had become someone else's? When those happy violins and triangles started up, it was Miki Drews who expressed delight. She had seen the movie, of course; she adored Audrey Hepburn. When we took the steam train to the border the following day, Drews shared his wooden bench with that inscrutable Japanese woman. (But that smile – I can't ignore her smile: bursting through that marble face and melting even the iciest jealousy.) Miki was at the window, smoking a succession of Kents, and it was to her that I gave descriptions of the sights passing by. She nodded appreciatively, absorbing the sights as she exhaled cigarette smoke, and it was through those carved eyes that Drews saw the sights and enjoyed them. Miki bought the dried squid for us to munch at the border. She withdrew from a neat wallet the green notes for the return tickets. When we plotted our blockbuster novel – to begin and end at that deceivingly placid border – it was Miki who sat on the floor filling in the boxes on the posterboard while Drews and I paced the room hurling out ideas. And before long, perhaps inevitably, I sought out my own Miki, finding him at a bus stop near the yacht club during a sunshower. In other circumstances, he might have been my life's great love; in any case, he loyally filled my cup until the jug ran dry.

And so, when we dreamt up *Orientweek* magazine behind those wide green drapes on countless nights drenched in impressive quantities of liquor, we were a foursome: me acting the id, Drews the ego, Miki the superego, and Kin Wah moving from kitchen to living room in an attempt to keep glasses filled. Two Asians, two *gweilos*; two pacing men, one marble-faced courtesan on the floor and a Cantonese boy at home in the shadows; one pair of heels by the door, two cowboy boots knocked on their sides, a small pair of proper English loafers (Kin Wah's) and two large peasant shoes of ripped, black canvas (mine). We were an odd group, for sure, but young, bound by love, infected with the ambitious energy of Hong Kong and able to stay up till dawn when the need arose and the booze allowed, which was often. If the *Review* had known the hangovers Danny and I dragged into the newsroom weren't mere symptoms of the journalist's disease – they were the brands of treason, pure and true. The *Review* supplied aspirin for the staff in those days, being a headachy place, stored in a box near the water-cooler. The Cantonese staff called it '*gweilo* candy'. If Danny and I owe the *Review* anything, and we probably do, it's a bloody large crate of Bayer aspirin.

It was on a summer evening in 1976, ostensibly a requiem party to mourn the passing of Burl Ives and Mao Tse-Tung, that we revealed to a choice assemblage of Hong Kong journalists our intention to start a magazine. Drews and I did the proselytizing; beside Drews was his Oriental empress, smoking inscrutably, and next to me was Nick Naversen in his raffish prime, who had insinuated himself with novel ideas on finance. Across the table sat the formidable Fran, nodding agreement with flashing spectacles. Kin Wah hovered near the door, helping the waiters. It was a private room at the Pine and Bamboo. In my memory, the excitement was completely infectious. But here comes a sting in my ear: there were worried looks around the table as staffers weighed the risk of abandoning secure jobs for a gamble called *Orientweek*. Someone even raised the issue of salary levels. This was not the night of *Orientweek*'s conception: that had taken place behind those green drapes. Nor was it the magazine's birth, which would take six months longer and be accompanied by PR hoopla (bullied by Fran Naversen) and historical levels of venomous scepticism at the FCC bar. At the Pine and Bamboo we merely announced the pregnancy. And when dinner ended and there was a disloyal rush from the private dining room, Evan Olcott approached me with a sympathetic smile.

'Your secret's out, my dear boy.' He pointed at the door, closing behind a pair of fast feet. 'They're on their way to the FCC, you know, as fast as their dirty little chappals will carry them.'

'We'll tender our resignations tomorrow.'

'You'll be sacked tonight. Hope you have nothing valuable in your desk.' Evan was old even then – he had been old for a decade. I had befriended him as a new China hand paying obeisance to the old. I had invited him to the dinner knowing he'd never contribute a thing to *Orientweek*, not a line of copy or a Hong Kong cent. Perhaps that's why Drews perversely named him chairman a few months later. I would later learn that Evan Olcott was more than an expired China-watcher, one of Hong Kong's rare shades, but a compelling anti-philosopher who, it can now be revealed, introduced me to the great poem of Khushhal Khan Khatak. It happened in India, Evan's India. Where, under the vast, empty globe of the Indian night, he read for me in that empty voice with the boyish lisp:

> *Roses, wine, a friend to share*
> *Spring sans wine I will not bear . . .*
> *Time hath all young lovers slain,*
> *Time is heedless, time is heartless –*
> *Saqi, fill and fill again.*

Yes, our secret was out. *Orientweek* was about to be born. The following morning, Drews, Nick and I found the contents of our desks in cardboard cartons by the *Review* lift. Drews kicked his with a cowboy boot and, with a hard expression, marched out of the lobby. Nick, stooping, bemoaned the loss of a half bottle of booze. I'd be lying if I didn't acknowledge a certain lumpiness in the throat when I saw those bloody cartons by the lift. We thought the hard part behind us that morning when we left the building, cartons in our arms. But we were foolish: the hard part is never behind you.

She was sitting at a desk, a woman smoking a languid cigarette, not so much concentrating as connecting to some sweet dream. That was Drews' first view of Miki. The desk was dirty grey steel. Miki's legs were crossed. There were other women in the newsroom in neater dresses and prettier hairstyles. But the other women rushed about, bowed nervously and giggled with hands before their mouths. They were scrawny and Kabuki-white. Their laughs seemed to pain the corners of their acute eyes. They were incontrovertibly and irredeemably Japanese. Miki was a native of her own particular land. She had a large, open face with a mouth that gave way to unabashed, wide-laned smiles. Her eyes were inevitably chiselled. But her genetic sculptor was a Mannerist, placing them in the centre of the face, on exhibit, not tucked behind tightly pulled lids. While other Japanese women seemed small even when large, Miki was the reverse. She crossed her legs. She smoked cigarette after cigarette, pulling from them calm or remove, the atmosphere of that personal, faraway homeland. When Drews approached, she looked up from the desk with slow puzzlement. There was no giggle, no scrape of the chair, no nervous honorific. Just a pulling away from that distant place and placid, questioning eyes. 'What?' she said.

Drews would soon learn: Miki was independent of habit, if not of mind, argumentative with her Japanese colleagues at whisky and beer sessions and she had a husky voice. She sang at the tiny bars, closing her eyes dreamily. She made love in a deep, grateful surrender. She was too old to marry in strict Japan. And so she was poised at a turning point, legs crossed, contemplating a decision she hoped to postpone until the world's supply of cigarettes expired. Her intention was to retreat to a bar in rural Japan to become a Mama-san for the rest of her nights. She would have been a fine Mama-san. She smoked and sang, crossed her legs and uncrossed them for strangers. She loved drinking and her laugh was vulgar by Japanese standards. And yet she had no real rebelliousness.

Her plan was that of all unmarriageable Japanese girls, or all unmarriageable girls who made love and knew hangovers. Miki was twenty-nine years old.

And so began the nights of Daniel and Miki Drews. They were nights without a room, for Japanese rooms are identical and featureless. They drank and made love on the tatami, mattresses and quilts jammed to the corners, Miki's head pushed against the sliding glass door. That was the face Drews came to cherish: those sealed, narrow eyes, black hair jammed to the window, features sculpted by the ivory light glowing through the glass. He cooked bacon in the tiny kitchen of his flat and spun intoxicating dreams. Miki listened with a cigarette between two fingers, absorbing it all in deep, thirsty draughts. For Miki was in need of fresh dreams. And Drews, the dreamy expatriate, had enough for both of them. He told tales of his round friend in Hong Kong and she nodded and laughed, sometimes with a slight, linguistic delay. She told of her past – the rural upbringing, the hard-earned scholarship to Tokyo, the terrible reward: nine fruitless years at a Japanese newspaper punching linotype tapes and filing photos in the library. That was the brick wall Miki spent her days blowing cigarette smoke at. And when she described her vigorous passage into that cul-de-sac, Drews saw the aged marble melt and, behind it, the country girl emerge, whose fine determination had yielded so little. That was the turning point: the discovery of the scholarship girl – his own discovery, his own girl – within the cigarette-smoking, hard-drinking, easy-fucking woman of the evening. He asked to see childhood photos. But she had only one: of the grandmother who revered books, a kimono-clad woman with snowy hair. Miki spoke of the frustration of her life. She said: 'I am weak.' She meant: *I am defeated.*

Drews said: 'You don't seem weak to me.'

'Not weak,' she replied. 'In Japan, I am very strong. But I can't do what I want.' Her eyes lowered, searching for the correct English words. They rose. 'You have so much. You are happy. I have nothing on my own. Her voice was smoky, even at dawn. 'That is my tragedy.'

And so, a woman scanning the horizon through cigarette smoke, despairing of the wave that would sweep her away, met a man who was trying, in youth and ambition, to gather tidal force. Drews married Miki, thinking he was giving her something while actually satisfying his desire for a mate he could possess totally. Miki would allow herself to be subsumed with intelligence, grace and without resentment. And Drews believed she would be his for all time. For who could again salvage her, as he had, from the ocean floor? Drews, in his cowboy boots and with his shiny black locks, felt himself the prince awakening the marble-faced princess. Two princesses: the husky-voiced adult whom the world knew and knew a little too well and the country girl within, who was Drews' alone.

That his princess was impure didn't trouble Drews. Quite the contrary. To Drews, Miki had a hard-earned view of the world, which he considered poignant and wise. In fact, Miki knew only the world of defeat, which is a very different thing: not wise, often desperate and ultimately unsubmergible, even under waves of contentment, success and love.

To Hong Kong they went. For Miki, life pulled back from the edge with glamorous speed. She was twenty again. She loved the young man who talked to her continually and uncondescendingly, who found her beautiful. She was intoxicated by his corona of ambient success. For the ambitious country girl lived on. The pit was behind her and the scholarship girl gained what she had always lacked – a little help – and what she had always desired – a wide horizon. Plus a love that showed all signs of permanence. Miki learned the secret of Drews' heart. He desired total possession and, in that oddly-formed heart, possession was incomplete if not mutual.

Drews' Hong Kong friends came to know the night-time Miki: the woman with the iffy English, the surprising smile, the rum and tonics and the succession of Kents, which she held before her like wands releasing a smoky veil. She was a woman not full of fun but at ease in it – that is, at ease in the cyclonic swirls surrounding Drews and Tim Marquand. Indeed, beyond a certain hour, it was hard to spot Tim or Drews without the cross-legged Japanese woman on the adjacent barstool. And when parties broke up and the shared taxi reached Conduit Road, it was always the three of them that disappeared into that mouldy building to talk about God knows what for heaven knows how long. And it was only then, and only before Drews and Tim, that the other Miki made her appearance. Sitting on the floor drawing the lines and boxes for the novel that would make them rich; dispensing earthy counsel on who could be trusted in the new venture named *Orientweek*; or merely talking about life with girlish animation and womanly strength under the rather too loud voices of Richard Burton, Gordon MacRae and Rex Harrison.

There were the inevitable jokes about Drews' Mongol or, from the catty, his mongoloid. She was tarred with that old, lumpy brush: the Asian bride, the weak Western man's harem of one. When Drews had risen to imperial status at *Orientweek*, and when he started spending most of his waking hours in the newsroom or in staff revels, Miki was considered a kind of consort in pearls dragged from Shu Fai Terrace for banquets and bacchanals only. They saw her as a decoration on Drews' chest that seemed too small. Tim Marquand refused to defend Miki in detail. All he would say was: 'If you only knew, my friends, then you'd know our Daniel Drews.'

And thus, Miki Drews became a long-term enigma in Hong Kong, largely because no one had cared about Miki, or more precisely, about Drews, in the mid-1970s. Then Drews was nothing but another journalist. No one noticed, or cared, that he left the *Morning Post* newsroom precisely at six each evening, sometimes early, and went home for lunch. No one saw the Drewses, or noticed, as they trod the muddy lanes of Stanley Market holding hands, Drews selecting the dresses. No one but Tim Marquand knew the education Drews was feeding Miki each evening, rushing home to quiz her on the ambitious novels he selected each weekend at Swinburne's, Miki at his side. Nor could they know of the excited, alcohol-driven nights in which the two discussed dreams of the future, interrupted only by the call of the mattress and even then, fairly often, returning in *yukatas* to the wicker dining table for more rum and beer and conversation. No one cared about the Drewses at that time. And later, when *Orientweek* was a reality and Drews had sprung, fully formed, as its deity, they grappled for the thread of plot not knowing they had taken their seats at the start of the second act.

Except Ellen Weigner, the veteran Tokyo correspondent for the *Reviewing*, and after 1976, *Orientweek*. Ellen was small, box-shaped, also fond of cigarettes, which her thick fingers always seemed to be stubbing out. She was divorced, with a weary, nasal voice. She was more *Review* than *Orientweek* and resisted Drews' crazed charm, which made him value her above all *Orientweek* staffers. As a rule, Ellen disapproved of Japanese women and their relationships with Western men, having seen it all and seen nothing but the worst. But she recognized the difference in the Drewses' marriage. Ellen was summoned to Hong Kong for the gala launch of *Orientweek* in 1976. And it was on a pleasure junk cruising through Aberdeen harbour, with Drews singing 'Hang Down Your

Head, Tom Dooley' on the top deck, that she found herself in an ardent discussion with Miki Drews. For Miki was drawn to Ellen Weigner; there was, in Ellen's personality, a sympathetic strain of defeat. She spilled the Drewses' secret: that they were trying to have a child.

'I never thought I could,' Miki said. Ellen nodded knowingly, stubbing out a cigarette. To see them smoking together was like viewing paired portraits entitled 'The High Life' and 'Smokers Beware!'

'And I know Dan will be a good father.'

'Your kid will stomp on desks before he walks. He'll be singing "Tom Dooley" from the crib.'

Miki shook her head. 'I keep thinking: the magazine and the baby. What more could we want?'

It was to Ellen Weigner that Miki sent a card announcing, in imperfect English, her pregnancy. And Ellen Weigner was the only *Orientweek* staffer to send Miki a note when she lost the baby four months afterwards. On her subsequent business trips to Hong Kong, Ellen stayed with the Drewses at Shu Fai Terrace (for Drews was notoriously tight about hotel bills). She shared their private dinners, often paired with Tim Marquand, and was invited to foursomes at the Conduit Road flat, rolling her eyes as Tim replayed the overture from *My Fair Lady*. Many years later, over an after-dinner drink in a Causeway Bay pub, Miki again revealed to Ellen that she was pregnant. *Orientweek* was thriving in the limitless Hong Kong of the early 1980s. Drews and Tim had abandoned the women for a last check of the newsroom, for it was deadline night.

'I need something of my own,' Miki said. 'Dan has the magazine. He loves it so much. They all love him. I need something.' Ellen nodded with tight lips, cognizant of the shift in Miki Drews' thinking from first baby to second. When Miki miscarried two months later, Ellen flew to Hong Kong. She stayed at the Drewses' flat and avoided the *Orientweek* newsroom, for both the pregnancy and the miscarriage were kept secret.

It wasn't long afterwards that Drews' newsroom affairs began. To Miki, the affairs seemed inevitable. She recognized the looks of love and devotion Drews inspired in his staff. She observed from her perch, her hallowed barstool, and thought of her own face in that tiny kitchen in Tokyo as Drews cooked his bacon breakfasts. She looked across the bar, to the mirror behind the bottles, wondering if that devotion still lingered on her face. But the mirror was faulty. It showed the familiar, large-featured face she had never liked, with a wave through the middle. Miki had turned forty-one. She lit another cigarette, exhaled blue smoke and watched her husband work the crowd with jokes and old routines. She absently fingered her beloved pearls. It had the appearance of a long night.

Despite the affairs, Drews' love for Miki was unaltered: an alloy that couldn't change shape once established. The long, alcohol-fuelled conversations continued deep into the nights, although never again interrupted, or concluded, by the call of the mattress. The threesome with Tim Marquand also lived on, although Canossa Hospital started claiming more of his time. (No one could persuade him to lessen his drinking for Timmy always had his poem to quote, in grand, stentorian manner in the middle of a bar or in the living room of his Conduit Road flat.

' "Abstinence I do abhor!" '

'Yes, Timmy,' said Drews, 'but your friends . . .'

' "Cup on cup, my *saqi*, pour." Kin Wah. Another for the gentleman.')

Ellen Weigner openly disapproved of Drews' newsroom flings and stopped staying at Shu Fai Terrace on her trips to Hong Kong. She refused dinners with the couple. She met Miki alone for lunch or when Miki returned to Japan to see her family. They remained friends, but their conversations rarely strayed from *Orientweek* gossip. For Miki had no real confidences to share with Ellen. Her life with Drews was altered in only one way and she was too shy to discuss sex with the formidably divorced Ellen Weigner. Ellen might recommend a drastic action that could threaten Miki's entire existence. And the woman who had flirted once with defeat was not yet ready for its frightening embrace. Not alone, anyway.

Life at *Orientweek* continued and improved. Circulation grew. Nick Naversen had long before decided to 'go it alone' in search of pastures that were, he suggested (with numerous, knowing nods from wife Fran), far greener than journalism. Tim Marquand's China coverage won awards. Salaries grew, although clamours for housing allowances were never heeded. Every year there was a celebration on *Orientweek*'s birthday – the only time Evan Olcott, chairman of the company, made his otherworldly float through the newsroom – and there was the famous cover story in which *Orientweek*, or Daniel Drews, called for the banning of ties in Asia. The Marcoses and the Philippines began to obsess Drews, culminating in his famed Imelda Diary in 1985. More and more female staffers started using that telling monosyllable, Dan. The entire staff continued to peer through the glass pane in his office door, waiting for their hairy leader to emerge and breathe some magic into the mechanical life of weekly journalism. They watched surreptitiously: he sat in his sacrosanct office, his gaze half-focussed on the Shaukiwan typhoon shelter, a pencil flickering ever-faster between thumb and forefinger, until it shot out of his hand altogether, ricocheted across the room and struck the glass pane of his office door.

Which startled everyone in the newsroom. And then came Drews' face grinning through the pane. He bowed, salaamed, bowed again, flung open the door and let loose the patented Drews bellow:

'Boys! Be ambitious!'

Or:

'Chuck, Chuck, Bo-buck, Banana-fana Fo Fuck . . .'

Or:

'Dolly! Where are those bleeding bananas?'

Or, tunelessly:

'We know we belong to the land! And the land we belong to is grand!'

Or when things went haywire, as during the increasingly serious hospitalizations of Tim Marquand, Drews deemed and accomplished an actual change in the newsroom's weather. The staff was assembled at the Ball, after midnight, before a deadline. Drews jumped from a standing position, cowboy boots scuffing the bar, and sang 'Joe Cool' in five verses ('Tom Dooley' having been subsumed into the past). The Cantonese bar girls with the rubbery nipples danced on unamused.

And Miki Drews sat on her barstool in a cloud of Kent smoke, legs crossed, pearls shining, smiling that same, elusive smile.

Drews' Imelda Diary landed *Orientweek* in legal trouble. A notoriously corrupt Philippine politician sued for libel and, after a protracted court battle, won. Luckily, the politician was as pompous as he was corrupt. He announced he wanted no damages from *Orientweek*. He didn't need the money – abundantly true after fifteen years with the Marcoses – and had merely wanted to prove a point. In lieu of damages he demanded that *Orientweek* take a Filipino on staff for training purposes, 'so the foreign magazine, and its troublemaking editor, could contribute something to the country they have tried for twelve years, in the spirit of evil mischief, to degrade and besmirch and drag through the mud of the blackest propaganda'. Drews, in the aforementioned spirit, pinned the news report on the *Orientweek* bulletin board, circled the words 'to clear his name' and wrote in red pen: 'Like all Filipinos, this man just can't resist a joke.'

Two months later, Gabriel Ledesma arrived in the *Orientweek* newsroom with a suitcase and three shopping bags. The receptionist brought him to the desk of Dolly Leung, who ushered him into Drews' office. She withdrew and closed the door behind her. Through the glass pane the staff could see Drews rise and shake his hand.

'He's a looker,' whispered Tisch McAuliffe. 'Too bad he's only here for six months.'

Marietta regarded Tisch with disbelief. 'I've never heard you say such a thing, Tisch. What would Philip say?'

'A girl can have her dreams, can't she? Oh God. I think I've been in Hong Kong too long. I'm starting to go for the dark ones.'

Dolly pointed at the shopping bags next to her desk and giggled. 'All the Filipinos carry shopping bags.'

When the door opened, all eyes were covertly peering over glowing terminals. Drews had his hand on the Filipino's shoulder: he liked him. Gabriel Ledesma was indeed a looker: he had coffee-coloured skin, a sharp brow, amused eyes and baby-soft black hair. His smile was that easy Philippine sunburst with a gap at the rear where molars were missing. He wore jeans and an open-necked shirt with a missing button. Later the staff would wonder: did he know in advance of the necktie ban? Or, as Tisch suggested, did he not own one?

Gabriel lunged to the copy desk – ten heads jerked toward their screens – and formally shook everyone's hand in turn.

'Meet Gabriel,' said Drews.

'Gabby,' said Gabriel.

Drews patted his shoulder. 'We have enough Gabbies in this news-room.' And the command was obeyed: Gabriel's nickname was no more.

'You've come straight from Kai Tak?' Tisch pushed to the front.

Gabriel smiled affirmatively, hands folded before him like a giant schoolboy.

'You work for the *Star*?' asked Marietta, who edited the Philippine stories.

Gabriel laughed. 'It's not like this.' He made a large, admiring gesture. 'We've nothing like this in the Philippines. This is terrific!' His accent was that peculiar blend of rolled r's, words rushed humbly and sentences punctuated by small explosions of GI slang.

'Did you cover the coup?' asked Kelvin. It became the usual newsroom rush with offers of lunch and drinks for the interesting newcomer, an assignment of a desk and terminal, a cup of tepid *Orientweek* coffee, until Gabriel Ledesma gathered his shopping bags and stood patiently at Dolly's desk, raising eyebrows at those who met his gaze. He and Drews were going home together. For Drews, in his anger at the legal defeat and in line with his traditional cheapness over hotel bills, refused to pay a single night's lodging for a trainee forced on him by a bent Philippine court. Gabriel Ledesma was to spend the next six months in the Drewses' guest room, across the hall from Drews and Miki's bedroom.

Drews came to like Gabriel Ledesma. He was an unobtrusive house guest. He spent hours away from the flat exploring Hong Kong. He appreciatively ate everything served by the Drewses, even Japanese food. He was kind to Rosemarie, the Drewses' Philippine maid, and they laughed in the kitchen over tales of Negros Occidental and Ilocos Norte, their respective provinces. Rosemarie directed him to the local Philippine provisions shop. He loved English and kept a diary filled with wisdom culled from all sources, including *Reader's Digest*. He produced it one night and Drews flipped the pages. 'Virtue is learned at mother's knee; vice at other joints. (Thomas Paine, 1737–1809)'. Another page, with stars at the top: 'The right thing at the wrong time is no better than the wrong thing at the right time.' Another: 'A bather whose clothing was strewed / By winds that left her quite nude ...' Over dinner, Gabriel described his eighteen months in prison under Marcos. He told the story with discordant humour: he had been a mere student leader, hardly a threat to the regime. Jail wasn't so bad. Coming from the robust, unscarred, easy-smiling Filipino, it was almost possible to believe. Drews thought of Gabriel's diary and the quote from Cardinal De Retz (1673): 'We learn from experience that not everything which is incredible is untrue.' In bed, he asked Miki: 'Do you think he lost those teeth in prison?' Miki said: 'He has to go to Stanley. He's worn that same shirt for a week.'

After four months, Drews said he might offer Gabriel a permanent job in Hong Kong.

Miki exhaled cigarette smoke.

'I think he's real *Orientweek* material. He gets along with everyone. Even the Cantonese.'

'What about his family?'

'It's the best thing for them,' said Drews. 'He can send money home. And we're only talking about the child. He's separated from his wife.'

Miki nodded.

'You heard what he said,' Drews continued. 'He was going to quit the *Star*. He couldn't make ends meet. But he's a born journalist.'

Miki said: 'Then offer him a job.'

When the announcement was posted on the bulletin board, Tisch rushed to Marietta's cubicle. 'We've got a reprieve,' she whispered. 'We're keeping the Filipino!'

'Tisch, you've really gone round the bend.'

'Don't say you don't find him attractive, Etta. And you already like native men.'

'Kelvin is not a "native", Tisch.'

'Well, you know what I mean.'

'Gabriel has a family back in the Philippines.'

'I've only heard of the child. "Smile". So sweet.'

'She has a birthmark on her face,' said Marietta, nose wrinkled in distaste. 'In the shape of an S.'

'I think that's sweet,' said Tisch. 'He's really a sweet man. The sweetest man on Hong Kong side. That's what I call him to Philip. Although it must be horrible to have a child with a birthmark on its face. You don't think it's one of those red ones? I'm sure they can be removed. In the States, I mean. By now.'

'Kelvin thinks he should have been kept on the industry beat.'

'But he knows politics. He was in *jail*, you know.'

'Tim agrees.'

'Oh, Tim is just jealous because Drews and Miki have a new friend. Fran Naversen saw the three of them in the Vietnamese Restaurant in Causeway Bay.'

Gabriel loved two things equally: working out and animals. He spoke frequently of his dog in Manila, more often than his daughter Smile. And when he brought a stray puppy back to Shu Fai Terrace, Drews could hardly object. The dog was already settled in a basket in the kitchen. Rosemarie eagerly accepted the walking duties. Gabriel claimed he was an expert in dog training and, indeed, the dog was housebroken in days. To Drews' astonishment, Miki accepted the dog and even petted it from time to time with the tips of her fingernails.

'What happens if it doesn't work out?' asked Drews. 'If Gabriel has to go back to the Philippines?'

Miki shrugged. 'He can take the dog with him. Or Rosemarie can keep it. Or we'll get rid of it.'

Drews and Miki brought Gabriel to the Conduit Road flat after an evening at the FCC. Tim was recuperating from a stay at Canossa. He sat massive in the wing chair, barking commands to Drews at the record player. The Filipino tried his best with tales of the Marcoses. Drews joined in with remembrances of the Agrava hearings and even Miki, awkwardly fingering her pearls, volunteered a story about Imelda, whom she had seen on an airplane. But the China-watcher, bloated beneath his bathrobe, was only interested in the music from the record player. Drews said: 'Timmy, yesterday was the tenth anniversary of Edgar Bergen's death. Remember your party at the Nullah?' But Kin Wah appeared at the door with pills and the three visitors descended in the lift in silence.

★ ★ ★

When Drews arrived home from Indonesia, he received a cold welcome from Rosemarie. The dog cowered in its kitchen basket. He said to Miki: 'The Missing Link drove me nuts.' Miki looked up from her cards – she had taken up bridge – and said: 'What?' For the rest of the week, Rosemarie avoided Drews' gaze. Gabriel spent long hours at the gym. Miki shuffled her deck. And one day, while looking for underwear, Drews discovered an unfamiliar handkerchief in Miki's jewellery drawer. He unfolded the handkerchief to find a small, rust-coloured stain. The discovery upset him, for he knew its meaning, but also puzzled him. The next day, when the flat was empty, he examined the guest room. Nothing was amiss. Gabriel's possessions were scattered on the book-shelves and the table. Beneath the bed were two blue dumbbells. Drews looked down at a dark Afghan rug. He understood. They had fucked in the guest room and for some obscure reason – secrecy? eroticism? – had sacrificed the comfort of the bed for the floor. Miki had been men-struating and Gabriel had thoughtfully covered the carpet with his handkerchief. For Gabriel was the most thoughtful of men. Gallant, some said in the newsroom.

He searched Miki's drawers again and discovered the white shirt, smelling of sweat, that Miki had once criticized. The following day the shirt had disappeared. He asked Rosemarie about it and she said: 'I don't know. He's washing his own clothes in the bathroom.' But Miki couldn't let go of that precious, stained handkerchief. Drews stole it and pored over it in his office, the door's glass pane covered by a worn sweater.

One night Drews lay awake, listening for his wife to rise. She gently closed the bedroom door behind her. Drews followed her. In the hall of his own flat, he dropped to his knees to peer through the keyhole of his own guest room. A keyhole has a constricted view, of course. Even if the couple had been *in flagrante*, Drews would have seen little. He saw a mere close up: Miki's face above that of the Filipino. He saw the marble dissolve into a special smile. It was that country girl Drews had rescued from Japan. Through a keyhole, he saw the happiness he had once monopolized pass to the control of another man. The mental shutter clicked, clicked again, clicked over and over like the banks of cameras at a news conference. Then there was a crash. Drews leapt to his feet and stood terrified in his underwear. He heard a smaller bang, more recognizable: it was the guest room bed scraping the wall. He lowered himself to the keyhole, steadying himself on the door jamb, and peered into the room. But the bed was empty. The two lovers had moved out of sight – onto the carpet. Drews stood and moved with silent steps to the toilet in his bedroom. He stealthily shut the door before he flushed. He returned to bed. After an eternity, Miki returned. She opened and shut the door with care and moved slowly to her side of the bed. Drews peeked: never once did she look toward him. Drews rolled over in feigned sleepiness. Miki took her place in the bed and the two lay motionless for a long time.

Behind the shield of the sweater, Daniel Drews began the first diary of his life. He chose an old notebook with scrawls from a reporting trip to confuse anyone who came upon it. We can discern a touch of melodrama in that action, excusable in an undeniably melodramatic situation. And hypocrisy: for Drews, in his heart, must have wanted and expected that diary to be read someday. Never had he written a word, or spoken one, or even thought one, that he desired to keep to himself.

The diary began in mid-notebook and mid-story:

> That night, with Gabriel's stained handkerchief in my pocket, I went to Bethany's apartment for the first time, unannounced. I fucked her on the couch, from behind, with her jeans and panties pulled to her knees. I fucked her two times more, each time thinking I was finished, only to be re-aroused by the thought of the two of them at home. I asked Bethany if she'd ever had a black or brown cock. She had – a soldier from Qatar – and I quizzed her as I fucked. 'This powerful? Could he touch you here?' When I left, Bethany said: 'You shouldn't drink so much, Dan.' I was satisfyingly sore in the cab. But when we turned into Shu Fai Terrace, I was aroused once more.

Drews started avoiding the flat, the Foreign Correspondents Club, even the newsroom, where Gabriel was sure to be sitting at a terminal projecting a sympathetic, guiltless smile. Drews returned home late, when lovemaking was sure to be over. He discovered a bar in Wanchai with a plaster elephant head above the door and there he wrote his diary.

After avoiding Timmy for a time, he slammed through the door of the Conduit Road flat one evening and laid the handkerchief upon Timmy's elephant-foot table. Drews was drunk and he'd remember little of that night. But he remembered Timmy rising from the wing chair, bathrobe pulled around his distended body, lumbering to the record player. He remembered Richard Burton singing in a defeated voice: *The way to handle a woman is to love her ...*

'That's it, you bearded cretin! Don't forget the love!'

The night, the tears, the booze, Burton's weak voice: *... simply love her ...*

'Get off your knees. Never sacrifice the love!' Timmy stood above Drews, illness shadowing his face. 'What else do we have, Danny boy, at the end, if we don't have our love?'

Drews escaped to the Philippines, of all places. He stayed at a shabby hotel in Ermita with no refrigerator, no television, a double bed with a large mirror on the wall and, to his delight, a neon sign outside the window that reddened the room. He avoided the journalist haunts – the Rat's Nest, the Cave, the Spider's Web, those well-named traps – and stood at the bar with the oilers at the go-go joints. A row of cowboy boots on the bar-rail below, a row of fist-covered San Miguel bottles above. He abandoned his scruples about paying for sex and chose the smallest girls available, desiring to feel large and white within them. He sat them on the linoleum platform beneath the mirror and fucked uncomfortably, watching his own contorted face. One day, he nearly succeeded in picking up a Japanese woman at the pool of the Philippine Plaza Hotel. He trawled the lobby that evening for more. His lust was a hydra: one head decapitated, hundreds more rearing and spitting fire. He watched in the bedside mirror as he masturbated: a beard ajar in lonely pleasure. The masturbation was an exaggerated gesture of self-pity, of course, for the roomboys were willing to provide any sexual partner he desired, except Japanese, for a modest sum. But Drews relished the sight of his pathetic loneliness: his face reddened with exertion, his long, gyrating legs. He wrote his diary with a loopy drunken hand.

> In countries like this, an old man sleeps with virgins in the hope that their sweet cunts will bring life to the gnarled, decrepit cock. I had always dismissed it as a bloodless superstition. Now I understand.

When he returned from Manila he found Miki dealing herself cards at the dining table. 'Where's Gabby? Working out?' Miki looked up, eyes opaque.

The guest room was cleared of Gabriel's possessions. On Drews' pillow was a letter. Gabriel begged forgiveness. He swore eternal professional loyalty. He insisted, over and over, on his love for Drews and, in a different way, his love for Miki. 'And I know the love she feels so deeply for me, however wounding it may be to you at this time, will always ...' At the end, the letter mentioned the dog.

'He's moved out?'

Miki looked up.

'Put down those fucking cards.'

The night became a hideous parody of the nights of the past. Miki wept silently and Drews made horrible, interminable sexual accusations. He read Gabriel's letter aloud, scorning each mention of the word love: 'How many *Reader's Digests* did he need for this masterpiece?' Drews accused Gabriel of adventuring. 'He thinks he's saving you from something. That's all he cares about: being the fucking knight in shining armour with a cock for a lance. How long do you think that will last?' He returned to the kitchen for more beer. 'What about the next housewife who rouses his pity? A younger housewife – a white housewife with blonde hair.' All Miki could say was: 'I don't know what to do.' Several times she said she'd go back to Japan to open a bar.

Drews agreed to meet Gabriel at the Nullah. He saw the tall Filipino, in his new Stanley Market clothes, walk confidently into the main bar. Everyone noticed Gabriel, men and women alike. *She's picked the best-looking man in Hong Kong. How the hell did she do it?* He winced: for he had brought Gabriel to Miki. With elbows on the table, Gabriel spoke of love. The last thing he wanted was to break up the marriage. Nor did Miki intend to leave Drews, he said. The affair had just happened.

'There was nothing we could do to stop it. You should have seen her when I touched her. She was actually trembling.' Gabriel spoke with innocent frankness. 'When I kissed her she kind of collapsed. I had to carry her into my room.'

After weeks of imagining, and despite rising nausea, Drews had to hear. 'You put your handkerchief over the rug.'

'Yes.' Gabriel sounded surprised. 'She was menstruating.'

Drews longed for information about the entry, to hear a description of Miki's cries. He needed Gabriel's dimensions, a precise image of them making love and he wanted to know how long they continued and whether they did it once or twice. For he had fantasized it all. 'Why the floor?' Gabriel solved the mystery: the bed banged the wall. Rosemarie would have heard. Gabriel talked of his failed marriage. His wife had deserted him for a policeman. He hadn't had sex since. For Gabriel was a true romantic. He fucked only for love and had been celibate for a year before Miki. Drews was dumbfounded: he had never heard of such a man.

'And Miki,' Gabriel asked. 'She hasn't had sex for four years?'

'Since the miscarriage.' Drews shifted on his bench. 'It was her decision, by and large. It wasn't me. I was willing. You can ask her.' Later, Gabriel talked about passion and Drews went into a rage. He mentioned the *Reader's Digests*.

At home, Drews said: 'Why did you have to tell him about the four years?' He agreed to allow the affair to continue but on one condition: that Gabriel resign from *Orientweek*. Miki rejected the condition. 'I can't work with the man every day,' Drews protested. Miki shook her head and stared at the table, foreseeing the ruin of Gabriel's career. And, she asked, how would he keep his Hong Kong visa? 'That's your fucking problem,' Drews said. 'I'm not responsible for visas for my wife's big-dicked Gabbies and JoJos and Ding-Dongs.'

The impasse continued for two weeks, including a second rendezvous at the Nullah. Gabriel started to weep and Drews stormed from the bar in anger. The next meeting was at Shu Fai Terrace, a summit, and Drews relented on the *Orientweek* job. He demanded that Miki and Gabriel meet outside the flat. Again, Miki shook her head. Gabriel wasn't allowed visitors in his rooming house. She refused to patronize 'love hotels'.

'I'll pay for the damn hotels, for God's sake.' Drews called an end to the evening and retired to the bedroom to allow the couple a private goodnight. After five minutes, he burst from the room, certain they were making surreptitious love. But they were standing in the living room holding hands and talking softly. 'Let's get a move on,' Drews shouted in his underwear at the end of the hall. Gabriel went to the kitchen to take his leave of the dog. He moved to the front door and took Miki's face in his hands and kissed it goodnight. Miki looked at him with a tragic smile.

When Miki came to bed, wiping her eyes, Drews said: 'I wouldn't trust a Filipino.'

'You're making this so hard.'

So Drews allowed them to make love in the flat. They were tormented nights for Drews, sitting at the elephant-head bar picturing their love-making through a mental keyhole. When he returned to the darkened flat, he checked the empty guest room for signs of passion. He examined the blinds to see which had been lowered. He peered at the couch cushions, searching for disorder or unusually deep impressions. But Miki always tidied up. Soon, he started coming home early, turning the key quietly in the latch, to catch a glimpse of a locked door, to hear sounds from within, or to get a peek through a keyhole. But he would find them at the dining room table talking in relaxed tones and playing with the dog. They invited Drews to join them. Miki was shyly silent. Gabriel was completely relaxed and once, to Drews' astonishment, said: 'So, is this how you normally spend your weekday nights?' At *Orientweek*, Drews kept an eye on Gabriel through the glass pane in his office door, particularly at lunchtime. When Gabriel was absent, he invented pretexts to go home, where he'd find Miki innocently occupied. Finally, one night, he told Miki he didn't think the arrangement was working. She phoned Gabriel. They battled anew. Drews gave them time to say goodnight but after three minutes his enraged shout came from the bedroom: 'Aren't you finished?' He appeared at the end of the hall. Miki and Gabriel were embracing lightly, looking sadly at each other. Miki's finger was tracing the line of Gabriel's chin: the way she had touched Drews' when they first met. He returned to the bedroom. When Miki followed, he walked past her. He brought a bottle of whisky to the dining table. She came out in *yukata*.

'I can't stand this,' Drews said. 'I think I'm going mad.'

He came home most evenings in an attempt to freeze, or obstruct, the affair. He lectured Miki: 'He talks of passion. But passion is only here.' Drews grabbed his crotch. Miki smoked and said she'd return to Japan to open a bar. On a particular evening, after drinking at the FCC, Drews made another unannounced visit to Bethany's flat. As he rang the doorbell, he checked his watch. It was 10 pm. If he returned home, he could interrupt Miki and Gabriel's lovemaking. Bethany opened the door, hair wet, a hand clasping the lapels of a bathrobe. Drews slid open the exterior gate with a metallic crash. He kissed Bethany, shut the door and moved her toward the living room with an urgent grip. He leaned her over a wicker chair and unbuckled his trousers.

'Wait!' Bethany's hand flailed, pointing blindly. 'The gate is open . . . the keyhole. Someone can see!'

Drews adjusted her and entered slowly, staring back at the keyhole in the front door. Facing him was a vertical hallway mirror. In the mirror, he found an image that dumbfounded him. It was Drews, the Drews everyone had known and tolerated for decades. He removed his shirt, fumbling with buttons, to further the image. Bethany was starting to moan in her usual fashion – 'Dan, Dan, Dan . . .' – but he ignored her. He watched the man in the mirror with the jeans at his knees, the cowboy boots, the tensed buttocks and black curls dangling onto his neck. He changed his tempo: the image in the mirror changed too. Tears welled in his eyes. He realized Daniel Drews retained his power, his command. He had only lost it for a brief, puzzling spell. He continued in this manner, gyrating with his mirror twin, mesmerized by the image of youth and power that he had believed dead.

When it ended, he hauled Bethany up from the chair with ostentatious tenderness. She had marks on her breasts from the wicker. 'Drews – Dan – I think you should go home.'

'I'm sorry. Really . . .' Drews ran down the curved street. From the taxicab, the buildings seemed taller, brighter than at any time in the past two months. He sprinted up the stairs to the flat and found Miki and Gabriel at the table. He stood before them and played his final, most desperate card. 'Come on!' He tried to control his quivering chin. 'What else are we going to do? Someone has to take control of this thing.' Miki was opposed but Gabriel put an arm around her. Drews allowed them to precede him to the master bedroom. He sat, tapping his foot, draining a can of beer. When he entered they were embracing on the bed. He saw the Filipino's figure, long and subtly muscled, in deep brown jockey shorts. His mental snapshot of the couple was nearly fulfilled. With deliberate noise, he removed his shirt, trousers and, already aroused, his underpants. He climbed onto his bed. Gabriel rolled over. Miki looked up at her husband, nipples wet with Gabriel's saliva. Drews said: 'Take off your briefs.' Gabriel obeyed, folding them carefully on the edge of the bed. Drews saw the erect cock, tapered at the end, and a black, sagging scrotum. Drews said: 'Kiss her again.' Miki extended her arms to Gabriel. Drews pulled her legs apart and entered her, relishing the gasp. Gabriel looked up from the kiss and smiled.

★　　★　　★

Back at the wicker table – three matching *yukatas*, three celebratory cigarettes – Drews said: 'I knew this was the only way.' He ran his hands through his curls. 'We needed some new weather in this relationship.'

'We all love each other.' Gabriel and Miki looked at each other.

'Some things are *not* out of your control,' Drews said.

A couple that reaches the heights of fresh, sexual love are impossibly and ridiculously happy. When that couple is three, the happiness is multiplied – along with the ridiculousness. To quote from the diary of Gabriel Ledesma: 'Mr Jones is such an optimist he lights a match before asking for a cigarette.' (Not to forget: 'The game of love has never yet been called off because of bad light.' And: 'A cute debutante from St Paul – Wore a newspaper dress to a ball . . .') The three lovers felt they had accomplished an impossible climb and they wanted their tricolour to be saluted publicly. Gabriel returned to the flat, to the delight of the dog, and the three started going everywhere together, even grocery shopping. They talked endlessly about their astonishing achievement. The conversations tended toward the same turn: so what if *they* find out? Valorous statements were made. 'We're not doing anything wrong; we're doing something *right* . . . At least we've got the guts.' Drews announced: 'I've never been prouder of anything in my life.' Miki, blowing smoke, said: 'I thought sex was over for me.' Gabriel, looking like an expectant father, said: 'Anyway, hardly anyone knows me in Hong Kong.' Miki learned Philippine dishes. She cooked extra quantities of Japanese rice, which, one night, Gabriel was forced to admit was superior to Philippine rice. Drews watched the two of them proudly, scooping into their rice.

Nonetheless, the three were scrupulous in keeping the full reality from Rosemarie. They waited for her to retire at night, or, in the daytime, darted from room to room with whispers and quiet lockings of doors. Gabriel was always in his bed when Rosemarie announced the new day with her distinctive banging of pots and pans. It was Gabriel who alerted them to the material debris of love – namely, condom wrappers – for he knew Philippine maids and their curious and insatiably optimistic attitude toward trash. He collected the wrappers, stored them in his room and disposed of them discreetly on the way to the office.

It was that early, proud period that brought Miki and Gabriel to Statue

Square one Sunday morning, walking hand in hand behind a small dog on a leash. It was Tisch's maid who spotted them, bestowing upon Tisch the greatest coup in the history of *Orientweek* newsroom gossip.

'That's why Drews has been so rat-assed,' said Kelvin, 'ever since he returned from Manila.'

'Poor Drews,' said Marietta. 'Who can imagine?'

'What do you think he'll do?' whispered Tisch. 'Philip thinks he might resign in shame. And he thinks someone from the business side should be given the editorship for once.' And then Drews and Gabriel entered the newsroom laughing at a private joke. Drews started whistling 'I Could Have Danced All Night'. He made his Monday morning demand for new weather in the newsroom, called Gabriel to his office and shut the door. Ten heads swivelled from their terminals. Marietta shot Tisch a betrayed look.

'Maybe he doesn't know after all,' said Tisch tentatively.

'That's why he's so happy?' said Kelvin. 'Because he *doesn't* know?'

'Maybe your maid needs glasses,' said Marietta. 'I told you the Drewses didn't have a dog. Miki Drews is not, by any stretch of the imagination, a dog type.'

They vowed to stay together always, moving to any point on the globe if necessary. They sealed that vow with constant lovemaking. Gabriel slipped into the master bedroom each morning and they fucked with honest vigour prolonged by a touch of masculine competition. At lunchtime, Gabriel and Drews stole home to do it again. Miki groaned when they pushed through the door but put down her cards with eagerness. At night, with the lubrication of liquor, the two men shared her breasts and simultaneously pushed their heads between her legs. Gabriel licked with ardently shut eyes; Drews' eyes were open, absorbing every image. The pattern from the first night was unalterable: Gabriel was responsible for the initial kissing and the foreplay, for it was he who aroused Miki now, not Drews. Drews waited, lying beside them, for the moment when he was allowed to join. Denied her kisses, Drews concentrated on her body and it was he who removed Miki's panties at the appropriate moment or when his patience had expired. And then he began his commands. When he was above them, thrusting slowly into Miki, he'd interrupt their sideways kiss. 'Let her suck you.' He decided when it was a night for sequential sex or frequent alternations. One night, he lifted Miki on top of Gabriel. He reached underneath her and grasped Gabriel's cock, inserting it inside her. When they were finished, they lay in bed smoking cigarettes and talking excitedly about themselves and their performances. Miki absentmindedly slapped Gabriel's softened cock against his belly. Gabriel told of his former wife's interest in anal sex and Miki said, 'Never,' making the two men laugh. Drews tallied up their lovemakings – each session counted twice – and volunteered to enter Miki in the *Guinness Book*. At the start, they lay in bed in a rigid formation: Miki between the two opposite-coloured men, tending to the Filipino. But time eroded that rigidity. It was Gabriel who first put his arm around Drews with brotherly casualness. Soon Drews responded. And when Miki returned from the bathroom one night, she found Drews sitting with Gabriel's head resting in his lap debating some newsroom controversy. The bearded husband with the sharp muscles and pitiless eyes: the brown-skinned lover with the languorous posture. She said from the doorway: 'You look beautiful.' Gabriel raised his head and smiled his tropical smile. 'Come here, honey.' (For that was his chosen term of endearment.) She took her place between the men, saying, 'I never thought two men could be beautiful.'

One morning, when they needed milk for coffee, Drews returned from the corner shop to find the master bedroom door locked. Gabriel let him in, shielding his private parts. 'You missed it, Danny.' Miki smiled from the bed. Drews removed his T-shirt and shorts. 'Dan,' laughed Miki, 'it's over.' Drews climbed onto the bed and said, 'No way.' Drews became obsessed with the idea of missing an act. For only Gabriel could initiate sex, only Gabriel could make love to Miki alone. When Drews was shaving and noticed an unusual silence in the flat, he ran naked from the bathroom to check Gabriel's door. He refused to go to the corner store alone again. His anxiety was boosted whenever they discussed the bad old days before the threesome. Drews quizzed them about all aspects of the affair, with emphasis on the sex. One day, on the way to the office, Drews asked: 'Neither of you are very interested in blow jobs.'

Gabriel said he could take them or leave them.

'You don't enjoy coming in a woman's mouth?'

They had only done it at the very beginning, Gabriel said, to minimize the sounds when Drews was sleeping across the hall. Drews recalled those nights alone in bed, listening for those sounds of love, unable to steal into the hall and look through the keyhole. For he had tried a second time and found the keyhole clogged with a piece of green notebook paper.

Drews imagined the image as it would have been seen through the keyhole. 'Could she take it all the way in?'

'I had to use my hand,' said Gabriel.

Drews cut back on business trips; he couldn't leave Miki and Gabriel on their own. When a trip was inevitable, he demanded a full debriefing on his return and felt joy if a night, or even two, had been sexless. He lived with a profound fear that the two were returning to the guest room in an attempt to recapture their joy before Drews' intervention. But they never did. Gabriel found the Drewses' bed more comfortable.

Ellen Weigner made a visit to Hong Kong and over lunch Miki told her about the threesome. In the newsroom that afternoon, Ellen stubbed out a cigarette and stared aggressively at the Filipino. That evening, Gabriel described the scene. Miki admitted her confession.

'Why, honey?' asked Gabriel. 'Why did you have to tell Ellen?' (For many months had passed and the threesome's desire for glorious exposure had evolved into a fear of the boat being rocked.)

'I haven't even told Timmy,' Drews said. 'God – I must go see Timmy tomorrow.'

'I had to share it with someone,' Miki said. 'You two have each other. You can talk things over. Ellen's the only woman I know well enough.'

'What did she say?' asked Drews.

'She said: "Let's see how long *that* will last."'

Gabriel rose on an elbow and stroked Miki's thigh. 'It will last forever, honey.'

One Sunday Marietta and Kelvin discovered Drews, Miki and Gabriel on the beach at Repulse Bay. They were walking a small dog. On Monday, Tisch said with triumph: 'I knew my maid wouldn't have mistaken Miki Drews. And Gabriel: she can spot one of her own. You know, like animals sniffing each other?' And so Miki's affair with Gabriel, several months late and after it had evolved unrecognizably, became a gossip item in the newsroom. Miki gained her nickname, 'Drews' Hiroshima'. But no one could fathom Drews' friendship with his wife's gallant lover. It was many more months before they realized that Drews was no longer romantically inclined to the new, female subeditors. But the pieces of the puzzle never came together. And Drews showered his new happiness on the *Orientweek* staff, further obscuring the mystery. Superb cover stories were written. Gabriel became a minor star of Hong Kong journalism. The boozy, Friday staff lunches grew longer and more amusing than at any time since the early days. Drews sang and jumped on tables. Everyone enjoyed themselves, including Miki Drews, smoking a cigarette at one end of the round table, and Gabriel, at the other, connected by smiles and nods frequently intercepted by sharp-eyed staffers. They were wonderful times and even Tim's absence, due to illness, was nearly forgotten.

The frequency of their lovemaking inevitably declined: first the lunch-times, followed by the mornings, for Gabriel, the sexual spark plug, was a groggy riser. But at night, their passion proved limitless as love and trust deepened. Gabriel started squeezing Drews' balls in mid-intercourse, for he desired the same. One night, while Drews was on top of Miki, he removed Gabriel's cock from her mouth and put it in his own, experiencing a rubbery, unsexual sensation. Miki's deepest satisfaction came when Gabriel was the finale. When Drews was the last, she lay with her face on Gabriel's chest or belly, Drews working from the rear, receiving Gabriel's consoling caresses. Drews' thrill was to lie beneath Miki, his head at her cunt, watching the brown cock pushing in and out. One night, he reached up and circled his thumb and forefinger around Gabriel's base, becoming part of their love. The gesture became an unspoken ritual.

Drews also enjoyed watching the couple make love on their own. They were beautiful together – perfect specimens of the passive Asian female and the strong male. They became totally involved in each other, even with Drews alongside. Occasionally he controlled himself and waited for Gabriel's long, brown fingers to find Miki's panties, test her moistness and remove them sightlessly, clumsily, involved in a deep kiss. Then Gabriel made the first entry. For Drews it was a return to the keyhole. An entry in Gabriel's diary read: 'In the orchestra, he plays first violin but at home, he plays second fiddle.' Drews recognized this truth: he heard it each time Gabriel's tapered cock entered Miki, pushing from her a needier gasp than his ever did. It was Gabriel's gasp now, which Drews could only overhear.

But Drews appreciated the excitements of his role, the relief of not being excluded and his remaining control over his wife and her love affair. The Drewses said farewell to Gabriel each night with long hugs and kisses (for Rosemarie was still shielded from the reality). One night, Gabriel fell asleep and had to be roused. He staggered to the doorway rubbing his face. 'You can never sleep like this when you go to your own bed.'

Long after the threesome's six-month anniversary, commemorated with an expensive meal at the Peninsula, Gabriel received a job offer from an American newspaper. It required a second man in its Hong Kong bureau. Drews bought champagne to celebrate. For weeks, they congratulated themselves, connecting Gabriel's professional success with that of the threesome. The job came with a housing allowance and they debated how to use the money. Gabriel wanted to take a flat nearby, where he could install a weight room and, perhaps, a larger double bed. 'Or you could take our bed,' suggested Drews, 'and we'll buy something bigger.' Miki wanted to save the money to fly around the world together. She wanted Gabriel to see Japan.

'Won't it look funny if I continue living here? To the paper?' Drews replied: 'Not after all this time.'

Gabriel found a place in a building painted a lurid swimming-pool blue. When Drews returned from a business trip to Korea, Gabriel had paid the advance. 'It's great, Danny,' he exulted. 'The servant's room makes the perfect weight room.' Miki nodded her agreement. She had been there, of course. Drews imagined them making love on the parquet floor. He peeked into the guest room: Gabriel's weights were gone. A new routine began. After work Gabriel trained at his flat, showered and rushed to Shu Fai Terrace with hair slicked back from his wide forehead. He immediately went to the kitchen to play with the dog. Often Miki had to prod, and Drews had to grumble, before he'd straighten up and join them at the dinner table. He stayed the nights: his clothes were still in the guest-room closet.

The new job kept Gabriel busy and his nights at Shu Fai Terrace shrank to three or four per week. The remaining nights were his 'sleeping' nights. Drews stopped by the flat one night and was surprised to find it fully furnished, complete with bookshelves. At home, he went straight to the guest room.

'He's moved his clothes.' Drews stood above Miki, who was dealing cards at the dining room table. 'And his books.' She looked at him impassively. 'We're not making love much. How many weeks has it been?'

Miki said, in a low voice, 'Three.'

'Since I came home from Malaysia.'

She nodded.

'Have you talked to him?'

She shook her head.

'Do you think there's someone else?'

They drank more.

'What about when I'm away?'

Miki looked at the table. 'It's normal.'

This was Drews' fear and they fought bitterly. 'What am I?' he demanded. 'Am I part of this or am I the fucking sugar daddy?'

Then, one night, the three of them were in bed. Drews was on top of Miki and Gabriel was stretched alongside. Drews made one of his suggestions – with sexual excitement it became a command – and Gabriel refused to comply. Drews made an alternate suggestion. Gabriel remained inert. 'Do you want to get a beer?' he asked. Gabriel shook his head. 'Take off your briefs.' Gabriel stood and went to the bathroom. Drews shouted at him from atop his wife. Gabriel came out of the bathroom fully dressed. Drews struggled into his underwear and Miki turned her head to the wall. Gabriel had the front door open. The dog peered timorously from the kitchen doorway. 'Get out!' he cried. Gabriel looked at him and turned. Drews slept in the guest room that night and left for work the following morning without a word to the woman at the dining-room table.

Drews sent Gabriel and Miki for a summit weekend in Macao. When she returned, Drews said: 'Well?'

'He says he doesn't know why. He's just not as interested as before. The job has lots of pressure.'

Drews laughed scornfully.

'His wife has sent Smile back to the province. He got a letter last month. He didn't even tell me.'

'So why doesn't he say something? To me?' Drews looked like a pouting child.

Miki shook her head.

'We've been together for almost a year. I think I deserve an explanation at least.' Drews returned from the kitchen with a fresh beer. 'How was the sex? In Macao?'

Miki said nothing.

'Well?'

'Normal.'

Drews raged and demanded that the dog be moved to Gabriel's flat.

Shortly afterwards the newspaper's Manila correspondent was evacuated for medical treatment in the States. Gabriel was sent to replace him. Miki saw him off at the airport. She returned home to the empty flat. Drews came home at eleven, said goodnight to Rosemarie, settled the dog in its basket and brought beer and a bottle of rum to the dining room.

'Manila is close,' Drews said curtly. 'Seventy-five minutes by plane. You can go for weekends. He can pay. He can afford it now.'

Miki shook her head, shuffling the cards before her. She knew the distance between Hong Kong and Manila. She knew the flight schedules, which Gabriel had collected from the airline offices.

'I'm sure he'll be true. To you. If not to me.'

Miki looked up.

'I tried my best. You know that. Someone had to take control. I made a superhuman effort.'

Miki nodded.

'He's the one that killed the threesome. Don't forget that.'

She nodded again. She looked up at him with a trembling mouth. 'What are we going to do, Dan?'

'I'm not to blame.'

That night, Drews tried to make love to Miki for the first time in five years. She turned on him savagely. 'Never!' And she cried so much, Drews moved to the guest room.

Drews received a letter from Manila, which cited Gabriel's undying love for both Miki and, in another fashion, for 'Danny'. It quoted Freud and *Reader's Digest*:

> *If you think you'll lose, you're lost.*
> *For out in the world we find*
> *Success begins with a fellow's will*
> *It's all in the state of mind.*

Then came Tiananmen, when Hong Kong was transformed from a

capitalist triumph to an accident waiting to happen. Gabriel flew back to Hong Kong to augment his paper's coverage. The threesome was resurrected unexpectedly one drunken night. But afterwards, Gabriel stayed away from Shu Fai Terrace. Miki met him at his hotel during the day. When Gabriel left Hong Kong for Manila, it was worse than before, as the general gloom of the colony obscured all rays of hope from the future. Then Tim Marquand entered his last days and Miki and Drews moved his bed, the abacus lamps and the long, green drapes from Conduit Road into the hospital room. Tim died before Drews could say farewell. His parting gesture was a vomited shower of congealed, black blood over his friends.

Each night, Miki smoked and played cards by herself at the wicker dining table. The dog paced the flat, sniffing around Gabriel's emptied room. The couple talked about their marriage. Miki affirmed her continuing, nonsexual love for Drews. She said she understood that in Drews' eyes she would remain ever-young, ever-beautiful, the most intelligent and loving woman in the world – as long as she was his. And, she said, with slow dignity, she was grateful.

'I did everything in my power to hold us together.'

'I know,' said Miki. Tears poured down a face that had been transformed, with frightening speed, from an elegant Japanese woman to a miserable, defeated country schoolgirl. 'But don't you see? I wanted something of my own.' The tears poured down splotchy cheeks. Her frantic hand jumbled the playing cards before her. 'Can't you understand that? You had your magazine. You had me. All I wanted was – can't you understand? – something on my own.'

'You still have me,' Drews said gently. 'We can . . .'

'Yes.'

'And you can still keep him, if you choose.'

Miki blew her nose. She shook her head. 'Oh God. I love him, you know. I do.'

Drews shook his head.

'God.' She wiped tears away. 'I had it all. Now it's all ruined.'

And now the bird can be released. Watch Memory fly, not toward the treetops with their pregnant clouds but back through the winding paths of the forest. I am sorry to see him go. I am dead, though hardly forgotten: there's my plaque in the Hilton Grill, my final cover framed at the Foreign Correspondents Club, photos on various walls and memories of my requiem parties for Chill Wills, Gypsy Rose Lee, Ramon Navarro, Edgar Bergen, Agnes Moorehead, all of whom will now spark remembrances of me every time they flicker across my friends' television screens. (Or, more precisely, every time they are recognized on my friends' television screens.) Memory goes searching for a new shoulder. I will miss him. I've had few more satisfying companions. But, I must admit, my ear has got bloody raw.

To prepare you for the remainder, I would like to fix Drews in a particular position. We must take a step backward. Let us picture him on that tree-shaded hilltop on the day of the second, and final, *Orientweek* Magazine Treasure Hunt. Drews spent the day on the border. Under his cowboy boots was Hong Kong, his home and his pinnacle. A stone's throw away was China, his trembling fate. Tiananmen was over but its tremors reverberated, nowhere more threateningly than in the Crown Colony. His closest friend was not yet dead but he was breathing his last in a hospital room fitted with familiar furnishings. Drews' marriage had endured but its nucleus had been invaded and left with a septic hole. His sense of love, which included dominance and possession, had been shattered. The ultimate shock had yet to come but the catfish were frantic and the dogs were starting to howl. The future of *Orientweek*, Drews' only child, had been stolen by the tragedy of Tiananmen. The child itself was soon to endure the most bizarre of custody battles.

And so Drews commanded his staff, including the core acolytes, to search the entire colony for a tarnished treasure: himself. He waited on that hilltop, towering over the landscapes of both Hong Kong and China.

But, in fact, Drews' gloriful mastery was waning. He was stuck in the centre ring, resplendent in the spotlight with luxurious curls and impressive boots, but his whip had lost its snap and the lions on the sidelines were grinning expectantly. I died. Drews' wife sat at a table shuffling cards, shooing away a timid, lonely dog. His staff continued to peer through the glass pane of his office door but with different expressions, for they knew the rumours of the magazine's sale. (Nick Naversen had seen to that. He sent a fax, with *Time* letterhead, which someone pinned on the *Orientweek* bulletin board. Drews ripped it down and stamped on it with his cowboy boots.)

So let us pause to contemplate my Danny, standing in his 'Asia Without Ties!' T-shirt, curls dangling down the back, gazing across the border into the People's Republic and snapping mental snapshots that signified nothing. Does he think back to those London days, when the existence below him was crumbling and Mrs Bottom fled barefoot up the stairs to catch a breath of unrotting air? Does he feel that disintegration pulling at him from the past? I did: my life was circumscribed by Mrs Bottom's thick walls. The Albert Court floor crumbled and down I fell, through to her bedroom and into her putrefying arms. Drews touches his right ear: does he feel a sting? Or is it the sound of a car – has he been found at last? And where will those saviours take him? To the Foreign Correspondents Club: back to the big top to sit beneath my final cover story and watch Nick Naversen laughing confidently at the bar? Then on to the elephant-head bar with its memories of his diary days? At the end, will they drop him home to the Japanese woman with her pearls and her tireless deck of cards? To the desolate double bed in one room and, across the narrow hall, the abandoned guest room with its worn Afghan carpet and its clogged-up keyhole?

Let us pity Danny, the ringmaster with the drooping whip. Let us pray! For now he understands: Does time tarry for thy prizing? I should say not. Or make speed for thy despising? Usually the opposite.

THE SUCCEEDING AGE

Drews received an aerogram addressed: 'Drews. Orientweek Magazine. Hong Kong.' It was from India. It read, in an old man's handwriting:

> I have a diary bequeathed to me by Tim Marquand. I've no use for it and believe you might both desire and learn something from getting it. I also believe you should have to find it. It may open your eyes as Tim's were opened.

The aerogram was unsigned. Drews knew the handwriting and knew of Evan Olcott's frequent disappearances into the subcontinent. They were legend, old legend, so old that their mystery no longer intrigued. Evan's message puzzled Drews. Tim had been Evan Olcott's friend, perhaps his only friend in Hong Kong. He praised Evan's sense of 'philosophy'. He had travelled with Evan an anniversary story of the China–India war, visiting all sorts of godforsaken border villages. The friendship was cemented in the mud huts of northern India.

Drews had never, in more than twenty years of friendship, known Tim to keep a diary. But neither would Tim have known about his diary, written at a time of particular need. Drews wanted the diary. As he studied the flimsy aerogram, he concluded the diary was written on that trip to India. That explained why it was bequeathed to Evan. What had happened in India that forced Tim to write his private thoughts? What was, after all, the philosophy of Evan Olcott, which Tim had praised for the next decade and a half? Drews couldn't recall. All he could remember were the over-familiar lines of the Pathan poem.

Drews decided to accept Evan's challenge. He put the aerogram in a drawer and did nothing. He knew from past experience, when Evan's disappearances coincided with board meetings, that he was impossible to trace in India. He knew the next step: to wait for a second aerogram with a dancing god on its front.

But Drews misread the old man's aerogram. It didn't occur to him that the learning Evan Olcott had in mind would come in the search, not in the diary itself.

Drews could hardly have known about the earlier aerogram sent to Nick Naversen, or the subsequent one, written in that same shaky hand.

Don't neglect the Morning Post Classifieds.

'What does he think this is?' cried Nick. 'A little game?'

'I've never liked games.' Fran frowned at the aerogram. 'I never win.'

'Okay, the old guy is addled. But why can't he find a pleasant little place to drool away his days? Like the Foreign Correspondents Club. Or this place?' It was early and Nick and Fran were the only customers in the Nullah. The Filipino band was setting up its instruments. 'Somewhere close to home?'

'I always read the classifieds.' Fran, gulping Guinness, vainly turned over the aerogram. 'After the obituaries.'

'Let's hope we find him there first.' Nick exhaled and tugged at his belt. 'I don't know how long I can jerk around *Time* magazine. They keep threatening to come out to "meet the principals".' He gave a scoffing laugh. 'I can't wait for that little meeting. One old madman, a Chinese catamite and Dan Drews singing "Joe Cool" on the bar. Followed by "Ninety-Nine Bottles Of Beer On The Wall".'

'Three point three million bottles of beer.' Fran's smile pulled her across the table. Her voice dropped to a conspiratorial whisper, the traditional sound of Naversen love. 'It's lucky I know India so well. That will make things easier.'

'What do *you* know?'

'I know Delhi, Bombay, Calcutta. I've been in the countryside. In the villages.'

'Searching for hare-lips, no doubt. No, no, the hare-lips come to you. It's the blind babies you have to ferret out. Can't read the classifieds.'

'Ha ha.' Fran recoiled in the wooden booth. Nick's sarcasm had fractured the intimacy.

'That country has always given me the creeps. The Indians don't like to let you in. Then they give you a hassle when you want to leave. Amazing, really.' He ordered another round of drinks. 'I much prefer the revolving door of Hong Kong. Although they're getting sticky with the tax checks at Kai Tak. Have you noticed?'

Nick withdrew a long fax from *Time* magazine. 'They've sent this seven times. Faxes, apparently, cost nothing when sent from Sixth Avenue.' The magazine's initial confidence in their ability to handle 1997 as a supra-national, meta-political entity had faltered. They wanted a quick deal. They asked Nick to search for a buyer for *Orientweek*'s printing press and pushed him to get 'top dollar'. They talked about plans for new management, meaning a new editor, and asked for a list of names.

Nick straightened his tie.

'Forget it, dearest.'

'It would be a feather. But with $3.3 million, who needs to run a fucking newsroom? They're animals at that magazine.' Nick raised an eyebrow. 'There are some fascinating creatures coming through the newsroom.'

Fran interrupted: 'Half of $3.3 million. And don't forget taxes.'

'You jealous old monster. So what's the plan?'

Fran recapped their position. Drews, Miki and Drews' banker were on one side; Nick, Fran and Saqi were on the other. The old man was the deciding vote. 'The new factor,' Fran said, 'is that *Time*'s patience is running short. We could lose the sale if we don't get to the old man.'

'How much do we offer the old man?' Nick spoke with exasperation. 'I don't think we can sway him with an offer of adoption. What a nice family that would be. You, me, Saqi and the old man. Think of the holidays.'

Fran sighed.

'Dad driving. Mum trying to fold the road map. The kids in the back seat. I'm sure we'd have to stop frequently for Evan. Those tired old kidneys.'

'It's just a promise.'

'I have tremendous faith in you, Big Girl, but if you think you can cheat a Cantonese . . .'

Fran shrugged. 'We're still in negotiations. With Evan, who knows? Let's find him.'

'Yeah.'

'Let's see if he wants to settle in India – that would cut costs. Maybe he's on his last legs.'

'Looked perfectly healthy when I last saw him. Very healthy thirst.' Nick looked up. 'What *if* he died? It's not a far-fetched idea. I remember my last trip to India. I hope he's not invited to the Oberoi buffet. That's what did it to me.'

'Housing is cheap there,' said Fran.

'It was, I believe, the shrimp cocktail.'

'Nick . . .'

'And he's an old man.'

'We can invite him to lunch there.' Fran's eyes glittered.

'I don't think we want to consider cold-blooded murder.'

'Who would miss him?'

'We would,' Nick answered. 'If he dies, Drews becomes chairman. And then he can appoint a new board member.'

The couple didn't have to wait long. At the end of April, a classified appeared in the *South China Morning Post*.

> Agree to sale but wish to discuss terms. Wait for me at the New Delhi Press Club. Lunchtime. First week of May.

Nor did Drews have long to wait. He received a second aerogram from India.

> I had the same misperceptions about India that everyone has. It's taken twenty years to dissolve them. It's an illusory land but beneath – underfoot, I'd say – I find a message worth proselytizing. Which reminds me of an old Indian story. A farmer went to the fields to perform a natural function. While walking back to his home he had an odd encounter. Severely shaken, the man went to the local police station. He said he'd tripped on a snake with a thousand heads! The snake had reared above him; its heads blocked the thousand stars in the sky. When questioned, the man's story altered. The number of heads on the snake came down. It became a hundred-headed snake, then fifty heads, then ten. The police persevered. It was a double-headed snake, a very large one. Finally, the man confessed that he had seen no snake at all. He had only stepped on something in the field, something cold and frightening in the star-filled night.
>
> I have studied the thousand-headed snake. I have stepped on something cold in the dark. But I have stooped and parted the grass.

Drews flipped the aerogram over.

If you want Tim Marquand's diary, please check into Claridge's Hotel, New Delhi, on the first of May.

The high, mighty sky of the subcontinent, so celebrated in word and song: who can imagine bloody India without it? Who can picture its mountains or its endless fields straining to anything less grand? Who can imagine the Indians, its 800 million wards, strolling to market with their staffs and cows, cross-legged and earringed at the tea shops, under a dimmer halo? See what happens when they transplant to the low skies of Clapham Common or Jersey City: how quickly the brown skin turns grey, those flashing eyes lose lustre, that inbuilt dignity dissolves into mottled flab. What conclusion can be drawn from this: that India's vast illusion, its aeons-old stage trick, is a function of the sun, the stars, the atmosphere? Can we test this by bringing a touch of Clapham Common to the blazing subcontinent – an eclipse? What are Indians like in their rooms? Surrounded by mud and tile, crumbling walls and insecure ceilings, with a cotton mattress thrown in the corner: isn't that where answers are to be found? Forget the mountaintops, the thundering monsoon, the omnipotent disc in the sky and its thousand night-time cousins. We will penetrate those thick-walled cubicles painted bird-egg blue or sunrise salmon. The mud ceilings hang impossibly low or, in painted plaster, oddly high and narrow. The doors: mere planks on two sets of hinges, held together by a bulky, brass lock. Even when secured, there are large cracks.

This was Evan Olcott's lesson, which I learned during our voyage to India in 1977. Perhaps I should have written it up in 8,000 words – it could have made a provocative cover story – instead of living it. Now Evan has expanded the syllabus. He plans a course of unusual intensity, the final chance of an old man to unburden his accumulated wisdom (if that is the proper term). He can find but one student who must be tricked into attending the course. Poor Danny. He's never known the essence of Evan Olcott and I am responsible. I held the key and kept it to myself, wrapped in an enigmatic poem. So I don't think it frivolous to suggest that Evan's chair in Indian Studies is a memorial chair with Timothy P. Marquand's name on it. Danny's scholarship is paid for in my blackened blood.

'I've always dreamed of India,' said Marietta. 'Oh look – our first cow!'

The plane was delayed. By the time Drews and Marietta got in the taxi it was a bright Monday morning on the roads of New Delhi.

'It's funny,' Drews said. 'Whenever I come here, I think to myself: This is a whole world. You know what I mean?' He gestured out the window. 'When I fly around the globe, I don't feel I'm seeing "the world". But in India, that's the feeling. Not a piece of the world. Not just a country.'

'A world of cows,' said Marietta. 'Look: that one almost got hit.'

'The images,' said Drews. 'One comes – and then another.'

There were small, square billboards off the road and ripped banners above with faded letters. The overhead traffic lights hung askew. The roads themselves, though made of the usual materials, lacked the established quality of roads elsewhere. They were tentative incursions into some pre-existing life, tolerated and needed but unsuccessful in their dominance. To a newcomer they appeared more than anachronistic: the remnants of a recent apocalypse, perhaps. The tiles of the centre islands were shattered, revealing naked, tangled wires and rusted reinforcing rods.

'I'm famished,' said Marietta.

'We can get a curry at the hotel.'

Marietta pressed a petite hand to her belly. 'It's 9.30!'

'Get used to it,' said Drews.

There was a Darwinian quality to the traffic. A full phylogenetic scale was present, from reckless ten-wheel trucks to wooden carts pulled by animals or half-naked coolies. Within each species, the vehicles were identical and, despite the seeming chaos, a pecking order prevailed. Predominant were the massive, dust-covered buses, crooked on their chassis, painted a putrid green and yellow. They jockeyed with narrow goods trucks, high off the ground like junks in the South China Sea. Sandwiched between were rounded sedans from the 1950s, beige and grey for civilians, inscrutable black for bureaucrats. Three-wheelers, public conveyances of the cheapest kind, bobbed bravely in the roiled wake, darting to the kerbs to collect or discharge passengers. Then came the motor-scooterists, determined fat men in humped helmets weaving sinuously and employing genteel hand signals. At the shoulder were the imperturbable cyclists, sweatless on even the hottest summer day. Last came the Japanese compacts, India's concession to modern times and the road's only dabs of primary colour. Newest on the scene, the Japanese cars had yet to establish their place. They nervously rode the waves, ever-vanquished by the buses and trucks and driven by sari-clad housewives, faces clenched with fear or defeat.

'What happened here?' asked Marietta. They passed a huge, twisted wreck.

'Bus crash into tree.'

'When did it happen? It looks ancient.'

'This morning.' The driver's eyes flashed in the rear-view mirror. 'Driver run away.'

Marietta surveyed the wreck. 'He *survived*?'

'Many die.' The driver laughed.

Drews gazed silently out the window. The shutter was open.

Life began impatiently at road's edge and, in India, every drive was a voyeuristic act. They passed a taxi stand with a domesticated look: the hulking metal taxis played the husbands and the drivers, bathing at spigots and coiling their long, deturbanned hair, the fussing wives. The taxi stand gave way to a refuse dump with grazing cows followed by an open-air urinal. Then came quarries with jagged sheets of marble followed by squatter dwellings of mud and corrugated iron. In the distance were the buildings of New Delhi: blocky residences in rain-stained yellows and tans, followed by government blocks with corroded coolers protruding from windows. Ancient silhouettes of brick rose everywhere and, in the bright haze, the eye was confused between actual ruins and the brick skeletons of buildings being erected. New Hindu temples shone in white marble; rounded Moghul tombs of blackened stone waited stolidly on the corners. And everywhere was the deep red of North India, the harsh, ochre stain of desert clay and desert stone. It was in the brick and on the facing of fancy hotels. It was painted on the houses. It burst from the potholes like old, dried blood, as if modernity was a cover for something more basic waiting to come through.

'This *is* amazing,' said Marietta.

Drews nodded. 'Look at the people.'

There were thousands of them in all attitudes of motion and repose.

Beggars slept on centre islands. Commuters chased after absconding buses. Male friends strolled hand in hand. The road had no chance as a mere conduit or place of transit. It was a site of life and, when an elephant ambled along, a spontaneous festival. Indian males wore plain trousers of grey or tan; their women counterbalanced with saris of peacock blue or vermilion. And everywhere there were flashes of pure white, India's cherished colour. The clerk's crisp shirt; the farmers' turbans; the tangled, diaper-like dhotis of old men; and, occasionally, the full, white robe of a priest.

'You know, Drews, I don't think I've seen so many handsome men anywhere. Am I mad?'

Drews shook his head.

'I never would have believed it. Why doesn't anyone write about it?'

'That's why you come to India. Indians are different outside.'

'I thought they were like those guards in Hong Kong. With rusty shotguns and orange hair. Look at her. Look at that hair! And those eyes!'

'The teeth. That always amazes me. How they do it — with their hygiene.'

When they checked into the hotel an envelope was waiting for Drews. He opened it, removed a sheet of paper and started to read. He lowered the paper. 'Let's go to my room.'

'I want a shower,' said Marietta. 'And something to eat. Let's meet at the coffee shop.'

'Please,' said Drews. 'We'd better read this first.'

In his room, Drews read the letter, pacing before the window.

'Get this. Rosy Pelican beer.' Marietta stooped at the minibar. 'Doesn't that sound foul?'

'Let's find out.' Drews shook his head and passed the paper to Marietta. She handed him the beer bottle.

What did you see? You saw the grey belly of a matron in a revealing sari. You saw a beggar with chalky, fingerless hands. You saw an entire family balanced on a motor-scooter. You saw patties of cow dung. You saw a fat Punjabi with a moustache and a gold necklace shoving food into his mouth beside his red car. You saw a tangle-haired *sadhu*. You saw dirty feet. You saw a toddler, eyes blackened with kohl, staring with accusation. You saw men squatting at the side of the boulevard, peeing contortedly. You saw a thin woman at a construction site in a crimson sari carrying bricks on her head. She was pretty. Very pretty, perhaps. She saw you. She stared.

Marietta said, 'Whew!' She accepted a glass of beer from Drews, sipped, grimaced and turned over the sheet of paper.

What do I see? I see a man walking to school with his children. They wear bright socks. I see a black banana peel on a sidewalk. I see people strolling past a temple and a man cycling to office. I see another man reading a tabloid. I see a woman with a shiny watch. I see a moustached motorist yelling at a fellow motorist. Their cars are stalled, with open doors, in the middle of an intersection. The motorist with the moustache raises his fist. I see trees and an old bitch with sagging tits. I see an elderly couple on a balcony drinking tea. I see a towel drying on a television aerial. I see a woman stop to remove a stone from her sandal. I see a traffic policeman in white scratching his bald spot.

You see the thousand-headed snake. Now you must look closer.

'What *is* this? He doesn't say a thing about Tim's diary.' Marietta turned the sheet over. 'He says nothing about a meeting. Not a word.'

Drews looked out the window. 'It's Evan's game now. I guess we'll have to wait.'

Fran and Nick Naversen emerged awkwardly from a three-wheeler. Fran carried a bottle of mineral water in each elbow. The three-wheeler puttered away and the couple stared at a nearly-collapsed building with a large sign: 'Press Club of India'.

Nick shielded his eyes with a hand. 'It looks like Evan was born here.'

'I'm not eating.'

'Come on, Big Girl. There's not an amoeba in the world that could defeat that iron belly.' He looked at her. 'We're spending quite a lot of time together these days.'

'I beg your pardon,' said Fran, inhaling her stomach.

'I mean, in Hong Kong whole years go by.'

'That's not what I meant.'

'Oh, the food. Never knew you liked Indian so much. For breakfast even. Waiters seemed impressed. Boggled, actually.'

Fran sighed and, rearranging her water bottles, trailed Nick into the building.

Inside there were grimy ceiling fans and tables with dirty-handkerchief linens. Caricatures hung on the walls, slipped in their frames, below streamers from some prehistoric celebration. The club was full of Indian journalists, a distinctive tribe: scruffy, conspiratorial, constantly laughing and pouring from thick bottles of local rum. Lunch was something brown and glistening served in steel spittoons with piles of flat grey bread.

At the far end of the room stood a group of white men and women. One man, dressed in extravagant Indian robes, was poking someone in the chest. It was the local contingent of foreign correspondents. The correspondent in Indian dress knocked over a bottle of beer. The bartender flicked a rag over the mess, splashed beer on the correspondent and suffered a sharp-tongued rebuke. The bartender begged the correspondent's indulgence. He folded his hands as in prayer. The correspondent turned away haughtily and, behind the bar, the bartender burst into silent laughter, accompanied by fellow waiters.

'That's us,' said Nick. 'God, we're everywhere.'

The foreign correspondents were a small group, defensive among the Indians but mildly excited at the same time. They had a story! The Indian government said yes; the Pakistanis said no. India said it was a long-standing policy not to comment on such affairs, but, at the same time, it would not be unfair to say that Pakistan had been firmly apprised of India's concern. In return, the Pakistan High Commission said this small Xerox would surely be of interest, off the record of course.

Nick rolled his eyes at Fran.

'According to Khan, the Indian press reports were "influenced" by the Ministry of Foreign Affairs,' said Georgette Vere, a wire service reporter. ' "Influenced." I really nailed him on that. I said, "Like you mean coached or pressure was put on the media?"' Georgette's eyes bulged when she related a story. They bulged as bulbously for boring press conferences as they did for assassinations, car bombs and blackouts at the Delhi bureau, which occurred twice daily. 'I mean, he wouldn't even say anything about the terrorist camps. And . . .'

Nick announced he was waiting for his friend Evan Olcott. Had anyone seen him? The correspondents responded blankly. None had heard of Evan Olcott.

'He's a member here, isn't he?' demanded Fran. The journalists shrugged and the conversation splintered into individual groups. Nick turned to a man standing beside him: 'Do you post, by any chance, the members who haven't paid their bills?'

'You say you're stringing for *Orientweek*?' The man was petite, pigeon-chested, with a wispy moustache and an outsized white shirt. It was Hubert 'Buck' Frye, a freelancer who wrote for trade magazines and an undiscriminating Middle Eastern daily. Buck Frye was perennially paranoid that his strings would be plucked away by someone new, younger, a little less lazy, a lot less alcoholic.

'I'm a director,' said Nick.

'So am I,' added Fran.

'Where were you posted before this?' blurted Georgette Vere, eyes bulging. 'I was in Cairo. I was in Beirut for the Marines.'

'We live in Hong Kong,' said Nick.

'Know anybody from Beirut or Cairo? From the wires?'

''Fraid not.'

She peered at him suspiciously. 'Jerusalem? My ex-husband's in Jerusalem. He lives across from Mary Magdalene's house. Total asshole.'

Nick smiled wanly.

'Baghdad?' Georgette Vere persisted. 'Teheran?'

Buck Frye slurped his beer and whispered: 'There's a tremendous amount of competition these days in Delhi. In the whole subcontinent. *Much* more than before.'

'I imagine so,' said Nick.

'But there are big business opportunities,' said Fran assertively. 'If you know what I mean.'

Buck stroked his moustache with worry. 'Hard living. Big start-up costs.' He shook beer from his fingers. 'I wouldn't move here if I were you. Wouldn't even consider it.'

'That's not true,' interjected a hatchet-faced correspondent in a stained fishing vest. The stains appeared to be old blood. 'Great stories here, Buck, hardly even touched.' He gave Nick a stare and pointed to the ceiling. 'Go north. With the *muj*.' When he turned away, Buck Frye poked out his tongue.

'We're not here for journalism, per se,' said Nick. 'We have some personal interest in India.'

'Antiques?' Buck Frye gave a prissy smile.

'Brought my own, thanks.' He gestured at Fran.

'Junkie?'

'Those are our alternatives?'

'Trekker?'

Nick leaned over confidentially. 'My ex-wife. She's here to *find* herself.' Buck Frye peeked at Fran, who was drinking a glass of beer in large gulps. He erupted in high-pitched girlish giggles. The other correspondents turned curiously. Buck ducked his chin into his shirt collar. No one recalled who bestowed upon Buck his ironic nickname – with his roomy white shirts and his spastic walk he was as uncowboy-like as anyone in India – but it stuck and at times he seemed determined to exploit all of its comic possibilities.

'Sorry,' he burped. 'Punchy today.'

Nick whispered again. 'Sure you don't know Evan Olcott? Old guy? Very old guy? Are you here every day?'

Lunch was served at three tables placed together. The hatchet-faced correspondent ate swiftly and intensely without utensils. He alternated between stewed yellow vegetables and a plate of raw chillies requested specially. When he chewed, he stared blankly as if the scarred wall of the Press Club couldn't halt a vision filled with mountains and sandy horizons. An Englishwoman in a sari asked about a woman named Gail and the man shook his head, blinked several times, cleared his throat – to signal the interruption of his reverie – and replied that Gail was travelling.

'Where?' demanded Georgette Vere. Beirut could be spied in her bulging eyes.

'Top secret.' The hatchet-faced man shook his head. '*Big* story.'

'Prentice's wife works for *Newsweek*,' explained the Englishwoman.

Prentice McGuinn nodded sombrely. 'Best job in journalism,' he said. 'All of Asia. Gail's really brilliant. Always been brilliant. You probably knew her predecessor. Small problem with foreign exchange dealings. Came close to being fired. That's what they say.'

'I enjoyed Gail's piece on dowry,' said the Englishwoman. 'And her recent piece on bride burning.'

'Brilliant stuff,' said Prentice. The faraway gaze had returned; it was as if, with proper concentration, he could spot his wife on one of those distant apexes, shining brilliantly, holding aloft a copy of her magazine, the 'Newsmakers' page flapping in the breeze.

'What do you do?' asked Nick.

Prentice fixed him with a pitying look and turned his profile.

'Prentice is writing a book,' explained the Englishwoman. 'On insurgencies, isn't that right Prentice? You are still working on that book?'

The profile nodded.

'Which insurgencies?'

Prentice glared at Nick. 'All of them.'

The correspondent wearing Indian dress leapt to his feet to rebuke a waiter. 'I said no ice!' His index finger hovered above a cloudy drink. 'No ice. No ice. No ice.'

The waiters throughout the club exchanged smiles. The bartender doubled over in laughter.

'If you're not eating those,' said Buck Frye. Fran pushed a plate of bread across the table.

'Huge breakfast,' said Nick. 'A good eater, the Big Girl. You should see her with corned beef hash. She can eat two cans.'

Prentice McGuinn gave a severe vegetarian's frown.

Georgette Vere, isolated and ignored, was bulging from the eyes. Prentice started flipping through a small, khaki-covered book, apparently a Bible. Buck Frye ate long after everyone else had succumbed to the daily argument. The topic was the rigours of living in India.

'You have to be married if you move to Delhi,' said Georgette. 'Honestly.'

'I've always disagreed with that,' said the Englishwoman in the sari. 'Delhi is very tough on marriages. For foreign couples it's like living in Alaska. And being married to an Indian is doubly hard.'

Nick whispered to Fran: 'She's stuck with a Gupta. Hundred to one.'

'Then single guys should have no desire,' said the correspondent in Indian robes. 'Leave their balls behind.'

'The women too,' said Georgette. She blinked nervously.

'No furniture,' said another hack. 'The dust!'

'No entrails,' said Prentice. 'Just ask Gail.'

'When you come to India, you should have no wonder,' said a solemn Buck Frye. 'Or this country will drive you mad.' The table became silent. 'Trust me: I've been here twelve years.' A closing bell rang at the bar and the foreign correspondents rose to leave. They were followed by the Indian correspondents. Nick returned from the toilet and found Fran alone with Buck, who was whispering: 'Will your husband be needing some help for *Orientweek*? On economic stories maybe?' His fingers and moustache were curry-stained. He departed, walking with fake confidence through the emptied club.

Nick drummed his lips with two fingers. 'What do you think would drive a woman like that to marry an Indian?' He gave a perplexed sigh. 'Any Asian, for that matter. She wasn't half bad, didn't you think?'

'European men marry Asian women,' said Fran.

Nick looked at his ex-wife. 'Stop the kidding, Fran, and let's get out of this dump.'

'Evan didn't show.'

'Can't blame him,' said Nick. 'Although the food was remarkably good.' He rubbed his hands together. 'I guess the old joker is going to make us wait until the very last day. Waiter? *She'll* pay.'

After two days, Marietta said: 'Come on, Drews. We can't spend our time gazing at the front door. Let's go out.' They saw forts and tombs. When they returned one evening, an envelope was waiting in Drews' keybox.

'Let's go to the bar,' Drews said.

The envelope contained an advertisement ripped from a newspaper. It was for a local cabaret. A drawing showed a woman dressed in Middle Eastern veils with an arched eyebrow. The hours were stated. Thursday had a special show and there was a circle around the word Thursday.

'Tonight,' Drews said.

Marietta examined the crude drawing. She shook her head.

'I can go alone.'

'I'm sorry, Drews, but you know how I despise sex shows. I simply can't imagine one in India.'

'I'm not looking forward to this.'

Marietta smiled sympathetically. 'Call me when you get back and we'll talk it over. Give Evan my best. You need this?' She offered the advertisement.

Drews smiled and put a finger to his temple.

'You've got the words or just the picture?'

Drews raised his palms to the ceiling.

'Get the bloomin' diary,' said Marietta, 'and let's go home.'

Drews travelled by a three-wheeler. He kept his eyes from the sights pouring past him. Evan Olcott's communications had made him feel deficient in his reaction to India. The thousand-headed snake: it was there at every corner. The journey ended at a neon-lit hotel and Drews was escorted to a large hall. Tables were crowded with men with hungry gazes. Drews shared one with a solitary man wearing rings on each pinkie.

Three musicians strolled onto a stage and handled their instruments. They chatted until one looked at his watch. He nodded and high-pitched, hypnotic music began. Strings twanged and drums beat: North India's equivalent of burlesque music. The lights went out. When they came on, a plump, smiling Indian woman was positioned on stage. She wore a full-length dress of worn black satin. She swung her hips wildly, yelping in cries of athletic exertion.

The audience hungrily absorbed the sight. Drews' tablemate had trouble concentrating on the ice cream sundae in front of him.

A waiter approached.

'Beer,' said Drews.

The waiter shook his head. 'No alcohol, sir. Would you care for a Limca?'

The combo changed tunes. The musicians played with eyes averted from the dancing woman.

After three songs rumblings arose from the back tables. The dancer, who had changed neither tempo nor movements from the first song, made a gesture extolling patience. On the sidelines, a man with an orange turban shouted. The woman gestured again. A voice from the back lent solidarity. The woman sighed and her tempo flagged.

Drews' table companion looked at his watch. 'My God!' he said.

'She's got all her teeth.'

'Teeth are very important,' said the man sombrely. 'But woman has more than teeth!'

The dancer moved an arm behind her and a middle section of the dress dropped to the floor. She jumped out of it heavily. Satin covered her breasts and her groin but a broad band of puckered stomach was exposed. The crowd fell silent. She performed new gyrations to highlight the exposed part of her anatomy. Her stomach was bound by a belt of thin silver digging into the flesh. Drews guessed she was a mother several times over.

The audience's contentment was brief. Drews couldn't tell whether they expected more or if complaining was part of the ritual. The man in the orange turban heckled. Voices in the back joined in. The dancer ignored the calls for a long time but finally her smile faded. She hissed at the audience. She made a spitting gesture. The turbanned man cried triumphantly. There was lusty applause. At Drews' table, the man with the melted sundae clapped his hands. He said to Drews: 'This place is bloody nonsense.' Several other tables emptied. The music was getting frantic and the woman danced faster and harder. But the mini-exodus couldn't be stopped. Waiters scurried to collect banknotes.

Then the music changed to recorded rock and roll. A younger, trimmer woman took the stage and revealed more of her body. The audience approved. She danced for a long time and was replaced by a yet thinner woman. The emptied tables filled again. Drews checked his watch. It was 12.30.

The music alternated between Western and Indian clamour. Each new dancer was thinner than the one before and each displayed additional flesh. Drews was surprised to see a woman with slanted eyes take the stage. She immediately removed a cloak. She was topless, with the small breasts of Japan or China.

'Excuse me,' Drews said. 'Where is this woman from? Thailand?'

'Nepal,' said his new neighbour, a boyish Sikh with his hair in a cloth-covered topknot. 'They're all from Nepal.'

And then the raunch began: wagging crotches, fingers inserted, all accompanied by undisguised venom from the women on the stage. One dancer shouted abuse at Drews, the only white man in the audience. At 2.30 he chose to leave. He strolled to the banks of a wide, dark river crowned by the silhouette of an iron bridge. He wondered about the show. The customers' palpable lust had impressed him, followed by the women's apparent abjectness. In India sex seemed needed, in short supply, worth pain. It stirred passions, so different from the blasé displays of Bangkok, Manila or Japan.

That silver belt, he thought. *How does she get it off?*

With the quiet of the water before him and the noise of the highway behind, Delhi seemed an ordinary metropolis. The bright stars, the crisp night air, a river, a shore, a naughty club. Perhaps India wasn't so different after all. The thousand heads started to diminish. A small boat floated downstream.

Feeling the need to pee, Drews started to unzip his pants. But what he had mistaken for underbrush was a carpet of ragged tents erected by a tribe of impoverished people. Looking down, he found huddled children stroking each other's hands. The entire riverbank, the whole Indian night, was sluggishly alive. Only the sky, with pinprick stars, was vacant. He recalled the platitudes about India as a crowded land. India was not just crowded on the streets or in the parks or in the cities. India had crowded riverbanks, roadsides, gutters.

On his way back to the hotel, he travelled through a prosperous neighbourhood. The houses were square, stuccoed brick with ugly gates and blackened windows. On one roof, illuminated by a light from a servant's quarters, stood a woman in a sari. She was motionless, her face at an oblique angle. Waiting for an assignation? Taking the night air? There was no way to guess. She was alone on the skyline in a sari of iridescent green. Drews craned his head to take in the sight and his mental camera clicked. She remained motionless. When Drews was quite distant, the light was extinguished and the woman disappeared.

Marietta was sleepy-voiced when Drews called and announced: 'No show.'

'Oh no, Drews. What went wrong?'

'He was there, Etta. I swear, I could feel him. He was watching me.'

'This is creepy,' she said. 'What does he want with you?'

'We'll see.'

At breakfast, Drews handed Marietta a letter. It had been left for him overnight.

The woman has a big belly with a silver belt. But take away the belt and it's just a belly, like your mother's. The girls are angry whores. But whores are whores whether they show the anger or not. The man beside you at the urinal has a black penis. He manipulates it for a long time, too long by your standards, to eject the final drops of urine. But it's just a penis. It goes nowhere unique; perhaps it goes nowhere at all. The woman on the back of the motorbike has big breasts bulging through her tight blouse. Look closely: she wears a bra like your Japanese wife. She takes it off for her man, like all women. The men are Sikhs but what does that mean? Hair? A bracelet? You are a white man with a shocking pink penis that you rush into your undershorts. You are shocking. You are dirty.

'This is disgusting.' Marietta held the letter with her fingertips. 'I think this reference to Miki is offensive.'

'Don't forget my poor mother,' Drews laughed. He sipped coffee and told Marietta the story of the thousand-headed snake. At that precise moment, an old man with white hair entered the lobby of Claridge's hotel. He greeted the black-suited man at the desk and made an inquiry. He proceeded to the coffee shop and peered through the glass door. A waiter tried to open the door. He backed away, a hand raised in apparent horror. He retraced his steps to the front desk and, after a bout of coughing, asked another polite question. The clerk nodded and glanced down to check a ledger. 'Yes. They're both from Hong Kong. From *Orientweek* magazine.' Then, gravely, the old man made his way out of the hotel, nodding respectfully at the liveried doorman. He walked slowly down the driveway and crossed the roundabout.

That evening, Drews received his final letter.

You were to come alone. What can I teach you with acolytes in tow?

Fran Naversen asked the Press Club waiter for more chapatis. 'Actually,' she said, 'I like this food. The price is certainly right.'

'It gets a little tired.' Nick pushed away his curry.

'If you're not eating that.' Buck Frye reached across the table.

It was the Naversens' fifth day at the Press Club. Evan Olcott hadn't appeared.

'I think he's dead.' Nick watched Buck shovel a piece of cold bread into his mouth.

'You said that three days ago,' said Fran. 'Should we have another beer? I'm not doing anything this afternoon.'

'The foreign press really ignores the economic stories,' Buck whispered.

Fran said: 'The gold price is 25 per cent higher than the world market. Why hasn't that been written up?'

'Exactly.' Buck smiled through a stained moustache.

'I mean, if you just wore a few of those gold discs, plus the chain of course, they'd never catch on. You just say it's your personal jewellery.'

'That's not what I meant,' Buck said primly. 'I was talking about liberalization.'

'But 25 per cent,' Fran smiled. 'That's easy money.'

'Some are suggesting an end to gold controls. I have my sources.'

'So we have to work quickly.'

Buck sighed impatiently. 'You have to know Indian customs.'

Fran leaned forward. 'That was my next question.'

'Really?'

'Well *do* you? Do you know anyone at Customs?'

'So how are things at *Newsweek*?' Nick spoke across the table to a pale woman with Botticelli hair. It was Gail McGuinn, who was conferring in a low tone with her vegetable-eating husband. She looked up with ostentatious courtesy.

'I hear *Time*'s giving you a big run for your money.'

'*Time!*' Gail McGuinn raised her chin and tossed back honey-coloured frizz. 'They have completely missed the subcontinental story.'

'Did you see Gail's piece on women in Pakistan?' asked Prentice. 'It was banned.'

'Briefly,' Gail said. 'They couldn't hold it back for long.'

'How are the women in Pakistan?' asked Nick. 'And I don't mean the little ladies with black bags on their heads.'

Gail McGuinn glared across the table. Nick accepted her glare. Then she looked abruptly to the ceiling. She moved a hand to her belly. She looked at Nick, then to her husband and she rose. She said: 'Excuse me.' Prentice stood and followed her halfway through the club.

'Pregnant?' Nick raised his eyebrow at Fran.

'Shouldn't waste her time,' Fran announced. 'In terms of cost-effectiveness adoption is the only answer. Here in India, I mean.'

Prentice McGuinn returned to the table. 'Amoebas,' he whispered. 'Probably from Afghanistan. Gail did a brilliant piece on the mujahedeen women.'

'Not my types,' said Nick. 'Sand in the sheets – nothing more irritating if you ask me.'

'Adoption is a very attractive option here in India,' continued Fran. 'Especially for working couples like yourselves. The red tape is nowhere near as bad as they say.' She smiled. 'But you need someone who knows their way around.'

'So have you decided to stay?' barked Georgette Vere. 'You obviously like New Delhi.'

'It's a good lifestyle,' said the Englishwoman in the sari. She had a red *bindi* on her forehead. 'Once you get adjusted.'

'No, no,' said Nick. 'We just wanted to get acquainted. To scout out the territory. In fact, *Orientweek* is going through some big changes. We have big plans. Millions of plans.'

Buck's eyes widened. 'You're opening a bureau?'

'We can't say about that,' said Nick. 'We're more on the administrative side. Aren't we, Fran?'

'With luck,' she replied. 'Which we're having conspicuously little of.'

On the way back to the hotel, Fran said: 'The plane leaves after midnight. We could come for dinner. It's his last chance to show.'

Nick said: 'This is a cat and mouse game. We're the fucking mice.' A young Indian woman with long hair drove by in a car. Her mother glared at Nick from the passenger seat. He groaned: 'Why couldn't Evan Olcott have fallen in love with Thailand?'

In India, most planes arrive or depart in the smoky hours of the early morning. New Delhi's international airport is a glamourized version of India with cheap marble, birds flying among the rafters and long, leather chaises occupied by dozing hippies with harassed expressions even in sleep.

Drews and Marietta sat on moulded plastic chairs at the departure lounge. Marietta said: 'I did enjoy it, Drews. Sorry I blew the whole thing. Perhaps we should have done an interview or two. We could have gotten an "Up And Comer".'

Drews said, 'Etta, look, we're not alone.'

'Evan? I can't believe it!' Marietta turned toward the security gate. She saw Fran Naversen arguing with a security guard over a bulky shoulder bag. Fran wrested the bag from the guard and walked proudly away. Nick slapped a newspaper against his thigh.

The four met in the middle of the lounge.

'Extraordinary coincidence,' said Nick.

'Isn't it?' said Marietta.

'You two are here on what?' asked Fran. 'A story?'

'Or just a little holiday?' smiled Nick. 'Nice hotels in India. I recommend the food at the Press Club if you're on a budget. The Big Girl put on fifteen pounds.'

Fran wearily dropped her shoulder bag.

'How are your friends at *Time*?' asked Drews. 'Someone sent a fax.'

'You tore it down from the bulletin board. I heard. With a certain, how do we say, pique? How's Miki?' Nick smiled broadly. 'Send her my best. Along with what's his name? The Filipino.'

Drews winced.

'So why were you here?' asked Fran.

'*Orientweek*'s stringer was arrested,' Drews replied. Marietta looked at him admiringly. 'It took some string-pulling. As you can imagine.'

'They're bastards,' said Nick. 'We had a fucked time at Customs. Fran's baby was almost confiscated.'

Fran sighed.

'Luckily it didn't cry. Can't cry too well. It has a hare-lip. Plus it's dead. Know anyone in Hong Kong who wants a dead Indian baby?'

Fran slammed Nick with her shoulder bag.

'Just kidding,' said Nick. 'Perfectly legitimate business. Unless you're from Interpol.'

On the darkened plane, Marietta said to Drews: 'We've been hoodwinked. *You've* been hoodwinked.'

'I know,' Drews said.

'But why? Why the Naversens?'

'He wants to sell his vote.'

'Why didn't he show?'

'He wants me. And he wants me alone. That's the only clear part.'

'But . . .'

'Etta, God knows what this is all about.'

'Is there a diary?'

Drews shook his head.

'There's no diary?'

'I don't know,' said Drews. 'I just don't know.'

Marietta was silent. She turned. 'Oh Drews, you're not coming back all alone to India? If there's no diary, why don't you just forget it?'

And that is the question, patient reader, but the answer is unfortunately clear. The student has been enrolled. Danny saw that school of staring Indians and he wondered what it expected from him. Did it want to cut his throat, marry him or just bring him home to supper? Or, in reverse order, all three? Drews had expected nothing from India, the topped-off land, filled to the brim with unexpected and irrelevant things. It was a world, as he said, it was life and life was a confusing mess. But Evan Olcott said he had a key: a way to strip the world to some essential, to

144

help arrange Danny's millions of mental snapshots. A key that had been, at one time, mine ...

Drews sipped brandy from a plastic cup. He said to Marietta: 'Evan wants something, for sure. But the diary might exist after all. Don't you think?'

Drews received a phone call in his office. He recognized the scratchy voice.

'My dear boy.'

'I know,' said Drews. 'You wanted me to come alone.' He manoeuvred around his desk to kick the door shut. He paused: one of those famous pauses in which one can actually hear Daniel Drews listening. 'This is a local call.'

The old man chuckled. 'The lines are impossible from India.'

'You're fucking with me.'

There was a deep silence. It was followed by an old man's intake of breath. 'You sound greedy, dear boy. That's hardly what I expected of you. Not from what I've heard all these years about Danny. Not from what I've read in Tim's diary.'

'You called Nick Naversen to India. Why?'

'Don't insult me. He wants mere money. I thought you were searching for something greater.'

'I want some proof about this diary. A Xerox of . . .' Drews heard a sigh and a single word spoken with the soft, distinctive lisp: 'Christ.' The line was cut.

Nick Naversen travelled by the MTR, which was largely a Chinese experience. There were signs prohibiting the carrying of roasted pigs – a circled, sketched pig with a diagonal line through it – and Nick mentally composed a snotty column protesting the policy. He was returning from the TVB studios. The Nullah was at the end of his journey. He daydreamed through the first few stops but the long journey through the harbour tunnel woke him. He looked around. The cars were orange with tall steel poles through the middle. There were Chinese boyfriends and girlfriends, nonsexual and undisturbing. The train pulled into a station. Outside the window, Nick saw a pair of Cantonese matrons in loose pants suits chatting volubly. Then he spied an old man with white hair. The old man smiled and waved slowly. Nick jumped to his feet. He pointed ahead to the next station. But the old man shook his head. He seemed to laugh. The train departed with Nick waving his arms like a referee. 'He was on this train,' Nick thought. 'He followed me.' Nick proceeded to the Nullah, of course, where he met a designer who said she enjoyed his column, sometimes. The morning came and he invited her to his flat.

'It's cozy, so to speak. Big enough for two. Plus my Chinese account-ant.' But she refused and Nick walked home alone planning a column on thick-ankled female expatriates who would be next to nothing in their own countries. 'Next to nothing,' he chuckled in the early-morning darkness, making a mental note. 'Especially after midnight.'

The door of Tim Marquand's flat on Conduit Road was unlocked. Drews pushed it open to find Kin Wah, in all his prescience, standing in the darkened living room with his hands folded neatly before him. Drews thought about love and beauty: how often the conjunction was stressed, how often the reality contradicted. He could barely recall Saqi as the boyish sexual conquest he once was. What had happened to that quiet university boy with the proud English, the big schoolbooks and the English loafers? Drews looked at Kin Wah's feet. He was wearing canvas *amah* shoes. Tim Marquand had always bragged that he accepted his cup in life and drank it proudly. But he had made Kin Wah serve that cup, night after night until the bottle was empty, the China-watcher was destroyed and the proud university boy had regressed a generation to become an ageless, bloodless Cantonese coolie.

'Hello, Saqi.' Drews reached instinctively for the light switch behind the door. The room was restored. The propaganda posters flexed their granite muscles. The green drapes masked the life outside. That mag-nificent view of the Hong Kong harbour: no one had appreciated it for twenty years. Kin Wah, perhaps, in the daytime. At night it was a room for looking backward.

Kin Wah moved to the kitchen. Drews interrupted him: 'I think we should talk, Saqi.'

Kin Wah turned. 'You haven't come for a long time.'

'I'm sorry. I've been travelling.'

147

Kin Wah shook his head and retreated to the kitchen. There was the sound of a beer can opening.

Drews went to the record player and chose innocuous jazz. When Kin Wah returned with a green can on a tray, he nodded thanks. 'Don't you want something? A brandy maybe?' Kin Wah shook his head.

'Sit,' said Drews.

'He's dead, you know. I know it. I am here every night. *Every* night – not just when I feel sorry for myself.'

'Please sit. Come on, Kin Wah. Sit down.' Kin Wah took Drews' place in the wicker chair. Drews sat in Tim's chair in the room's centre.

'Sure you don't want . . .'

Kin Wah shook his head.

'Cheers.'

The hour was late, as always, and the room was sealed. It was a room designed to immerse Drews in his past: the velvet drapes, the records in their crumbling sleeves, the photos on the walls.

'I got your letter about the rent increase. Henry'll take care of it.'

Kin Wah stared as if he hadn't heard him. 'I knew you'd be coming. Fran said so.'

Drews leaned back in the chair. 'Ah, Fran. I should have known she'd make an appearance. What about Nick? Doesn't he keep you informed? With a steady stream of faxes.'

'They're good people.'

'They're vampires.'

'They're good to me.'

'So am I,' protested Drews. 'The flat, everything else.'

Kin Wah shook his head.

'Saqi, Fran and Nick aren't the . . . they won't honour a single commitment they make.'

'No money.' Kin Wah made the fussy gesture of a bazaar merchant.

Drews looked surprised.

'No money's changing hands.' Kin Wah shook his head defiantly. 'No money.'

'They want your vote and nothing else? They must be promising to pay you.'

Kin Wah shook his head.

'So what do they offer? Their friendship? Through the next board meeting?'

148

Kin Wah fixed Drews with a defiant stare. 'They're getting me to the States.'

'How?'

His eyes flickered to the floor.

'Oh Lord.' Drews exhaled heavily. 'How would the Baby Lady get someone to the States? Through adoption, maybe?'

Kin Wah nodded.

Drews sat forward. 'You think they've found an American willing to adopt you? If you really believe . . .' His hands froze halfway through his black curls. '*They're* adopting you?'

Kin Wah met Drews' eyes.

'Saqi – you have to be crazy!'

'She's an American citizen.'

'Once the board meets they'll drop their promise. They'll laugh in your face.'

'What does it matter to you?' Kin Wah stood and his face entered a shadow. 'Whether they adopt me or not is my problem. The magazine is your problem.'

'But think of . . .'

'Don't try!' Kin Wah walked around Drews, wringing his hands. He stood in the kitchen doorway, his appointed place in the house. 'There's nothing you can say. The shares are mine – Tim left them to me. Fran is right: the shares are no good unless they're sold.'

Drews sunk back in the chair. 'Could you get me a beer, Saqi? Please.' Kin Wah went to the kitchen and returned with an unopened green can, which he shoved at Drews.

'Let's look at it another way. Think of this magazine. We created it. You were here. It's our child: Timmy's, mine, *yours*.'

'And Miki's.' Kin Wah's tone was provocative.

Drews opened the beer. 'Yes. Miki too.'

'That was the past.'

'The magazine is not in the past. It exists. It's just like a child and you want to sell it, for God's sake.'

'The magazine will be fine. The Naversens said so. *Time* magazine will own it.'

'*Time* will ruin the magazine. Tim despised *Time*.'

'I said, Tim is dead.'

'What if he was alive? What if it was the Naversens against Timmy and me? How would you vote then?'

Kin Wah's hands flipped nervously. 'You can think of nothing but yourself, you *gweilos*.'

'Don't you call me a *gweilo*,' Drews said in a low tone. 'Or I'll call you a chink. And Timmy will come down and smite us both, I swear!'

'Timmy, Timmy, Timmy,' snarled Kin Wah.

'Stop it.'

'You'll get money too,' Kin Wah implored. 'You're being stupid. The Naversens said so. You can retire!'

'I'd like to be here, in this room, to hear you say that to him. "Don't worry, Tim. All you have to do is retire." ' Drews stood and marched to the record player. He pulled a familiar album from a sleeve and, with agitated hand, poised the needle above it. Someone grabbed his wrist. Kin Wah was beside him with hate-filled eyes. 'Don't,' he said. 'I hate that music.'

'I know the money's important, Saqi. And you deserve those shares.'

Kin Wah's glare was unchanged.

'But can you think of me? The magazine is my life – it was Timmy's life. You're taking away everything I have left. If you joined us, if you vote with Miki and me – Timmy would *not* allow you to do this to me.'

Kin Wah smiled, a knife flashing in the dark. His hand remained on Drews' wrist. 'If it wasn't for you,' he said slowly, 'Tim would be alive.'

'I loved Timmy. You know that as well as . . .'

'No,' interrupted Kin Wah. 'I loved him. He loved you. And you . . .' He shook his head. 'I was . . . you know.' He made a wanking gesture at his baggy pants. 'You were the main act. For twenty-two years Tim waited for you.'

'Stop it.'

'I heard him in his sleep.'

'Saqi . . .'

'For the last ten years, we didn't even . . .'

'I said stop.'

'And that's why he died: because you couldn't love him.'

'What could I do, for God's sake?'

'Did you love him enough to stop him from drinking himself to death?'

Drews pulled his wrist from Kin Wah's hand. 'Did you?'

'Yes,' said Kin Wah. 'But it wasn't enough. *You* would have been enough.'

They faced each other.

'I can help you get a US visa, Saqi. I can try. I know people at the consulate.'

'A visa is nothing without the money.'

'The money,' said Drews. 'That's everything to you, isn't it? I can't believe this. You'd betray Timmy for the money. If he was lying in the hospital right now ... wouldn't you?'

'For the future,' Kin Wah said.

'For the money,' said Drews. 'That's why Tim couldn't love you. Because you were a greedy Cantonese.'

Kin Wah hissed a Cantonese obscenity.

'That was Tim's tragedy. He should have found a Filipino. At least they come with hearts. Not just passbooks.'

'Get out of my flat.'

'*Orientweek*'s flat, little millionaire. The rent stops tomorrow. Move in with your good friends, the Naversens.'

Kin Wah stood in the living room, teary-eyed, next to the wing chair. 'I'm throwing everything out!' He gestured around the living room. His hand pointed at the photo of Drews and Tim at the London kebab stand. Drews gave it a final look.

'Did you really love him?' Drews asked. 'Look into your tiny heart.'

Kin Wah folded his arms.

'Because if you did ...'

'Did you love your wife?'

'That's a cheap shot.'

'Timmy told me everything.'

'Congratulations. You must have enjoyed it.'

'I heard she's leaving Hong Kong.'

'She may go to Japan for a while. To her family's.'

'I heard she was moving to Manila.'

'Timmy didn't tell you that.'

Kin Wah shrugged.

'The Naversens told you that. Admit it, shithead.'

Kin Wah laughed. 'I told *them*. Everyone knows. It's all over town.'

There was a letter from Evan Olcott on Drews' desk.

The rumour mill is working overtime, dear boy, and its judgement is rather harsh. It's a hard thing to lose everything in life, especially a wife. I think you should reconsider my offer. By the time you receive this I will be in India. I advise you to follow me. I have much to explain to you. Timmy understood me, as his diary will show. Regrettably, I shall not be able to meet you in the city this time. You will be contacted and, in due time, we will meet.

There is also the matter of the upcoming board meeting. I believe I am the deciding vote. To make sure, I made a social call on Tim's 'friend' on Conduit Road, who seemed quite clear-minded. I am carrying the proxy form. The Naversens, our partners, have made me an offer which is, I'd say, still low. But at my age and with my experience one views money in a very different, perhaps idiosyncratic, light. I would enjoy hearing your side on the issue. If you choose to find me.

And, of course, if you find me first.

And so, one Monday morning, Drews failed to appear at the magazine to make the ritual call for new weather in the newsroom. His office door, with the glass pane, was locked. On Tuesday, the door remained locked. Marietta called Miki. She said Drews had gone on a business trip to Malaysia.

Questioned, Dolly said she had no knowledge of a business trip. Marietta called to Kelvin across the newsroom: 'Check the Comwire.' Kelvin punched some buttons.

'There's a memo here from Peter to Drews. Something about expenses.' Kelvin squinted at the screen. 'Drews questioned his last expense report? That guy will never learn.'

'When was it sent?'

Kelvin pushed a button. 'Last night. Monday evening.'

'He's not in Malaysia,' Marietta said. 'Send a query just in case. Dolly – could you open this up please?'

A search of Drews' office produced nothing. The drawers of his desk were locked. Marietta pushed shut the office door, sat in Drews' chair and punched buttons on the telephone. She talked for a long time, swivelling in the chair and tossing her hair from shoulder to shoulder. She opened the door and said: 'Kelvin? Would you come in here please?'

On Wednesday morning, the staff was surprised to see Ellen Weigner march through the newsroom carrying an aged leather briefcase. Tisch McAuliffe said: 'Ellen! I didn't know you were in town. How are things in Tokyo?'

Ellen, sturdy in her business suit, frowned. She stood next to Dolly's desk clutching her briefcase. She put her hand on the doorknob of Drews' office. It was locked. She said: 'Dolly?'

'What's going on?' asked Tisch.

'I'm taking over for a few days,' said Ellen. 'And I don't like it any more than you do.'

'Where's Drews?'

'That,' said Ellen, 'is the million-dollar question.' She went into his office and closed the door behind her. Through the pane, they could see her light a cigarette and pull on it with a disgusted frown. She picked up the telephone. The calls went on for an hour. Then Ellen appeared at the office door and said, in an inarguable tone: 'Dolly? Do you have keys to this desk? Or do we call a locksmith?'

Ellen Weigner is in Drews' office, making a fruitless search of a clueless desk. She finds a stack of foul cartoons, rows of ant-like staples, a handkerchief with a stain that looks like rust. She makes the kind of calls made when a fresh death needs announcing. The butts in the ashtray are piling up. Marietta and Kelvin are whispering in the library behind fourteen years of bound *Orientweeks*. Tisch and Philip are eagerly spreading the news on the business side. The Naversens are meeting for lunch at the Foreign Correspondents Club and it promises to be a good one. Nick has received a call from a mole at *Orientweek*, someone on the business side. Fran will undoubtedly pick up the tab. Miki Drews is at the wicker table in Shu Fai Terrace shuffling and dealing her tireless pack of cards. She's taken a dislike to the little dog: he spends most of his days in the kitchen. Her pearls lie tangled on a Philippine Airlines schedule. Gabriel Ledesma: what is he doing after all this time? A typhoon has hit the central Philippine Islands. He's driving in a jeep past miles and miles of devastated thatch houses. He looks like a Philippine movie star rather than a journalist and the villagers are thrilled to tell him their pathetic stories. He dutifully takes the details down, for Gabriel is the most gentle and considerate of men. Evan Olcott is in a blue room, eating a humble curry from a small steel bowl. The house is large and rambling, once grand but now rain-stained and structurally unsound. A servant stands waiting for the old man's command. Evan seems uncharacteristically happy these days. He walks with a slight bounce. He seems to be waiting for something: a cheque in the mail, a change in the weather, although the summer is still in high attendance. It's a new Evan Olcott and the servants and villagers are surprised. For they've known him, the old Evan, for nearly fifteen years.

Drews is somewhere between. In transit, shall we say, searching for something. A diary. A proxy form. A future.

'**I** can't stand people who are late,' grumbled Ellen Weigner, stubbing out a cigarette.

'You've been in Japan too long.' Marietta pulled her hair into a bun. 'Have some beer.'

'One of our group *is* a Japanese,' said Ellen. 'Don't forget.' Marietta poured from a tall green bottle. Ellen said: 'Thanks.'

The door to the room swung open. A waiter's arm appeared, gesturing impatiently within. Miki Drews rushed into the room with stilted bows and apologies. Drews' Hiroshima. The two women returned her formal greetings.

'You look very pretty, Ellen.'

'So do you, Miki.'

She sat with instinctive humility and, looking around, said: 'This is the same room.' Her tone was awed. 'As that night.' It was indeed: the same private dining room at the Pine and Bamboo in which Drews, Tim, Nick Naversen and assorted consorts announced their plan to start a magazine called *Orientweek*. Miki had sat next to her husband, smoking constantly, as he spoke with youthful evangelism. Fran Naversen sat across the table next to Evan Olcott and Ellen Weigner. Kin Wah stood with the waiters. The excuse: a requiem for Mao Tse-Tung and Burl Ives. The reality: the dawn of a dream. And now the sun was setting, spreading violent colours across the horizon.

'I love the food here,' said Marietta. 'Kelvin does too.'

'We used to come here so often.' Miki settled herself. 'In the old days.' She was as always: composed, neatly dressed, sporting impressive pearls on her neck, her ears, her ring finger. She lit a cigarette and exhaled as if anxiety could be expelled along with cigarette smoke. It was that same wide, marble face: a façade, perhaps, but uncracked. Her huge social smile appeared at regular intervals. She crossed her legs and affected calm. But how could she not be nervous? For the first time,

155

Miki Drews was in the spotlight or, at least, would have the spotlight aimed at her at regular intervals. She was the defendant. The victim: her demigod husband. The judges: her only friends in seventeen years in Hong Kong.

'We can't begin yet,' said Ellen. 'We're still short one. Miki, would you like to order a drink?'

'I thought we were . . . I thought it was just us.'

Ellen shook her head. 'At the last moment I found something. I was calling around. And then a call came through. A fluke. So I've invited . . .'

A plump woman with dark skin, dressed in a gaudy shirt, pushed into the dining room. She spoke with the breathlessness of a court messenger. 'She's coming!' The dark woman pressed a hand beneath her panting bosom. 'The stairs!'

The door swung open. A waiter's arm appeared again, slower and more solicitous. He guided into the room a tall, stooping woman with pure white bangs above a horsy, paper-coloured face. The woman looked at the assembled group with a shy, conciliatory smile. Her hands hovered nervously above a bulbous belly. 'I'm sorry.' The voice was the whisper of a weak little girl. 'Don't get around much anymore. If you know what I mean.'

The three women rose automatically.

'This is Alice Giles,' announced Ellen Weigner.

'What's left of her,' Alice smiled.

'How are you doing, Alice?'

'I'm doing great!'

'I think you know Miki.'

'I saw you in the hospital,' Alice said. 'Please sit. Please.'

'And this is Marietta Allen. One of our mainstays at *Orientweek*.'

'I've seen the byline. Hello Marietta.'

Marietta gave a wide-eyed half-curtsy.

'Perhaps I have no place . . .' said Alice.

'You're our main attraction.' Ellen sat abruptly. 'You've got the last piece, Alice, in the jigsaw puzzle.'

'I had to call. The grapevine was buzzing. And I was concerned. Drews is such a nice man. I don't know him well, of course. But I heard so much from Tim. And Drews was there nearly every night at Canossa. I used to see him coming in.'

'Exactly,' said Ellen. 'Miki, Etta. Sit down.'

The brown woman stood at the doorway like a sentinel.

'This is Yrlinda.' Alice gestured to her companion. 'My maid.'

Yrlinda giggled explosively.

'She's concerned about my food. But I can eat anything. I hope you ordered.'

'Dolly, our librarian, ordered this afternoon,' said Ellen. 'So let's get on with it. Would you like beer or tea?'

Yrlinda rushed forward with a large thermos.

'Never mind, Yrlinda. I'll have their tea. Thank you.' Alice gave her imploring smile. Ellen looked down at the table as if searching for notes.

'Tim talked about you.' Everyone looked up. Miki had spoken. 'You brought him music. At Canossa.'

Alice nodded.

'Jazz,' said Miki.

'Some old things,' Alice replied, 'I thought he would like.'

'Something. What?' Miki concentrated. One hand fingered the pearls around her neck. 'Something about an old piano?'

Alice laughed. '"I'd Like To Tinkle On An Old Piana".'

'That's it!' Miki gave her wide smile. 'He used to sing it. On Conduit Road. He bought the record.'

'It's Fats Waller.'

'But something else. Oh, I can't remember.'

'He loved Gordon MacRae.'

'Ah!' said Miki. ' "Love Potion No. 9"!'

Alice blushed. 'Yes.'

'From my teenage days,' said Miki. 'I remember.'

' "Love Potion No. 9"?' asked Marietta.

'It's one of my favourites,' said Alice Giles. 'After all these years. You must play it late at night. It dispels the demons, believe me.'

The food was served by swift, impatient waiters. The maid stepped forward. Alice said: 'I'm all right, Yrlinda.'

'Okay,' said Ellen, putting down her chopsticks. 'Let's get to it. Drews has disappeared.'

Miki fiddled with the remains of her rice.

'I've checked all the bureaus,' said Marietta. 'He hasn't shown up anywhere.'

'This is totally unusual?' Alice looked to Miki. 'I'm sorry. But there are men, husbands . . .'

Miki nodded.

'It's unusual?'

'Yes,' Miki said.

'It's never happened before,' said Ellen. 'This is no dirty weekend, if that's what you mean.'

'Sorry.' Alice smiled solicitously at Miki.

'As you all know, the magazine may be up for sale. Maybe that's a good thing, maybe it's bad.'

'The staff thinks it's bad,' protested Marietta. 'They think it's disaster. I mean, most of them.'

Ellen stubbed out a cigarette. 'Drews thinks it's disaster and that's the point. Am I right, Miki?'

Miki nodded through cigarette smoke.

'We all know where he is,' said Ellen. 'The question is how to get him back.'

Alice said: 'Could you explain, please, the progress of the sale?'

Ellen lit another cigarette with impatient fingers. 'The best guess is that *Time* will buy it. If the board approves.'

'And the board?' Alice straightened in her chair.

'As you know, there were three original partners of *Orientweek*. Drews, Tim Marquand and Nick Naversen.'

'Each had two seats on the board,' said Alice.

'Yes,' said Ellen, yielding to the veteran business reporter. 'The shares are held by the three: Drews, the Naversens and, these days, Kin Wah. You know Kin Wah, don't you Alice?'

Alice nodded. The brown maid nodded eagerly behind her.

'The board seats are more complicated. The Naversens and Kin Wah have three; Drews and his banker have two. Tim named Miki as one of his directors. That makes three.'

Alice said: 'Three against three. But Evan is the chairman. He has the deciding vote.'

'Evan Olcott,' said Ellen, 'is our problem.'

'He'll vote to sell, of course,' Alice said. 'Nick and Fran will pay him. I'm sure he needs the money. He's old. Being old is a . . . none of you know it, but it's a particular state of mind. Or need. But tell me again. Drews has gone to India? To dissuade Evan?'

'Not quite,' said Ellen. 'Marietta? Could you explain?'

'Well,' said Marietta, 'I can try.' She refilled her teacup. 'But it's all pretty foggy.' She described the trip to India with Drews. She talked about the diary and Evan's letters. She described Evan's disappointment that Drews wasn't alone. The table fell into silence.

'Dan loved Timmy,' said Miki. 'He'd want that diary.'

'We don't really know if a diary exists,' insisted Marietta. 'Even Drews doubted it.'

'It's not the diary,' whispered Alice. 'I'm sorry. It's not a question of money. Not with Evan.'

'But the Naversens were there,' said Marietta. 'At the same time.'

Alice nodded and bit her lip.

'Tell us about Evan,' said Ellen. 'That's why you're here, Alice.'

Alice sat back in her chair. She gave a deep sigh. 'I don't know him well. I never have. What I know is an old ... oh, an old story. Tell me more about Drews. Why would he follow Evan? That's crucial. What does he have to gain? The vote?'

'Drews has had a hard time,' said Ellen, with nervous eyes. 'The sale has been tough.'

'He is weak,' proclaimed Miki Drews. The other women stared at her. She said stonily in her chair, a cigarette burning in her hand.

'Drews is weak, Miki?' asked Marietta. 'I don't think that's fair.'

Ellen shifted uncomfortably.

'I mean weakened,' said Miki. 'Recently. I have to tell you.' She turned to the old woman with the white hair. Alice adopted a sympathetic smile. But her eyes were eager and pulling.

'He loves the magazine. He loves me.' Miki Drews pulled on her cigarette. 'Both are – what do you say? – endangered.' She exhaled blue smoke.

'I'm sorry,' said Alice. 'I didn't mean to pry.'

Miki shook her head. She started to speak and then shook her head. She looked up suddenly: 'I may be leaving Hong Kong.'

'I don't think we have to go into that,' snapped Ellen. 'Let's ...'

'He's a man who didn't have defeat,' continued Miki. 'Until now. He used to be ... you know ... the strongest.'

The table fell into silence.

'The truth is hard,' said Alice softly. 'But it's all we have. I'm sorry. But I think I understand more. Thank you. And when did Tim die?'

Marietta stated the date.

'Yes.' She slowly rose from her chair. 'I don't mean to be dramatic but I don't know any other way. Is there beer? I'd like a glass.' Ellen poured a glass of beer and put it on the turntable. She revolved it: Alice drank half in two gulps.

'I've known Evan Olcott for decades,' she announced. 'I wrote about him once. I'm not his friend. I think he had few friends except, I understand, Tim Marquand. But I've been in Hong Kong a long time. I know many things. It's got to that point: I'm a repository.'

Ellen and Marietta looked at the table. Miki stared at Alice through shatterproof eyes.

'I'm sorry.' Alice grasped her chair. 'I think Drews might be in danger. A strange kind of danger – I can't explain it. But I know Evan Olcott's story. I heard it from an English diplomat so many years ago. When Evan was freed from prison.'

'In China,' said Ellen. 'We all know that story.'

Alice shook her head. 'Not the whole story. China was such a terrible place then. It still is: witness Tiananmen.'

The three women looked at her.

'Perhaps I should sit. Yrlinda?' The brown woman helped her into her chair. 'Could I have a little more beer? I never drink, but ...' Miki obliged. 'I never liked beer. But there are times.' Alice drank greedily.

'Anyway, as you all know, Evan Olcott worked for the *Guardian* in Hong Kong. He made an illegal trip across the border and whammo, he was in a Chinese jail. It was a horrible time: so many foreigners were jailed. There was so little the foreign governments could do. It's unimaginable now. But Mao was like that. He'd keep people in prison for decades. Evan was lucky. It was less than five years. I've forgotten how long. But the others, my God, they were in prison for ten years, fifteen. Some of them still live in China. They're spotted at receptions: horrible old ghosts in the corners of high-ceilinged reception rooms, brought out to terrorize the British legation or the American nuclear power merchants. They stand there with their mai tai glasses saying, "Thirty years. Yes, it is a long time." No one writes about them. There are others, Evan types, who escaped China but never recovered. They live in Hong Kong or Cebu or Bangkok.'

A waiter brought dessert.

'The longer you stay in Hong Kong,' Alice said, 'these things resurface. We live in this constant swirl . . .'

Ellen interrupted. 'Tell us about Evan, Alice, please.'

Alice grinned bashfully. 'I'm sorry. But when you've been here so long . . .'

'We're worried about Drews. That's why we're here tonight.'

'I understand. Anyway, Evan was put away like all the rest. A journalist – Evan Olcott was never a spy, everyone knew that. He was a fine journalist. But the Brits could do nothing. He was in Wuhan, or somewhere like that. A decent prison by Chinese standards. Not by ours. The Brits finally found a lever. I can't recall what it was: an international agreement, something like that. They demanded the release of the *Guardian* correspondent. I think a deputy minister was planning a visit. I wish I had kept my files! Anyway, the Chinese were against some wall. A week before the minister's visit they agreed to release the British "spy". No strings attached. He would be delivered to the British Embassy in Peking just in time to be whisked away before the minister arrived.'

'So he was imprisoned by the Chinese,' said Ellen. 'Way back when. It did something to his mind . . .'

'Wait,' said Alice. 'There's more. Evan was in total isolation for what – two years? Three, maybe four?'

'The hostages in Lebanon . . .' said Marietta.

'Stop!' Alice made an uncertain attempt to stand. Yrlinda pulled back her chair. 'We're not talking about a news story. We're talking about a man. A mind. A soul. You have to understand!'

The room became silent. Marietta nodded contritely.

Ellen said: 'But then . . .'

Alice held the back of her chair and took a deep breath. She started to cough and the maid rushed to steady her. But the cough ceased and Alice waved a hand. 'The Chinese said he would be freed by a certain day. Wednesday, say. There's no way to check it. Evan never wrote his book, about China or the Chinese jail. All of the others did. Evan couldn't.'

'Why?' asked Ellen.

Alice paused. 'The British Embassy was poised to receive him. The deputy minister was almost on the plane. Another plane was standing by to fly Evan out of the country. But the Chinese never told Evan he was being released.'

'And?'

'On that morning, they removed Evan from his cell of five, or four, or three years. They moved him, without explanation, outside.'

'To a car,' suggested Marietta.

'No,' said Alice. 'They moved him to a courtyard. They stood him against a wall. A squad of riflemen was arranged on the other side of the courtyard. They blindfolded Evan, waited several minutes, and then shot at him. The rifles were loaded with blanks. Evan collapsed. Later that day, he was delivered hurriedly to the British mission in Peking: a body, I imagine, in the back of a car. He was sent immediately to London.'

There was a silence at the table.

'The government paid for his hospitalization. The *Guardian* gave him a pension.'

The silence continued.

'He was completely mad, of course,' said Alice. 'For a good, long time.'

Miki said: 'But he recovered?'

'He wrote a column for the *Standard*.' Alice finished her glass of beer. She returned gingerly to her chair. 'Of course he returned to Hong Kong. Everyone returns to Hong Kong. But only after several years.'

'Did Drews know?' asked Marietta.

'No one knew,' said Alice. 'Except Tim. He said something to me when he was dying. At Canossa. I don't know why it's such a secret. But it is. Humanitarian grounds, perhaps. It would be cruel to let that out. Think of what it does to a person. To a human mind! As I said: to a soul.'

Alice continued in her whisper: 'Life is hard. We all carry its imprints. They get deeper with the years until you think there's nothing left of your original self. Or nothing recognizable. But who can imagine Evan's experience? To feel yourself killed! To feel your very being destroyed! Then to find yourself in a sedan with a smirking Chinese soldier beside you. Or in an embassy bedroom. A hospital in Surrey. It's your worst nightmare come true. You know what they say about dreams. You never really die. Evan felt his own death. I'm sure he felt the bullets.'

'But he's led a fairly normal life,' said Marietta, 'for so long.'

'I wouldn't say that.'

'He wrote a column.'

'It was a very irregular column.'

'So what does he want with Drews?'

Alice shook her head.

'Then what's your guess?' asked Ellen testily.

'He's an old man,' said Alice. 'He has little time left. This is his last chance to ... oh, I don't know. To get revenge, you might say. No, that's not it. To unburden himself. To take a man and somehow do to him what was done in Wuhan.'

'A firing squad?' asked Marietta incredulously.

'I'm sure it's nothing like that. But I'm certain he chose Drews deliberately and not only because he has some leverage with him. Because Drews is desperate. Don't you see? The magazine, his brainchild, is being stolen from him. His best friend died horribly. And, well ...'

Everyone looked at Miki. She stared at the ashtray.

'Evan knows all that. He's an old correspondent. He finds things out. I can understand that: I'm the same way. To be old, alone.' She smiled. 'All we've got is our notebooks.'

Ellen stubbed out a cigarette and started to talk.

'Wait!' said Alice. 'Evan has found someone vulnerable. He's planning something wrong. I can feel it! I just can't fathom ...'

'In India.' Miki's voice was low and husky.

'I don't see how we ...' said Ellen.

'The rootless man.' Alice's interruption was a barely audible whisper. 'That's what Tim called him. That's what Evan called himself. What could a rootless man find in India? It seems the least likely place for him. And yet, he was always disappearing into India. No one knew what he did. After a while, no one cared.'

'Maybe he's found some roots,' suggested Marietta.

'Maybe he's found a way of pulling roots up,' said Alice. 'Someone else's roots. Finally.'

The women left the restaurant together. Alice led the way down the stairs, aided by her bossy, brown-skinned servant. On the pavement there were formal thank-yous. Ellen stood apart with obvious dissatisfaction. Marietta had the duty of flagging taxicabs. Alice said: 'My car is around the corner. I still drive.' In the distance were the encircling skyscrapers of Hong Kong.

Miki approached to offer formal, Japanese thanks. Alice bowed with elderly ungainliness.

'Evan is a demon.' She spoke in her urgent, girlish whisper. 'A demon of nothingness.' She stared at Miki, trying to gauge her reaction. But Miki's face was white and polished with a formal expression of concern. 'Does Drews have nothing?' Alice implored. 'There must be something you can . . .'

'Thank you very much for tonight,' Miki replied. 'I'm very, well . . .' A taxi was waiting. Miki bowed into it and the red car pulled away toward the Happy Valley racetrack.

Alice stood at the kerbside next to Ellen. 'I don't know,' she whispered. Ellen threw a cigarette into the street. 'Here's one.' She exhaled heavily. 'Good night, Alice, and wish us luck. I'm not sure, but it seems we're off to India.'

'Where?' asked Alice. 'When?'

But the cab door slammed and Ellen and Marietta sped toward Central.

Perhaps life was not such a vacuum, mused Evan Olcott. There were lads to be taught, or a single lad ready for the lesson. Evan was lordly atop a deteriorated rural palace, his white crown hovering above an ancient landscape. He swayed on the crumbling rampart. It was an actual rampart: battles had been commanded from its modest height. Now it held Evan alone, the only king of the district – a sprinkling of rupees had assured that – waging an obscure campaign that would benefit no one. No peasant, no merchant, no local landlord. Only an old man eager to impregnate, so to speak, at the end of his days. To impregnate a mind. To pass along, before dying, the harsh lesson of his life. It was a lesson few had ever learned, or few had survived, which gave Evan a certain pride.

'I am not in the best of health,' he announced to the air. He adjusted the intonation. 'I am not in the best of health, dear boy.'

Evan was exhilarated and it was an odd sensation: the feeling of sap rising in his old veins. From where, he wondered? For if sap remained it suggested roots. And roots were illusory: the metaphor was a lie. Roots suggested deep, smothering soil and Evan knew the human mind had no such constriction. China had proved this in a clamorous instant swelled by cordite and the experience of mortality. In the next instant, the swelling subsided for all time. India had confirmed the lesson over the years. He looked at the distant fields. There they went, the peasants, dismantling their instruments. Bound to the soil? He laughed gently. Bound to the charpoys in the dark, mud-formed rooms. To the willowy women who moved in and out of the rooms like brightly-coloured shades. To the past and the present, for sure, to the future, insincerely, when they sentimentalized about swollen-bellied kids, naked, with black strings around their waists. Tied most of all to the piece of bamboo with the crumpled bills and heavy coins stored in its cavity. But not to the soil. Man was not a lentil, Evan knew. He was a totally free spirit, freer

165

than he cared to realize. If only the truth were known. Or properly taught.

India! Evan surveyed the darkening landscape. *If people would see it bloody clearly.* The farmers were walking back to their homes, craning their heads to see the old man, seemingly laughing, on top of the crack-plastered palace. India could have been created for Evan Olcott, or more accurately, might have been created in the same way: through a trauma too deep for anything to survive but the most scattered of sparks, muscle spasms building to nothing greater in the damaged ganglia. And that, in Evan's eye, was the world. Little sparks adding up to nothing, one thousand momentary reflections misperceived as the iridescent heads of a snake on a dark, paranoid night. Could Drews be led down that final path of revelation? He was, Evan knew, primed for the lesson. For Evan had done his homework in Hong Kong. He had discreetly followed Drews for several nights. He had collected authoritative gossip about the marriage. He had confirmed the precarious state of *Orientweek*, Drews' surrogate child. And he recognized the trauma of the death of Tim Marquand. In Evan's mind, Drews had learned the treachery of the future as a long-term student of Hong Kong. He had learned the tragedy of the present as a good husband, and of the past as the bosom buddy of Tim Marquand. Drews seemed ready for the firing squad and Evan was anxious to call the order – and, subsequently, to remove the blindfold.

Evan became a tongue of white beneath the deep blue Indian sky. He didn't apply his mind to the final aspect, which was power. For power was one of those illusions Evan had supposedly forsworn. But that desire, it seemed, lived on in the roots, even of those who consider themselves rootless. The contradiction was there but Evan Olcott was deliberately oblivious. For he was an old, miserable man who didn't want to die as he had lived for twenty-four years. He had considered his obliteration in Wuhan complete. When a blade of grass finally pushed its way through the scorched surface, Evan didn't have the bravery, at the end, to pluck it up, roots and all, and watch it expire.

At Claridge's Hotel, the black-garbed man at the front desk said: 'Welcome back, Mr Drews. I believe ... yes, there's a package.'

Drews' fingers probed the rough envelope and discerned cardboard and wire. 'One second,' he said. In a corner of the lobby he opened the envelope. A notebook slid out with script in Timmy's hand. Drews slowly replaced the notebook in the envelope, rose from his couch and finished the registration formalities. 'Would you like this morning's paper?' Drews shook his greasy black curls. 'You'll probably want your rest. You've come from Hong Kong?' Drews looked up with pained eyes. 'From Hong Kong?' repeated the hotel clerk.

In his room, Drews sat with the envelope on his lap. He rose, turned on CNN and returned to his chair. It was an old-style *Orientweek* notebook, dating back at least ten years. It had aged as only notebooks and newspapers can. The corners were disappearing: the hasty scrawls on the cover were forever and heartbreakingly cryptic. Even Timmy, alive, wouldn't have recognized their former significance. He turned it over. A phone number was written diagonally on the back: a number with the old New Territories prefix. Had this notebook really come from India, Drews wondered? He looked for the scars of a notebook carried around too long: the collapsed spine, bent spirals. But the notebook wasn't battered, it was merely old and faded. He turned the cover. The first page was a series of hastily-written quotes with careful notations of the beginning and ends, double paragraph marks for para-phrases: Timmy's old code. Several of the quotes contained Chinese characters. He flipped the page: the interview continued. He continued flipping. The interview ended abruptly and blank pages intervened. The next section was a series of closely written paragraphs, the first draft of a story written in a taxi or airplane analyzing leadership changes in the People's Republic circa 1979. After a page and a half, the draft ended in mid-sentence. Drews closed his eyes and saw Timmy lumber out of a red Hong Kong taxi, fumbling for bills in his pocket. He saw him shoot through the tube of an airplane, wreathed in his characteristic impatience, blue Olivetti case dangling from his beefy hand. He waves a stout hand to the passengers waiting to emplane on the other side of a glass barrier. Drews opened his eyes and continued to flip through the notebook, finding nothing but a succession of blank, green-tinted pages.

How did Evan get one of Timmy's notebooks?

He closed the notebook, flipped it over and opened the back cover. The first page had a single line written in the centre of the page:

'Diary, Proxy, Revelation . . .'

This is Evan's handwriting.

Drews flipped the page and found a notation in the same spidery script:

'. . . TK.'

TK – newsroom shorthand for 'to come'.

Saqi, Drews thought. *Kin Wah gave Evan the old notebook. When he visited the Conduit Road flat.*

And so Drews waited. *TK,* he thought. *It will come.* He watched karate movies on the television and ate chilli-cheese sandwiches. He strolled the neighbourhood with its placid, tree-lined boulevards leading to roundabouts where peace surrendered to angry vehicular warfare. At dawn one day, in the coffee shop, Drews was startled to hear one waiter say to another: 'TK.'

Drews called them over. 'I'm sorry. But did you just say TK?'

Both waiters nodded.

'What does it mean?'

'Teekay,' said the turbanned waiter. 'It means "all right".' The second waiter gyrated his head in approval. ' "Fine," ' he said. ' "Okay." It's Hindi. Are you speaking Hindi?' Said the first waiter: 'More tea?'

'Teekay,' smiled Drews.

Late one afternoon, there was a knock on his door. It was a short young man with a motorcycle helmet under his arm. 'I'm from Mr Olcott. You're to pack your bags.'

'Now?'

The young man nodded.

'Okay. Like to come in?'

The young man stepped into the room and walked around with unabashed interest. He parted the curtains, saw a view of the hotel kitchen and let them drop with abandoned curiosity. 'Ready to make a move?'

After checking out, Drews said: 'Are we going far?'

'No.' The young man fumbled with his helmet.

Drews clambered on the back of a motor-scooter, jamming his over-nighter between himself and the young man. The man tilted his helmet in a gesture of interrogation. Drews nodded exaggeratedly, allowing the nod to pass through his shoulders and chest. With a start, they pulled onto the boulevards of New Delhi.

'Where are we going?' Drews lightly grasped the man's shoulders.

The man pointed ahead. They circled a roundabout.

'Is it a hotel?' he shouted.

The black helmet shook.

Drews turned his eyes from the gritty summer wind. 'Do you work for Evan?' The scooter weaved between two sedans. The black helmet shifted slightly and the man's shoulders moved. Drews felt the reply through his fingers. They were communicating by vibrations and Drews felt a queer thrill at the intimacy. He was touching India: it was responding.

The young man drove with reckless confidence. He circled a monument that looked like an ancient smokestack. The driver called something into the air.

'What?' Drews turned his ear forward.

'The Qutab Minar. Very famous!'

Then the scooter entered a timeless bazaar-town hidden at the edge of the modern city. The streets were narrow and cluttered. The driver refused to reduce his speed, playing chicken with approaching scooters, with groups of children walking from school and with a menagerie of placid, street-wise animals. Drews saw tailor shops with plate-glass windows; sweet shops with sweating globes streaked with silver; small, wooden booths occupied by cross-legged vendors, idle and curious about all that passed their small worlds. They plunged dangerously into a group of men with caps.

'Is this a Muslim neighbourhood?'

The man pointed. Drews could catch a single word: '. . . mosque.'

'Is this still Delhi?' But the cycle made a swift turn, brushing a woman whose face was covered by a black cloth and the answer was lost in the peril of the moment.

169

Then the scooter turned into a maze of alleys and the bazaar became a cramped Indian village. The driver increased his speed. Drews saw a succession of snapshots, all in close-up: doorways with sagging charpoys; women squatting in gloomy rooms churning cooking pots; children picking lice from each other's scalps. The alleys curved and made sudden, ninety-degree turns. The scooter stopped short and Drews fell forward onto his overnighter. A lustrous black buffalo with a soiled anus ambled up the alley. They manoeuvred gently around the animal; Drews pulled in his knees. And then they sped off. They went up a steep lane with gutters on each side. The cycle halted. The driver dismounted swiftly, pulling off his helmet. He shook his hair.

'This is it?' Drews saw a row of dilapidated dwellings made of thick, plastered brick. A young girl peered at him from a gateway.

'We get the keys here.' The man marched into a small courtyard. He beckoned. There were three rooms reached by plastered stairs. The walls were covered with aquamarine paint. He could see women, long-haired shadows, within the rooms. The driver pulled a collapsible lawn chair into the shade. 'Water?'

Drews shook his head.

The man climbed to one of the rooms and disappeared inside. Drews heard voices in inscrutable tones: murmurs suddenly rising into near-argument. One of the green walls had a poster showing a Bavarian cottage in wintertime. Drews rubbed the dust from his eyes. The man returned dangling keys. 'This way.'

They walked past the motor-scooter and down a lane. Drews could see fields at the end of a plastered tunnel. At a low door, the man fumbled with a lock. A gutter ran outside the door and a current, caused by the incline, pulled its water toward the distant field. Drews saw tumbling faeces and a struggling, deflated condom.

The man threw the door open and Drews stooped through the doorway. He lowered his overnighter to the floor and waited for his eyes to adjust to the darkness.

'I'll be making a move,' called the man.

'You're leaving?' Drews returned to the sunlit alley. The young man was walking to his scooter. 'Hey – you're not leaving?'

The man nodded. He placed the helmet on his head and flipped up the visor.

'What am I supposed to do?'

'Take a rest.' The man manoeuvred the scooter in the opposite direction.

'For how long?'

He shrugged.

'Did Mr Olcott send a letter? For me?'

The young man shook his head.

'Did he send any message?'

'Yes. I forgot. He said you should stay in your room.'

'*My* room?'

'Don't go out.'

'But, I mean, for how long? This is ridiculous.'

The man smiled – a sympathetic, white flash splitting his profile – and kickstarted the scooter.

'Wait! What's your name?'

'Sanjiv.' Then the motorcycle sped down the alley.

Drews retraced his steps feeling tall, hairy, expensively dressed and oddly exploitative. He could see human figures at the far reaches of the alleys: field workers, naked children, swatches of bright saris flipping out from doorways. He ducked into the room. He saw a plastic light switch the colour of old ivory. He turned it on.

It was a single room the size of two jail cells. A large, Western-style bed with a faded floral spread was against one wall, leaving little room on either of its sides. On the opposite wall was a shelf with a primus stove, several battered pans and a single box of precious-looking matches. On the wall opposite the door was a low platform for sitting or working. The walls were plastered with variegated, deteriorating colour: venerable yellows and oranges devouring the more recent blues and greens. A poster of a film star was next to the bed; an Indian god was enshrined near the door. Thick shelves were built into two walls and they were jammed with books, piled on top of each other, in Hindi and English. All the books were on accountancy. At the foot of the bed was a black and white television seated on a battery of electrical devices with dials and plastic buttons. There was a door in the far corner and Drews manoeuvred around the bed to open it. Outside was a walled-in lot with scattered bricks, a broken tricycle and firewood. At the wall was a spigot and a plastic bucket. There was a small hole in the wall that led to the gutter outside.

Do I have to shit here?

Drews returned to the room. Next to the bed was a table covered in brightly-covered fabric. He lifted the cover. Underneath was an ancient sewing machine. He looked up and saw a fan. He traced the wires with his eyes and found the switch. He sat at the foot of the bed and tried to calm himself. Someone played Indian film music in a nearby house. A woman shouted something in Hindi. Gravelly footsteps came toward his room and continued onwards.

Drews returned to the door and opened it. The light was failing and the noise in the neighbourhood seemed to be rising. A teenaged girl turned into the lane carrying a heavy bucket. She saw Drews and started to run, water sloshing from the pail. Drews shut the door. He found more light switches and tried them. Nothing happened. He took off his boots and lay on the bed.

There was a banging on the door. Drews opened it and found a woman standing outside in the near darkness. The woman nodded and moved forward. She went to the primus stove, bent under the shelf and withdrew a series of bottles. She brought a pan to the spigot outside. Soon she handed Drews a glass tumbler of sweet, thick tea. She motioned at the stove and said something in Hindi. Drews realized: there was more tea in the pan.

She walked quickly to the door.

'Wait! What about dinner?' He made a motion: a scooped hand at his mouth.

She turned and nodded. Then she left the room.

One mystery solved, Drews thought. *I have a cook.*

Several hours later the woman returned carrying a steel lunchbox with round, stacked compartments. She placed it on the plaster shelf and motioned Drews over. He stood next to her as she dismantled the contraption, pointing out two curries and, in the top compartment, folded breads. Drews looked at her: she was small, in her mid-twenties, plump-busted and wearing a red *bindi* on her forehead. She gave Drews an unshy look. He returned a smile. She reached for the end of her sari and put it to her face. Suddenly she stuck out her hand. 'Money?' Drews asked. He took out his wallet and put fifty rupees on her palm. Her plump fingers closed quickly on the bill. She walked to the door, opened it, gave him another bold look and left.

After eating, Drews looked around the room. It had grown less evil and the sounds of the neighbourhood less strange. *Who lives here?* Drews looked at the stacks of accountancy books. *Middle class. So this is the Indian middle class.* (Which *Orientweek* was in the habit of glorifying.) *Or the bottom of that class.* He started rummaging through the accountancy books – dog-eared paperbacks with crippled spines – and took them down from the shelf. Soon all the books were stacked on the wooden platform and the tall man was separating each one, peering at the lurid covers. For Drews knew that if there was a message for him in this room, it would be among the books. A message from Evan Olcott.

Sure enough, in the middle of one of the stacks, Drews found a single non-accountancy book. It was a literary magazine with an orange cover. He turned to the table of contents. There was a fiction section, poetry, reviews and articles. The title of one article was circled. Drews turned to page 47. He read: 'Bessie Head: Two Letters'. There was an annotation at the top in Evan's spidery script. It read: 'Been to India . . .' – the word India was scratched out with annoyed strokes – '. . . Africa, dear boy? The so-called "Heart of Darkness"?'

There were two letters from Bessie Head – whom Drews had never heard of – describing her life and the inspiration for her novels. Drews read them quickly. Then he put the magazine down and returned all the books to the shelves. He removed his clothes and got into bed to reread the letters.

'Perhaps I should first give a brief summary of the fatal paths people can travel, moving from one calamity to another,' Ms Head wrote. She described a brief marriage, wrangles with the South African government and a teaching job in a rural village in Botswana. 'I felt a "presence" walk right into the hut where I lived,' she wrote, 'and I began to have very disturbed experiences. I would apparently be sleeping and a long nail would be hammered through my head from one side to the other. I would wake up with the impression of violence done to me but be quite alive the next day.'

Drews looked around the room. To his right was an evil-looking wall with hellish, melded colours.

She lost her job and became a refugee in Botswana, a 'nightmare world' in which she wrote her first novel, *A Question of Power*. She heard shouts. The shouts were of three kinds:

' "We don't want you here. This is my land. These are my people. You keep secrets."

173

' "You are a dog. You are filth. You are a coloured dog."
'The other shout became an obscene roar: "When I go I go on for one hour. You can't do that. You haven't got a vagina ..." '

Drews stopped reading again. *When I go I go on for one hour.* He thought of Miki and Gabriel. He saw them through the keyhole, hours and hours at the keyhole. He turned and saw the evil patch on the wall.

> I had stumbled upon a world of evil that was eternal and would live forever ... People then began to tell me of things I had lived through in *A Question of Power* which are normal everyday events for black people. They told me there are two kinds of witches in the society, day witches and night witches. The day witches are people in the society who are evil and who can be identified. The night witches are hidden. They are the *baloi*. They enter the body of a sleeping victim and from then on the victim feels a pain. It is either a pain in the head or a pain in the chest accompanied by disturbed sleep. The obscene and hideous is the great joy of the night witch/wizard. The other great joy of the wizard is to open the mouth of a sleeping person and poke his finger in it.

Drews peed in his courtyard, bending forward shyly, and watched the urine fall through the hole to the lane outside. He turned off the light and tried to sleep. But the neighbourhood noises – the sudden shouts, the otherworldly music – disturbed him. He dreamt of a nail through his head, a finger poked in his bearded mouth. He had erotic dreams, seen through an unvanquishable keyhole. 'When I go,' said a disembodied voice, 'I go on for one hour. You can't do that.'

He was awakened by the woman, who came to make morning tea. She turned her face from Drews' bare chest. He spent the morning reading. At noon the woman returned with lunch. Again, she requested payment. At dinnertime she returned, unpacked the dinner and Drews reduced his payment to twenty rupees. She stared at the bill but accepted it. She lingered in the room. Drews said: 'What's your name?' She giggled and shook her head. Drews pointed at his chest and said: 'Dan.' He pointed at her. She giggled again and moved to the door. 'Teekay?' said Drews. She looked at the floor and then pointed outside. She said something in Hindi. And then she was gone.

174

Asleep, Drews was awakened by a gentle knocking. He opened the door and saw the woman. He let her into the room and turned on a light. He was in his underpants. She moved to the bed and sat deliberately. She kicked off her sandals, slid up to the pillow and lay on the bed. She pointed at the light. He turned it off and groped his way to the bed. He felt her hand on his arm. She refused to remove her sari but Drews coaxed her out of her blouse, freeing the constricted breasts. It was teenage sex, with parted clothes, a darkened room, a single position. She refused to be kissed but was otherwise an ardent partner, hungry and, Drews imagined, aroused by the novelty of a foreign man. He tried to satisfy her, imagining once more his wife and her brown lover united through the keyhole. Her moans started to worry him: he imagined them echoing through the alleys outside. He even slowed his tempo. But, in frustration, she moaned louder. Afterwards she dressed hurriedly and stood by the door. She put out her hand. Drews found his wallet and withdrew two hundred-rupee notes. She looked at them with awe, separated the bills with two fingers and shoved them into her blouse. When she returned the next morning she was relaxed and cheerful. Drews motioned her to the bed but she refused. Apparently, that was a night duty.

He spent the morning rereading Bessie Head. *When I go I go on for an hour.* But after the night with the woman, the horror refused to take hold.

At lunchtime, he answered a knock on the door and was surprised to find the motor-scooterist, helmet under his arm.

'Come,' ordered Sanjiv.

'Where are we going?'

He gestured with his chin in the opposite direction.

They drove very far, through the centre of New Delhi and to its dusty outskirts. They passed low, modern industrial parks. Sanjiv pointed and shouted to the rushing air.

'What?'

'Vultures.'

There was a flock devouring a buffalo carcass.

'Doesn't anyone kill them?' Drews averted his face from the hot wind.

'. . . lots of vultures in Delhi.'

They were riding on a high road of dust, the land sloping away to fields and modest villages. Sanjiv stopped the bike at an abandoned tea shop. He pointed at a steep gully. 'You're to ask for Om Prakash.'

'Om Prakash?'

Sanjiv nodded.

'He has a message for me?'

'Watch out!' Sanjiv wrapped his arm around his face. A dust storm swirled around the string beds outside the tea shop. Drews struggled against the storm and descended a gully sloping into the most primitive village he'd ever seen. On either side of the gully was a long but low expanse of old brick. These were the houses: uniform in design, attached, but queerly discordant. Each house was square with an open doorway in the brick. But something had gone wrong with the village. Drews laboured to see the problem. The lines, ostensibly straight, all veered at the wrong moment. No corner was clean. Drews wondered if it was the crumbling of the brick. Or the crazy gullies, pocked with slime-filled craters, that split each picture up the middle. The sky was low and yellow with dust.

It looks like an industrial accident, Drews thought. A wind blew down the gully and Drews covered his eyes. He climbed a mound of dirt and hugged a wall. *I'll find corpses behind these walls.*

Drews felt something at his leg. It was a street dog. In the distance, a child darted into the gully, looked in his direction, and vanished.

This is a bad dream. Drews proceeded further and found himself in the centre of a maze of crumbling brick. Another dust storm arose; an infant wailed behind a wall; and when the dust receded, he decided to return to the main road. But he had lost his bearings.

As he wandered, Drews became aware that the colony, which seemed so eerily uninhabited, was filled with life – behind the brick walls. It started with a small flash at the end of a lane: a girl with ragged clothes and wide intelligent eyes. Then the girl disappeared. The doorways would be empty, then suddenly occupied: first the farthest, then the one across the lane, then a nearer doorway. They were brief flashes of face and colour: a naked boychild, a protective mother whisking him away with a flourish of poly-chrome sari. *They're hiding from me*, Drews realized. *Somehow they know when I pass.* He stopped and turned. In two different doorways, women stood staring. They put hands to their faces and disappeared.

Are there holes in the walls? He turned. Another figure vanished into its brick warren.

The dust storm accelerated. Drews heard a shout and looked up a lane. He saw an old man waving. Drews struggled toward him.

'Are you Om Prakash?' he shouted.

The man bowed once, twice, put a protective arm around Drews and ushered him through a small courtyard and into a modest house. Prakash shut the door. Drews was offered a seat. He wiped dust from his face. A young man fetched a tumbler of water. A woman squatting on the floor dished something white from a pot. She put it on a steel plate and passed it to Prakash. He placed it in front of Drews.

'Today is a holiday,' he said. 'Please. Eat.'

'What is it?'

'It's a sweet. An Indian sweet. Please – you are our guest.'

'I'm looking for Evan Olcott.'

Prakash nodded. He retired to an adjoining room and returned with a paperback book, which he handed to Drews.

Drews examined it. *A Passage to India*?

The old man nodded.

'Oh Christ.' He flipped its worn pages. There were sections underlined in Evan's hand.

'A very famous book,' said Prakash. The others in the room nodded with respect.

'Is there no other message?'

The old man said something in Hindi. A young man seated along the wall reached up to a shelf and pulled down a binder. He gave it to Prakash, who passed it to Drews.

'This is the story of our colony.' He motioned around. 'The story of our lives.'

The binder was filled with news clippings. Drews started to read one. He looked at the grainy photo.

'That's you.'

The old man nodded. 'I am the head man in this colony. We are mostly *harijans*.'

'*Harijans*?' Drews asked. *Untouchables*.

'*Harijans*. We are from Bihar.'

Drews read quickly through the clippings. 'You were resettled here?'

The old man nodded.

'And promised houses.'

He interpreted for the assembled crowd, who shook their heads with approval.

'And then the . . .' Drews flicked through the binder. 'The *patwari* . . .'

The word sent a charge through the room. Several men stood.

'What is a *patwari*?'

The *patwari* was the local land surveyor – the lowest rung on the ladder of the Indian bureaucracy. It was on this rung that the government had hung its population-control programme. The *patwari* was rewarded if he delivered a certain number of sterilizations, female and male. His reward: cash, cooking equipment, gilded trophies. So the *patwari* struck a deal with the *harijans*. They could get land but only if they surrendered their fertility. They all obeyed, buying their futures with wombs and testicles. But then the *patwari* reneged. He refused to surrender the land titles. For the land had become valuable due to its proximity to Delhi. And the sterilized *harijans* were being forced from their houses.

'The police are with him,' said Prakash. 'He has *goondas*. They come to the house. They threaten us.'

Drews was inundated with piles of documents: small, green booklets and large sheets of aged paper with identification photos attached. They were sterilization certificates. The women shouted at Prakash and pointed their fingers at their names on the papers.

'I don't understand,' said Drews. 'People are selling their sterilization certificates? Why?'

'They get the money. And other people get the land.'

'You mean these papers, these certificates, are like land titles? Is that legal?'

Prakash shrugged.

'And now,' Drews continued, 'there's a black market in sterilization certificates?'

Noise came from outside the house. Drews heard shouting, both female and male. Everyone rushed outside. There was a crowd of four bulky men and five angry-looking ladies.

'Who are they?' asked Drews.

'The *patwari*'s people. They discovered you were here.'

'What are they saying?'

'Bad things.'

'Like what?'

'They say the press are a bunch of liars. They say the press will never help. They say the press is corrupt.'

'Oh,' said Drews. The women in Prakash's courtyard started shouting at the ladies outside. 'What is this all about?'

'They say bad things about our women. They say our women are whores. But they are the whores. They are well known in this area.'

A scuffle arose between two men, but was calmed.

'I think you should go,' said Prakash. 'My son will walk you.'

'Is everything all right?'

'When you leave, everything will be all right. When someone from the outside comes, there's always trouble. That's the order of the *patwari*. Wait. I have one more thing for you.' He returned with an envelope and patted Drews farewell.

'What about those articles?' Drews asked. 'Did they help? Did the government do anything?'

The old man shook his head.

'Is there anything . . . I'm editor of a magazine in . . .'

The old man put his hand on his shoulder and walked him through the doorway. Drews turned to wave goodbye but the lane was already empty.

Sanjiv was waiting at the tea shop, reclining on a charpoy. The dust storms had ended. Drews said, 'Wait one minute.' He opened the envelope and read Evan's familiar scrawl.

We will meet in a few days. Keep your eyes open. I've spent many happy hours in this colony.

The scooter pulled away with abrupt speed. Drews looked behind at the receding village. He saw a small girl dart from the gully and stare after him. He waved but the girl stood frozen.

'Khassi colony,' shouted Sanjiv.

'What does that mean?' called Drews.

'Khassi means castrated. It's just a nickname.'

He was relieved to return to the room with the floral-patterned bed. That night, he started thinking once more of the finger in the mouth, the nail through the head, mass vasectomies and hysterectomies for a gilded trophy. *When I go I go on for an hour. You can't do that . . .* He waited anxiously for the woman's rap on his door. At midnight, he heard it and the night became normal.

179

Over the next few days, Drews tried to absorb the lesson Evan had set out for him. But he found himself becoming comfortable in the small room. He learned to work the television; he became accustomed to squatted ablutions in the private courtyard with the warm summer sun on his shoulders. The woman visited every night, always waiting for her two hundred rupees at the end. On his fourth day Drews broke Evan's admonition and took a tour of the village. He visited the mosque and made friends at a tea shop. He bought cloth for Miki. At the edge of town, he found a spirits store and purchased two large bottles of rum. When the woman came at lunchtime, he pointed at the bottles. He tried to communicate via sign language but she went away puzzled. An hour later, there was a knock at the door.

'Sanjiv!' said Drews.

Sanjiv was altered. He wore a plaid *lungi*, the Indian sarong. His toes showed through plastic sandals. 'You have rum?'

'I thought we could have a small party. For the neighbourhood.'

Sanjiv pondered. 'Okay. After dinner.'

Drews went out again to buy snacks. After dinner, a knock sounded on the door. Sanjiv entered the room with three male friends. There were introductions. Sanjiv poured rum for all. A steel jug was filled with water. One of the men had a cassette recorder. Soon the room was filled with music. The young men sang favourite refrains from Hindi films in uninhibited voices. There was conversation, interpreted through Sanjiv, and the men inspected Drews' cowboy boots with admiration.

The door opened again to admit the Indian woman, followed by two friends and four young children dressed for an occasion.

'They want to dance.' Sanjiv pointed to the children. He barked a command to one of his friends and cassettes were switched. 'Disco dance. They like to disco dance.' The children clambered on top of the wooden table and started dancing with sombre expressions.

The drinks were replenished several times. Drews found a male arm around his shoulder. He made eye contact with the Indian woman, who smiled shyly from the opposite corner. A crowd of neighbours stood in the doorway, swaying and clapping. Soon Drews was on the table, his curls grazing the ceiling, singing a capella with theatrical soulfulness.

Met her on the mountain.
Asked her to be my wife.

180

Met her on the mountain.
Then I killed her with my knife.

Drews stabbed with an imaginary dagger and the group laughed and applauded.

Hang down your head Tom Dooley,
Hang down your head and die.
Hang down your head Tom Dooley,
Poor boy, you're going to die . . .

Then the children were allowed a finale. They stood on the wooden platform and the Indian woman yelled at the man with the cassette recorder. The music began – banks of glissando violins – and the children sang, earnest and well-rehearsed: '*Ek, do, teen* . . .'

The woman returned later that night to sleep with Drews. Afterwards she refused the payment and gave Drews a fond kiss, as if to say goodbye.

The next morning, Drews was visited by two men with gold neck chains and moustaches. They took seats on the wooden platform. They introduced themselves as estate agents. They offered Drews a lease on the room. For a certain price.

'Who stays here?' asked Drews.

The men made dismissing gestures.

'But surely someone already lives here? The books. The sewing machine.'

The tenants, it transpired, were a young couple. The husband was an accountant. The wife was not working. They were trying to save money to bring their daughter in from the countryside, where she lived with grandparents. The child needed an operation apparently. A 'nose operation', according to the men. But the couple didn't pay enough rent.

'We will evict them,' said the lead man. 'No problem, boss. We can throw them out in a morning.'

'I'm not here for long.'

The agent continued: 'If they give us problems, we will break everything. We will break her face.' A local politician was on their side. How much was Drews willing to pay?

Drews got rid of them and went out to the courtyard to look at the broken tricycle. In the afternoon, he was interrupted again. Sanjiv was at the door with his motorcycle helmet.

'Pack up,' he said.

He dropped Drews at Claridge's Hotel. 'A car will be waiting early tomorrow morning. To bring you to Mr Olcott.'

Drews tried to chitchat with Sanjiv in the hotel driveway. He asked what he did for a living. Sanjiv said he was an accountant: he taught students at his own private school.

'That's your room?' asked Drews incredulously.

Sanjiv nodded.

'Where did you stay? These nights.'

Sanjiv shrugged dismissingly.

'And your wife?' Drews asked.

Sanjiv spoke through his helmet. 'She was the one who served your meals. And your bed tea.'

Drews stammered.

'We're saving.' Sanjiv kick-started his bike. 'I want her to get a job.'

Drews reached for his wallet but Sanjiv had already shot down the drive, giving a backward wave in farewell.

The Press Club of India was redecorated. One could feel it. But it was hard to pinpoint specific changes. Were the distempered walls a shade brighter? Perhaps there were new lights or bulbs finally renewed? The caricatures seemed straighter in their frames, or a few of them. Those shrivelled buntings along the shadowed ceiling: were they from some less ancient celebration? The tablecloths, yes, the tablecloths were new or possibly laundered. Like India itself, the Press Club was hardly a stagnant place. It accomplished its functions (except on strike days), it ran the smallest of deficits, it *worked*, or, at least, it endured. But change at the Press Club seemed to follow in the rear, never to lead.

Gail McGuinn, swathed in tired Indian cottons, stood at the bar rhythmically flipping her mantle of blonde frizz. Husband Prentice was reading his khaki-covered book – was it really a Bible? – lips moving involuntarily within his square-cut beard. His arm rose autonomously, fingers poised to flick a gnat from the miniature page. Buck Frye was enjoying his second bottle of beer, gulping nervously. His name had been posted for overdue bills and he was drinking as much as possible before his credit was guillotined. Unexpectedly, he leapt in the air like a yanked puppet.

'Christ!' His legs scissored as if on fire. 'Can't someone get rid of that cat?'

'Uh oh.' Gail McGuinn flipped her hair. 'They're back.'

Nick and Fran Naversen smiled from across the dining room. Nick hoisted a hand in greeting. Fran struggled with two bottles of mineral water.

'That woman is abominable,' said Gail.

'They must be opening a bureau,' murmured Buck.

'I'm not standing any beers,' said Prentice. He returned his gaze to his book. 'Gail – no beers.'

'Something's going on,' said Gail. 'I can feel it. Something funny at *Orientweek*.'

'The gang's still here,' bellowed Nick. 'I know a doctor who could separate those feet from the bar-rail in a jiffy. Absolutely painless.'

Prentice glanced up with hooded eyes.

'Getting toasty.' Nick showed two fingers to the barman. 'Fran's sweating like a hog.'

Fran sighed with disapproval and lunged at the beaded bottle of beer.

Buck Frye inched closer and gazed up with devotion. 'If you need any assistance,' he whispered, 'any assistance at all.' His eyes widened with inspiration. 'This round's on me!'

Nick gave a sharp clap of appreciation. Buck beamed with the virgin gratification of generosity. Gail and Prentice McGuinn looked on with unsuppressed astonishment.

In her office that afternoon, Gail struggled with a story on the miserable women of Bangladesh, which she was writing cover-length despite New York's unaccountable lack of enthusiasm. She turned from the computer, picked up the telephone, dialled twelve digits and said: 'Drews, please.' She waited. 'Could I speak to Drews, please?' She listened. 'What do you mean? Hello? Hello – I was looking for Drews. This is Gail McGuinn from *Newsweek* in India, in New Delhi. I . . . Ellen? What are you doing in Hong Kong? How are you? How are things in Tokyo? I was trying to get Drews.' She listened again. 'I see. Well, Ellen, I was just kinda curious. We have these *Orientweek* people here in Delhi . . . they're practically camped out at the Press Club.'

There was a squawk from the phone.

'They say they're looking for a man called Evan Olcott. Who is Olcott?' She listened. 'He's chairman of *Orientweek*?' She reached for a copy of *Orientweek* and flipped quickly to the staff box. 'Ellen, what is this all about? You can't find your own chairman? What's he doing in India?'

Ellen Weigner pulled on a cigarette and hollered. 'Dolly – get me Marietta. At home.' She stubbed out the cigarette and picked up the phone.

'Surprise, surprise. The Naversens are back in New Delhi. When does the plane leave?' She lit another cigarette. 'I think you're going to need some help on the ground. As unpleasant as it may sound.' She gave

Marietta contact numbers for Gail McGuinn. 'And you have to move quickly. If the Naversens don't show up at the Press Club tomorrow, we may have lost them.' She tapped her cigarette on the ashtray. 'No, don't mention him. Gail's gunning for a story. As far as she knows, Drews is on a business trip in Malaysia. Make her think it's all about Evan. You're searching for the lost chairman. That'll satisfy her.' She listened and sighed. 'Yes, she's heard about the sale. She said as much. Say what you want but Gail's a sharp journalist. Prentice, on the other hand . . .' She frowned with displeasure. 'I know, I know, Marietta. You'll have to say she's Drews' representative. Say she's Evan's old friend. Say anything – but don't say that Drews is missing or we'll all end up in the pages of *Newsweek*.' Ellen snorted. 'Yes, I couldn't agree more. Better us than our bylines.'

It was 4 am but the lobby of Claridge's Hotel was brightly lit. Weary passengers were disgorged from their humped taxis, counting luggage several times over. Marietta rubbed her eyes with petite hands and placed three passports on a marble counter.

'Uh, yes,' she told the clerk, 'three rooms.' She thought for a second and went across the lobby. Returning, she said: 'I'm sorry. That's a mistake. We need only two rooms.'

'Adjoining, Madame?'

'No,' Marietta said. 'That's not necessary. In fact, could you separate the rooms a bit?'

As the new arrivals attempted sleep in their rooms, one guest was preparing to depart. Drews exited the elevator at 5.30 carrying his overnighter. He paid the bill and stepped into the night. There was a single car parked at the rim of Claridge's drive: an Ambassador painted chocolate brown. He knocked on its window. The driver roused with a start, opened the door and slowly pulled himself from the car.

'From Mr Olcott?'

The driver nodded sleepily. Drews threw his suitcase in the back seat. He put one leg in the car and looked at the darkened streets. Dawn was still distant.

'Well,' Drews said, inhaling. 'Let's go.'

An hour later, as the sun made its portentous appearance, Fran Naversen slowly walked through the hotel lobby, grimacing with each step. In the coffee shop she lowered herself gently to a chair and ordered tea and dry toast. 'Very dry,' she demanded.

'Very dry, Madame,' said the waiter. He offered a newspaper; she glanced at it, saw a large photo of the Prime Minister nibbling a white sweetmeat and waved it away. When the tea and toast was served, she sighed heavily. Thirty minutes later she called the waiter back. 'Maybe I'll have an omelette. Plain. No chilli. *Please.* I'll have that newspaper now. And how about a big pot of coffee? And yeah – a side order of bacon. Lean. You know what I mean? *Lean* bacon.'

The waiter nodded. 'Teekay.'

Nick joined her at eight, patting his belly.

'I'm not going anywhere with this stomach,' said Fran. 'Honestly.'

Nick settled at the table. 'Then we may be here a good, long time.' He accepted the menu with a nod. 'Do they have a health club?'

'Nick, I've been miserable. I spent the whole night in the bathroom.'

'Prefer the bed myself.'

'Didn't you hear me?'

'Fran, we're on different floors.'

'I wouldn't be surprised if they could hear me in Calcutta.'

'Mmmm,' said Nick. 'They'd probably recognize the sounds. In Calcutta.'

'Not a wink of sleep.'

'Didn't see you at the bar. Didn't see anyone at the bar, as a matter of fact. Took a little stroll. Found some guy squatting in the bushes. Over there.'

'Oh, please!'

'Stared at me just as boldly as you could imagine. Could see his dickie dangling down.'

'Nick.'

'Big one.' He folded the menu. 'On such a small guy. Which one of these moustaches is ours? The one with the tea cosy on his head? Nice colour.' He waved over a waiter. 'Bring me one of those omelettes. The ones with chilli.'

'I hope we're not here for another week,' said Fran.

'Someone recommended the disco at the Sheraton.'

'Someone?'

'Someone at the bar. Import-export. They're all import-export. Or jelly-filled cables. They get it in their mother's milk. Import-export. Jelly-filled cables. And then, when the double chin comes in, it's off to Daddy's office. To make the jelly-filled cables. Poor fuckers.'

Buck Frye sashayed across the coffee shop, bowing slightly when he reached their table.

'Early.' Nick bisected his omelette.

'I'm up with the sun.' Buck settled next to Fran. 'Making contacts. Calling sources. The freelance life, you know.'

'I thought everyone drank tea until eleven,' said Nick. 'Come to Hong Kong. Then you'll learn what it is to work. Order anything you'd like. On us.'

Buck chose chicken livers on toast and a Bloody Mary. Fran groaned.

'So.' Nick stared assertively across the table. 'Do you really know the countryside?'

Buck, chewing bread, nodded Indian-style.

'We have a bit of a setback,' Nick said. 'Fran's got the shits.'

Fran exhaled defeatedly. Buck moved his chair a few inches away.

'But I think the Big Girl'll be ready when the summons comes. She's a soldier. Marches on her stomach and all that.' He leaned forward and his voice dropped to a whisper. 'I told you, didn't I, that this mission is a bit touchy? Hush hush. We have to wait for the precise time to strike.'

Buck nodded with full mouth.

'Otherwise we could lose everything. And Fran wouldn't like that. No she wouldn't. And when Fran gets angry . . .'

'Nick stop it.'

'The tricky thing,' Nick lectured, 'is that we don't know where we're going. It's all a kind of . . . game. That's why we need a little local help. We can't get caught in some goddamned town not knowing how to wipe our asses. That's where you come in.' Nick stood and tucked in his shirt. 'And now, I'll leave you two to discuss terms. I have to make a call.'

Fran stared. 'To whom?'

'Just a little gamble. Not much hope, really. But nothing ventured . . . Took a little waylay to the Sheraton last night. It's not half bad.'

Buck watched him stride from the coffee shop. He turned to look at Fran.

'I feel better.' She smiled and rubbed her hands. 'Let's talk business.'

★ ★ ★

When Nick Naversen strode across the lobby toward the elevator, he failed to notice the bearded, khaki-clad man sitting behind the potted palm. But Prentice McGuinn kept a careful eye on Nick Naversen. At ten he was joined by his wife Gail and they had an earnest discussion. Gail walked to the elevator and disappeared behind its doors. An hour later she reappeared.

'We have to watch them. They're our only lead. I'll stake out the Press Club. You stay here.'

Prentice crossed his legs and withdrew from a pocket his khaki-covered book to demonstrate infinite patience.

At 3.30 she returned. 'They didn't show.'

Prentice nodded sagely. 'They haven't left the hotel. She had lunch in the coffee shop. Alone. I rang his room. It sounded as if he was napping.'

'Our friends?'

'Chinese restaurant. Then the pool.'

Gail nodded. 'Keep the watch. If they don't leave by sunset, it'll be tomorrow. And watch the front desk. Marietta says they're waiting for a message. A summons. From Evan Olcott. Try to get a copy. Spread a little money around, Prentice. *Newsweek* will pay. If this isn't a story – a big story! – I'm not a journalist.'

New Delhi's blood-coloured monuments were far behind them. Gone were the four-lane highways linked by disintegrating nineteenth-century bridges. Meerut was a memory. Drews was entering a new India, linked to the old by a ceaseless tide of Indians travelling in both directions, trapped behind bus windows with expressions of imprisoned curiosity. The country and the city: in all lands that divide was paramount. In some, the visitor could comprehend the desire or need that brought people one way or the other. In India, Drews found himself clueless. The weekenders were obvious, of course, in their Western clothing accompanied by difficult children who snacked constantly. And the truckers: black, emaciated men in prehistoric rags. But the rest: who were they? Where were they going? Why? The questions loomed in Drews' mind because of the stares that constantly met his. The curiosity of the Indians seemed exactly reciprocal: who was this bearded, dark-curled Westerner shooting with reckless speed into the heart of their subcontinent? Where was he going? And why?

The interior of Drews' car, including its ceiling, was lined with synthetic, brown carpeting. The seats were covered in vinyl tiger-skin. Tiny curtains, white with brown piping, decorated the rear window. A wooden box attached to the ceiling held two empty cassette cases. From the dashboard dangled a long cat's tail, purple wisps of nylon with plastic eyes that jiggled with each bump. The summer had arrived and the wind outside was hot and stinging. Within the car, the temperature was several degrees higher.

The driver was slack-jawed with tobacco-coloured skin pierced by millions of tiny pockmarks. Like most Indian drivers, he cowered behind the wheel in a bowed slump. His rump and lower back were rooted to the tiger-skin seat. His hands grasped the steering wheel loosely, spinning it with a tentative touch. He stared at the road as if it was barely familiar. His body seemed to be resting — in preparation, perhaps, for some strenuous driving demand in the future. His only display of muscular coordination was a tiny twitch made with a thumb: to honk at everything registering on his retina. Drews wanted to lean forward and check his legs, but didn't dare. He feared they were nowhere near the brake or clutch – or weren't there at all.

Drews' initial attempt at conversation yielded little. 'How long is the drive?'

The driver shook his head. 'No.'

'What town is this. *This* town.'

An enthusiastic nod of the gleaming hair, which smelled of burnt coconut. 'Okay!'

'Can we stop here? Here? Stop?'

A refusal: 'No okay!' Further conversation confirmed the obvious: 'no' and 'okay' were the driver's two words of English.

The towns slowed them down. It was morning market time. Squatting vendors sold every commodity imaginable: fowl, massive padlocks, pink buckets, a lasso-type green vegetable. Their displays ate into a road already clogged with oxcarts and jerry-rigged, smoke-belching vehicles. The towns were identical and the sights recurring: piles of gunny sacks, tobacco stands on stilts festooned with foil packets, stained eggs stacked in high-rise layers and pale brooms sticking stiffly out of tin buckets. Placid donkeys were driven by skinny men in white squatting atop wooden carts. The walls were covered with election posters, torn and defaced, and fresh film advertisements with shouting men and thick-eyebrowed ladies. The towns were a blur of three colours: the dusty green of roadside crops, the ochre of piled dirt and the worn driftwood grey of everything else.

Between towns, however, they drove beneath canopies of flowering trees. At the roadside, the sugar cane was in season, tossed in the hot breeze, interspersed with neat patches of thin stalked plants. 'What is that?' Drews asked. '*That* one.'

'Dal,' said the driver.

'Dal?' said Drews. 'In English?'

The driver shook his head. 'No. Dal.'

'The dal you eat?' Drews said. 'In restaurants?'

'Okay,' said the driver. 'Dal.'

Drews opened Evan's copy of *A Passage to India*. He had read the book in college but remembered little except the mysterious Marabar caves. He scanned for Evan's underscorings. The first came in the scholarly introduction:

'... the places Forster visited included Bankipore (the model for Chandrapore), the Barabar caves (which suggested the Marabar), near Mayapur ...'

The car decelerated and pulled bumpily onto the road's shoulder. The driver extricated himself from the car. Drews waited for him to enter the bushes and relieve himself. Instead, he turned his pockmarked face and pointed.

'What?'

He pointed commandingly.

Drews splayed the book on the seat and joined the driver on the roadside. He squatted slowly and shook his sweat-dampened curls. The driver shook his finger. Drews looked.

Between bushes was a low square of plaster with a royal blue border. In the middle was an inset aquamarine square. It was thin paint that allowed the plaster to come through in streaks. In the middle of the central panel was a primitive figure in fluorescent orange. It appeared to be a tree with two branches forking symmetrically from a central trunk. Above the tree were two orange discs – one crescent-shaped to represent the moon, the other, wobbly round, the sun. The execution was rough and garish. Drews squatted in the dust to see it properly. *It's hideous*, he thought. He pointed at the orange tree. 'What is that?'

'Shiva.'

'Shiva? The god?'

The driver nodded. He pointed at a white plaster cylinder at the base of the painting. 'Shiva lingam!'

'Lingam?' Drews recalled the *Kama Sutra* he found on Mrs Bottom's shelf in Albert Court. Timmy had read it aloud at hashish parties. *The sex organ?*

'Okay!' said the driver.

Back on the road, Drews flipped through *A Passage to India*. Midway through the book he found brackets. It was a passage describing the Marabar caves, setting them on the timeless edge of the Dravidian plain. 'They are older than anything in the world. No water has ever covered them ... If flesh of the sun's flesh is to be touched anywhere, it is here ...'

The caves were natural bubbles in the ageless rock, linked to the outside world by man-made tunnels. Drews read and recalled the famous passage about their mirrored walls: 'The two flames approach and strive to unite, but cannot, because one of them breathes air, the other stone . . .' Senior year of high school, an English exam – that was the passage used to test the boys' reading comprehension. Drews paused in his reading. *And here I am*, he thought, *tested again by the same words. What did I make of them in 1966? What am I supposed to make of them now?* A section was underlined in Evan's hand:

> But elsewhere, deeper in the granite, are there certain chambers that have no entrances? Chambers never unsealed since the arrival of the gods? Local report declares that these exceed in number those that can be visited, as the dead exceed the living – four hundred of them, four thousand or million. Nothing is inside them, they were sealed up before the creation of pestilence or treasure; if mankind grew curious and excavated, nothing, nothing would be added to the sum of good or evil.

A later passage was underlined twice, as Forster's characters finally enter the mysterious caves. It described the caves' echo:

> Whatever is said, the same monotonous noise replies, and quivers up and down the walls until it is absorbed into the roof. 'Boum' is the sound as far as the human alphabet can express it, or 'bou-oum', or 'ou-boum' – utterly dull. Hope, politeness, the blowing of a nose, the squeak of a boot, all produce 'boum'.

Drews shifted uncomfortably and turned the remaining pages of the novel, finding no further markings. He returned to the marked passages. 'Boum,' he said aloud, testing the sound. ' "As the dead exceed the living . . ." ' He went back to the beginning to read the book properly.

At around eleven, the car slowed and stopped before a wooden stall with a corrugated iron roof. A man with a shaved head sat on a platform behind a battery of cooking pots.

'*Chai.*' The driver pointed. '*Chai,*' Drews responded. '*O-cha.*' The driver got out slowly, flexing his thin limbs. Drews followed. He went behind the tea stall to pee but found a group of children playing with goats. He walked up the road and stopped between trees covered with thorns. He unzipped his pants. A woman walking from the field watched him. Drews shifted position to find a bicyclist pedalling towards him.

He looked to the other side of the road. There were farmers in the field, a teenager leading a buffalo. *Where can you pee in this country? There are people − eyes − everywhere.*

Drews finished his tea. The driver motioned him to the side of the stall. He pointed. It was another roadside deity: an irregular-shaped rock covered in silver foil with a single eye − black iris and pupil surrounded by ivory white − recessed in the centre. Red slashes of paint portrayed the tri-limbed tree.

'Shiva?' said Drews.

'Okay,' exulted the driver. 'Shiva.'

Back in the car, Drews thought: *'Boum.' Belly dancers with the belts of silver. Roadside gods of rock and paint. What is Evan getting at?*

By late afternoon, Drews was half-way through *A Passage to India*. The car passed a small railroad station and pulled onto a path. Drews saw rounded hills covered with lunar craters. The car jolted down the rutted path. The hills came closer and he saw they weren't craters: they were hundreds, four thousand, four million massive boulders strewn across the hills as if by a careless giant. There were no signs of human habitation.

'Where are we going?'

The driver nodded his head. 'Okay.'

Could Evan Olcott live here?

The road ended at an official-looking building under a shade tree. The door of the building was padlocked. A footpath led into the hills. The only vegetation was browned grass growing between boulders. There was a sign, royal blue and gold, announcing fines for desecrations. But the Indian Archaeological Survey didn't bother to identify the national treasure it sought to protect.

'What is this?' Drews expected no answer. He was surprised when the driver responded: 'Barabar.'

'The Barabar caves?' Drews returned to the car and reached through the window. He flipped open the first pages.

'... the places Forster visited included Bankipore (the model for Chandrapore), the Barabar caves (which suggested the Marabar), near Mayapur ...'

'Is this Mayapur?'

The driver pointed down the rutted road. Drews recalled the railroad station.

'So these,' he said, 'are the mysterious Marabar caves.'

'Barabar,' corrected the driver.

'Barabar,' said Drews.

'Okay!'

Drews climbed, feet slipping, through a monochrome land of stone. *Forster was right*, he thought. *It's a landscape from the sun.* Drews and the driver squeezed between two rounded boulders and came to a clearing. Another sign from the Archaeological Survey issued the same rusty warning. Before them was a massive, submarine-coloured rock sunk into the ground like a half-buried whale. Two square doorways were cut into the flank of the rock. The first was adorned with carvings in high relief: a lintel, a pair of decorative columns and a frieze of marching elephants – the hand of man, creative man, not some ancient swirl of gasses.

Forster fudged it. Drews stared at the elephants and the black rectangular doorway with its fine-cut lines. *On the outside, at least.*

He ducked and found himself in a high-ceilinged rectangular chamber with a wall reflecting the light from the doorway. There was a peculiar smell – the brine of cut rock with the dust of decomposition – and Drews instinctively breathed through his mouth. He stepped back out of the cave. The pockmarked driver was now squatting patiently.

Drews mimed the striking of a match. The driver reached into his pocket. Drews returned to the cave and went to the far wall. He lit a match and watched for Forster's reflection. But he failed to rouse the spectral twin. He looked at the doorway, with its light pouring in. He moved to the opposite wall, which was in shadow, and tried several more matches. None produced the effect described in the novel.

'Well . . .' he said. And the echo began. It was as Forster described: low, deep, coming from the buried portion of the rock, not the tall ceiling. Drews stamped his boot. The echo issued forth. Drews called: 'Boum!' Boum came back to him. He struck a match. The sound was too faint to summon the echo. Then Drews noticed something at the far end of the rectangular room. It was a second doorway, lower than the main entrance and unadorned. He walked to it, lit another match and thrust his hand inside. The chamber was empty. He stepped within. It was small and round with a low, scrabbled ceiling. The walls were unpolished. No light came through its entrance. The dust-death smell was heavier and Drews began to cough. The match expired and he hurriedly lit another.

This is a Marabar cave. This is what Forster saw.

When he exited he found two men awaiting him: his driver and a half-naked holy man carrying an iron trident. Drews marched to the second cave. The interior was the same as the first. He didn't try the matches and played briefly with the echo. The three men walked around the head of the rock and found a third entrance. Drews scanned its flank. There was only one blackened doorway. He said to the driver, 'How many . . .'

A noise came from within the cave. Drews recognized it: *boum*. He took a step backwards and said: 'Hello.' Again: *boum*. He stepped back again and, in the bright sunlight, clicked his fingers. Another sound came from the cave: *boum*. The Barabar caves could pull sound inside. He examined the cave swiftly, which was smaller than the first two, and rejoined his guides.

'Are there any more?'

'Okay,' said the driver.

They moved down the hill, climbing between boulders. They came to a square-cut shelter in a smaller rock. The driver pointed. It was open to the air: no entrance, no mystery. Just cut, grey rock where one might wait out a rainstorm.

'That's it?' asked Drews. 'That's the Barabar caves?'

The driver nodded with satisfaction.

Where are the undiscovered caves? Where are the natural bubbles? These are all man-made.

'Hold on a minute,' Drews said. 'I want to go back to the second cave.' He pointed uphill. 'The second one – I didn't see it thoroughly.'

This time the driver entered the cave with Drews. He watched as Drews lit matches. He pointed out a puddle in the cave's corner.

'What is it?'

The driver said something in Hindi. Drews looked at the puddle. The rains were not expected for weeks.

When he approached the doorway to the inner chamber, Drews felt a scared, whirring presence. He jumped back.

'What is it?' The echo started to reverberate. 'Was it a bat?' He flapped his arms. He enunciated: 'Bat?'

'No,' said the driver. Drews could hardly hear him over the echo.

'What *was* it?'

'No,' repeated the driver. 'No okay.'

Drews pointed at the chamber. The boums were joining forces. He had to shout: 'Is there something in there?'

The driver pointed at the puddle on the floor. *An animal? Animal urine? Is there an Indian bear in that chamber?* Drews lit a match and moved toward the opening. The driver said: 'No!' The echo took up the word and transformed it. '*Boum . . . boum . . .*' Drews walked backwards until he was beside the driver. He looked at him, match burning in his hand. 'Let's go.'

They descended the rocky hills and Drews made for the car. But the driver beckoned to him. He brought him around the base of the hill. There was no path; they clambered over more Barabar rocks. Finally, the driver pointed. It was another small shrine, a crop of low rocks with foil sheets and more red paint. Again, Drews saw the tri-limbed tree etched in vermilion paint. There were more staring eyes. The rock had ten or more sheets of foil, ten or more eyes.

'Evan Olcott wants me to see these. Doesn't he? This is Mr Olcott's orders.'

'Okay,' said the driver.

He looked at the stupid squares of foil, the hideous slashes of red paint and felt nothing but tiredness and disgust. *They're so low*, he thought. *Why is everything in India at knee level?* He stumbled away and came to a stream. Next to it was yet another shrine, different from the rest. It was the size of a shoebox, square, made of smooth, grey mud. It had a conical top. This shrine was free of the garish decoration speaking of ignorance and hopeful superstition: the eyes, the foil, the red slashes. It was timeless, hardened mud with a square door. Drews squatted and looked inside. In the centre of the interior he saw another round lump. Next to it was a toy trident, small and straight, unweathered and firmly stuck in the smooth floor. The metal was cut precisely. The middle prong was straight and long; the prongs on either side were smaller and curved with sharp symmetry. He reached in and flicked the trident with his fingers. It remained firm.

'It's Shiva,' said a voice. 'Of course. In this part of India. Cow country.'

Drews looked up. Across the stream was a white man seated on a boulder. His gauze trousers were rolled at the ankle. He was shirtless with pale feet immersed in the stream. 'They do love Shiva. And I mean who can blame them? Ram, Krishna, Buddha. I mean, that guy had *lives.*'

Drews nodded.

'*Capisce*, Cowboy Boots?'

'I guess.'

The man plucked a colourless shirt from the pool, wrung it out and laid it on a boulder. 'Buddha was his last incarnation – that's what they say. But I mean there's no proof, is there? Is there? Jesus Christ seemed like a Shiva type to me. Had that Shiva *je ne sais quoi*. Jim Morrison, man. Keith Richards – he's even got the blue skin.' The man laughed privately, the laugh of a man accustomed to being ignored. 'Sam Walton. Charles Manson. Yeah, Chuckie even had his own Parvati: Squeaky Fucking Fromme.'

'What's this symbol? On all the shrines? This tree.'

'Not a tree, man. That's a trident. Shiva never left home without it.'

Drews thought of the metal trident in the mud shrine.

'Essential equipment for wandering in the forest.' The man's eyes narrowed. 'Or is it Vishnu? I always get those two guys confused. Too many incarnations in this place, that's what I say.'

'Are you, uh, travelling?'

'That's me, man.' The man raised his arms and fluttered his hands. 'Paddling the great stream, Cowboy Boots. Bobbing in the vast Hindu ocean.' He was wiry and pale with a severe crewcut and black eyes with tight corners. Drews recognized the counterculture glare: a look filled with lentils and hashish, guitar riffs and sleeping bags, with glints of madness and defensive contempt. His look, his patter: it was an ageless thumb-jerk from a soul stuck forever on the shoulder of a long, fast highway. 'Renounced the world of BMWs and cable TV. Couldn't take another sun-dried tomato. The hardest part was leaving behind my microwave. And my excellent haircuts.'

Drews spoke demandingly: 'Did Evan Olcott place you here?'

The man laughed scornfully. 'Man, this ain't no cocktail party. This is India.'

'You're sure you're not with Evan Olcott?' Drews crossed the stream, stepping carefully on dry rocks.

'Give me a break, Cowboy Boots. I'm on my fucking own.'

'Dan Drews.'

The man's eyes narrowed at the name. He regarded Drews' outstretched hand as an exotic curiosity. With a sigh, he reached and shook it. 'Dave,' he said. 'Of Goa. Via Kathmandu and Poona. Actually, I may skip Goa. It all depends on Poona. You going to Goa?'

Drews shook his head.

'Where are you going?'

'I'm not sure.'

'Go on.'

Drews nodded.

'No shit,' said Dave. 'You got a car, a driver and, I don't know, credit cards and you don't know where you're going?' He gave a high laugh. 'Sort of says it all, doesn't it? I mean, when you don't have the wheels you get stuck on the road. But if you spend your life getting those wheels – and fucking *succeed!* I mean, you *get* your wheels, they're sitting there with engine racing and a full tank and, like, CD and everything – you forget where you want to go. Amazing, isn't it? I mean, you and me, man, sitting here on this rock: we're the world.'

'Tell me you don't have a credit card.'

'Here maybe.' Dave patted his pants pocket. 'But not here, man.' He placed a hand on his heart.

Drews touched his temple. 'What about here?'

'Chapter Eleven all the way.' Dave gave his hysterical laugh. 'And proud of it.'

'What are you doing in this place?'

'These are the Marabar caves. *The* Marabar caves.'

'I know.'

'This is boum land, Cowboy Boots. The heart of darkness, India style. Everybody has to come to the Marabar caves. To blow their noses. To scratch their matches. To squeak their boots. This is where our path ends, man. Or maybe where it begins. Yeah, where it begins.'

'Hope,' said Drews.

'Fucking politeness,' said Dave. 'Yeah, you've read the book. I got here Wednesday.'

'You've been here three days?'

Dave nodded.

'Where did you stay?'

He shrugged and rearranged the shirt drying on the rock.

'Christ,' said Drews. He walked around aimlessly. 'Is this place in the guidebooks?'

'The guidebooks?' Dave spoke dismissive. 'Douchebags' India. I mean the Taj Mahal: that's designer India. Ajanta and Ellora: fucking arts and crafts. Kitschy Rajasthan. Even Varanasi – I love Varanasi, the bhang shops on the river, man, you can spend years there – even Varanasi is a drag if you really think about it.' He touched his temple and stared at Drews aggressively. His eyes were so narrowly chiselled he might have been mixed-blood. 'I mean, what's the difference between Varanasi and Our Lady's fucking chapel? It's like lighting candles all day long, if you go deep. *Really* deep. Although no one took a shit in Our Lady's chapel. Not in my suburb, at least.'

Drews laughed.

'So, Cowboy Boots, what are you doing here?'

'I'm on a kind of tour.'

Dave shook his head.

'A special tour.' Drews' driver appeared and made a gesture. 'I think I have to go. Can I offer you a ride?'

Dave leaned over and felt his shirt. 'I don't think we're quite ready. And I think we're going opposite directions.'

'You don't know which direction I'm going.'

Dave laughed. 'Don't fool yourself, Cowboy Boots.' He leaned down and scooped water in a palm. He offered it to Drews.

'Is it safe?'

Dave gave an ironic look. 'Man, a little water isn't going to hurt us. Not at this point.'

Drews nodded and drank from the man's hand. Dave took another palmful and slurped it up. Water dribbled down his chin. He said: 'How's the magazine? Are you really being bought out?'

Drews stood back.

'Okay, okay, I should have said something. I'm Dave Erdman.'

'Dave Erdman from Bangkok?'

He nodded.

'You used to write for me.'

'You fired me,' Dave said. 'The old heave-ho. The lead handshake.'

'Yes.' Drews blinked. '*That* was long ago. During the Chinese invasion of Vietnam. You disappeared.'

'Yeah,' said Dave. 'I didn't have my act together in those days. I really didn't. I admit it. Personal problems, you know.'

'Where did you go? We never did find out.'

Dave shook his head.

'You don't want me to ask?'

'I'm not sure I recall. Somewhere poor. I think it was a city. There was definitely a girl involved. Yeah – a girl.'

'You were married to Dinah.'

'Yes indeedy,' said Dave.

'Did you really try to kill her? In Bangkok.'

'Oh man – that's *her* story. And it was KL, not Bangkok. And if you have to know, it was mutual, believe me. There were nights, I can tell you, I wondered – I really wondered – if I'd wake up in the morning. She'd slipped across the border, yes she had. The border that doesn't require any visa.'

'She married a banker, you know.'

'Major turkey.'

'They've adopted a baby.'

'What did I say?'

'Didn't you go to that energy wire in Singapore?'

'Oh man, don't remind me. Don't fucking *remind* me. That was a tragedy. Big housing allowance, swimming pool, expense account. I was free from Dinah at last: for the first time in years I could sleep with my eyes fucking closed. But man, I couldn't hack it. I thought I had my act together, but, well, you know. Also, I didn't know a *thing* about energy. They kept saying, "Dave, you got that story for us?" And I'd look at the light bulbs in the office and think: "What fucking story?" "Dave," they'd say, "that *story* . . ." They used to say it in my dreams. I mean, I was not into energy in the least.'

'Then what happened?'

'Oh, I went back to Bangkok. But, you know, Bangkok is a heavy scene. Indisputably heavy. It sort of sucks the life out of you, sucks it out real slowly. Not so slowly, actually. It sort of sucks it out immediately.' He made a loud sucking sound. 'And then the rest is drugs and sitting around in coffee shops with the girls and these really heavy hoods. Dangerous places those coffee shops. Those guys: they'd take your passport and then you kind of . . . disappeared. I saw it happen. These guys would come from Holland – always from Holland – and work as disc jockeys. And then: they'd be *gone*. Totally gone. Their parents would come looking for them, from Holland, and you'd see their pictures in *The Nation*. Heavy, white-haired fathers searching for their sons among whores and pimps and hoodlums. Back to Holland alone – *The Nation* never reported that – and then three months later there'd be another story, another photo of a white-haired Dutchman in *The Nation*. Even the journalists. Remember Chris Fallon?'

'Yeah,' said Drews. 'He wrote for us.'

Dave clicked his fingers. 'Without a trace. Ionosphere. His whole organism disintegrated into subparticles, man. Nothing left but his chromosomes lodged in little brown bastards in Patpong.'

'I thought Chris was at UPI in Utah.'

'Fuck.' Dave shook his head. 'Same thing.' His eyes narrowed. 'I thought his name was Chris Fallon. Or was it Malloy?'

'So where are you now?'

'I'm kind of in between addresses, if you know what I mean.'

'Are you still writing?'

'Of course.'

'Journalism?'

'Nah,' said Dave. 'That life didn't work out for me. I had trouble with the suspension of disbelief thing. The suspension kind of, you know, *gave*.'

'So what are you writing?'

'A novel, man. It's all right here.' He touched his temple again. 'It's inevitable. And everything's gonna be in it. Everything about us. You and me and the Pussycat and the rooms with the mirrors next to the beds and the sinks clogged with vomit and ... suspenders. Yes, fucking suspenders! And designer baseball caps. And shock guards for wrist-watches: indispensable for foreign correspondents, who lead very bruis-ing lives. And lots and lots of Asian girls.'

'The blow of the nose?'

'Yeah, drugs too, and Anton Vavasour and Tim Marquand and Claire Hollingworth and all of your buddies at the FCC, those guys who ball their amahs in the dead of night in the room behind the kitchen. "Her skin was smooth as silk ..." '

'And it will all go boum.'

Dave laughed. 'You're not as bad as I thought, Drews, I mean Cowboy Boots. I don't know if it'll go "boum", as in, you know.' He clicked his fingers. 'But we'll all go boom, that's for sure!' He raised his arms in a gesture of explosion. 'That's where we're all headed, isn't it? That's what this is all about, man! That's fucking life – I mean, after your thirties.'

The driver appeared again. Drews prepared to leave. 'Dave ...'

201

'Enjoy your tour, Cowboy Boots. Maybe we'll meet in Goa. Or the ashram in Poona.'

Drews crossed the stream and looked back. He called: 'Boum.' Dave winked a narrow, black eye. Drews passed the mud shrine with the trident within. Back in the car, he bumped over the unpaved trail. When the car passed the railroad station, the driver slowed and pointed. Drews saw a cow out the window. Above the cow a sign read 'Mayapur.'

The driver said something in Hindi. He seemed excited. 'Barabar!' he said. 'Barabar!'

And Drews realized that the presence he had felt in the second Barabar cave, the moment that had brought him closest to Forster's evil magic, was a cow. The puddle on the floor was cow piss.

The sun was failing and shadows slipped down the mountainsides in irregular, mossy parabolas absorbing everything in their paths. Darkness was triumphing and soon the hills and valley would be masked. Not obliterated, however, but transformed into velvet cushions for a miracle in the making: a city high in the sky! A constellation of artificial stars was flung across the violet mountain range, which wavered through the final heat of a summer's day or, during winter, through viscous mists. It was a remarkable piece of magic that occurred every evening signalling that the dark Indian night wasn't quite so opaque or impenetrable, or not always or everywhere – not here, at least, for there were diamonds studding the clouds.

Deep in the valley, Evan Olcott stood on the highest point of his crumbling palace with his back to the lengthening shadows. The nightly magic didn't affect him. Evan's habit was to dismiss the city in the sky with a practised phrase. 'The British built it to get away from the wogs. Like all hill stations.' Or: 'It must have been considerably more enchanting before fluorescent light.' His life's desire was to unmask magic in the sky or on the earth. He stood with his back to the shadows, to the heavenly city coming to life, his eyes on the road leading from the plain.

'Soon, sahib,' whispered a moustached, middle-aged Indian man standing close beside him. 'There's no need for worry. They'll be here soon.'

'It must be the traffic.'

The Indian man nodded agreement, as he did for all of Evan's utterances. One hand fiddled nervously with the disintegrated cement of the balustrade; the other adjusted his shiny leather belt. 'The government says the new road has helped. But the truckers say it's costing them lakhs in . . .'

Evan turned and walked toward the stairs. 'Call me, Rajinder, when they've come.'

The Indian man followed him solicitously, talking rapidly about the preparations. Evan raised a hand.

'We've gone through it all, Rajinder. Everything should be ready.' He walked carefully down a set of deteriorated steps. At a lower rooftop he paused for breath.

'If I hadn't bought the vegetables personally . . .' Rajinder grabbed the old man's elbow. 'That bloody vendor . . .'

Evan lifted a weary hand. 'Bring some chairs up. I think we'll have cocktails on the roof.'

'Imported?' asked Rajinder gravely.

'Local.' Evan stooped through a stone doorway and concentrated on a flight of narrow, unlit steps. He faltered briefly and Rajinder tightened his grip on the old man's elbow. 'It's all Indian for our guest.'

The two men stopped suddenly. They heard a motor sound. Then shouts from the garden. Evan turned his head, a tight smile visible in the close stairwell.

'They're here,' said Rajinder.

'He's here,' lisped Evan. He turned clumsily in the narrow passage, pushing Rajinder aside. 'I'll be waiting on the roof. Please have Bhawani bring the chairs. Manoj can get the glasses and the ice and the rum.'

'What about the documents?'

'Leave them where they are for now.' Evan squeezed past. Rajinder watched him climb slowly back to the square-cut doorway. He paused at the top, out of breath. 'I have a few last hoops for our guest to go through.'

Drews said to the pockmarked driver: 'This is Evan Olcott's place?'

The driver yanked the parking brake. He turned in his seat. 'Okay!'

Drews pulled himself from the car, his back aching, and walked a few steps toward a rambling whitewashed structure. It was a grand palace, or formerly grand, built in sections over the centuries. The entrance was a scalloped plaster arch over a plank door with brass inlays. Above it was an aged wooden balcony with trestles and hanging bougainvillea. From the main wing jutted a variety of extensions in different shapes and different colours. Drews turned and walked in the opposite direction. He saw square green fields studded with irregularly spaced trees shrinking into the distance. He returned his gaze to the house and looked up: directly above the house was a city slung across the mountaintops. The lights were coming on, shining like some celestial decoration in honour of his visit.

'You are most welcome. Most very welcome. We were just waiting for you.'

Drews turned and saw an Indian man with a thin moustache, eager eyes and an exaggerated ramrod posture. He was dressed in pressed grey slacks, a white shirt and a club tie. His black oxfords were highly polished. A hand shot out and Drews received a lengthy, hard handshake.

'I was admiring the view.'

'It's a hill station.' The man moved closer to Drews. 'Haven't you been to our hill stations? We've so many hill stations in India. Mussorie, Ooty, Nainital. We can go there tomorrow.' He pointed to the mountaintop. 'It's not a long drive.' He shook his head to dispel this unspoken misapprehension. 'Not long at all. You will enjoy the beautiful vistas.'

'I can't imagine they're prettier than this. It's one of the most amazing things I've ever seen.' The Indian man continued to nod in agreement. 'It reminds me . . .' Drews lowered his gaze to the palace. On the rooftop he saw a head with white hair. The head pulled back. Drews looked to the Indian man, who had witnessed the same scene.

'Evan?'

'Mr Olcott is awaiting you. As I told you before, we've just been waiting. This is a big occasion for us.'

'For me too.' Drews checked the rooftop but it was empty.

'We have few visitors.' The man's voice dropped confidentially. 'Mr Olcott prefers to be alone.'

'You've been with Evan for a long time?'

The man nodded with satisfaction, placing a fist in the small of his back. 'We've been here for nearly fifteen years. My name is Rajinder. Major Rajinder Rana. Ex-army.'

Drews gave a mock salute. Rajinder, pleased, took a step closer.

'Does Evan own this place?'

'I'm afraid I can't answer a question such as that. There are laws, you know, here in India.' He looked around suspiciously, as if the police or the very Indian Army might be hidden in the bushes. 'You'll have to ask Mr Olcott. Once the slightest suspicion gets out . . .' He looked Drews in the eye. Drews looked back, waiting for the sentence's conclusion.

Rajinder winked. Then he rubbed his thumb and forefinger together. He smiled as if the gesture brought him pleasure.

'I see,' said Drews.

The man suddenly grabbed Drews' elbow and held it firmly. He pointed at the main wing and whispered: 'This part is ours.' He pointed at one of the extensions and shook his head with disgust. 'Not that part.' He fixed Drews with a look that demanded the deepest sympathy.

'Not that part,' Drews repeated, pulling subtly to break the grasp on his elbow.

'My uncle,' Rajinder whispered. He pointed at the extension on the other side. 'And that's his brother.'

Drews went to the car. He reached inside for his overnighter. He felt Rajinder's hand on his arm.

'That'll be taken care of.' Rajinder shouted suddenly: 'Manoj!'

'Let's go.' Drews walked toward the main door. He stopped suddenly. 'You might have had one visitor. Back in 1977. Tim Marquand. From Hong Kong.'

'Oh yes.' Rajinder was obviously delighted by the memory. 'Mr Marquand came long, long ago. He enjoyed himself very much. Very much. He helped us renovate. We were expanding the section for the cows. That part.' He pointed. 'I remember him singing all the time. Very lovely singing voice.'

Drews smiled.

'What was the song? An old song. He was singing it when he cleaned the cow pens.'

Drews laughed. 'Well, Timmy could shovel it with the best.'

'He was a lovely man. Yes, quite a lovely man. Enjoyed his food. And his drink.'

'He died last year.' Drews spoke bluntly. 'Of liver disease.'

Rajinder shook his head knowingly. 'Everyone dies. Not only in India but everywhere else. Everyone dies. And if it's not the liver, it's the heart. And if it's not the heart . . .'

'Yes.'

'And the doctors.' Rajinder spoke with awe. 'The bills!'

Fatuous idiot, thought Drews. *I hope this isn't part of Evan's philosophy lesson.*

They climbed wide plastered stairs. 'The electricity,' said Rajinder. 'It should come on soon. But India's a very poor country . . .'

On the second floor they went past a succession of empty rooms and silent, staring servants, frozen like statues in gestures of work: stirring, polishing, bending to haul something heavy. There was a spartan bedroom and a sitting room with an old, upholstered couch and a carved stone mantelpiece. A carbine was fixed on one wall. Rajinder waved Drews onto a patio completely circumscribed by blue plastered walls.

'This is a bit of a secret.' Rajinder opened a wooden door. 'A secret passage from the old days.'

They entered a narrow flight of stone steps. Rajinder grabbed Drews' elbow from behind. 'Mr Olcott is fond of the rooftop.' His voice boomed in the close space. 'He comes up here all the time. Summer, winter. He sits looking at the mountains, hour upon hour, and laughs.'

'He laughs?' Drews stopped climbing.

'Yes.' Rajinder spoke fondly, as if swapping tales of a mutually admired genius. 'Laughs.'

'Lots of laughs in . . . what's the name of this place?'

'Mayapur.'

Drews turned in the close stairwell, pulling his elbow from Rajinder's grasp. 'Mayapur? But that's miles away. Where the Barabar Hills are.'

'Mayapur is the name of this.' Rajinder slapped one of the stone walls. 'Mr Olcott named it. Fourteen years ago. Just the house. Our section. The town is Tanda. And the district is . . .'

Drews came out of the stone tunnel. The first things he saw were pinpricks of light on the mountaintop, stronger now, a delicate crown in the sky. Below them was the palace in all its confused glory. From the outside, it had appeared a feudal fortress: the forces inside defended from those without. But from above, it had a new aspect. It was a vast labyrinth designed by a civilization waging war within. There were numerous wings, all separated; there were rooms at all levels with tiny windows; countless courtyard patios, all empty except for a few tired dogs. Running up the centre of the palace was a narrow, brown channel, presumably for drainage. The walls were bird's-egg blue in one wing, cream yellow in the next, green in the adjacent. The roofs were browned with age and dirt: some were plaster, others corrugated iron with bricks and scrap metal dumped on top against the wind. Rajinder waved Drews to a small series of steps open to the sky. Drews climbed. He reached a square rooftop, the pinnacle of the palace. Directly opposite was a white-haired man sitting in a lawn chair. The man's back was to Drews. His gaze was

207

not on the mountaintops but straight before him at a stained wall. Above him, unseen, was the artificial constellation, blinking for attention.

'Evan.'

The old man's head jerked as if with surprise. He stood slowly and turned. The city in the sky hovered above him. Evan extended both arms. 'My dear boy, I've just been thinking of you.'

Drews felt Rajinder close behind him. He said: 'Tim Marquand never wrote a diary.'

'Is that how you greet your old chairman? After such a long time? Such a challenging trip?' He cleared his throat. 'Such interesting times, as our Chinese friends say. Interesting for you. Interesting for me. Interesting for *Orientweek*.'

'Evan – you know why I'm here. What's all this crap about Tim's diary?'

' "Timmy", I think you mean. I think that's what you called him.' Evan shifted his chair with a faltering hand. 'Timmy and Danny. How we heard about them all those years in Hong Kong. The names that were on everyone's lips. The journalists of our generation. And a lovely couple to boot. As long as it lasted.' He motioned abruptly. 'Come, dear boy, come sit.' Rajinder rushed over and positioned a second chair for Drews. 'We'll go through all that later. In the meantime, shall we watch the sunset together?'

'There's no diary.' Drews slapped his arm suddenly.

'It's mosquito time. Gets worse with the heat.' Evan paused to regain his train of thought. 'No, Daniel, alas, there's no diary. That was a bit of a fib. As I think you knew from the start.'

'I did not.'

Evan chuckled. 'Hope springs eternal. Usually in a somewhat younger breast.'

Drews turned and walked to the steps.

'The car is gone.'

Drews looked to the old man. Evan's face was expressionless. He walked to the edge of the roof. The car had departed.

'No need for ugly looks. I fooled you about the diary. I wish there *had* been one – things might have been much easier.' Evan lowered himself into the chair, craning his neck to address Drews. 'We have other things to discuss, Daniel. Do you mind if I call you that? I think we should get beyond this "Drews" business. I always found it a bit boarding-school.' His eyes connected with Drews'. 'Come sit with an old man.' He patted the empty chair. 'We have things to discuss. The magazine. Other things. I have many memories of Tim I'd like to share with you. From here.' He gestured to the mountaintops. 'Will you join me?'

Drews walked slowly toward the chair.

'Rajinder? Please leave us for a while. Manoj will bring the drinks? And some coils? The mosquitoes are bothering our guest.'

Rajinder retired reluctantly, shooting Drews a smile. Drews stood over Evan. 'Just tell me what this is all about.'

Evan gestured at the city above them. 'It's about that, Daniel.' He gestured at the landscape in the opposite direction. Drews saw a smoke-stack protruding from a field. 'It's about that.'

'A finger in the mouth? And caves . . .'

Evan laughed a bony, satisfied laugh. 'A finger in the mouth. I did like that.' He slapped his knee. 'Sit, boy, sit. We have all the time in the world.' A servant deposited a tray on a table. Another squatted to light a mosquito coil. 'And the nail in the head. *Incomparable*. Have you had the Indian rum?' Evan poured rum. 'Boiled water.' He poured from a thick, ceramic pitcher. 'You can't be too careful, especially near the hills.'

'I didn't come for drinks.'

Evan looked at Drews with disappointment.

'What is that?' Drews pointed at a far corner of the palace, where a shadow protruded from a pillared pavilion. 'That bird.'

'That, dear boy, is a buzzard. Our pet bird in this district.' Evan laughed. 'You come to enjoy them over time. *Memento mori*, so to speak.'

Drews took the seat beside Evan. 'Vultures?'

'Did you know they live to ninety?'

The bird was motionless with relaxed, heavy wings and a sinuous neck. Its tiny head was watching something in the distance.

'You don't chase them away?'

'Lovely birds. Very gentle.'

'They don't cause . . . trouble?'

Evan shook his head. 'And no one bothers them, you know. That's very unusual in India. It's live and let live for the buzzards and the buzzards alone. Did you know it's the only bird humans can't digest?' He looked at the motionless bird. 'Presumably that's why they are left undisturbed.'

'Creepy fuckers.'

'I've often wondered,' sighed Evan, 'what they would say if they could talk. What if God had given them a tongue, instead of, say, the idiotic parakeets? We have them too – they like that particular tree.' He stared at the buzzard. 'I don't know about the rest of you, but I'd listen.' Mosquitoes hovered around Evan's hair like a halo.

Suddenly Rajinder was beside them, smiling hopefully. 'You called?'

Evan, watching the buzzard, gave a small smile.

Rajinder looked to Drews. 'You didn't call?'

Drews looked at Evan.

'It must have been the peacocks, Rajinder.' Evan turned his gaze, fixing Drews with an odd look. 'They dance on these balconies when it rains. There, there and there.' His hand pointed.

'Really?'

Evan nodded. 'Personally, I prefer the buzzards.'

'You didn't call?' asked Rajinder.

'Rajinder, I'm sure Manoj needs some help.' Rajinder walked away backwards, hoping for a last-minute reprieve. When he was gone, Drews said: 'He's been with you for fifteen years?'

'Retired from the army. A very loyal man. Indian to the core. All his values in the right place.'

'Where is that?'

Evan laughed sardonically. 'In his hip pocket.'

Drews saw the mental snapshots passing by his automobile window: the women on the construction sites in gaudy saris, the men on bullock carts with twisted dhotis. 'Most Indians don't even have hip pockets.'

Evan turned again to the buzzard. He guffawed. 'Balls,' he said.

The two men sat unspeaking as the night descended. Evan had his hands folded in his lap. The cloud of mosquitoes buzzed around his hair. Drews was sprawled with his legs crossed at the ankle. His intention was to make Evan uncomfortable. But the old man seemed content sitting on his rooftop watching nothing. At one point he began to hum along to the film music issuing from servants' huts below. Suddenly he sighed. He rose and walked to the edge of the roof. He looked up at the city in the sky.

Drews slapped his arm.

'The coil.' Evan spoke in a low voice, staring in the opposite direction. 'It has died.' His voice dropped away.

What is he thinking, Drews wondered. *What's going on?*

Evan clapped his hands suddenly. He moved behind Drews and grasped his shoulders.

'Please, Daniel, relax tonight and enjoy the famous hospitality of India. You're our guest. And I want to talk to you. I want to tell you about India. My India – the India I introduced to Tim. No, there is no diary. I admit that was a somewhat cruel trick. But it worked: you are here, where your friend was, at this house, twelve years ago. I have memories you will enjoy. You were his closest friend, after all. You should know what Tim learned here.'

Drews nodded hesitantly.

'I remember those evenings.' Evan squeezed fingers into Drews' flesh. 'Tim talked about you. About your meeting in London. Your landlady – a Mrs Bottom, I recall. Albert Court. I strolled by it once to take a look. More than once actually. That wall between your bedrooms. Yes, the wall. Tim was much taken with walls. Your deep "friendship".' Evan lifted a hand and ran it lightly through the end of Drews' curls. Drews froze in his chair. 'Sweet stories – I remember them all. Word for word. Let's reminisce tonight, you and I. I'll write you Tim Marquand's India diary. In his words.' The old man's hand rose in the dusk. 'Words written on the evening air! With the stars as our company. The stars and . . . that!' He motioned to the city in the sky. 'Isn't that better than an old notebook?'

Drews rose awkwardly from his chair. But Evan was determined. He threw an arm around his shoulder.

'But tell me, dear boy, how have you found India?'

Buck Frye was trying his best to be assertive but the taxi-wallahs at Claridge's Hotel had the advantage. They were tall and robust with brilliant turbans and sumptuous beards. They negotiated en masse. Two were dressed in loincloths, having just finished evening baths. They coiled their hair as Buck listed his demands. Ostensibly the men agreed with everything Buck requested, including the best car at their disposal, perfectly maintained, and the most talented driver. 'He must speak English,' Buck insisted, stamping a cardboard loafer in the gravel. 'I can't bring these people to the depths of India and get lost with a driver who doesn't speak a word of English!' He received a torrent of assurances, pledges of obedience accompanied by large hands placed reverently on beefy breasts. 'No problem' was the key promise, repeated liturgically. 'No problem, sahib.' But years of experience had taught Buck to expect any old car the following morning. The driver would be the most junior, thanks to the early starting time, with no concept of geography outside his native Punjab. He wouldn't speak a word of English and his driving skills would be wretched. The Naversens would spend the entire ride with hands covering their eyes, horns blasting terrifyingly in their ears. And Buck would be blamed. He imagined a box to his ears from Fran along with rudely personal comments from Nick. Perhaps they would cut his fee. Buck's fears were confirmed when he marched away from the taxi stand with the utmost grace and courage. Behind him he heard the sound of manly Punjabi laughter.

He met the Naversens in the Chinese restaurant.

'It's all arranged,' he said breathlessly. 'Tomorrow at 5.30.'

'You're sure they know the route?' Fran, mouth full, didn't offer Buck a seat.

'They said so,' said Buck nervously. 'I pointed it out on a map. It seems somewhat straightforward. Until we get to the mountains.'

Fran's chopsticks froze in the air. 'Who said anything about mountains?'

Nick groaned. 'Bloody Evan. Mountains, yet.'

Buck shifted from foot to foot. 'We don't actually go into the mountains . . .'

'God willing,' said Fran.

'Tyres willing,' said Nick. 'First thing tomorrow, Big Girl, get out your knee pads and check those treads.'

Prentice McGuinn enjoyed a better rapport with the taxi men of New Delhi. He had a swagger they enjoyed. He spoke several words of Punjabi, including a few curses. They approved of the steel bracelet he wore on his left wrist. So he was welcomed at the Claridge's taxi stand. He sat on a charpoy and got all the information he needed. Someone helpfully fetched a map. Then he slapped some backs, took a final draw on an old man's hookah and returned triumphantly to the hotel lobby.

Where he ran into Buck Frye.

'What are you doing here?' Buck pulled Prentice to a dark corner of the lobby.

'I'm waiting for my wife, Buck.'

As if on cue, Gail McGuinn came through the lobby, throwing her frizzy hair over her shoulder. She approached the two men.

'Are you spying on me?' Buck whispered. 'This is *my* job. Don't you go and ruin it for me. You've got a salary, after all. Or at least you do.' He pointed accusingly at Gail. 'I'm a freelancer. These kinds of jobs don't come along very often.' He pondered. 'Any kind of job, these days.'

Gail said: 'I don't know what you're talking about. We've come for a drink. We have to discuss a big story I'm working on.'

'All of your stories are big stories.'

'Hey, buddy.' Prentice grabbed Buck's shirt collar. 'That's my wife.'

Buck's jaw started to quiver. 'I don't believe you two. Just let go.' He wrenched himself free and walked prissily across the lobby and out into the night.

'Well?' asked Gail.

Prentice smiled. 'I've got the information. They leave tomorrow at 5.30.'

The two conferred.

'Arrange our car,' said Gail, 'from the same stand.'

'Done already.'

'Make sure our driver is related to theirs. His cousin or brother.'

'Did New York call?'

'They're fired. But they're giving me a first-class runaround on the Bangla women story. They want to shrink it to a box. Can you believe that?'

'Fuckers.'

Gail stood, shaking her head. 'I'll go tell the Hong Kong group. Give me ten minutes.'

'They can't be late,' Prentice warned. 'We have to leave exactly on time.'

Gail turned back. 'They'll be ready.'

'That is your room, Daniel.' Evan pointed over the rooftops to a square structure jutting from a far wall of the palace. It was a single room set behind cream-coloured columns. A rusted antenna protruded from its top. Directly below was an enclosed garden with vines climbing an arch. Beneath the garden on the ground floor was a series of walls punctured with holes to form screens; another courtyard containing a well, a hand pump and several plastic buckets; and then the long, narrow central channel of the palace, equipped with narrow gullies on either side and enclosed by walls stained an evil brown.

'What is that?'

'The house's guts,' Evan replied. 'That's the only common part of the whole place. Everything passes from there. I wouldn't advise a visit. But your room – shall we see it before dinner?'

Evan led Drews through the labyrinth, down long columns of steps, up shorter sequences, down again.

'Who designed this place? A madman?'

'History,' Evan said, 'was our architect. Watch this portion here.' The old man stepped gingerly. 'With proper vision you could see the history of an old, noble family in this structure, my boy.' He stopped, and raised his arms. 'The history of India – the history of mankind!'

They ascended a spiral staircase with chute-like walls.

'Finally.' Evan was out of breath. 'Quite a climb, this part.' He threw open a pair of plank doors. It was a simple room with blue-green walls. In the centre, as if enshrined, was a narrow bed with a dangling mosquito net gathered in a pink knot. Next to the bed was a table covered with a white cloth. There was a recessed area above the bed with a statue of a cow. There was only one window. Its shutters were closed. 'The loo is over there. That's why we've put you up here. It's isolated.'

They left the room and stood between two columns, gazing over the variegated palace. 'It's an interesting story,' Evan said, 'complicated on

215

the surface but simple at heart.' He described a landowning family, revered as lords by villages reaching to the far horizon – in an older time. Then India gained its independence. Land reform cost the family its fields, its serfs and its future. The patriarch died and the brothers fell out. Finally, one of the brothers died mysteriously. 'He died in that room. See?' Evan pointed. 'The one with the light. Poison, presumably.' The murdered man's second wife claimed ownership of the entire palace on behalf of her sons.

'How?' said Drews. 'I thought it was divided among the brothers?'

'Apparently our patriarch was sloppy in his legal formalities.' The three branches of the family became mortal enemies and walls were erected dividing the palace in three. 'Rajinder was in the middle.' Evan sighed. 'These things get very complicated. Everyone said he should relinquish his claim because he has no children.'

'He never married?'

'It didn't last. When I met him he needed money to fix this part. Army salary, you know. For legal reasons the house had to be physically occupied. I gave the money and lived here a good part of the year. We signed papers. Now we are partners. Legal partners, you understand.'

'He divorced?'

'No,' Evan said. 'He's never considered it.'

'Why?'

'He refuses to pay the lawyers.'

'And that's how it stands in the family?'

'Heavens no,' Evan chuckled. 'The evil second wife was usurped by one of the brothers. Terrible scene. I was here. Threw her right out of the place. Furniture and all. Tremendous hollering.' The wife took the ultimate revenge, Evan said: she sold her rights to the place – the entire structure – to a local farmer. 'A "new Indian". Love that term. Man with piles of money, political connections, a gang of hoodlums. That, dear boy, is the "new Indian". The case has been going on for years.'

'And they live like enemies?'

'Actually, the court case has pulled the family together. Understand: the house can't go to someone from the village. That's impossible. This family used to rule this area. They were kings. They can't lose their ancestral land to a farmer, a former serf. This family had a glorious past – their Original Age, let's say – and, for them, it's simply too soon to leave. There are certain caste considerations but let's not get into that.'

'So the cousins are on good terms?'

'Not exactly. Each has their own telephone. Their own servants. Their own televisions.' He gestured at the antennas on the roofs. 'They never visit one another. And there's no common entertainment, of course.' He paused. 'Not since the poisoning.'

'It's terrible,' said Drews.

'But please,' said Evan, 'don't say anything to Rajinder. Especially about his poisoned father.'

'His father?'

Evan nodded.

'So Rajinder's stepmother is fighting the case?'

'Indeed.'

'He died over there,' Drews pointed. 'The room with the light. He was poisoned by that brother? The brother from that wing?'

Evan shrugged. 'The details, my boy, are not important. Only the essence.'

It was totally dark. From the opposite rooftop, they heard a call.

'That's Rajinder. Dinner is ready. I'll lock up.'

They descended through a different set of blackened corridors and stairwells – 'Hold the wall,' Evan instructed, old man's fear in his voice – until they reached a courtyard on the ground floor. Rajinder awaited them. They exited the palace. A table was set up beneath a clump of trees.

'That's my family temple,' Rajinder said. 'You will see it tomorrow.' Servants stood at attendance. A few steps away were curious children and adults.

'Are they villagers?' asked Drews.

'Please, get comfortable. More coils, Rajinder.' Evan turned. 'It's always amazed me. Even in the greatest heat the mosquitoes survive. Great surviving machines.'

Drews pointed to the city hovering in the sky. 'It reminds me of Hong Kong. The Peak.'

'A bit,' Evan said.

'A Hong Kong that is . . . cut free. That floats above all the . . . I don't know.'

Evan chuckled. 'Rootless. Yes, a rootless Hong Kong. What a charming notion, Daniel. I think this was your glass.'

A servant scooped food onto plates. Another brought hot, flat breads.

Drews started to eat and Evan said: 'Now, Daniel, tell me: what did you see in your room. In Delhi.'

Drews' hand, with a piece of gravy-dunked bread, descended to his plate. He looked at Evan curiously.

'Yes,' Evan said. 'Let's start.'

Drews said: 'India?'

'Well, yes, India.' Evan nodded. 'But tell me about the room.'

Drews put the bread in his mouth and chewed slowly, looking at the city in the sky. He swallowed and, without looking at Evan, said: 'It was a medium-sized room, neat but dirty, tall ceiling with a patterned curtain that disguised a storage space. Double bed, primus stove, table – a low, Southeast Asian-type of platform table – a sewing machine. Perhaps the wife makes money sewing. Books – many books – but not real books, trade books. The walls were interesting. Stained in an odd way. Very evocative stains.'

Evan sat back in his chair with his eyes closed. 'Yes, the stains. Like clouds. You can see anything in them. At night. What did you see? Let me hear, Daniel. What did you *see*?'

And so it began. The two men talked in a low, emotionless murmur. The servants went back and forth with food, bread, pitchers of water, bottles of amber rum. The villagers watched in respectful silence. The night was black with only a few sources of light. Yellow auras from the thick-walled palace windows; in the valley, a fluorescent tubelight in a farmer's house; the lights of the hill station above, crowning it all.

'. . . a room for small lives,' Drews said. 'But there was nothing evil, Evan. No nail through the brain. I got to like the room. I felt at home.'

'Exactly.' Evan sounded satisfied.

'What was I supposed to feel, Evan? What about the finger in the mouth, the nail in the head? What was all that crap?'

'That was Africa. The heart of darkness. I wanted you to feel the contrast. This is India, my boy. India is no heart of darkness. No indeed. Quite the opposite. That's my point exactly. You get a star.'

They discussed Khassi colony, the land of dust and crumbling brick, where untouchables traded their fertility for housing.

'In the end it seemed like just a story to me.'

'A story?' Evan sounded surprised. 'A fairy story?'

'No,' said Drews. 'A *story*. Journalism. You know: politics, corruption, exploitation. The same old story.'

'You didn't feel sorry for the poor people?'

'Of course. Anybody would. But in the end, I mean, it was nothing but . . .'

'What?'

'Money.'

Evan smiled in the darkness.

'I felt the same about that cabaret. You were there, weren't you? That night?'

Evan nodded.

'I mean, the women were sad and disgusting and angry.' Drews stopped. 'That was unusual: the anger. But it was all a matter of money. No heart of darkness. No heart at all. Just trade. Everything was . . . sort of flat.'

'Shiny, colourful, a great surface,' said Evan. More film music issued from the workers' huts. 'That's India, my boy. The great surface. Durable. Extremely durable. Plastic shoes – did you notice, by any chance, the popularity of plastic shoes in India? And what about my Barabar caves?'

'I couldn't get anything from them,' Drews said. 'They were nothing.' He raised his glass to his mouth. 'Except for the echo. That was extra-ordinary.'

' "Utterly dull," ' said Evan. ' "Hope, politeness, the squeak of a boot." That's what Forster wrote. The squeak of a plastic shoe, I would add. "All produce 'boum'." I wish I had shown Tim the caves. But I hadn't discovered them. Everyone who comes to India should see them. Instead of the Taj Mahal.'

It was the servants' turn to eat. They squatted at a distance, sharing their food with the villagers. Rajinder interrupted to light another mosquito coil. He smiled at Drews and withdrew.

Evan had become silent. Drews noticed a smile on his face.

'Did she sleep with you? In the room?'

Drews looked at him.

'Well?'

He nodded.

'I know that couple, or, I should say, their parents. Nice young people. Saving money – daughter has some medical problem. Very enterprising. Love marriage, which is unusual.'

Drews said: 'Sanjiv. And . . .'

Evan shook his head. 'Can't recall.'

Drews thought: *I never asked her name.*

'I hope she didn't take more than a hundred rupees. That was my specific instruction.'

Drews realized: *Evan arranged everything. Even the sex. All with money.* He spoke in an angry tone. 'You know, I think this has gone . . .'

Evan raised a commanding hand. He called Rajinder. 'I think it's time for you to bring those documents from my room, if you don't mind.' Rajinder rushed away. 'Don't be angry, Daniel. I have something important for you.' Several silent minutes went by. Evan tapped the arm of his chair to the beat of distant music. Rajinder appeared before them, breathless and smiling, holding two documents with blue backing. He proffered them to Evan.

Evan motioned to Drews. 'They're for him anyway.'

Rajinder reverently placed the documents in Drews' hands.

'This is . . .'

'A proxy, dear boy. Made out in your name.' Evan leaned over and poured himself another drink. 'I've decided to give you my vote. So your precious magazine is saved. It won't be sold.'

Drews turned to the second document. Rajinder stepped forward to explain: 'Copy.'

Drews flipped to the final page. 'It's not signed.' He checked the second document. 'This one too.'

'We have time, Daniel, for the formalities.'

'But why? Why are you giving me the proxy?'

'Let's say old time's sake.'

'I'm sure the Naversens offered you money.'

'My needs are different from other people's. I'm sure you know that.'

Drews looked doubtful.

The old man put his hand on Drews' shoulder. 'I own this place.' He gestured expansively, taking in the black hills and the invisible farmlands in the valley. 'With Rajinder, of course.'

Rajinder nodded eagerly. He smiled as a parent encourages a child to thank someone for a gift.

'I don't get it.' Drews shook his head. 'You brought the Naversens to New Delhi. In April – when you called me here. I met them. The only reasons they would have come . . .'

'My negotiations with the Naversens took a rather humiliating turn.'

Evan spoke with disdain. 'At my age. I'd rather not go into it. Have nothing to do with them.'

Drews laid the documents in his lap and looked out at the valley. 'I'm not sure I believe this, Evan. The magazine is saved? So easy?'

Evan gave a strange smile, displaying his overlapped front teeth.

'And then this tour of India? Fingers in mouths, women paid to sleep with me ...'

'In a room with stained walls.' Evan leaned back in his chair. 'I pictured the two of you in that room. Sitting up there.' He pointed. 'But that's something entirely different, my boy. That's education. This' – he leaned to pat the documents – 'is mere business. The future.' Evan clicked fingers and Rajinder removed the documents from Drews' hands. 'Of course, I'd expect to be retained as chairman. But we can complete the formalities tomorrow. Tonight I want to talk more about India. About Tim. I introduced him to that poem, you know. *"Roses, wine, a friend to share ..."* '

'Of course,' said Drews.

'We sat here night after night talking. He should have written a diary. He was very impressed with my vision. But I believe he took that poem in the wrong spirit. Misunderstood. What I mean is I'm rather sure I failed to make my *point*. But now, Daniel, here, with you ...'

Rajinder interrupted. Behind him stood a semicircle of shadowed figures. The villagers, Rajinder said, wanted to meet the new sahib. Drews stood awkwardly. The villagers drew closer, their faces emerging from the night. They raised hands in salaams. Drews responded with a low, Japanese bow. One of the men stepped forward with a bottle. The other men laughed. The women drew veils over smiles. Drews leaned backward, raised eyebrows at Evan and collected his glass. They bustled him to a charpoy and started pouring. The sound level rose and Rajinder struggled to interpret all the questions. Someone produced an instrument. There was a shout: the transistor radio was silenced. The sound of a single flute began in the darkness. A child ran from the row of houses, holding something. Then a second flute joined in. More voices rose. Additional children appeared. All the usual questions were asked of the visitor: age, marital status, number of children. The men slapped Drews' muscular shoulders with approval. The women remarked on his beard and his boots. Drews' glass was filled and refilled and he grabbed the bottle to reciprocate the courtesy. Ultimately, he was standing, his back to the house and his head thrown soulfully back.

'*Met her on the mountain*,' he sang. '*Then I killed her with my knife.*' He stabbed downwards. The children recoiled with alarm. The men applauded. Drews commanded Rajinder to interpret the lyrics.

> ... *About this time tomorrow*
> *Reckon where I'll be*
> *Down in Lonesome Valley*
> *Hanging from the old oak tree.*

Under his tree, Evan sat like a statue. Drews finished the song, grabbed his bottle and returned. He tried to fill Evan's drink. But it was full.

'This is wonderful!'

Evan looked up at him.

'Why don't you join us, Evan?'

'I had hoped . . .'

Drews threw himself in his chair. 'It was like this in Delhi, you know. In Sanjiv's house.'

Evan turned with an interested expression.

'The final evening we had a party.' Drews scrabbled underneath the chair. 'Can you find that pitcher?' Evan passed the water jug. 'The whole neighbourhood crowded into my room. Sanjiv's room. This is the last of the water.' Drews laid the jug on the ground.

'I'll tell Rajinder.'

Drews described the party in the room with the stained walls: the music, the drinking, the women huddled excitedly in the corner. He told of the children and their solemn disco dance. Drews' voice dropped to an excited whisper. 'The wife – you know, Sanjiv's wife – it wasn't what you planned, Evan. She enjoyed herself. With me. She didn't do it for the money. At the end, she refused it. They weren't greedy people. I hadn't known Indians were so warm.'

'Christ.'

'Honestly.' Drews was called back to the group. The music had become raunchy, with drums and a harmonium. Drews joined a group of men dancing wildly. Evan balanced a drink motionlessly in his hand. Suddenly he hurled the glass to the ground. He struggled to stand. Rajinder rushed over and Evan hissed at him: 'Never bloody mind.'

Rajinder collected the jug on the ground and started to trot toward the house.

'Rajinder.'

He halted and turned.

'Come *over* here.' Evan wrenched the jug from his hands. '*I'll* get the bloody water.' Evan marched toward the house. Rajinder followed. 'Go back to the group!' Evan continued his slow walk to the palace.

The kitchen was empty. Evan slammed the jug on an old table. He picked up a wooden spoon and threw it, with a shaky overhand, at the far wall.

'Disco dancing! Parties! Tender bedmates!' He strode to the window. Drews had started singing again, his arms outstretched in hammy passion. The villagers and servants were clapping. Rajinder was tapping his foot. No one noticed the white-haired man leaning out of the square, yellow window.

'Thick as a plank!' A sleepy man appeared in a low doorway, one of the junior kitchenboys. Evan shouted: 'Bugger off!' The man disappeared.

Evan steadied himself against a wall. He started talking in a low, urgent undertone.

'The man has an iron skull. He's hooked on love and kittens and . . . disco dancing.' Evan paused with a hand on his chest. He started to chuckle. 'I offer the view of life. And instead' – the hand weaved through the air – 'he sees dirty little urchins dancing to a Japanese radio!' And there he stood, arm poised, barely breathing, for a very long time. Then Evan Olcott's head nodded several times. He returned to the wooden table and reverently picked up the water jug. He crossed to a doorway leading from the kitchen. He scrabbled for a light switch. A small bulb illuminated a blackened, furniture-less dungeon. The floor was scattered with brass cooking pots. Evan stooped to a tap and filled the jug until it overflowed. He straightened, wiped a hand on his vest and exited the room, carefully extinguishing the light.

He spoke to the empty room, his tone one of reason. 'You simply haven't understood. And in such a case, the lesson will have to be hammered in.' From the window the scene was unchanged. Drews was winding up the final verse of 'Joe Cool' in Spanish. Standing in the middle of the empty kitchen, Evan raised the water jug. 'I'm so sorry, dear boy. But we have far to go. There isn't that much time.'

Evan walked from his palace with slow dignity. He circled around the tree and went straight for Drews, who reclined on a charpoy with his arm around the shoulders of one of the servants. Drews was talking. Evan stood before him holding the pitcher.

'Drink, dear boy. This is all the entertainment we have here.'

Drews struggled to sit. 'I know you want to talk . . .'

Evan shook his head. 'Drink now. We will talk tomorrow. All day.'

The villagers opened a new rum bottle. 'Not too much,' said Drews.

'Let him have a lot of water,' said Evan, filling the glass.

Rajinder rushed over with Evan's glass. He took the water jug from the old man.

Evan shook his head. 'Tonight I'll take mine neat. Thank you. Yes, that's enough.' Rajinder again tried to pour water in his glass. 'No, Rajinder. Let me try it neat for a change.'

'Look at that.' Drews pointed to the glowing city on the mountaintop. The servants nodded and explained something in Hindi. Rajinder laboured to interpret.

Evan took a sip of his drink. He stared in the opposite direction.

$\mathbf{F}$ran Naversen insisted on carrying her bags to the waiting car. She shouldered away a grovelling bellboy. 'Tip not necessary,' he implored. 'Complimentary, madam.' Fran lowered the bags to the driveway and glared through spectacles gone pink and blue in the dawn.

'You think I haven't been in India before? You think I don't know what happens to *bags*?' She hoisted them and glared at the hired chauffeur, a Sikh in a magenta turban, who stood by the car picking at long, white teeth.

'If you don't mind!'

The driver gave a tug to the front of his trousers and strolled to the rear of the car. Fran drummed fingernails on the black steel. He gave her a wide, interested smile. Fran slammed the trunk with an impatient hand.

Nick emerged from the lobby carrying a newspaper. He shielded his eyes, arched his back and scanned the horizon.

'Where're your bags?' demanded Fran.

'They're coming.' At that moment, Buck Frye emerged from the lobby hauling two black suitcases.

'Careful,' said Nick. 'If those bottles break we'll trail gin fumes down the length of the Grand Trunk Road.'

Buck staggered beneath the bags.

'Not to mention,' continued Nick, 'a certain thirst that is likely to develop later this evening. In our cosy quonset hut.'

Gasped Buck: 'You must have gold bars in here.'

'Don't you wish.' Nick adjusted his belt. 'Don't I wish? Try her bags.'

Fran glared at the driver. He shrugged and tugged open the trunk.

'Tell him to be careful,' called Nick. 'Babies are so-o delicate.'

'Shut up, Nick.'

'But she's packed them well.' Nick smiled at the Sikh. 'In popcorn.'

Buck collapsed at the car with Nick's bags.

'Can barely hear them screaming. Buttered popcorn, I think. Big hit with young 'uns.'

Fran scolded the Sikh for carelessness. Buck wondered aloud whether there'd be enough room.

'I believe in travelling heavy.' Nick pointed at Fran. 'Obviously.'

'I can't take much more of this, Nick.'

'Sure you can, Big Girl. You can take anything. 'Cause you can smell it – admit it, dear, you smell it! That pot of gold at the end of this yellow dirt road.'

'Tell me, um, more,' Buck said, 'about this pot of gold.'

Fran slammed the trunk. Her spectacles flashed yellow: the sun had risen. 'You.' She pointed at Buck, who froze with fear. 'You're in the front. Got the maps?'

Buck nodded timorously. Nick spasmed in a small belch. Fran opened the rear door.

'Nick – step to. Let's get out of here.'

As soon as the Naversens' car departed, winding around Claridge's traffic circle, an identical car pulled into its place. The driver wore an orange turban. The lobby door opened a crack: a bearded face protruded and quickly glanced in all directions. A hand followed. It chopped the air. Several minutes later, both doors swung open to disgorge Prentice McGuinn, in serious correspondent khakis, and wife Gail in faded batik. They were followed by lovely Marietta and two bellboys carrying suitcases. Prentice conferred with the driver in broken Punjabi. Gail directed the bellboys with the bags. Marietta looked at her petite, gold watch.

'Are they coming?' said Gail, 'or what?'

'I knocked on their door,' said Marietta.

'It's going to be a squeeze.' Gail looked at the horizon. The sun was rising. 'And it promises to be a long drive. Does the driver know where we're going?'

'It's his cousin,' called Prentice.

'Did Buck see you?'

Prentice shook his head proudly.

'I hope there's a phone,' said Gail. 'Or a telex, at least. This story could get hot fast.'

Marietta sighed. 'I just hope Drews is still there.'

The lobby doors opened once more.

'Finally,' said Gail.

'Good morning,' called Marietta. Prentice opened the car door.

'Let's get going,' said Gail.

Drews was in the bedroom with the blue-green walls. The mosquito net dangled above him in a giant knot: no one had untangled it the previous night. A sword of light stabbed through a crack in the window shutter. Drews' eyes opened suddenly, pink and narrow with pain. He sat up groaning. He was fully dressed. Only his boots had been removed.

He unlatched the door and stepped barefoot into the glare of his private balcony. The insane house, with its warring courtyards and surrendering rooftops, was abandoned. He found an Indian-style commode. He felt bites all over his body: on his palms, under his beard, on his ankles. Drews squatted a long time. He staggered back to the bed and stared at the ceiling. A lizard pursued a cottony moth caught in a medallion of light. Drews' glance followed the shard of sunlight, with its dancing particles of dust, until it settled on a silent figure staring from a shadowed corner. He heard a single word spoken in a gentle lisp: 'Yes.'

'Evan.'

The old man, seated on a stool, nodded gravely.

'What?'

Evan swallowed slowly. 'I've been waiting.'

'I need . . . could you get some water?'

Evan leaned against the wall and crossed his legs. 'All night.'

'I think I need a doctor.'

Evan's head shook slowly.

'I'm sick.'

Evan uncrossed his legs. 'Rajinder will come.' He stood and carefully secured a bottle and tumbler against the wall. He lifted the wooden stool and carried it to Drews' bedside. 'Sooner or later.'

'I have to go to the bathroom.'

Evan fluttered a hand. 'Go.'

When Drews returned, he was shivering. Evan produced a blanket from a wardrobe and laid it atop him. He returned to the stool and looked at the bearded man searchingly.

'Daniel,' he said. 'Have you read of the Original Age? The Succeeding Age?'

Drews smelled rum. 'A doctor, Evan. I feel like I'm dying.'

The old man shook his head. 'Balls.' He sat silently, mouth pursed. 'Too much disco dancing.' Then he spoke in a low, insistent tone. 'The Original Age, Daniel? Think. Open your eyes, please. *Please?* Thank you. The Succeeding Age? Make an effort to understand.'

And so it began: the towering cliff that Evan Olcott had made of his life, on which nothing caught including light, crumbled and disintegrated beneath the pressure of a vast, hidden reservoir. The barren rock, incapable of supporting the stealthiest weed, had been bubbling imperceptibly through all the years. A lake had risen. And now it was pouring through the breach in a corrosive river of wisdom mixed with gall. The morning was new but the old man intended to talk until he was dry. He had waited twenty-four years since Wuhan. He had sat through the night with his rum bottle waiting for his captive to regain a sliver of consciousness − without accompanying energy − through which Evan could inject his lesson. Only once before had the stream been released and that was when Tim Marquand occupied the same blue-plastered room. But Tim Marquand had bobbed along on Evan's bilious ocean, singing and bellowing and refusing to jettison the pathetic ballast of his life: in particular, his frustrated love for the man with whom he had shared servants' quarters in long-ago London. Tim capsized and drowned but that wasn't Evan's plan. He had wanted him to invite the rising water into his lungs and learn to walk through it, with the inevitable slowing of step, as Evan himself had. Now it was Drews in the sealed room, on the bed, where he rocked in pain with no friend waiting on the opposite side of the plastered wall. No hope; no love worth keeping. Nothing on his horizon but the rising tide of the Succeeding Age.

'It's from the Mahanirvana Tantra,' said Evan. 'The Succeeding Age is characterized by anxiety and perplexity, a constant distress of mind.'

There was a knock.

'Please,' implored Drews.

Evan shut his eyes.

'For God's sake, open the door.'

Evan stood and walked to the door. Rajinder entered and moved to the bedside. He looked down with sympathy.

'It must have been bad water,' Drews gasped. 'I drank from a stream at the Marabar caves. The Barabar caves.'

Rajinder shook his head knowingly.

'Can you . . .'

'Get water, Rajinder.'

Rajinder nodded and turned away.

'I have to . . .' Drews struggled with the blanket.

'Rajinder.'

Rajinder helped Drews to the balcony. Drews shrank from the morning sun. They walked clumsily toward the toilet.

'Rajinder?'

The Indian turned back. Evan was standing in the doorway shielding his eyes.

'I'll fetch the water.'

When the two men returned to the room, Evan was in the corner again, on his stool, with a small jug of water positioned next to his rum bottle. A fresh drink was balanced on his knee. On the bedside table was a separate pitcher. With Rajinder's help, Drews drank two glasses of water. He collapsed back on the bed.

'Leave,' Evan said.

'I'm just bringing some curd.'

The old man drained his drink. 'No bloody curd.' Rajinder stared with surprise. Evan picked up his stool and moved to the head of the bed.

'Tim never understood,' he said. 'He continued to cling to . . . things. "*Roses, wine. A friend to share.*" But you . . .' Evan snapped his head toward the door. 'I said bloody leave!'

Rajinder secured the door behind him. Evan threw the latch, raising a violent metal sound.

The old man talked about Tim and the failure of his life: Kin Wah, of course – 'love in a pair of *amah* slippers' – the China-watching and the inevitable tragedy of expatriatism. 'I taught him the Succeeding Age. But he never learned to make peace with it. He took my idea and blended it into, oh, a coda to his life. A coda, yes: some sentimental finale. The Succeeding Age became a melody, a *tune*.' The old man hissed with disapproval. 'Slow and stately, harmonized with all the earlier themes of his life. The alcohol theme.' Evan twisted his drink in the dusty light. 'A perky tune, as I imagine it, instantly recognizable, which grows darker and more complex until it gives way to timpani and the final crash of the cymbals.' He turned to Drews. 'Tim, I understand, swelled like a buffalo before he died.'

Drews shook his head with pain-tightened mouth.

'No way for a man to die.'

Sweat poured down Drews' face. He kicked frantically at the blanket.

'And "Danny".' Evan laid his hand on Drews' arm. 'The "Danny" theme: the most variable, most important, most moving in the piece. The symphony will live or die on the Drews theme.' Evan moved his face closer. 'As, indeed, its composer did.'

Drews grappled for the water jug. Evan held the glass while he drank. 'Yes, Daniel, your friend died of drink and you were the cause.'

'That's what they say.' Drews' eyes were lustreless yellow.

'But I don't agree. Oh no, I don't agree at all, dear boy. What could you have done, after all?' Evan gripped Drews' arm. 'You loved him. Isn't that right? Just not in the same *way*.'

Drews' eyes were squeezed shut.

'I mean, what would they have had you do? In the circumstances?'

Tears came from Drews' eyes.

'Yes, Daniel, you weren't to blame. Your friend was.' Evan stood up. 'The Succeeding Age is not a bloody song. That's what Tim couldn't accept. It's a foreign landscape, a new existence, not the final chapter heading. This is what you must understand. All that came before ends. *Bang!*' Evan slammed the top of the stool. 'You've lost everything, dear boy, as everyone does sooner or later. You must let go as Tim refused to – *which was the cause of his painful death*. The roots rot. Hope, love: stoop and pluck them out! Your best friend, your marriage, your magazine: tick them off. Even our pitiful Crown Colony: six million people exiting the Original Age. You need a new home and I am your escort. I will point out the austere beauties of the Succeeding Age. Clean living. Inexpensive, for sure. Unhurried. No more rented tuxedos. And your nights, dear boy, are all your own.'

Evan was at the window, chuckling at his joke. He had opened the shutter and was gazing at fields beyond. 'Now, Daniel, let me tell you about Wuhan.' He adopted a more gentle tone. 'Where I collected my ticket.' He turned back. The bearded man on the bed was asleep.

'God's blood!' said Evan. The door slammed noisily but Drews remained unconscious.

★　　★　　★

Drews was awakened frequently by spasms of pain and explosions of light from the door. Consciousness and unconsciousness blurred; disturbing dreams entangled with Evan Olcott's ceaseless phantasmagoria. Drews was in the newsroom, leaping from desk to desk, when his boot missed its fall and he hurtled face-first to the ground. Timmy's voice shouted: 'Let's get some *weather* in this bloody newsroom!' He was in the tub in Albert Court, relaxed, soaping his penis, which was suddenly longer, uncircumcised and brown. His gaze lifted to the ceiling, penetrating the yellow mist, to find Evan Olcott grinning malignantly through the pantry windows. An old, scratchy voice intoned terrible things about his wife. *The breasts of the Japanese are small – but so are their wonderful, dark triangles. That makes one feel large, doesn't it? They like to be dominated. But once unfaithful they are the most faithless women in the world, isn't that so, dear boy?* Drews saw again, through that unvanquishable keyhole, his wife's smiling face above that of the Filipino. 'But she loves me!' Drews cried. And Evan's reply: 'She doesn't love you alone.' He opened his eyes, searching for Miki's wide, knowing smile. Instead, he found Rajinder smoothing his hair and helping him with a glass of water. Rajinder withdrew the blanket. Drews pushed off the sheet with his legs. He became frantic about his boots. Boots became the most important thing in his world. He leaned out of bed and scrabbled at the floor. But the boots were not there. He heard the low, intrusive voice: 'You've lost everything. Your best friend, your marriage, your magazine: tick them off . . .' Drews rose and shouted: 'But you said the magazine was saved!' He glared around the room with wild eyes and a sweat-soaked face. He was alone.

The door opened again. It was night. Evan wiped his hands on his trousers. 'The heat simply refuses to break.'

Drews whispered: 'The documents, Evan.'

But the old man had no time for *Orientweek* or documents, for the long, hot day and the steady rums had jarred him loose from the present, from India, from the Succeeding Age and propelled him back to the Chinese jail cell that had been his world for nearly five years. He remembered and drank and talked. And Drews, half-conscious, travelled back with him to Wuhan. 'You can see it, can't you, Daniel? That cool light from the tiny window. A cell.' He sighed heavily. The landscape was bleak, he said, but lovely in its monotony. It was a quiet place for a prison. Remarkably quiet. Evan whispered a phrase in Chinese. 'That's

dialect. Remember it still. Tim and I conversed in it. Most enjoyable.'
He repeated the Chinese phrase until Drews knew it, until it became a
chant. 'That's what they told me, Daniel. That morning.' Drews practised
the phrase while Evan gripped his bicep. 'Very good. Quite awful, isn't
it? *Your life has ended, white devil!* Once again, please.' And Drews followed
Evan Olcott as he paced that hard prison cell with the tiny window. He
smelled the fetid bucket on the floor with its yellow slops and faced the
malign smiles of the Chinese guards. He heard, repeatedly, their taunts
of the imprisoned white spy. 'Personal things. Unspeakable, really.' He
ticked off the remaining seconds of Evan Olcott's life, in descending
order, in dialect. 'Excellent, Daniel, you've an ear, yes you do.' He
walked that final walk and saw the steely sky. 'No cigarette, I'm afraid.
No final meal. No padre. Just the walk. The pole on which they tie our
hands. No blindfold, Daniel. We will watch them aim their rifles, steady
and straight. One soldier: he actually smiled. I knew him. Quite cruel.'
Drews breathed with Evan a high, frantic breath and then he experienced
the shot without hearing it, as is the case. After which Evan allowed a
reverent pause and refilled his drink. He sat on the stool, looking away
abstractedly. Finally he spoke with that soft, boyish lisp. 'Yes. Yes indeed.'
Drews lay with eyes averted from the old man. But the voice resumed
and Evan reconstructed the aftermath: the rough treatment by the guards,
the bustling into the car, the flight to Peking and the drive to the embassy
with the white spy prostrate in the back seat. The final insult: *Your life
has ended, white devil!* And scornful laughter by the Chinese soldiers. Of
course, it was mere reconstruction for Evan had no memory of the
events succeeding the rifle fire that did, in its way, end his life.

'The moment that delivered me from the Original Age, Daniel. Do
you understand? Open your eyes. Please. Dear *boy*. Thank you. Don't
you hear that shot ricocheting in your life?'

Drews pleaded weakly.

'Yes, Daniel. We will sign the documents tomorrow, as I said. In the
meantime . . .'

'This is tomorrow.'

'Drink some more.' And then Evan continued. 'There's an amusing
subplot, which may surprise you. I was, actually, a model captive. Strong
constitution: I kept my sanity.' He stood for a stroll. 'And, believe me,
many did not. There was a certain Frenchman . . . Oh, we don't have
time. I did the usual things: multiplication tables, food fantasies, picking

up the local lingo. Sex of that sort. I would walk through the house of my boyhood, room by room, smelling the different smells and feeling the differing textures beneath my feet. Amazing, really. Wood, carpet, the metal dividing strip at the doorways. I could picture classrooms from my youth and place students by name. Memory: no one knows how powerful it is, how preserved, until it's needed. Until the horizon looms large – until the future, so to speak, packs up. Fascinating. Now, I've told no one this, only Tim before you, but you see, I wrote my book. Yes, wrote it from first to last. "Prisoner of Mao", that type of thing. I started after I was imprisoned. And as time went on, and new events transpired, Chapter Two would become part of Chapter One. And then Chapter Three. And then Four. So many things kept happening. Telescoping, you'd call it. It would have been quite the book. Far superior to "Prisoner of Mao". I even did the Chinese translation of the book – all up here.' Evan touched his temple. 'Memory. It's still here, I could dictate it to you. But it hardly seemed worthwhile, afterwards, to write it.' Evan sipped his drink. 'It was the past.' He turned to Drews and whispered: 'It's astonishing. For five years I was on the brink of renewing my life. I could have gone *back*. And then . . .' He exhaled heavily. 'Actually, it could be viewed as nothing but a practical joke. For those with, shall we say, a Chinese sense of humour. Cruel people the Chinese.'

Drews was asleep. Then he was sitting and Rajinder was stealthily feeding him yoghurt. 'Hurry.' Rajinder helped him to the toilet: the city in the sky had faded to a few dim lights. The night was almost exhausted. Then the unstoppable voice resumed.

'It is India, understand, that finally taught me. It took time to see beyond the spectacle. Quite extraordinary: everyone comes to India to find something, even if it's just the Taj Mahal. "Found" each day by thousands. Spirituality, identity. They see the snake's thousand heads, shining and colourful, and reach for them. Then comes disappointment. For India has nothing for us to find. That's its beauty, don't you see? That's what brings us here. It seems to have everything' – Evan gestured around the empty room – 'and, at heart, I believe there's no emptier country on the globe. This tired old religion, adding a totem whenever the mass needs a fresh thrill. Two hundred million gods. Think, Daniel, how thin a religion can be spread. Scratch the surface – and find nothing. No heart of darkness; no roots that go beyond a millimetre. A perfect land of decadence and materialism, of plastic shoes, of idiotic shrines to two hundred million gods, where marriage, and love, is a matter of rupees. Naipaul writes: "... always the rupees: the rupees are always necessary." Good man, Naipaul. Excellent on India. The thousand-headed snake: reach down, part the weeds – they come up in your hands.' Evan's hands were before him, fingers tautly curled. 'Look for it – grab! And up you come with that cold, dry stick in your hands.'

Drews' fever continued to rage. Rajinder was finally barred from the room. Evan had locked the door.

'Bloody India.' Evan paced the room. 'Near here is a very special man. We've met him: Rajinder and I visited one afternoon. He has the longest fingernails in the world. Just imagine. The nails are three feet long, brown, curled, rather unusually grotesque. He's been growing the nails since the 1950s and they made him famous in these parts. That's the intention of course: a little attention for a little man living in a decidedly unheeding world. You can find him in the *Guinness Book*, been there for decades. The government planned stamps, one for each Indian in the *Guinness Book*. Never came off. Perhaps the fingernail man was the stumbling block.' Evan snorted. 'Think of that stamp! Anyway, I found something poignant in this man. I admired his achievement. But we read in the paper he's become dissatisfied. He didn't get his stamp. Hasn't slept well since the 1960s – that's what the paper said. So he's announced that his nails, his lifelong fame – hard-earned, as anyone would admit – are up for sale. For cash. Someone planted the idea, patently, and inevitably it has grown. The fingernail man has gotten greedy. He refused $100,000 for the nails – imagine what $100,000 would buy in India – because he wants more. Two hundred thousand. Refuses to sell for less. He blames taxes: he wants to *clear* $100,000. So now he's taking out ads, which he can hardly afford. I've seen his rooms. He'll run through his savings. Ruin his family. All to get *more* for his brown fingernails. And then no one will buy them. Rather sad, I thought. He was satisfied with fame. And then came greed. It happened in Bhopal, you know. Those poor people, the whole world was with them. Union Carbide was a global villain. They deserved anything they could get. Until they got the same idea. They became money-crazy. All they thought about was compensation, more compensation. The government settled with Carbide, pitiful amount, and the victims kept crying for money, more money. No one pays the least attention. With reason: they've become greedy buggers.'

Evan waved his drink.

'Not far from here, there was a nasty incident. Middle-class couple from the city were motoring from the hills.' He motioned to the ceiling. 'By mistake, they hit a young boy on the road, a villager. They stopped their car: very decent but a mistake. Significant mistake. Villagers surrounded them and a scene ensued. Emotions were high. The couple wanted the police but they were restrained. Finally, the crowd came to a decision. They opened the car door and pulled from the back seat one of the couple's young sons. They chose a boy who was roughly the same age as the accident victim, who lay on the roadside with, I imagine, open, dead eyes and a body twisted as bodies don't naturally twist. The crowd murdered the young boy and the incident was resolved. No one thought of harming the father or mother or the daughter or the second son, who was, quite fortunately, several years younger. Justice, they called it, but what they really meant was retribution.'

Drews groaned.

'You have to see it from an Indian perspective. A son is valuable. That's the point: asset value. The son will support the family one day and this goes for rich families as well as poor. When the poor family lost that valuable commodity, retribution had to be made. Had it been a small girl who was killed – well, an apology may have sufficed. Daughters aren't assets in India. They're liabilities. There are so many stories here, all the same at root. "... always the rupees: the rupees are always necessary." That's Forster's boum, dear boy, although he misinterpreted, mystified, that childish romanticism of my homeland. But you've seen the real Marabar caves. They hold nothing spiritual – don't you agree? Nothing above or beyond the surface: nothing whatsoever. Just that deadening echo. Boum: the sound of a celestial cash register, Daniel, Indian-style. It's the tinkle of a rupee coin – or a payment in blood. A murder, a nose-blow, the squeak of a plastic shoe, to paraphrase. Boum.'

Drews drifted in and out of Evan's eternal summation.

'... It was the usual sort of roadside eatery, or *dhaba*. You passed it on the road here. It did wonderful business; I think that's part of the story. Until the police closed it down. The proprietor was selling human meat. He escaped – "absconded" in the local lingo – and at first the police thought customers paid extra for human flesh. Kidnapped children, largely. But, of course, the explanation was simpler: children were simply cheaper sources of curry meat. Margins. Little fuss: a couple of paragraphs. I call this man the king of his flim–flam land. These are the stamps I'd issue: the *dhaba* owner in Kanpur, the roadside mob. Not to mention the dowry killers: the sound of greed raised to a burning shriek. Women ignited for a pile of rupees. Wives ignited! We had a case near here recently . . .'

Drews started vomiting and Rajinder had to be summoned. Several hours were lost.

'Even foreigners,' said Evan, 'get infected by the local spirit. Diplomat family in New Delhi. Loved the place. Kids got a kick out of the elephants. Forget their nationality. Usual crowd of servants: houseboys, gardeners, cooks, chauffeurs. One autumn, they adopted a street puppy. It grew and, being a wanderer, had its own litter. The kids loved the puppies, the servants' kids loved them, the servants, of course, fed them and wiped up the piddle. One day, the mother bitch started choking as if she had a bone stuck in her throat. The chauffeur brought her to the vet and returned with upsetting news. The bitch had rabies. Common here: avoid those dogs on the street. So the father took the afternoon off and accompanied the chauffeur to the vet. The poor bitch was put down. But there was a problem with the puppies. The disease might have been spread to them. They had to be inoculated and temporarily quarantined. Similarly, there was a danger to the humans in the house. Anyone who had kissed or been licked by the puppies had to get shots. Not so bad, you know, as in the old days. Series of five in the arm or the old, you know, buttocks.'

Evan patted his seat.

'So the father hustled everyone into taxis. Everyone had played with the puppies: the chauffeur, the houseboy, the houseboy's kids, the neighbour's kids, the washerman, the sweeper. Off they went to the doctor. The foreigners and the neighbouring children – middle-class Indians – sat in the waiting room. The servants huddled outside, excited and a little proud to be there. Now, a problem arose. Rabies shots are no longer painful but they are expensive. The father was given an estimate. Remember, it was a huge crowd: a grossly extended family. So he made a dicey decision. He, his family and the four neighbouring children were administered vaccines imported from France. The servants and their children were given an Indian vaccine, one-tenth the price. Buyer beware: the Indian vaccine, according to the doctor, was not as effective as the one from France. At home, the wife became extremely upset. 'What if someone dies?' Said Papa: 'It would have been a fortune! Our home leave money!' So they lived in fear that one of their servants would suddenly start choking like the poor dead bitch. It is quite a fear, believe me. Rabies is an unattractive disease by any stretch of the imagination. In addition, it's incurable. And, indeed, a few days later, the houseboy's eldest daughter exhibited the symptoms. Terrible turn. Bad disease, extremely painful. Hydrophobia is one of the symptoms. The poor little girl died like a dog. They all attended the cremation. The diplomat's wife was frantic. She said: 'What happens if they find out? That they got the Indian vaccine?' The diplomat said: 'Stop getting hysterical.' The wife said: 'They'll do something to the children!' And indeed, a few days later, one of the neighbouring children, a middle-class brat, quarrelled with the diplomat's son over a new kind of water gun and, in revenge, let the cat out of the bag. He told the servants they were given the cheap vaccine. The foreign family was petrified. They lived with these people! Their clothes were washed by them. Their toilets were scrubbed by them. Their food was cooked by them. The houseboy had keys to the wardrobes. The driver could actually steal the car, which was imported. So they waited, terrorized, for reprisal. The mother wanted to send the children home to New Hampshire or Kyoto – I can't recall the nationality. But Dad thought that would provoke the servants into a rushed revenge: a slaughter! The mother became troubled. I believe she had problems with pills. The father couldn't work. Finally, they had a summit with the chauffeur, whom they trusted most. He was surprised at their concern. The servants didn't blame them at all. They were grateful they got any injection at all. 'You saved my life,' the driver said, tears in his eyes. They all deemed the diplomat's decision sensible and generous, even the houseboy who lost his eldest daughter. Because the imported vaccine was notoriously expensive. However, they were bitter about the Indian doctor. They suspected him of switching the vaccine – injecting water – to make a bigger profit. Equally, they blamed the Indian manufacturer of the vaccine. They presumed that deadly profit was made somewhere, by someone, perhaps by a chain of greedy Indians. Wouldn't be the first time. Reprisal had never occurred to them. And even if it had, there would have been practical problems. For they were servants, you see, and when servants get in any kind of trouble the police do appalling things to them and, often, to their entire families. Happens constantly. Unless the police can be bought off. But servants don't have the cash and most employers would rather fire them than incur the additional expense.'

Evan shook his head. 'That one made the papers. But not all stories end so happily ...'

The night silence gave way to birdsounds. Light showed through the cracks in the window shutter. Rajinder brought sweetened tea. Drews sat up, hair matted and eyes glowing with fever.

'Tell me you saw it, Daniel. Didn't you see the rupees – "always the rupees" – in front of those shrines? Indians forced to pay off their gods? Two hundred million collections every day? And what do they get, the Indians – certainly you've seen that? The greatest, longest-running, most successful flim-flam in the history of human civilization. The very gods are in on it, with the doctors, the police, the parents, the neighbours. And the spouses, of course.' He mimicked the lighting of a match. '*Whoosh*. Till death do us part.'

On the bed, Drews' vision narrowed to the dimension of a keyhole. He saw his wife's smiling face above that of the Filipino. He heard Miki's voice in memory, tear-choked: 'You don't believe. But I love *him*. I'll always love you – but I love him. You must believe that.'

'But what about ...'

'Wait,' said Evan. 'Let me guess, Daniel. What about love?'

Drews stared.

'Boum!' cried Evan. 'The squeak of an old boot. Love is the toenail of life, dear boy. You cut it, it continues to grow, it gets thicker and yellower ...'

'Wait,' Drews said, rising to the challenge. 'I saw a shrine. The picture: it's here.' He touched his head. 'It was lovely.'

'You saw no lovely shrine.'

'Not one of your shrines. It was at the base of the Marabar caves. The Barabar caves.'

Evan shook his head dismissingly. Drews extolled its simplicity, its colourlessness. He described the toy trident standing guard over the lingam. There was no pile of rupees, he said.

'Too piss poor.'

'No.' Drews described the message he read in the shrine: some private dedication or timeless devotion. 'It touched me.' Drews pulled the

239

blanket up. He was shivering again. 'I found it . . . I told you, beautiful. With the colour washed off.'

'But the colour, my boy, that's what it's all about. The thin silver foil. Do you know how flat that silver foil is pounded? Mere molecules. That's India. That's the thousand-headed snake. A shiny skin glinting in the brutal sun. Until the sun kills it finally. You merely found a dead one.'

'It made me think of Timmy,' Drews said. 'I wondered if he had seen that shrine.'

Evan glared at his captive.

'Especially after those vacant caves.' Drews coughed. 'Is there water?'

'You've learned nothing.' Evan stood above the bed in anger. 'We are almost out of time.'

Drews slept again and was awakened by a commotion. Servants and villagers surrounded him. There was a smell in the room: he had fouled his trousers. They carried him from the room and, with much shouting and manoeuvring, down through the crazy palace. Drews saw fields going by and a temple. They stripped him at a pump and washed him. Rajinder directed the operation. Then he was alone once more. Drews' shaking hand moved and discovered the taut ropes of a charpoy. It moved to the wall and found smooth, clammy mud. He opened his eyes and saw low walls, a thatched roof and a primitive doorway. Sounds could be heard in the distance: servant talk and rancorous Indian music. Drews looked at his body: he was dressed in Indian peasant's clothes. He was alone in the hut.

The sun was high over the guest house and the locals, along with their animals, were sensibly asleep. Only the foreigners were about, as foreigners always are.

'That was delicious.' Nick Naversen burped.

'That was foul, Nick.'

'Mistaken, Fran. Fowl was dinner. And breakfast. Remember: you were the one who demanded a new menu.' Nick fanned himself with a menu. 'Damned hot.'

'They try their best.' Buck Frye's right hand, brown with curry, dangled before him. His brow was beaded with sweat. 'Fresh meat isn't always available. It's not like the city.'

Nick licked his lips. 'Tasted fresh to me.'

'Stop,' cried Fran.

'What kind of animal was that? Human?'

Fran covered her ears.

'Which caste? Perhaps that's the question.'

Buck spoke emphatically: 'Lamb.'

'An intelligent little lamby.' Nick wiped his hands with a handkerchief.

'Or,' said Buck uncertainly, 'goat.'

'An intelligent goat?' Nick rose from the table. 'It's funny – I thought the Big Girl would enjoy her brain curry. Although I would have skipped the peas. Jarring visual combination. Peas and brains. Brain à la pea.'

Fran removed her spectacles. She wiped her face.

Nick put a hand in a pocket. 'And the other dish.' There was an interior earthquake in his trousers. 'I'm feeling stronger already.'

'That was goat,' said Buck triumphantly. 'Goat testicles. It's considered a delicacy among Muslims.'

'Among Muslims?' Nick frowned, trying to formulate a circumcision joke. His concentration was snapped by an attractive servant clearing the table. 'I wonder if they have any, um, talent in these parts.' His hand stirred in his pocket.

'Nick, please.'

He shrugged and started tapping his teeth with a finger. 'Pea à la brain and goat's balls. Sounds like some correspondents of my acquaintance.'

'I'm totally revolted,' Fran said. 'And I'm famished.'

'Have another cutlet. Totally free of body parts. Except a stray finger or two.'

Fran laboured to put on her glasses. Buck Frye looked away nervously.

'Main ingredient seemed to be oil,' Nick said.

'They're all gone!' Fran glared at Buck.

'Hungry.' Buck stroked his moustache. 'Not much with brains. Never have been. Since schooldays.'

A servant entered the dining room to announce a visitor.

'This is it,' said Nick. 'Ready, Big Girl? Buckeroo? This is what we've been waiting for. The summons from our crackpot chairman. His trusty native messenger. And Fran, don't call him Gunga Din again. That went out with the Moghuls.'

'I'm getting tired of this,' snapped Fran. 'It's so damned hot.'

But the man who entered the room wasn't an Indian. He was a foreigner with a severe crewcut and a defensive smile. He wore gauzy cottons and gave an ironic Indian salaam.

'Fucking reunion,' the man announced. 'In the wilds of India. Hello Naversen.'

Nick squinted.

'Dave Erdman. Your old buddy from Bangkok. Don't you remember that night at Soi Cowboy?'

'Good lord,' said Nick. 'Erdman. What the hell are you doing here?'

'Karma, man.'

'And, to answer your question, I don't recall a thing about that evening if you don't mind. Wouldn't know her name if I heard it. Five hundred baht: that I remember.'

'And the clinic the following day.'

'The sores finally healed.'

'When was this?' asked Fran aggressively.

'Nineteen oh nine.' Nick shook hands with Dave. 'After our divorce.' He introduced Fran.

'I've seen your ads,' Dave said.

'You have?' Fran asked eagerly. 'In the *Bangkok Post*? Or the *Straits Times*?'

Nick laughed. 'The ones with the scratch-and-sniff strips?'

'Cut it, Nick.'

'Actually, we're on a little buying trip. Good cost advantages in the subcontinent.'

Dave Erdman looked from Naversen to Naversen.

'Shipping connections need to be improved. By the time the babies arrive, they have moustaches.'

'Nick . . .'

'And those are the girls.'

Buck coughed in request of an introduction. He said: 'You're a journalist? Not contemplating a move to India, I hope.'

'Former journalist,' Dave replied. 'I'm living in the forest now. Renounced this vale of tears, man. Deadlines, man, they'll do you in.'

Buck pulled his chair closer.

'Breaking news. How I hated fucking breaking news.'

Buck gasped.

'And energy. Fuck, never get involved with energy. Energy is the pits.'

'Lots of energy stories on the subcontinent,' breathed Buck. 'And shipping.'

'They're all yours, man.'

'They do get technical.' Buck was grave and thoughtful. 'But with the proper reference books . . .'

'I never found them.'

'I mean . . .' Buck grew frantic. 'What does one do when one stops being a correspondent?'

Dave laughed.

'Seriously!'

Dave looked him in the eyes. 'Everyone knows. Fucking freelance, man.'

'No, no,' implored Buck, 'I mean after freelance.'

'Depends on local law, I guess.'

'Huh?'

'I mean, like, whether they allow life-support systems to be turned off.'

'Old correspondents never die,' announced Nick. 'They just scrounge away. I penned a little column on that theme once. Most unpopular. Near riot at the FCC.'

'How is the old FCC?' asked Dave.

'No amnesty for unpaid bills if that's what you're asking.'

'Hard luck for both of us, man.' Dave stared at the Naversens with sharp-cornered eyes. 'So what's this: a little family holiday?'

'Oh no.' Nick smiled. 'Much more than that. Kind of a honeymoon, actually. Romance, moonlight, Taj Mahal. And goat's balls: lots and lots of goat's balls. Good for the strength. You must know that. After Bangkok.'

'Yeah.'

'You see' – Nick pointed at Fran and Buck – 'these two have just got married.'

Fran sighed.

'I'm chaperoning. Demanding job. Condom checks and all. Smelly work, truth be told.'

Buck tittered.

'Have to make sure the heat doesn't get too much.' He motioned to Buck. 'He generates the heat.' He pointed at Fran. 'The Big Girl brings the dust.'

Dave was delivered a beer. 'Quite a reunion.'

'Mm,' said Nick. 'That *was* some night at Soi Cowboy. Little row with a Lufthansa stewardess, I recall.'

'Not us, man. I mean this *Orientweek* reunion. You must be meeting up with your founding editor.'

Nick and Fran stared at him.

'Drews. The Wanchai cowboy. I bumped into him. Such a fucking shock.'

'You bumped into Drews?'

Dave nodded.

'When?'

'Two days back.'

'Where?' demanded Fran.

'I don't think you'd understand. Probably the heaviest place in India.'

'Fran might enjoy that,' said Nick.

Buck stroked his chin. 'Why would you conclude that we were, uh, necessarily meeting up with Mr Drews?'

Dave leaned back in his chair and laughed.

'Okay,' said Nick. 'We *are* meeting Drews. Just a little business.'

'In the centre of fucking India,' said Dave. 'Routine conference. Like, next year Patagonia.'

'Would you like something to eat?' interjected Fran.

'What do they have?'

Buck started to giggle. Nick said: 'Today's specials are highly recommended.'

Fran interrupted forcefully: 'Cutlets.'

Dave ate two portions of cutlets. He wiped his mouth and said: 'Must be an important *Orientweek* gathering.'

Fran said: 'Administrative.'

'Of course, it wouldn't have anything to do with the sale.'

Nick contemplated the ceiling and whistled the first eight notes of the 'Colonel Bogey' march.

'And a big gathering,' Dave continued. 'Nick and Fran Naversen. Daniel Drews. The elusive chairman . . .'

Fran shifted nervously in her chair.

'. . . plus foxy Marietta . . .'

Fran lunged forward.

'. . . whom we all loved from afar . . .'

'Etta? What's this about Etta?'

'I had breakfast with her. And her group.'

'Her *group*?' said Fran.

'Down there.' He motioned out the window. 'We stayed at the same guest house. Just ten minutes away.'

'Christ,' said Nick. Fran glared at Buck, who was wringing his hands. She gave a significant grunt.

And Buck, with childlike eyes, said ruefully: 'Well, I guess we have to face it: we've been followed.'

At the other guest house, Gail McGuinn was pacing the porch with annoyance. 'I can't take much more waiting.'

Prentice nodded without looking up from his pocket Bible.

'I wonder if the edit has come through on the Philippine abortion story.'

Prentice flipped a page.

'They can't hold it another week.'

Prentice's lips moved as he read.

'And if we have to stay another night, I want a new room. I don't want to hear those two grunting and groaning.'

Prentice looked up.

'You didn't hear it?'

He shook his head.

'Well I did.'

'Big one?'

'Oh, I don't know. At first I thought someone was crying. I think it's rude.'

'Um . . .' Prentice pointed with his jaw. Marietta was walking toward them, twisting her hair into a ponytail. 'No word yet?'

Prentice shook his head.

'Strange to come all the way out here and just wait. And it's so hot.' She fanned herself with a newspaper.

'The Naversens are waiting too,' said Prentice. 'That's the important point. They're there. We're here. All of us are waiting.'

Gail flopped into a chair.

'I just wonder why,' said Marietta. 'The Marabar caves: I can't imagine how Drews ended up at the Marabar caves. It's so odd.'

'Why don't you check again.' Gail waved an annoyed hand. 'With the driver.'

Prentice closed his book. 'We have to wait. As soon as the Naversens leave, the messenger will come here to let us know.'

'And you told him to hurry?'

'I told him to hurry.'

'And you offered enough? The more you offer, the faster he'll come.'

Prentice glared with offence. 'Gail, I've been twelve years in the Third World. I've been in every insurgency in the world. I know how to handle natives.' He turned to the mountains, showing his profile, in mental contemplation of all the natives he'd handled in the past.

Gail turned to Marietta. 'Is everyone ready? We have to move as soon as we get word.'

'We're ready.'

She tipped her head toward the rooms overhead. 'Those two?'

'All of us, Gail.'

Drews opened his eyes to find Rajinder standing over him.

'How long . . . ?'

Rajinder wagged his head comfortingly.

'Rajinder, can't you find me a doctor?'

'It's almost over.'

'Evan has gone mad.'

Rajinder shook his head. 'He's just an old man.'

'My clothes . . . my wallet . . .'

'How are your motions?'

Drews squinted, as if listening to an interior melody. 'I'm . . . I have trouble concentrating.'

'Wait,' said Rajinder. 'I'll just be going.'

Drews closed his eyes. He opened them after a lengthy sleep. Rajinder was standing above him.

'I said I'm going to make a move. I'll just be back. No need for worrying. I am keeping your wallet.'

Rajinder walked through fields and past peasant huts. The palace came into view. Evan was on the roof, peering intently. Rajinder waved. He mimed a sleeping posture. Evan pointed in the distance. Rajinder walked to a sedan and climbed into the rear seat. The car rolled down the dirt road and shuddered with the engine ignition. Rajinder lectured the driver on the price of commodities appearing outside his window: the vegetables on portable carts, dry goods in stores. He lambasted economic liberalization, which, he said, only brought inflation. Government, he said, was entirely to blame. The town ended and they were on the highway. They approached a shop with large slabs of marble leaning against each other. Rajinder asked the driver to stop. He conversed with the owner. His hand gestures grew more agitated until he returned to the car with an angry walk.

'We're planning renovations,' he said. 'But not from that thief.' He chose a mildly vulgar epithet. For Rajinder was a former military man and, in India, the military knew better.

It was late afternoon when he arrived at the guest house. Buck Frye was sitting on a porch picking at a sandalled foot.

Rajinder gave a formal bow. 'I'm coming from Mr Evan Olcott. Are you Mr Naversen?'

'Good lord no,' tittered Buck.

'Very sorry,' said Rajinder. 'My mistake.' He started to walk away.

'Wait!' Buck scrambled out of his chair, hopping to adjust his sandal.

'I'm with the Naversens. I'm their guide. Are we going?'

'Yes,' said Rajinder. 'It's not far. Just over there.' He pointed to the city on the hill, which was starting to flicker alive above its mountain.

'This was rice fields,' said Miki, 'when I was growing up.' Drews saw strips of new asphalt and uniform houses in tan and white stucco. A Japanese matron cycled by. Slender pines shook in the distance, protecting the land from the sea. 'With tiny little frogs.' Miki squatted to search for frogs. She looked up with her amazing, incandescent smile. 'I'm old, *ne*?'

Drews opened his eyes. Amber light outlined the hut's door: the day was ending. The ropes of the charpoy dug into his back. He put his hand to the wall to shift position. It was warm with the accumulated heat of the day.

The door opened and a servant entered with a tray.

The prisoner is soon to be released. Drews ate curd and drank a yoghurt-like drink. *With his proxies. His magazine.*

Rajinder entered the room and inquired about his appetite and his 'motions'.

'Where's Evan? Where are the documents?'

'He's just coming.' Rajinder looked to the door. 'Please wait for Mr Olcott.'

They waited in silence, Drews propped against the mud wall in his peasant clothes, Rajinder ramrod straight at the door. A cock was crowing. Rajinder checked his watch. Several minutes went by. He closely examined his fingernails.

'I'm getting up.' Drews slid across the charpoy. 'This is absurd.'

'You have to wait.'

The door opened and Evan Olcott stooped through. He was dressed as if in celebration: a collarless shirt with freshly-ironed vest. His white hair was wet and brushed back from his bony face. He carried two long documents backed with blue paper.

'Dear boy, you are looking much better.'

'I don't know, Evan. I think I still need a doctor.'

'You should get back to the city.'

'When can I leave?'

'Whenever you please.' Evan spoke casually. 'We'll soon accomplish our final piece of business.' He waved the proxies. 'I don't think the countryside has agreed with you.'

'It must have been water.' Drews sat wearily on the charpoy.

'Rajinder?' Evan motioned outside. The Indian man disappeared and returned with three wooden stools, placing them before the charpoy.

'Now, dear boy, I'm afraid I have ... *Daniel?*'

'I'm listening.'

'Rather unnerving.'

'I hear you.'

Evan sighed. 'Well, I'm afraid you'll think I've played a rather nasty trick.'

Drews' mind jumped from the mud hut to the city, through Indian doctors and plane rides and he was back in his newsroom at his rejuvenated magazine ushering in an entirely new climate on the most promising Monday of his life. The most promising cycle, as issues are known in the magazine trade. One cycle ends – gloriously, poorly, disastrously – and it can't matter because another cycle inevitably begins. Drews was home in his flat, drinking beer with his card-shuffling wife and, perhaps, her paramour. Who was, it had to be admitted, the finest rival a husband could wish for. If Miki was happy, they all could be. Perhaps the magazine *would* have to be shifted. Drews and *Orientweek* could hardly expect to dictate the future of Hong Kong. Maybe the printing press should be sold, or disassembled and moved to a more stable place. Maybe Manila: Miki would be pleased and there would be a definite saving in staff salaries ...

Evan's scratchy voice interrupted. '... to learn, finally, what it all comes down to in the end.'

Someone snorted. 'Moolah.' It was a new voice in the room, snide and familiar.

Drews opened his eyes and found Nick and Fran Naversen standing in the doorway. Nick was grinning. Fran squinted behind her spectacles.

'Please sit,' said Evan. 'These are for you.' The Naversens approached the stools. Two men followed them through the doorway. Drews recognized Dave Erdman, who salaamed. The other man was unfamiliar: a timorous man with a wispy moustache he tugged at.

250

'What are you doing here?'

'Same as you, old bean.' Nick craned back to Evan. 'To meet the chairman.'

'A kind of board meeting,' said Fran.

Nick fanned himself. 'What is this, Evan? The guest dungeon?'

Evan placed the documents on the vacant stool. He sat next to Drews on the charpoy. The ropes sagged, forcing the two men against one another.

He whispered: 'Welcome to the Succeeding Age, Daniel.' He shifted to a Chinese dialect and spoke familiar words: 'Five, four, three, two, one.'

'You sign here, Evan.' Fran flattened the proxy on the stool. Rajinder stepped forward and proffered a fountain pen.

'Excuse me one second.' Evan squinted at the document and signed in a spidery hand. He straightened up and looked at Drews inquiringly.

'And here,' Fran said.

'Rajinder,' said Evan, 'you will witness?'

Drews wiped his brow. A sudden nausea had risen. 'Those are not for me?'

Nick laughed. Rajinder signed with sombre formality.

Drews turned to Evan. 'You had two sets?'

Evan nodded.

'Why did you bother? You knew you'd give them to Nick and Fran.'

'It was possible you'd see my vision without my using, shall we say, the big gun. Alas, that was not to be.'

'You wanted the money.'

Evan shook his head. 'India's a very reasonable place to live.'

Rajinder looked up as if to disagree.

'Then why?'

Evan glanced at the assembled group. He hesitated. Then he leaned sideways and whispered in Drews' ear:

'You weren't getting it. This is what it all comes down to – once you accept that hope and love and dreams are the thousand-headed snake. This is the cold stick in the grass, that which remains on the stage when all the mirrors and wires are dismantled. A small pile of rupees.'

Nick Naversen snorted again. 'Sorry. Couldn't help but overhear. A small pile of rupees?' He gave a forced laugh. 'Speak for yourself.'

Rajinder replaced the fountain pen in his shirt pocket. 'Don't be forgetting taxes, Mr Naversen. Taxes are most important.'

'Remember that, Fran, would you?' Nick looked at his watch. 'It's getting late.'

'See you back in Hong Kong,' said Fran. 'At the board meeting. Don't worry about Kin Wah. We'll bring him.'

'Saqi's a good square. Should have gotten to know him better through the years.' Nick adjusted his belt. 'Might have been a passport to new and interesting friendships.' At the door, he turned back. 'Wish it could have been otherwise, Drews. In a way. Okay, Big Girl. Let's get you in the car.' The Naversens disappeared through the door. Buck looked from left to right, giggled and tripped after them. Evan patted Drews' shoulder and stood slowly. He walked to the door, accompanied by Rajinder, and turned in the doorway. He showed Drews a malignant smile. His mouth contorted and he spoke in rough, high-pitched Chinese tones: *'Your life has ended, white devil!'*

The only person left in the room was Dave Erdman, who moved to one of the stools.

'Well, man, here we are again. Stuck on the rock.'

'Oh lord.'

'I mean, like this is boum. This is a big boum. Maybe the biggest!'

Drews' eyes were closed. He spoke in a low tone: 'Leave me the fuck alone.'

Dave rose, squinting with offence.

'Just find me a car. I'll pay anything to get back to Delhi.'

Dave spoke from the doorway. 'The only thing I know, man, is that you've made my novel. You're right here.' He touched his temple. 'Man, I'm going to make you famous.'

In robbing Drews of his magazine, Evan Olcott had chosen and aimed his charge well. It was a cannonball that struck Drews squarely and propelled him a great mental distance. The hut was nearly dark – the door was open but dusk was falling – and the low shadows of the room engulfed the motionless man on the charpoy. He felt the ropes on his back and recalled the dying Punjabi warrior bidding farewell to his saddle, his flintlocks, his women, with an unmartial cascade of tears. *'He died with reins in his hands, remember, Danny boy?'* He saw the green drapes, the abacus lamps and the hospital bed from Canossa, emptied and stripped. But when he opened his eyes, there were only blackened roofbeams. He watched the light fade and the mud walls sink from sight. He rose and crossed the room to find intersecting walls, warm to the touch. *This is where I will stay*, he thought. *Until someone comes to find me.* He lowered himself to the ground, knelt, and memory brought him to that keyhole, the central image in his photographic recollection of the past. His wife, yet again, smiled atop another man. '*I love him, you know. I do.*' That was Drews' barrier, even during the threesome. He had tried to entwine the love of three into one and failed. For if Miki loved the Filipino she couldn't be Drews' in the old manner. The old was destroyed, not succeeded, by the new. Drews turned and sank back into the corner. His hand caressed one of the walls and he heard his own words from the very first day at Mrs Bottom's: '*My bed is on the other side. If you knocked, I'd hear it.*' Drews made a fist. He knocked gently, as he never had in London. '*What else do we have, Danny boy, if we don't have our love?*' He knocked again on the mud. Tears poured from his eyes. Drews felt the failure of his life and his power as editor, lover and friend but couldn't comprehend the cause. They had all been in love, hadn't everyone always said so? Drews had never stopped loving Timmy, and Miki, and even Gabriel. Wasn't it love that had failed them? Why was it that love could only be enjoyed in its original form and, when time worked its omnipotent heartlessness, became a kind of vanquishing torture? Even the love of a parent, which was said to be changeless. Drews thought back to England, to a house in a northern village, where Timmy's father sat beside him in a reading chair. Drews was engrossed in a mystery, boots crossed at the ankle. Mr Marquand had his paper. They heard the sound of the front door closing. Timmy entered the room, the only son, and a glance ricocheted from Mr Marquand to his son to his visiting friend. It was a look of irrepressible contempt. It was a new memory: Drews wondered if it was real. But something about the mud hut made it come alive and Drews cried for the doomed love of man and woman, parents and children and old friends.

He heard a car noise outside. The darkness of the hut had become a comfort. *Light no lamps*, Drews prayed, *not on this night, my friends.* 'Okay men,' he whispered. Those words: their strange power. He started to sob.

Should Drews have been a stronger man? It hardly seemed possible. Should he have been weaker? Evan's prescription – to eradicate the past – was inhuman. But his distinction between an Original Age of hope and love and a Succeeding Age was proven true. Drews felt a hostage in that age. But hadn't there been a vow? Hadn't Timmy said he'd rescue him from such a plight? 'Gary, Indiana' was on the record player. Timmy had ripped the needle off the record. '*I would find you,*' he bellowed. '*That's what I'm here for!*' Timmy knew India, knew the palace, knew what Drews was going through. They had shared almost everything in life and Timmy hardly seemed dead to Drews in the darkness of a hut in a land of two hundred million gods. Drews gazed at the plain, colourless walls and felt himself growing small. He was inside the tiny shrine at the Barabar caves. He was alone: a forgotten lump in the corner. Where was his trusty trident? Someone to stand guard through eternity? Would the two friends never have a chance to prove their love? Timmy's role: to find Drews. And Danny's: to allow himself to be found as Timmy had desired to his dying moment.

The hired car was still moving, kicking dust and crunching gravel, and Gail McGuinn's door was open. She raced toward the palace, hair and skirt flying behind her. Prentice struggled out of the car: he had been jammed between Gail and the driver. 'I better follow. She's fearless, my Gail.'

Marietta opened her door. She stretched and looked at the city in the sky. 'It reminds me of Hong Kong. Sort of.' She was forced to shout: birds in a nearby tree were deafeningly mourning the end of their day. Marietta looked at the whitewashed palace. 'There's a man on the roof. Looking at us.' She squinted in the falling light. 'Neither Drews nor Evan.'

The palace door flew open and Gail raced out, followed by Prentice. They ran away from the car. Gail turned and pointed in the direction of a field. She fumbled at a camera hanging around her neck.

'Oh lordie.' Marietta pulled her hair into a ponytail and turned. 'Come on. They're somewhere over there.'

Drews dreamt of Tim Marquand walking down a jungle path lined with decapitated heads on staves. He calls: 'I'm coming, Danny. Hold on, Danny!' The sun is high and strong and Timmy is perspiring. The heads on the stave are familiar. Mr Marquand. Evan Olcott. Nick Naversen with a death grin and Fran with closed, puffy eyes. He comes to a mud hut and pushes the door open. The room inside has lamps made from abacuses, Chinese propaganda posters, photos of journalists in scuffed wicker chairs and green velvet drapes stretching from wall to wall. A record is playing 'You Did It'. In the centre of the room is a massive man in a bathrobe with slumped head. It is Timmy and he is dead.

Drews groaned and awoke. There were noises outside the hut. A figure appeared in the doorway.

'Hello?' It was a woman's voice. The figure fumbled at the door jamb and a single bulb came on below the blackened beams.

Drews shrunk from the light.

'Drews?'

He squinted up.

'Good God, Drews.'

A man entered the hut. 'Let's get him up.'

'Wait,' commanded the woman. Drews rubbed his eyes. A flash lit the room.

'One more.' Gail looked at the lens ring of her camera. 'I hope I've got this right.'

'Who are you?'

'Gail McGuinn. From *Newsweek*. Look away from the camera.'

'Don't . . .'

The bulb flashed.

Drews struggled to his feet. 'Get out.'

'We've been travelling for days.'

'Out!'

'This is a big story!'

'A story?'

'I'm on deadline.'

'I'm no story!'

Prentice intervened. 'You need help. Let us help you. Where are your clothes?'

'My editors are waiting,' said Gail. 'They want to know what's happening with *Orientweek*.'

'Fuck your editors.'

'You look dehydrated, man. You need fluids. And Gail's on deadline.'

'Leave!' Drews was getting hysterical. His eyes were wild and he was shaking with the effort of standing.

The McGuinns started to withdraw.

'Turn off that light.'

He could hear them whisper outside. Her voice: 'I've got to get to Delhi.' And his: 'Give him time. We'll come back.'

The door opened again. The silhouette of a man filled the doorway. Drews turned his head. He thought: *It's them.* And then, with shut eyes, he heard the one word he had been waiting for:

'Danny?'

Drews started to choke.

'Danny? Are you in here?'

'Timmy . . .?'

The man stepped into the room. 'We're here to take you home.' The shadows shifted and Drews could see his face.

'Gabriel.'

'You're all right now.'

A woman was standing in the doorway. One hand was raised to her mouth. The other was held a few inches from her body. Cigarette smoke floated upward into the shadows.

'Honey,' said Gabriel. 'He's in the corner.'

Miki faltered in the doorway. She was joined by a smaller woman.

'You'll have to help, honey. He's very weak. Is there a light?'

Marietta found the light switch. 'Drews! What have they done to you?'

'Oh Dan!' said Miki.

Drews sat in the corner with vomit stains on his peasant clothes. He had trouble speaking: his lips were flaky and his throat seemed out of control. The odour of faeces pervaded the room. Gabriel helped him stand. Miki approached and the two embraced. She felt him tremble.

Drews pulled away. 'It's all over. The magazine is lost.'

Miki pulled his head to her shoulder. 'Don't cry, Dan.'

They helped him through the fields to the palace. Rajinder and the McGuinns were at the door. Gabriel bathed him and placed him on a couch. Rajinder had a servant bring water and curd. Prentice poured salt in the water. 'He's definitely dehydrated.'

'Could it be typhoid?' asked Marietta. 'Or cholera?'

'He's had high fever,' said Rajinder.

Gail McGuinn pieced the story together from Rajinder and Drews. 'A day's missing.' She consulted her notes. 'What did you do all of yesterday?'

'He was sick,' said Rajinder. 'We were taking care of him.'

'That doesn't make sense,' she said. 'He was sick today, too.'

'Maybe he was very sick,' said Prentice.

'Yes,' said Rajinder. 'Very sick.'

Drews shook his head. 'Evan wanted to talk.'

Gail frowned. 'To talk?'

'All day. And all night. More water, please.'

'About what?' asked Gail. 'Can you talk?'

Drews nodded.

'What did he talk about?'

Drews shook his head.

'Was he harassing you?'

Drews closed his eyes. Gail gave Rajinder an aggressive stare.

'He's an old man,' said Rajinder.

'He was . . .' Drews shook his head. 'He tried to educate me.'

'All night?'

Rajinder smiled indulgently.

'Where is this Olcott?'

'He left in the first car.' Rajinder pointed toward the road. 'Just now. With the rest. I'll just be getting more water.'

The McGuinns had to leave immediately. The others decided to spend the night so Drews could recover. But Drews awoke in the darkened room, thinking: *Evan is in the house.* He opened the door and announced: 'We're leaving now. Find a car. Any car.'

Rajinder surrendered Drews' clothes, neatly washed and folded, but the cowboy boots had somehow disappeared. Drews hobbled barefoot to the car. Rajinder saw them off in the darkness. He pulled Miki aside and produced Drews' wallet from his front pants pocket. 'Please count. Just to be sure.' He invited them for a return visit when the palace was renovated. And he counselled them to pay the negotiated price for the car and no more. He waved as they pulled away, stiff-backed and smiling graciously.

The roads were dark and the driving dangerous. The driver guided the car as if in a trance, his thumb on the horn. Between towns the headlights caught on a canopy of branches, creating an endless tunnel to New Delhi. They passed a town with a stopped clock tower and Drews broke the silence.

'The Barabar caves are near here. The model for the Marabar caves.'

'*A Passage to India*,' said Miki.

'Do you want water?' asked Marietta.

Drews watched the road, waiting for the familiar turning. He thought of the small shrine with the toy trident. He wanted to see it, or, at least, its road. 'Down a path like this.' He pointed. 'With different trees.' In the daytime he could have found the turnoff easily, for Drews had a photographic memory. But night masked the landmarks and Drews was left in the back seat with memory alone.

Gabriel turned from the front seat. 'How are you feeling?'

Drews nodded wearily.

Gabriel squeezed his knee.

Miki spoke gently. 'Dan, I know it's bad. But don't worry.'

'It's a crime,' said Marietta. 'The magazine will be ruined without Drews.' She discussed the potential for a staff strike.

Drews looked at the blackened landscape.

'It's not all over.' Miki looked to the front seat. Gabriel smiled sympathetically. 'We haven't lost everything.'

'We have each other,' said Gabriel.

Marietta blinked curiously.

'And we'll have money. From the sale.' Miki leaned forward, peering at her husband with concern. 'With money we can start over.'

Drews shook his head.

'It's a lot of money, Dan. What else do we need?'

Drews turned to her with yellow eyes. 'Evan Olcott told you to say that.'

Miki looked with surprise.

'Always the rupees. Always the rupees.'

The other three exchanged glances.

'Dan,' said Miki. 'Look at me.'

But he didn't. And until Delhi, not another word was said in the car.

We were young in London: young and so blissfully, bloody stupid. One night, sitting in Mrs Bottom's kitchen, Danny described a sport he called 'bolting'. The black chimneys of South Kensington were etched on a charcoal sky. Mum was in bed with her vodka bottle. There was school in the morning but it took more than school to stop the talk between Danny and me. Nothing could stop it: of that I'm eternally proud. Danny was at the kitchen table draining a beer tin. I was pacing the kitchen with restless energy.

'Bolting,' said Danny. 'This ought to appeal to you. A blow to the bourgeois class.'

Bolting was a young man's sport. You entered a bar, according to Danny, in a group. Good friends, many drinks. The buoyant conversation of youth. Innocent miens beneath new, patchy beards. The night was young – but nights were eternally young in those days. When the group was sated and the vulgar jokes exhausted, someone rose and disappeared. Then another. And another. The group discreetly dispersed. Stealth was necessary and it was propitious if there was an exit near the loo. Finally, the table was empty and the group was reunited at some parking lot around the corner, happy and laughing over a free night of booze at Trip's or the Church Key or Dead Eye Dick's. You sped away, of course, with tyres screeching and a powerful radio spreading a song into the balmy summer evening. I imagine it, somehow, as a summer sport.

'Appalling,' said I. 'Never. If I had less than a tuppence and a thirst from the Gobi.'

'Come on,' said Danny, the reckless American.

'I might do it in your land. Not mine.'

'Why?'

'Because it lacks honour.' I sliced the air with Mrs Bottom's salad spoon. 'And here, in this country, in our "bars", we still have our honour.'

'Bullshit,' Danny laughed. I can see him with his new beard, his Lacoste shirt, his sparkling leprechaun eyes. 'In this country they make you pay before they surrender a drink. Bolting was probably invented in England.'

'At least, my friend, we saw how to curb it.'

'Bolting, racism and peas: peas were definitely invented in England.'

At the end, I did the dishonourable. I bolted and stuck Danny with the bill. I stood up at the fortune-teller's and Danny was dealt my card, which read: 'Long die thy happy days before thy death.' I believed the bilious lesson of Evan Olcott and chose, in response, to seize the day. *Time hath all young lovers slain* – I thought the revelation was mine alone – so cup on cup my Saqi poured. I seized the day too roughly and lost it all, including those happy nights with Danny on Conduit Road where we had, if nothing else, our pasts. As for the future, that ruthless thief, no amount of vigilance was sufficient. Few have taken greater pains to batten the hatches, bar the windows, plaster over the skylight. But at the end, I, like everyone else, found myself cleaned out.

After the sale of *Orientweek*, Nick Naversen was appointed Executive Editor. He offered Ellen Weigner the managing editorship but Ellen said: 'That's a job I wouldn't wish on my worst enemy.' So Dave Erdman was appointed – receiving the first housing allowance in *Orientweek* history – and he packed the staff with members of his wandering tribe, the freelancers of Asia. *Time* weighed in with a new editorial policy saying all stories had to be about Asians with emphasis on Asian businessmen. Which led to a spate of stories about Sunny Wong stitching pocketbooks in Kwun Tong and Baby Hernandez's roast pig restaurant in Bicol. Buck Frye reported on the titans of India's jelly-filled cable industry. The banned words, 'revealed' and 'colony', starting appearing in print. No one called for new weather in the newsroom on Monday mornings and soon everyone was coming to work in a tie. Earless Ho continued to empty *Orientweek*'s garbage, oblivious to the changes. Saddam D'Souza felt neglected and combed the classifieds for a new job. Dolly Leung soldiered on as librarian and newsroom secretary. It was Dolly who prompted tales from the old days of desktop stomps, nights at the Ball, Drews and Tim and hunts for treasure. She giggled behind her hand and provided forgotten details. 'Remember the guy with the bananas? How he peeled them with his toes? What was his name?'

Fran Naversen opened an immigration consultancy that prospered in the run-up to 1997. She reneged on her promise to adopt Kin Wah, as she had always intended to. But she secured him an immigration visa for Australia and gave a discount on the consulting fee. Kin Wah was rich and free of Hong Kong's threatening future. He opened a gay bar in Melbourne for Asians and the Australian men who favoured them.

Evan Olcott used his windfall from the Naversens to make legal claims to the entire crumbling palace. Pending a resolution, he and Rajinder renovated the middle section, including a new kitchen with a microwave oven. Their servant Manoj married. His wedding present from Evan and Rajinder was a pair of imported cowboy boots several sizes too large.

Marietta and Kelvin were also married at a ceremony at City Hall attended by the entire *Orientweek* family, old and new. The reception was at the FCC and Drews gave his blessing with all five verses of 'Joe Cool'. But a year later they separated. For Marietta was involved with a banker on the Peak; it was a long relationship she failed to sever after her marriage. Lovely Marietta's reputation suffered and she followed the banker to a new posting in Jakarta. In shame, Kelvin resigned from *Orientweek* and joined the *Review* business desk.

And what about my Danny, the man on the bar, cigarette dangling, who once had the love and admiration of an entire colony? Tito and Santa Claus rolled into one: the paragon of youth, idealism and success after seventeen years in the Far East and, despite wrinkles around the eyes, hardly middle-aged?

Time offered Danny a position in New York but he graciously retired the day *Orientweek* was sold. He needed a break, he announced, after fifteen years of weekly deadlines. A vacation. A suntan. It was a lie. Danny was set on revenge. He dreamt of a competing magazine. He declared to Miki: 'We have to think of our old readers.' (Danny and his readers: he always believed they were out there, waiting and needing him.) He flew to Europe to meet with bankers and tried to recruit Ellen Weigner, who said: 'I'm too old, Drews, to go through that again.' He negotiated with newspaper groups in Hong Kong and, from his own money, purchased a shell company. The negotiations were promising. One day, Danny read that *Orientweek*'s printing press was for sale. He bid in the name of his shell company and won. But the negotiations in Hong Kong broke down. He negotiated with the *Straits Times* in Singapore. A government official said the last thing Singapore wanted was an uncontrollable news magazine. Then *Time* announced it was pumping more money into *Orientweek*. Danny's bankers pulled out and his dream of a new magazine died. He was forced to sell the printing press, losing $400,000 in the process.

He abandoned journalism and bought a house in Manila. Danny and Miki shared a bedroom and Miki was careful to wake up each morning in the conjugal bed. He bought a second house in the Visayas. But the beach quickly bored him. One night, Danny announced he needed his own passionate affair and Miki and Gabriel gave reluctant approval. He pursued love with vigour. A famous Filipina got him to buy her a boat. Another took over the house on the beach. He invited a Finnish diplomat for a cozy foursome at the house. Miki cooked; Gabriel poured the drinks. But the affair soon ended and Danny said: 'I missed the language barrier.' Soon he was agitating to move. Rio attracted him. But Gabriel didn't want to quit his job and Miki agreed. 'We have enough money,' Danny insisted. 'The important thing is to stay together.' There was a bitter disagreement and a punch was thrown. Danny flew to Rio alone. And then he returned. A former central bank governor asked him to start an economic newsletter. But the idea never got off the ground. And now Danny spends his nights at the jolly brothels of Mabini where everybody knows him and where he's allowed to stand on the bartop and sing. The girls join in on the choruses of 'Joe Cool'. They like the song. They love Drews. He's cute, they say, and he has such a nice beard. He leaves without saying goodbye. No one watches him make his way home.

At the end, there is Alice Giles. Despite frequent stays at Canossa, she endures. She lives with Yrlinda and her daughter in a Midlevel flat with a panoramic view of life in the frenetic streets of Hong Kong. Alice is a veteran of the Succeeding Age: love gave her the cold-shoulder early on. But there is nothing dead about the old girl. (That is the accepted term after all these years: the old girl.) Life engrosses Alice and she watches from her bedroom window, or from the bar at the FCC, or from the newly franchised Friendly's, with all the awe and pity of an adolescent. I was a mere China-watcher: China is much too small for Alice Giles. The hour is late but her bedroom is lit. The stereo is playing 'Love Potion No. 9', Alice's favoured late-night song. She peers out her window with hope, perhaps, that life will extend its hand and offer one more turn on the dance-floor. But if it doesn't, Alice will remain in her chair along the wall, singing in a schoolgirl whisper, grateful to be able to watch.

Time hath all young lovers slain indeed. Life is a bloody cremation ground. But not everyone is blinded by the smoke. Alice pushes it away, blinks back the tears and keeps her eye on that thousand-headed snake: inscrutable and venomous, with two thousand fangs to fear, but at so many angles iridescent and beautiful. I admire the old girl: I should have accepted my own reprieve with such grace and, yes, joy.

July 1992
Taira, Japan